The

WOMAN
on the
ORIENT
EXPRESS

ALSO BY
LINDSAY ASHFORD

The Color of Secrets
The Mysterious Death of Miss Jane Austen
Frozen
Strange Blood
Where Death Lies
The Killer Inside
The Rubber Woman

The
WOMAN
on the
ORIENT
EXPRESS

A Novel

LINDSAY JAYNE ASHFORD

LAKE UNION
PUBLISHING

Published by Lake Union Publishing, Seattle

www.apub.com

Amazon, the Amazon logo, and Lake Union Publishing are trademarks of Amazon.com, Inc., or its affiliates.

ISBN-13: 9781503938120
ISBN-10: 1503938123

Cover design by Shasti O'Leary-Soudant

Photograph of train by Tim Stocker Photography / Getty Images
Photograph of woman by Sasha / Getty Images

Printed in the United States of America

For my parents, Janet and Graham Molton, and my brother, Tim.

Also in memory of my mother-in-law, Yvonne Lawrence: February 20, 1936–February 22, 2016.

PROLOGUE

August 1963

He comes from the river. Steals into my garden without warning. I am sitting in the camellia grove above the estuary, waiting for the sunset, watching a pair of oystercatchers at the water's edge, and trying to work out who is going to murder Major Palgrave. The lapping of the tide lulls me to sleep, so I don't see the boat heading for the mooring.

"Mrs. Christie?" His shadow falls across my face.

"Who is it?" My eyes snap open. I lean forward. With the light behind him, it is difficult to discern his features. Do I know him? He is tall and slim with a mane of dark hair. He is wearing tennis shorts and his legs glisten with droplets of water.

He holds out his hand, steps toward me. The movement unmasks the sinking sun, whose fiery glow blinds me. As I blink away a flurry of green disks, he trips over the syllables of his name. It is a name from long ago. A name that carries the scent of Turkish cigarettes and hot desert winds.

"I'm sorry to barge in on you like this." His voice is gentle, like a doctor giving bad news. "I had to see you. You're the only one who can help me."

I say nothing. I can hear the oystercatchers calling to each other, the sweet piping sound echoing across the water. He has come here for the story I promised never to write. A mystery that began more than thirty years ago when I stepped aboard the Orient Express, bound for Baghdad.

He moves closer. I must say something, anything, to get myself out of this. I ask him if he realizes he is trespassing on private property. Then I drop my eyes to the small patch of grass that separates us and say that anyway, I haven't the least idea what he is talking about. Even to my own ears it sounds unconvincing.

He already knows enough to have tracked me down, to have taken the risk of cornering me in my own garden. Would it be wrong to tell him? Must a promise be kept when the author of the secret is dead and gone?

"I have a photograph." He reaches inside the knapsack slung over his shoulder and hands me the evidence. Exhibit A: Myself three decades ago. When I still had a waist and could swim without shame in nothing but a pink silk vest and a double pair of knickers. I smile from under the fronds of an overhanging tree. I have my arm around Katharine, who stares straight at the camera with that same bold, quizzical look she gave me when we first met. We have draped ourselves in towels to cover our modesty, but our hair, plastered to our heads, gives away the fact that we have only just clambered up the banks of the Euphrates, which lies, out of shot, to my left.

I turn the photograph over. There, in Katharine's small, meticulous handwriting, is the date, December 1928, and the words "Agatha and Self in Mesopotamia." I flip it back and stare at the image again. There is a ringing in my ears—something I get these days when my blood pressure rises suddenly—and I can feel my heart pumping.

"Do you remember?" The man's voice has an edge of urgency now. He is afraid that age has addled my brain. No doubt the sight of me asleep with my mouth lolling open encouraged him to think so. I could easily play on this; send him away with a handful of half-baked tales of my travels in the Middle East. But the truth is that I recall that December afternoon as if it were yesterday. The shock of what happened that day in the desert still lingers, even after all these years. And something in Katharine's eyes—that brave insolence—dares me to tell the truth, the whole truth and nothing but the truth.

"When did you find out?" I pass the picture back.

"A few months ago. I wrote but you didn't reply."

I shake my head. "I'm sorry. I do get a lot of letters. I have an assistant who—"

"It's all right." He waves it away. "I understand. But I had to talk to you. You do see that, don't you?" He hesitates. Bites his lip. "May I sit down?"

I take a breath. I need time to think. "Let's go to the house, shall we? A pot of tea and some cake?" I grab my stick and ease myself up from the wooden bench. But he is delving into the bag again.

"There's this other one—but there's nothing written on it apart from the place and date. I thought perhaps you . . ." He trails off, blinking as he hands it to me, as if the sight of it is too much to bear.

This one is more timeworn than the other. The right-hand corner has been bent and straightened out. And the sharp black-and-white has faded to sepia tones. The words written in the border have faded, too: Venice Lido—April 1928.

A group of men and women: young, tanned, and posing for the camera. They stand in a semicircle, close enough for arms and legs to touch. Nancy looks out from center left. Her wavy dark hair is half-covered by a close-fitting striped beret. Her eyes have an intense expression, at odds with her casual holiday attire of linen culottes and blouse. She looks tiny beside the muscular man to her right, who clasps her hand while his other rests on the shoulder of a smiling woman in a kimono.

At the far end of the line, on the right, is a man in a patterned toweling robe and buckled canvas bathing shoes. He stands in profile, looking not at the camera but back at the line of friends. He is so tall that he can see over the heads of the others. His face is beautiful, but the set of his mouth and eyes has an obsessive, almost cruel quality. It could be a trick of the camera, but he seems to be staring at Nancy.

"Do you know who they are?"

I could say that I have no idea. I am not in the photograph, and in the spring of 1928 I was hundreds of miles away, in London, humiliating myself in court. I close my eyes to shut out the image, but that face—that one face—is branded inside my eyelids. Even now, after all these years, it pierces me like broken glass.

"You recognize somebody?"

I have given myself away. If I lie now, he will know. But if I let it out, I'll have to tell him everything. Can I face that?

"Please." He takes my hand. There is no pressure. His touch is as gentle as his voice. "If there's something, *anything* you could tell me. You see, there's no family left now—no one who knows."

You must tell him.

Whose voice was that? Not Katharine's or Nancy's, but a man's voice: the one I tried to shut out of my mind all those years ago when I climbed aboard the Orient Express.

There was a sister. Maybe a brother now, too. You can't deprive him of that. Think what it did to Rosalind.

Oh, that's cunning, using my own daughter to prick my conscience.

I start for the house, beckoning the man to follow. With one long stride he catches up with me. His smile would melt any woman's heart. I have around ten minutes to decide just how much I should tell him.

CHAPTER 1

October 1928—London, England

Can we be haunted by those who are not yet dead? In the weeks that followed Agatha's divorce from Archie Christie, a ghostly part of him seemed to follow her everywhere. Sitting in an empty house, she would hear his footsteps on the stairs. Waking in the night, she would feel the weight of his body in the bed. Opening the wardrobe, she would breathe in the familiar scent of shaving soap and cigarettes, even though his clothes were long gone. It was as if her senses had joined the conspiracy to push her over the edge.

The trip on the Orient Express was an attempt to banish the ghost of Archie. She told everyone, including herself, that it was just a holiday. But for the first time in her life, she was traveling abroad on her own. Everything she would do in the next two months would be entirely of her own choosing. She would find out if she could do it. If she could stand being alone.

Agatha knew how fortunate she was, having the money—and the time—for this escape. Having just delivered the final draft of *The Seven*

Dials Mystery to her publisher, there was no need to be in England to start on novel number ten. The original plan was to sail to the West Indies and Jamaica, but then, just days before she was due to go, something changed her mind.

Invited to a dinner party in Mayfair, she very nearly left within minutes of arriving because of a whispered conversation she couldn't help overhearing. As the drinks were being served in the host's conservatory, a woman on the other side of a giant tree fern was saying Agatha's name. Two other female voices chimed in with words of disbelief.

"Yes," the first one hissed. "It's definitely *her*."

"The one who faked her own death?"

"And pretended she'd lost her memory?"

Agatha moved closer to the trunk of the tree fern, wishing she could disappear.

"They say she only did it to sell more books."

A pause and then: "I read an article—the *Daily Mail* I think it was—said she'd cost the taxpayers thousands with all those policemen searching for her."

"It's the husband I feel sorry for."

"Ah, but they say he had a mistress!"

"I wonder why she chose to disappear to a town in the middle of nowhere?"

"No idea. But I'm amazed she has the nerve to show her face after a stunt like that!"

Agatha wanted to run from the room, but there were people everywhere. By keeping her head down, she managed to get as far as the hallway. If she could just make it to the front door without bumping into the host, she could slip away unnoticed. But as she crossed the hall, she was hailed by someone coming down the stairs.

"Mrs. Christie!"

She turned to see a tall gray-haired man she didn't recognize, smiling as he pulled something from his jacket pocket.

"Would you be so kind as to sign this for me?"

Agatha gave him a dubious look.

"It's for my mother. She's bedridden now, and she does love your books. She'd be thrilled to have a signed copy."

It was *The Secret of Chimneys*. As she fanned her hand to dry the ink, he told her how much he, too, had enjoyed reading it. Before she knew it, they were being ushered into the dining room, where, thankfully, she was seated between him and the host.

He told her he was a military man who had been stationed in Iraq. Soon they were chatting about what was in the papers, of the new discoveries made at Ur by Leonard Woolley and the treasures being unearthed there.

"I've always been fascinated by archaeology," she said. "I do envy you, living there. I'd love to visit Baghdad."

"Oh, you must go!" he said. "You can get there by the Orient Express."

His words had an almost magical effect. She found herself telling him how she had seen this train as a child, catching sight of the distinctive blue-and-gold livery when her mother took her to live in France before the war. She had watched men and women walking along the platform with rapturous faces, greeted by immaculate stewards standing to attention outside every carriage. She saw boxes of oysters glistening on ice, whole sides of bacon slung on hooks, and cartloads of every kind of fruit being loaded on board.

And so, the day after the dinner party, Agatha went to Cook's and canceled her tickets to the Caribbean. It took less than a week to sort out the visas for Syria and Iraq, and by the weekend she was boarding the train that would take her on the first leg of the journey, from London to Dover.

Her friend and assistant, Charlotte, came to see her off. She thought it very unwise for a woman to be traveling alone to the Middle East, but she knew Agatha well enough not to try talking her out of it. As they said their good-byes, she cautioned her friend about the men she was likely to encounter in Baghdad.

"You'd better be careful," she said. "Those blue eyes of yours will turn heads, you know."

Agatha smiled at this kind, clumsy attempt to make her feel better about herself. On her wedding day, what seemed like a hundred years ago, Archie had said her eyes were incredible, like the sky when you flew above storm clouds. After the service, as they came out of church, he'd squeezed her arm and said, "Promise me one more thing, will you? Promise you'll always be beautiful."

She remembered laughing and kissing him, then crossing her heart with her finger. "You'd love me just the same if I wasn't, though, wouldn't you?" she said. His own smile had disappeared as he replied. "Perhaps . . . perhaps I would. But it wouldn't be *quite* the same."

Somehow that promise had been broken. What was it, she wondered, that had made her cease to be beautiful to him? Was it having a baby? Failing to lose the four or five pounds she had put on with pregnancy? Or was it simply that love had blinded him, and he had woken up one morning with the realization that he could have done better?

"Don't forget my Turkish slippers!" Charlotte yelled as the train sounded a warning blast.

Agatha waved through the window, the sulfurous smoke of the engine filling her nostrils. To her it was a good smell. An exciting smell. She was turning a page. Agatha Christie, wife, was about to become Mary Miller, adventuress.

~

The morning sunshine pierced the lace curtains on the second floor of number six, Connaught Mansions, dappling the stack of green leather suitcases on Nancy's bed. She took two hatboxes from the top of the wardrobe and added them to the teetering pile of luggage. Then she walked across to the window. In the park below, people were already on the move. Two uniformed nannies in shiny black straw hats pushed perambulators through drifts of dry golden leaves. A milkman on a horse-drawn cart shouted something through the railings, and one of the women looked round, smiling and shaking her head. Somewhere in the bushes, a dog barked, and ducks cackled as they rose from the pond. In the distance Nancy could see Buckingham Palace, the Union Jack fluttering in a light northwesterly breeze. This was a view she was never going to see again.

Her room looked forlorn with the cases piled on the bed. The dressing table was stripped of everything familiar: the jewel-colored bottles of perfume; the silver hairbrush, comb, and hand mirror; the crystal jars of powder and cold cream. And the precious photograph that was in her handbag, wrapped in a scarf ruined by moth holes. When she had pulled out the square of peacock print silk, she had caught a faint whiff of lily of the valley. The scarf had belonged to her mother and retained a trace of her favorite scent. The smell had undone Nancy. The tears she had dammed up came flooding out. She could hear her mother's voice as she lay weeping into her pillow: *Come on now, darling: a true lady should always be able to control herself.*

In a moment she would go downstairs to the morning room, where the man she was about to leave forever would be sitting at the table behind his copy of the *Financial Times*. He would look up absentmindedly as she passed his chair. The paper would be laid aside only when Redfern brought in his breakfast of poached eggs, sausage, mushrooms, and bacon. As he ate, he would probably ask her what she planned to do today. He never actually listened to her replies, so she could very likely dispense with the lie she had prepared. He would go off to his club with no inkling that she was about to embark on a journey halfway round the world.

By the time he was eating his lunch, she would have boarded the train that would take her to Dover. When he got home, she would already be in France. She reached inside her handbag and pulled out the tickets she had bought by pawning the diamond necklace and earrings she had inherited on her twenty-first birthday. Yes, this was really going to happen. The day had arrived, and she must be on that train. It was the only solution. Tonight she would be sleeping in a foreign country. And by the end of the week, she would be in Baghdad.

Nancy had no idea what it would be like to live in such a place. All she knew had been gleaned from magazines and her cousin's letters. In her wildest dreams she had never imagined setting up home in a city in the middle of the desert. But where else could she go? Who else would take her in?

Her gaze rested on the two nannies, who were now sitting, chatting on a park bench. With a sharp intake of breath she turned away from the window, thrusting her hand back into her bag. The silk shroud slithered to the floor as she pulled out the photograph. There he was. Her insides surged at the sight of him.

"Please come," she whispered. "Please don't make me do this on my own."

~

On the other side of London, a woman with wisps of blonde hair trailing from her hat was walking up the steps of the British Museum. She had a copy of the *Daily Express* tucked under her arm, purchased hastily from a boy on a street corner. She was not in the habit of buying a paper and would not normally have chosen this one. It was the headline scrawled across the front of the newsstand that had propelled her across the street: *Riddle of Newlywed's Suicide.*

Katharine had been unable to look at the boy as she handed over the money, fearful that her photograph would be there on the front page. As soon as she was out of sight, she unfolded the paper. The breeze tugged the pages, making it difficult to handle. Beneath the fold was a photograph of Bertram in his regimental uniform. After just two paragraphs the report petered out, to be continued on a later page. Impossible to look at it in the street. She must wait until she got inside the museum.

"Good morning, Mrs. Keeling." The doorman gave her his customary greeting, the ends of his walrus-like mustache sliding into a smile. She nodded and looked away. Had he seen the paper, she wondered? Would he know? Would the porters be talking about her over their morning tea?

She lowered her head as she made her way to the place where she knew she'd be safe from prying eyes. In the basement of the British Museum, an Aladdin's cave of ancient objects waiting to be catalogued, was the office shared by the Mesopotamian dig team. She prayed no one else would be there this early.

To her relief the room was empty. She sank onto a chair and spread the newspaper out on the rough table strewn with shards of pottery and beads from necklaces buried in desert sand for thousands of years.

There was no photograph of her on the inside page, just another shot of her late husband, this one taken more recently, in Egypt. He was with a group of other men, sitting in the courtyard of the building that had been his headquarters in Cairo. His smile pierced Katharine's heart, unleashing a flood of guilt: for being alive when he was dead, for turning the sacrament of marriage into a death sentence.

Her eyes stung as she scanned the text, cringing at the obvious relish with which the journalist reported the awful story. Bertram had died nearly five years ago, but it had taken this long for the legal process to run its course. She had been warned that she might have to give evidence at the inquest—something she absolutely dreaded—but in the end she had not had to appear in person. The coroner had accepted her written statement of what had happened.

The verdict was that Colonel Bertram Keeling had taken his own life while the balance of his mind was disturbed. The report drew attention to the fact that he had served his country with distinction during the Great War. So many men had returned from the conflict with shattered minds. It was easy to blame the war—but that was not the real reason for Bertram shooting himself. She knew it and the journalist obviously suspected it. The coroner's verdict had been a disappointment, so the story had been spiced up with sly innuendo as to why a man married for just six months would take his own life.

No one would ever guess the truth, because she was the only living person who knew it. The doctor—that stupid, stupid man—had died himself, just weeks after Bertram, of cholera or typhus or something. Divine retribution, some would say.

Katharine folded up the newspaper and tossed it into the bin in the corner of the room. Darting across to shelves stacked with books, she pulled out three slim volumes and tucked them into her bag. Ten minutes later she was back outside, striding down the steps and hailing a cab. In an hour's time she would be on the train that would take her far away from nosy reporters and their prurient readers.

Inside the cab, she closed her eyes and conjured the desert landscape she so longed for: the vast, uninterrupted swathes of sand and clear blue sky; the scent of wood fires and spiced meat; the sonorous, lilting call to prayer at sunrise. This time next week she would be there.

There would be that other business to attend to first, of course. The wedding in Baghdad. The thought of it sent an involuntary shudder down her spine, as if someone had walked on her grave.

When Bertram died, she had never imagined taking another husband. But the dig's high-minded backers had given her no choice. Marriage was the only way they would allow her to continue working in a camp full of men.

She had accepted the archaeologist's proposal with one crucial condition: that their union would never be consummated. To her surprise he had agreed with only a momentary hesitation. No doubt he thought he would be able to make her change her mind once they were man and wife.

Poor fool. She heard Bertram's voice as clearly as if he'd been sitting next to her. If only she had known. If only she had been to a doctor *before* their wedding night . . .

"Off somewhere nice, miss?" The cab driver broke into her thoughts.

"The Middle East," she replied. "Mesopotamia."

"Blimey—can you go that far from Victoria?"

"Certainly you can. You get off the train at Dover and take the Orient Express at Calais. The railway goes all the way to Damascus. Then you get a coach across the desert to Baghdad."

"How long does that take?"

"Only five days."

Five days and nights. How many waking hours was that? Less than a hundred. Not very long to work out how she was going to keep this new husband from her bed.

CHAPTER 2

London to Paris

Agatha didn't venture far from her compartment on her first night on the Orient Express. She'd never been good on boats and was worn out with seasickness after the Channel crossing. The excitement of boarding the train gave way to exquisite relief as she climbed up a tapestry-covered ladder and slipped between damask sheets, knowing there would be no more sea travel until they reached Istanbul.

The steward said she would have the compartment to herself as far as Belgrade, and so she lay in her bunk without pulling down the blind, watching the darkening landscape as the train rolled through the fields of Normandy. Past black fingers of trees newly stripped of their apples, past silhouettes of horses startled into life by the snort of the engine. It looked so tranquil, so untouched by time. Hard to believe that a decade ago this place was ravaged by war.

She thought of Archie soaring over these fields in his Cody biplane. One of the few qualified pilots in Britain when war broke out, he was lucky to have survived. He had written to her from France before they were married, wanting to know if she was worried about his flying. She had read between the lines—seen that what he really wanted was to reassure himself about the danger of what he was doing. She had sent him violets and a Saint Christopher with the letter she wrote back. She told him she was not in the least bit worried because she had seen him in the air and knew how good he was. She was careful to avoid any reference to what dominated her life back home, to the broken bodies of the men and boys she tended every day at the hospital in Torquay.

It's a filthy job, nursing. I hate to think of your doing it.

He had written those words the week before his first leave. And because he couldn't bear it, she never mentioned her work to him again. Her letters became dreams of home, of the life they would have when the war ended.

Their wedding took place in a rush on Christmas Eve, 1914. They were staying at his mother's house, and after telling her the previous evening how wrong it would be for them to marry with a war on, Archie had marched into her bedroom at eight o'clock the next morning to announce that he'd changed his mind: they must do it immediately. He had just forty-eight hours' leave, so there had been no time for buying a dress, choosing flowers, even making a cake. Agatha had married in the jacket and skirt she had worn for her interview at the hospital. Their witness was a friend who just happened to be passing the church after the vicar had been located and paid eight pounds to grant their desperate request. And then, after just one night of honeymoon, Archie was on his way back to France.

Agatha closed her eyes, summoning images to blot out the memory of his hard, lean body sinking into her soft white flesh. She traveled back in time, to a place in her head where it was always summer, never winter, to the beach at the foot of the cliff in Devon where she had spent endless carefree days fishing for crabs in rock pools and feasting on hard-boiled eggs and fish paste sandwiches.

After a while she drifted into sleep. She woke because the train had stopped. Where were they, she wondered? Paris? Or farther than that? Dijon? Lausanne? Agatha raised herself on her elbows and peered through the glass.

She glimpsed the figure of a man on the smoky moonlit platform. There was something horribly familiar about him. The high sculpted cheekbones and diamond-bright eyes. It couldn't be . . . could it? She blinked, craning her neck. It was months since she'd seen him, but somehow Archie was there now, outside the window. It was as if he'd followed her across the sea, lost her somewhere around Calais, and then, with supernatural speed, overtaken the train.

He was looking, not at her, but at something further along the platform. There was an air of impatience about him. His lips twitched, then parted, as if he was speaking, though she could see no one near enough to catch his words. Suddenly she heard his voice inside her head.

Running away again, are we? Perhaps you'll make a better job of it this time . . .

Agatha closed her eyes tight, telling herself it wasn't him: it couldn't be. He was in England, tucked up in bed. Probably dreaming of *her*, of what he would be doing in a few days' time, after the wedding.

When she stopped torturing herself and opened her eyes, he had disappeared. She told herself that her imagination was working overtime. As the train began moving again, she settled back against the pillow, making herself breathe in and out to a slow count of four. Each breath brought the comforting scent of freshly laundered linen. Then she made a mental list of all the treats in store on the train: the food, the music, the places she would see. There was something so very safe about being on a train. She was not really alone—she had only to ring the bell and a steward would appear.

Agatha thought about where she was headed, and her stomach did an involuntary flip. Could she really do it? Could she really go all that way by herself? Yes, she whispered, of course you can do it:

you're thirty-eight years old and you're not going to the moon, just to Baghdad. The word sounded the way a shiver felt. At the dinner party in London it had been a shiver of excitement, but now it held a frisson of dread.

She knew precious little about the place. She had been to Egypt once with her mother, and she imagined it would be something like that. At eighteen years old she had squandered her time there, far more interested in men and dances than the pyramids and tombs.

There had been one man—a very kind, rather handsome colonel a good deal older than herself—who had asked her mother for Agatha's hand in marriage on the boat back to England. She was cross when her mother told her, feeling cheated because she thought the question should have been put to *her*. By the time she found out about it, they were back in Devon. Now his face hovered in the semidarkness of the wagon-lit. If she had married him instead of . . .

She tried to stop thinking, to concentrate on the rhythm of the engine and the sound of the wheels on the track. And she prayed that when she fell asleep, she would dream of anything but Archie.

~

Nancy moved from the window to the door and back again, pacing the small compartment like a caged animal. From the moment the train had pulled into Paris's Gare de Lyon, she had pressed her face to the glass, desperate for a glimpse of him. But it was too dark and too smoky to see properly. There were knots of people along the platform, some waiting, some ready to climb aboard. She wanted to jump off the train and run among them, aching to see his face. But that would be too great a risk. She might miss him—or worse, the train might set off without her while he was already on board.

At every stop on the journey so far she had hoped he might appear. At Victoria station, as other passengers were bidding fond farewells to their loved ones, she had remained, alone, on the platform until the guard had practically shooed her up the steps, his eyebrows raised in a look of pity.

Then, when he was not at Dover, she had walked round the decks for the entire crossing in case he had made a last-minute dash for the boat as it was about to sail.

At Calais, where the Orient Express was waiting, she was prevented from lingering on the platform by the very attentive steward who insisted on showing her where everything was, how everything in the compartment worked, and taking her through the list of supper dishes available that evening. In other circumstances she would no doubt have found it thrilling—but she was too worked up to take it in. By the time he had finished, the train was already pulling out of the station.

"Your companion, madame," the steward asked in his soft, foreign accent, "will she be joining you in Paris?"

"Er . . . yes. In . . . er . . . Paris." Nancy was embarrassed at being confronted with the lie she had told. She had paid double the price for her tickets, booking a whole second-class compartment in the hope that he would come. Only passengers of the same sex were allowed to share, so she had informed the man at Cook's that her traveling companion was a Miss Muriel Harper.

She felt a flush spread from her neck to her face as the steward smiled at her. She suspected he saw right through the lie. Knew it was a lover, not a friend, who had let her down.

Poor little rich girl. She could almost hear him thinking it.

Paris was her last hope. There was just a chance that he had got there before her, planning to board the train in darkness to avoid being caught out by the steward.

She glanced at her watch. They were due to leave in less than five minutes. She heard a door slam. Footsteps in the corridor outside. A woman's voice, speaking French. Nancy sank onto the bed, her mouth so dry she could barely swallow. As she reached for a tumbler of water, she heard a soft clicking sound. Whipping her head round, she saw the handle of the door move up and down. With one bound she was there.

"Oh, darling!" She fell into his arms, tears prickling her eyes.

"You'd better let me in." His lips brushed her cheek as he took her by the shoulders, moving her sideways as he crossed the threshold.

"Where's your luggage?"

He wasn't looking at her. He sat down heavily on the bed, his eyes fixed to the floor.

"I can't stay," he said. "I'll have to get off in the morning."

"But—"

"Don't ask me, Nancy—not yet. Let's make the most of this night together. Lock the door and come and hold me, will you?" He reached out with both hands, and her body melted into his.

Afterward, as she lay on the narrow bunk in the darkness, breathing in the scent of his damp skin, she heard the steward knock softly at the door. She called out that there was nothing she wanted. The words mocked her. The very thing she wanted most in the world was lying there beside her, but in a few precious hours he would be gone.

She heard the steward's footsteps recede down the corridor, and she reached out for the warm body beside her. But the spell was broken. He was sitting up. A match flared as he lit a cigarette. Now he was going to tell her what she dreaded to hear.

"I had to come, Nancy—I couldn't let you down." He inhaled deeply, blowing out a plume of smoke that drifted across her face. "But it's difficult at the moment. You do see that, don't you?"

She felt a hysterical bubble of laughter rise from her stomach at his words. Difficult? How could anything he had to contend with be any tougher than what *she* was facing? But she made no sound. Said nothing. Waited for him to explain it if he could.

"I think she suspects," he said. "I'm worried she'd go to the papers if she knew for sure. Think what that would do to us."

"But it wouldn't matter, would it? Not if we were in Baghdad." Nancy couldn't see his expression. The only light was the red glow of the cigarette.

He let out a low grunt of a laugh. Almost a growl. "Baghdad? What on earth would we do in Baghdad?"

"I . . . I don't know. Just . . . ," she faltered. "Just live, I suppose. We love each other, don't we? Isn't that enough?"

His silence told her what she feared most.

She wanted to tell him everything then. Oh God, how she longed to let the secret out. But she couldn't. Wouldn't. Unless he came willingly, because he wanted her, it would never work. She had enough sense to realize that. And despite everything that had happened in the past few months, she still had some pride. She was not going to resort to emotional blackmail.

"You know how much I care for you," he whispered. "Do you think I'd have risked coming here if I didn't?" He leaned across her to stub out his cigarette, nuzzling her head as he shifted his weight. "If you can just lie low out there for a few months . . ." He was stroking her neck with his cheek, sending delicious shivers through her body. "We will be together—I promise."

Nancy closed her eyes as he slid his body against hers. She wanted so badly to believe him.

CHAPTER 3

Lausanne to Milan

The next morning Agatha woke with great excitement, glimpsing the Alps through the window. The snow on their peaks reflected the rising sun, blankets of coral and pink drawn up against a perfect sky.

She dressed quickly: the Sonia Delaunay jacket in bold autumn stripes over a camel silk blouse and matching wool skirt. When she went to put on lipstick, her reflection in the little round mirror above the basin caught her by surprise. The red tint in her hair was quite striking in bright sunlight. The hairdresser had warned her of the likely effect. *You are a natural blonde,* she said, *so the color will be very different.*

She smiled at her strange self and reached for the spectacles that completed the disguise. The labels peeping out from the luggage rack above her head confirmed her new identity: Mrs. M. Miller of Greystone House, Drewsteignton, Exeter.

She opened the door of the compartment and stood for a moment, paralyzed at the thought of entering the dining car. All those faces. What if she was recognized?

But her stomach came to the rescue. The smell of hot buttered toast and bacon and coffee came wafting along the corridor as a door opened somewhere. *There is nothing like a good breakfast to banish the nerves,* her father always used to say. Her insides rumbled in happy anticipation as she followed her nose.

The headwaiter seated Agatha with her back to the engine and asked whether she would prefer Indian or Chinese tea. He went to fetch it while she perused the menu: eggs Benedict, kedgeree, or pancakes with maple syrup? Delicious indecision. By the time he returned with a pot of Darjeeling, she had made up her mind.

The newspaper, carefully ironed, was laid out beside silver cutlery that glinted where the sun caught it. She unfolded it, reaching for her tea. As she lifted the monogrammed porcelain cup to her lips, she spotted a girl at the table opposite.

No more than twenty-five, Agatha guessed. Dark wavy hair and delicate features, well-cut, unfussy clothes, and just a little makeup. The sight of her gave Agatha a strange sense of déjà vu. She felt sure she had seen her somewhere before but couldn't place her. Thankfully, the girl was not looking up. It gave Agatha a chance to conceal herself behind the pages of the paper. But as she opened it, she saw something plop onto the piece of toast on the girl's plate.

She was crying.

As Agatha watched, the tears fell in a steady stream. The girl made no sound and no attempt to wipe her face, as if she was paralyzed by grief. Agatha picked up her cup and set it down again, her fingers working furiously on the handle. Should she pretend not to notice? Would that be the correct way to behave? No, she decided, she must go to her.

But at that moment the girl glanced up. She was not looking at Agatha but at something at the far end of the dining car. She moved her hand slightly. It was the vaguest shadow of a wave, as if she was afraid of being observed.

It would have been rude, of course, for Agatha to twist her head round to see who she was waving at. But a strange trick of light revealed who the girl had seen. Agatha blinked as a ray of sunshine slid a reflection across the window: a face framed in the doorway of the dining car.

His face.

He was not a ghost; she had not dreamed him up. He was here, on the Orient Express.

Agatha's hand began to shake, her teacup catching the saucer. But the sound was drowned by the sudden whoosh of the brakes. The train began to slow down. Suddenly, there were wooden houses with frost-rimed windows, carts driven by people with fur hats and pale, pinched faces.

The train came to an abrupt halt. The door at the end of the dining car swung open. She saw the back of his head as he walked away.

Was it him? Was it *really* him?

Agatha glanced at the girl. She was staring at her plate, her hair falling forward, curtaining her face.

If that was him, then who was she?

The carriage gave a little shudder as the engine pulled away. Agatha twisted her head to catch the name of the station, but the sign flashed past before she could make it out. She guessed that they must be in Switzerland or Italy. Why would Archie be getting off a train in either of those places?

She turned to look at the girl, but as she did so, the waiter arrived with breakfast, blocking her view. In the time it took him to lay down the plate, unfurl her napkin, and ask if anything else was required, the girl had left the dining car.

Could this be Archie's mistress? It suddenly struck her how little she knew of the woman who had stolen her husband's heart.

Her name: yes, she knew that. She had even seen her once. He had brought her to the house for the weekend with a group of his golfing friends. But Agatha was laid up with the flu. She had heard them all in the hall as she lay in bed. She wanted to get up, at least to say hello, guilt-ridden at being such a rotten hostess.

Probably there was nothing going on at that stage, otherwise Archie wouldn't have had the nerve to invite her. On the Saturday morning, Agatha had left her bed to go to the bathroom and glimpsed two men and a woman in the hallway. They didn't see her. It struck her how attractive the woman was: slim, with dark wavy hair. She had asked Archie, when they'd all gone, who she was. *Oh, Nancy,* he said. *Not a bad handicap, for a woman: she plays off ten.*

Agatha never saw her again after that. Never even thought of her until a year later. It was the summer of 1926: the night before Rosalind's seventh birthday. That was the night Archie chose to tell her there was someone else: someone who meant more to him than his daughter and his wife.

So was this her? How Agatha wished she had a clearer memory of the woman in the hall at Sunningdale.

She picked up her knife and fork and tried to do justice to the eggs Benedict, but her insides were in knots.

When she rose to leave the dining car, she lingered by the place the girl had occupied, scanning the table for clues. A handkerchief, perhaps, with an initial? But there was only the crumpled napkin and a few crumbs of toast.

You're letting your imagination run away with you. Her mother's voice this time.

Agatha paused in the corridor, pressing her face against the cool glass of the window. Her breath blurred a landscape of meadows sprinkled with snow. This was not meant to happen. She had come on this journey to heal, to move on.

The sight of pine trees whizzing past made her dizzy. She closed her eyes, enveloped by an awful sense of emptiness. It was as if she were back in that hotel room in Harrogate, all alone, waiting to be found. Longing for Archie to come for her, to want her back.

It had been nearly two years since she'd boarded that train to the north of England without telling anyone where she was going: a gray December morning four months to the day of Archie's bombshell about the new love of his life. She had begged him for more time, for an attempt at reconciliation. On that Saturday in December they were supposed to be going for a weekend away together in Yorkshire. To a hotel in Harrogate. But on the Friday night he hadn't come home. She had waited and waited—and in the end something inside her had just snapped.

Running away again . . .

She heard a door open and turned abruptly away from the window, afraid of what people would think if they saw her. The train took a sharp bend, and she grabbed the handrail to steady herself. In her confused state she opened the door of the wrong compartment. Or so she thought when she saw a woman stretched out on the banquette.

"Oh—I'm so sorry!" Agatha backed out, shaking her head.

"Mrs. Miller?" The woman looked as if she'd stepped out of the pages of *Vogue*. Tall enough to have to duck beneath the luggage rack as she stood up, she was dressed in pajamas of white silk with a border of black Egyptian hieroglyphs at the neck, cuffs, and hips. As she moved toward Agatha, her clothes wafted a heady, unfamiliar scent. There was vanilla in it and something like jasmine or narcissus.

She held out her hand with a dazzling smile, revealing perfect teeth. She appeared to be wearing no makeup other than lipstick, and her skin was flawless. Her hair was thick and glossy—a Scandinavian pale blonde—and her eyes were a deep blue, almost violet. They reminded Agatha of the harebells that used to grow in the fields beyond the garden of her mother's house in Torquay.

"Katharine Keeling." Her handshake was as firm as a man's. "I do apologize for alarming you. I had to get them to move me. Bedbugs, would you believe!" She arched her eyebrows and gave a little shudder, which made her bosom shift beneath the silk pajamas. "You wouldn't think it, would you? Not on the Orient Express. I'm told it's all the woodwork—they burrow into it and come out at night." She sank down onto the banquette and patted the upholstery. "Now, come and tell me all about yourself."

As Agatha sat down, she saw that the compartment had been completely rearranged in the time it had taken her to eat breakfast. None of her things were in evidence. Her hairbrush and dressing case had been removed from the table under the window. Her nightdress no longer hung from the hook on the back of the door, and her hatbox had been turned on its side and crammed into a corner of the luggage rack.

She had chosen a second-class cabin because there was so much more space than in the single-berth, first-class compartments. Now she wondered if she had done the right thing.

"What a divine jacket!" Katharine ran a long, elegant finger over the fabric at Agatha's wrist. "Is it Sonia Delaunay?"

"Yes, it is."

"I thought so. I worked for her once."

"Really?"

"I'm a commercial artist." Katharine nodded. "I've worked for fashion houses in London and Paris."

"You must be very talented," Agatha said. "Are you traveling for work or pleasure?"

Katharine threw back her head and laughed. "Do they have to be mutually exclusive? I love my work more than anything." Reaching across to the table under the window, she picked up a silver cigarette case and flipped it open. "Would you like one?"

"No, thank you—I don't smoke."

"Hope you don't mind if I do." She pulled something from the pocket of her pajamas. A cigarette holder, black with a silver tip.

Agatha's heart sank at the thought of sharing a compartment with a smoker. In the years with Archie she had got used to the smell of cigarettes. But sleeping in a room with no lingering scent of tobacco was the one pleasure of being single again.

"They're Turkish," Katharine said. "Rather good. One of my colleagues brought them back from Baghdad. I must get some more."

"Is that where you're going?" It seemed an odd destination for someone from the world of haute couture. Agatha had assumed the woman would be leaving the train at Milan.

Katharine blew out a plume of smoke as she lit the cigarette. "I'm going on to Ur. I'm working on the dig there: drawing the finds. It's my fourth season."

"You're working with Leonard Woolley?" Agatha's voice rose in awe.

"I am." Katharine rolled her eyes, as if the name conjured something unpleasant.

Agatha wanted to ask what she meant by it—whether the great man was difficult to work with or had some unfortunate personal habit—but that would have sounded disrespectful. Instead, she told Katharine how fascinated she had been to read about the dig in the papers and how it had influenced her decision to travel east instead of west. Then she asked which of the many treasures was her favorite.

Katharine tapped her cigarette over the ashtray. "I suppose it would have to be Queen Shuabi's headdress. It took me two months to reconstruct it—an absolute nightmare with all those tiny beads—but it was worth it."

She described how the team at the dig unearthed burial sites that had lain undiscovered beneath the desert sand for three thousand years. The headdress of the Sumerian queen was one of many magnificent grave goods found in the inner chamber of the tomb they had excavated last season.

Katharine's description of the process of piecing together fragments of gold, lapis lazuli, carnelian, and agate drew Agatha into another world. She hardly noticed the mountain landscape beyond the window giving way to the plains of Lombardy, so transfixed was she by the images of what had been discovered at Ur.

A sharp rap on the door of the compartment startled her back to reality. It was the steward with their morning coffee. He asked Katharine if there was anything still to be moved from the compartment she had previously occupied. He addressed her as "Mrs. Keeling," which surprised Agatha, as Katharine wore no wedding ring.

When he had gone, Katharine said, "You've been naughty, Mrs. Miller, letting me go on and on about my work: now tell me something about yourself." She spooned sugar into her cup and lifted it to her mouth. When she replaced it in the saucer, there was a perfect arc of coral lipstick on the rim. "Baghdad is an unusual destination for a woman traveling alone . . ." She trailed off, the implication obvious. She wanted to know why Agatha was taking such a holiday without a husband.

She took a breath before replying. She had anticipated curiosity of this kind and had a ready answer. But she wanted to make sure it sounded convincing. She told Katharine that her daughter had gone away to boarding school—which was true—and that she missed her terribly and needed a distraction. Then came the lie: "My husband . . . He's . . . he was killed in the war."

She had practiced in the mirror. Told herself over and over that it was better to pretend to be a widow than admit to the shame of divorce. It felt awful, though, saying it for real, as if she were wishing he really *was* dead. And that face reflected in the train window, haunting her before the lie had even been told. Was that her punishment? The latest cruel trick of her senses, to see things that weren't really there?

Katharine reached across the seat and patted her hand. "I lost my husband, too."

The words made blood surge into Agatha's face. Now she felt doubly guilty. *You wicked, wicked woman,* Archie hissed.

Katharine's eyes went to the window. "We met when I went as a nurse to France."

"France?" Agatha echoed. It was hardly possible to imagine an exotic creature like this in the blood and mud of a field hospital. Nursing soldiers in Torquay had been bad enough. She could only imagine the horrors Katharine must have seen.

"We were only married for six months." Katharine reached for another cigarette.

"War is so cruel." A platitude—but experience had taught Agatha not to probe too deeply.

"When it ended, I went nursing again," Katharine said. "I was in Egypt at first, but then I went to Baghdad. That's how I came to work on the dig."

Agatha waited for her to go on, but after lighting her cigarette, Katharine fell silent. There was a weight of expectation in the air, as if, having sketched the circumstances of her marriage, Agatha must now do the same.

Agatha sidestepped it by telling her that she, too, had lived in Egypt. They talked of the places they had seen, a decade apart. Then Agatha launched into a description of her time at the hospital, playing up the humorous moments. She told Katharine how she and her friend Eileen had taught themselves chemistry between shifts on the wards, and how they had accidentally blown up the coffee machine in the process of using it to practice Marsh's test for arsenic.

She didn't tell Katharine that she had married Archie the weekend after the explosion happened, that the patients had teased her about her new status on her return, and a soldier from Glasgow had called across the ward that he preferred Nurse Christie to Nurse Miller, because it was a Scottish name.

It had been so strange, going back to work as a married woman after just one night with Archie, not knowing when or even if she would see him again. He had proposed just days after they met, sweeping her off her feet at a Christmas ball. Tall and slim with wavy golden hair, he had a careless confidence about him that captivated her. And he was a fabulous dancer. They had had a waltz and a foxtrot together, and he asked her for another dance, but her card was full. With a wave of his hand, he had told her to cut the other partners.

It had been the same when he had proposed and she had told him she was already engaged to a gunner, Reggie Lucy, who was away with his regiment. *What on earth does that matter?* He'd brushed it away as if it were no more than a stray hair on his collar. *I'm not engaged to anyone else, but if I was, I'd break it off in a minute without even thinking about it.*

And so she had written to Reggie—kind, gentle, patient Reggie, who had insisted on waiting at least two years to walk up the aisle—to tell him she was going to marry someone else. She had been so contented, so peaceful, with Reggie. He was a safe foot on the shore—a good companion, not a grand passion. But now she was swimming out into deep water. She had fallen in love with a stranger, a man who fascinated her because he was her polar opposite: practical where she was romantic, logical where she let her imagination run away with her, and hard-boiled where she was sentimental. And she had ached to marry him. It was unbearable when her mother had told them they must wait until he was earning enough to support her.

"You'll hate Baghdad, you know," Katharine said suddenly.

Agatha turned to her, bewildered. "Why do you say that?"

"It's full of memsahibs. You might as well be in Surrey. It's all tea parties and tennis clubs. You must avoid them if you want to see the real Mesopotamia."

"Oh . . . I . . . er . . . I've booked a room for five nights at the Tigris Palace Hotel, but I have no real plans beyond that." Agatha stopped short of saying that she was hoping to visit the dig at Ur. She didn't want to appear to be inviting herself to stay with someone she had only just met.

After an awkward silence, Katharine said, "Well, you must come to us."

Agatha wondered whom she meant by "us."

"There's an annex to the dig house for guests," Katharine went on. "Leonard's not very keen on tourists, but he won't mind me showing you around."

Agatha thought Katharine's use of her employer's Christian name rather too familiar. It implied a lack of respect for someone who was a world-renowned figure. She wondered if this was something peculiar to the life of an archaeological dig—that in such a closed world different rules applied.

"You're very kind," she said, "but I wouldn't dream of imposing on you at your workplace. The man at Cook's said I could hire a local guide to take me to places of interest."

"Nonsense!" Katharine grunted a laugh. "I love the Arabs, but they can be very tiresome unless you know the ropes. Really, I insist: you must come to us. It would be an absolute pleasure for me. I'm surrounded by men for five months at a stretch, and one does crave a little female company."

There was something in the way she said it, something that defied contradiction while at the same time hinting at vulnerability, almost a fear of what she was going to. And yet she had said this was her fourth season at the dig.

Agatha had a strange sense that for Katharine, this journey was the exact opposite of hers: that for all her talk of loving what she did for a living, something menacing awaited her in the desert.

CHAPTER 4

Milan to Venice

As the train crossed the bridge over the Ticino River, Agatha began writing a letter to her daughter. She planned to compose it in stages, describing her impressions of each country they passed through on the way to Istanbul, where she would post it.

The thought of not seeing Rosalind for almost three months was hard to bear. If she had not taken this holiday, she would have been able to visit her at school a couple of times during the autumn term. The girls were allowed to be taken out on Sunday afternoons—a maximum of four times per term. These rationed visits would, of course, have to be divided between herself and Archie.

Her sister Madge, knowing how Agatha felt about the prospect of Archie's forthcoming marriage, had kindly offered to visit Rosalind if she decided to go away. Rosalind loved Aunt Madge, but it didn't make Agatha feel any less guilty about not being there for her daughter.

The train stopped at Milan just before lunch, and a number of people, including Katharine and Agatha, disembarked to stretch their legs while the locomotive was changed.

The frost and snow of the Alps was far behind them and they stepped out into sunshine. As they wandered up and down the platform, Agatha shaded her eyes with her hand, scanning the groups of passengers for the girl she had seen in the dining car. There was no sign of her. Perhaps she had left the train before Milan. It had stopped at two other stations since breakfast—Brig and Domodossola—places Agatha had never heard of. Had she gone after the man who got off in the mountains?

As Katharine chattered away about the sights they would see when they reached Baghdad, Agatha told herself for the umpteenth time that the man she had seen in the window couldn't possibly have been Archie.

She made herself consider the matter as a lawyer might when interviewing a potential witness in a court case. Of her two sightings of the man, the first had been at night on a smoke-filled platform and the second a mere reflection on glass. No jury in the land, she told herself sternly, would convict on evidence like that.

When they got back on the train, she stared at her own reflection in the window, silently berating herself for getting into such a state over something that was pure fantasy. She knew very well where Archie would be at this moment: at his desk at Austral Development Ltd. in London. A creature of habit, he would probably go for lunch at the Criterion in Piccadilly. Then, in the evening, he would return to the place he was renting in West Kensington.

He was getting married in a few days' time. There was no earthly reason why he should be traveling anywhere this week—let alone on the Orient Express. He hated trains. Couldn't stand riding in anything unless he was in control. A plane or a car was fine—but not a train. Never a train.

As they pulled out of the station, Katharine announced that she was too exhausted to contemplate lunch. "Those wretched bedbugs kept me awake all night," she said. "I think I'll just order a sandwich and then lie down for a while. You don't mind, do you?" She flashed another of her dazzling smiles. Clearly, she wanted the compartment to herself for a couple of hours. Agatha was beginning to realize that Katharine was the kind of woman who was used to getting her own way.

As she made her way to the dining car, she tried to imagine her fellow traveler on an archaeological dig site in the middle of the desert, the only woman in a team of men. With looks like hers, it was a situation likely to spell trouble. She guessed that Katharine's combination of charm and steely determination was the armor she had developed for fending them off.

Lunchtime on the train was much busier than breakfast had been. The headwaiter asked Agatha if she would mind sharing a table. He seated her opposite an elderly lady from Canada who said she was on her way to see her son, who worked for an oil company. She was very deaf, so the conversation was limited.

"Don't feel you have to talk, my dear," she said, brandishing a fork-ful of Wiener schnitzel. "The food is so marvelous, it really deserves one's full attention."

Agatha ordered French onion soup, followed by rillettes of duck. This was served with a half bottle of claret, which she was going to send back because—to her disappointment—alcohol had never agreed with her. But her dining companion seized it before she could catch the waiter's attention.

"Don't you want it, my dear? May I take it? So nice to have a little something in hand. I do hate disturbing the stewards late at night."

Agatha smiled to herself, picturing the woman pouring wine into the glass she probably kept her false teeth in.

When the old lady got up to leave the table, she was quite unsteady, grasping the edge as she attempted to walk down the aisle. Agatha went to her aid and offered to walk her back to her compartment, but a steward appeared before they had taken more than half a dozen steps.

As she made her way back to the table, Agatha caught sight of a familiar profile. It was the girl from breakfast. She was two tables back from hers, facing toward the engine. She was looking down at a book that lay open beside her plate. Even if she had looked up, she would not have seen Agatha without twisting her head at an uncomfortable angle. So she lingered over getting back into her seat, taking a good look at the girl. Her right hand was on the table, beside the book, but the left was out of sight. Agatha had not noticed, at breakfast, whether she wore a ring.

Archie's wedding was taking place on the Saturday after next. She knew the date because Rosalind had come out with it after a weekend visit. She wanted to be a bridesmaid, but her father had told her it wasn't going to be that sort of wedding. For that, at least, Agatha was thankful. It would have been unimaginably cruel, sending Rosalind home with a request like that.

She went back to her half-eaten plate of duck, took a mouthful, then pushed it away, no clearer in her mind about the girl's identity. She was the right age, certainly. And there was something hauntingly familiar about her face. Agatha told herself she must be someone else she had met before. But not *her*. Not Nancy.

Through the window she saw a flat expanse of water. A sign flashed by: "Lago di Garda." Soon they would be in Venice. For some inexplicable reason, Hercule Poirot appeared in her mind's eye as she gazed across the lake. What, she wondered, would her little Belgian detective do in a situation like this?

The answer came back in a flash. *You must use the little gray cells.*

Yes. Of course. But how, exactly?

The irony of it didn't escape her. There she was—sitting on a train that she had already decided would feature in one of her future novels—waiting for a figment of her imagination to tell her what to do. How is it, she thought, that one can create a character who is more intelligent, more observant, more perceptive than oneself?

She had intended to take coffee in the saloon after lunch to while away the time Katharine needed for her nap. But she decided to stay put for the time being. She wanted to see which way the girl went when she left the dining car. That would narrow down the location of her compartment, which would be a start.

She moved into the aisle seat and took out the compact she kept in her bag. By appearing to powder her nose, she was able to see the comings and goings behind her. She didn't have long to wait. The girl stepped out from the table, then darted back to pick up her book, as if she had almost forgotten it. She had her back to Agatha, heading for the same portion of the train that Agatha and Katharine occupied.

There were only two wagon-lit carriages between the engine and the dining car: one was first class, the other second. Would Archie's future bride be traveling first class? Agatha thought it unlikely. She had a strong suspicion that money—her money—was part of the reason he had stopped loving her in the way he once did: she had become a different person from the girl he had married—an independent woman with an income of her own.

It was time to put the second part of her plan into action. She asked to speak to the headwaiter, telling him that she thought she'd recognized a fellow passenger but was reluctant to approach her in case of embarrassment if she was mistaken.

"Which table was it, madame?" He spoke with a very slight accent, which might have been French or something else.

She pointed it out, and he went to his station at the other end of the carriage to consult a list. She hovered in the aisle, feeling like a criminal as he came toward her.

"The name is Ann Nelson, madame." He smiled at Agatha inquiringly. She wondered if he could hear her heart thumping in her chest. *Ann.* That was not good enough. Because an Ann could still *be* a Nancy, couldn't she? Agatha had nursed alongside a woman called Nancy in Torquay, and the letters she received had always borne the first initial *A*. It was one of those peculiar English habits, to christen a girl Ann and call her Nancy, just as all the boys called Jack were really Johns.

"Ah . . . er . . . Nelson . . . ," she mumbled. "That must be her . . . er . . . her married name." It was not the name of Archie's lover, but it was very similar. She was a Miss Neele—or so he'd told her. Could she be traveling under an alias? It seemed unlikely.

But you're doing it. This time the voice in her head was her own.

"Would you like me to send her a message?" The headwaiter was positively beaming at her now. "A happy coincidence, is it not?"

"Oh . . . no . . . thank you. I'm . . . er . . . I'd like to surprise her." She gave him her brightest smile. "If you could just give me the number of her compartment . . ." She was trading shamelessly on the fact that people never suspect middle-class women the wrong side of forty to be engaged in anything underhanded. And although she was not yet that old, Agatha was sure she looked it in those spectacles.

"But of course, madame." He summoned one of the waiters, addressing him in French. The compartment number was duly scribbled on the pad that hung from the waiter's belt.

She had been right about the location: it was in the second-class carriage, not the first. She was at the far end, nearest to the engine, while Agatha was in the middle.

She made her way to the saloon, clutching the scrap of paper, her mind racing. If she went to the compartment and knocked on the door, what would she say? She could hardly ask the girl outright if she was her husband's mistress. Neither could Agatha demand to know if she was traveling under an assumed name.

She decided that a direct approach was likely to create a good deal of embarrassment and would probably get her nowhere. She was going to have to be more subtle about it, await an opportunity to engage the girl in seemingly casual conversation. Off her guard, she was far more likely to reveal something that would give Agatha her answer.

A steward seated her at the only unoccupied table in the saloon and brought coffee and petit fours. She bit into a heart-shaped morsel of chocolate-covered cake. Raspberry sauce oozed from the middle onto her tongue. It was a most comforting sensation. At the other end of the room, a pianist struck up the opening bars of Chopin's *Fantaisie*. Through the window she spotted a town on top of a hill, terra-cotta rooftops clustered round an ancient bell tower. She glanced at her watch. Less than an hour, now, until Venice. The Orient Express would not leave until nine o'clock that evening, so there was plenty of time for sightseeing. She had been looking forward to exploring the place; she must not let this . . . what? This *possibility* ruin it.

The man at Cook's had tried to persuade her to book a place on a guided tour, but she had come on this journey to avoid that kind of thing. She much preferred the idea of seeing the city from one of the water buses used by local people to get around. She had a Baedeker's guide and thought she would do pretty well by herself.

It suddenly occurred to Agatha that she might engineer a conversation with the mystery girl by following her when she got off. By positioning herself near the girl's compartment as they pulled into the station, she could watch her disembark, then follow at a discreet distance.

You're obsessed. Why can't you leave it alone?

Archie's voice, low and menacing. It reminded Agatha of the night he'd left the house at Sunningdale for the very last time, furious with her for refusing to divorce him. She would never forget the look in his eyes. It was as if a stranger had taken over the person she thought she knew.

He was demanding a divorce, but he flatly refused to allow Nancy's name to be mentioned in the proceedings. Instead, he wanted to fake some sordid encounter in a hotel in Brighton as grounds for ending their marriage.

Agatha felt that if he'd been honest about it, if he and Nancy had had the guts to admit to what was going on between them, she would have caved in earlier than she did. It seemed doubly unfair, having to appear in court herself while Nancy remained untouched by scandal. And when she had to break the news to Rosalind that her father wouldn't be living with them anymore, her little girl had turned away, saying, "Daddy likes *me*, doesn't he? It's *you* he doesn't like."

A man's voice—real, not imagined—brought Agatha back to reality.

"Would you mind if I joined you?" Brown eyes smiled from a young, tanned face with a neatly clipped mustache. "Forgive me for the intrusion, but I'm afraid there are no other seats available."

"Oh, yes—please do sit down."

He looked about the same age as her nephew, Jack. Although nearly thirty, Jack—she was sure—would have been mortified at the idea of having to make polite conversation with an unknown, older woman, but this young man seemed totally at ease. He told her how much he was looking forward to seeing Venice and asked if it was her first visit. Soon they were comparing guidebooks and discussing the relative merits of vaporetti and gondolas.

The pianist finished the Chopin piece and stood up with a little bow.

"Oh," Agatha said, "what a shame."

Her companion nodded. "Do you play?"

"I used to. I don't have as much time these days."

"There's a recital in Saint Mark's cathedral this evening: Do you like Wagner?"

Agatha's eyes lit up. "What is it?"

"The *Siegfried Idyll*."

"Did you have to book in advance?"

"It's free," he said, "but I would get there early if you want a seat."

She found herself telling him how, as a girl, she had been introduced to Wagner by her sister Madge, who took her to Covent Garden. It had sparked a teenage dream of becoming Isolde, of making a career as an opera singer. "I think it was the death scene that did it." She smiled, shaking her head. "When they're both lying there and it's her spirit singing. I could actually *see* the wings—the colors in them . . ." She broke off, embarrassed at having disclosed something that sounded so fanciful.

"I know exactly what you mean." He nodded. "I get that sometimes with music. It liberates the mind, doesn't it? Like blowing on a dandelion."

She nodded back at him. This wasn't like talking to Jack—not at all. She wondered what sort of life he had led, to be so perceptive. Then he told her that his grandmother had been an opera singer in Brussels and sang as Salomé in the first performance of Massenet's *Hérodiade*. So music was in his blood. As she listened to him, Agatha couldn't help smiling at the thought of finding herself in conversation with a mustachioed man of Belgian descent when Hercule Poirot had been on her mind just half an hour earlier.

When the steward came to advise them that they would be disembarking in five minutes' time, she peered at her watch, surprised.

"I do hope you have a pleasant evening." As he rose from the seat, her companion's hand went to his head to doff a nonexistent hat. Realizing his mistake, he blushed and made a hurried exit.

It was only when he'd gone that she realized he hadn't told her his name or where he was going. She wondered if she would see him again after Venice.

~

As the train slowed to a crawl, Nancy pulled down the blind. She didn't know if the Lido would be visible from the train. Just catching a glimpse of it would be bad enough. But robbing herself of the view only served to stoke the embers left by her other senses. The scent of wet sand. The sound of music and laughter seeping through the wooden walls of the beach hut. The taste of sea-drenched, sun-warmed skin. And the touch of his fingers. Hard to believe that it was more than six months ago.

She had been so utterly miserable at the start of her honeymoon in Venice, but he had come to her rescue. Saved her from a marriage that was doomed from the start.

It had been her husband's idea, to join a house party at an Italian villa a couple of weeks after the wedding. He had made it sound like such fun. But it was a setup: an elaborate plan to betray her in the worst-possible way. Looking back, she couldn't believe how naïve she had been. Felix had been too drunk to make love to her on their wedding night. He had come to her the next evening, but had insisted on going back to sleep in his own room afterward and had failed to appear at breakfast the following morning. A fortnight into her marriage, she had felt humiliated and bewildered by his casual disregard for her feelings. It was only when they arrived in Venice that she discovered what was really going on.

On the second night, when he insisted on staying up late to play cards, she had lain awake. She had decided to surprise him, creeping along the corridor to his room when she thought he was in bed. He was in bed. But not alone.

She had stumbled out of the villa, stunned by what she had just witnessed. One of the other guests—a tall, fair handsome man she'd only been introduced to the previous day—had caught sight of her. He was sitting alone on the terrace in the moonlight, smoking a cigarette and had jumped up, offering her a handkerchief and asking if she had hurt herself. When she told him what had happened, he had not asked any questions, just sat and listened.

They had watched the moon set and the morning star rise over the sea before they said good night. He had taken her hand then and kissed it, holding her eyes with a lingering glance before padding back across the dew-covered cobbles to his room.

The next day he knocked on her door, bringing a tray of coffee and peaches from the garden. She invited him in, secure in the knowledge that her husband would certainly not come looking for her. He had made her laugh with stories of the people he had flown out from England to work with. And then he had asked if she would like to go bathing—which soon became part of a daily ritual.

At the Villa Rezzonico few members of the house party ventured out of bed before midday. But she would rise at eight thirty to meet him for a morning dip. On the second day he swam to her beneath the surface of the water, as lithe and quick as a fish, skimming her hips with his shoulder as he swerved past. She almost lost her balance, but he was there, lifting her up above the waves. She bent to kiss his wet forehead, tasting its saltiness. And he tilted his head back until his lips met hers.

They had lain in the sand at the water's edge, her skin on fire where his fingers traced the curve of her arm. They had not spoken about it—hadn't planned what they would do—but the next morning, after their swim, he produced the key to a beach hut. It smelled of dry seaweed and olive oil—an empty bottle of which lay on the rough wooden bench that served as the only piece of furniture. He spread his towel on the sandy floor and they dropped onto it, limbs entwined, still slippery from the sea.

Three days later they were lying in the shade, eating green figs and melon when he took her hand, his eyes clouded. "Darling, there's something I've been meaning to tell you."

She sat bolt upright, trembling as he told her about his wife and daughter.

"I should have told you at the beginning." He reached out to stroke her hair. "But I wanted you so much." His eyes searched her face. "You have every right to despise me, I know. But I don't regret a single moment. Do you?"

She was prevented from replying by the sound of a saxophone. A hundred yards away, on the bandstand in front of the Excelsior Palace, a jazz quartet struck up and a tipsy-looking woman in pink silk pajamas began dancing barefoot in the sand.

"We'd better be getting back," he said. "They'll notice if we're late for lunch."

That afternoon, because it was their last day, everyone posed for a photograph on the beach. Unable to be near him, she couldn't smile. The shot had caught the tension in her. She looked like a cornered animal. And he was looking straight at her, not at the camera. There was a fierce, restless look in his eyes, as if he was sick of the charade the holiday had turned into.

And then they had met, just two weeks later, in early May, at a cinema in Leicester Square. It was easy to arrange because they had discovered they lived within a mile of each other. Perhaps if he had not been so close, if he had lived hundreds of miles away, she might have been able to forget him. But it had been pure torture, looking out across the blossom-filled trees of Green Park, knowing that he was just a few streets away.

Now the distance between them was growing by the minute. He was on the night train to Calais. Tomorrow he would be back in London. And Baghdad was so very far away.

We will be together, I promise.

Would he have said that if he didn't mean it? Nancy lay down and closed her eyes.

~

When Agatha opened the door of her compartment, Katharine was still in her pajamas. She was lying on the banquette, covered with a blanket, her head propped on a stack of pillows and a book open on her lap.

"Aren't you getting off?" Agatha asked, reaching up to the luggage rack for her hatbox.

"I don't think so." Katharine yawned and stretched. "I couldn't get off to sleep: too many doors banging everywhere. It'll be quieter when we stop. And I've seen Venice half a dozen times."

Agatha opened the door of the cupboard that contained the wash-basin, checking her reflection in the mirror. There was a smear of choco-late on her lip. Her insides curled. She wondered what the young man must have thought of her.

As she moved her head, she caught Katharine's face reflected in the mirror. The contrast did nothing to lift her spirits.

"Are you taking a tour?" Katharine looked up from her book as Agatha delved in her handbag for a lipstick.

"I don't really like crowds. I prefer to see the sights on my own."

"Very wise," Katharine replied. "People can be very trying, can't they? It will be such a relief when they've all cleared off."

Agatha could have taken offense at this remark, as she was the primary obstacle to Katharine's peace and quiet. But it was said with such a sweet smile, it was impossible to feel slighted in any way. "Are you enjoying your book?" she asked.

"Oh yes!" Katharine pulled out a bookmark and closed it up. "I don't usually read this sort of thing—but it's rather good." She reached across to deposit the book on the table under the window.

It was upside down, but the image on the cover was as familiar to Agatha as her own front door. An elegant foot in a red satin shoe stepping from a car onto the pavement. Black lettering against a threatening sky. A surge of adrenaline shot through her body.

"It's called *The Murder of Roger Ackroyd*." Katharine had turned away from her to plump up the pillows. "It's by Agatha Christie. You know: the one who ran off to Harrogate and had half the policemen in England chasing after her?"

Agatha snapped her handbag shut and seized the handle of the door, mumbling something about needing the lavatory before the train pulled into the station. When she reached the end of the corridor, she locked herself inside the tiny cubicle and sank down on the seat. The train, already slowing down, made a sudden lurch. As her fingers shot to the handrail, she saw that they were shaking.

What a fool, to think you can escape.

CHAPTER 5

Venice

As the train shuddered to a halt, Katharine leaned across to pull down the blind. People were already spilling onto the platform, eager to see as much of the city as possible in the few hours ahead. She moved the blind sideways, watching through a slit of window, seeing without being seen. It wasn't long before she spotted him.

"Oh, Max," she said to herself, "you just can't keep away, can you, darling?"

She saw that he had lost the beard he had grown last season. She thought the mustache looked better. He had lost weight, too. Quite handsome in that suit. So different from the scruffy student, fresh from Oxford, who had joined the dig three years ago.

Katharine watched him until he disappeared into the crowd. Letting go of the blind, she sank back onto the bed, images of him slipping through her head like a silent movie. Max had always been her favorite. In that first season in the desert, she had ensnared him, sending him on ten-mile treks to buy her sweets and cigarettes, rewarding him with nothing more than an invitation to brush her hair. She loved the way he did it, so firm and yet so gentle.

When they were alone together in her room, the atmosphere was electric. He wanted to touch her: she knew that and it thrilled her. But he was afraid of overstepping the mark, of going any further than she permitted him to. And that was more intoxicating still, to wield such power over another.

As she closed her eyes, she imagined his hands traveling over her body. She allowed herself this fantasy because it was safe. A make-believe man could do her no harm. The real Max, given half a chance, would be dangerous.

She hadn't expected to see him on the train. There was no need for him to travel out east this early. He could have left it another week at least. She wondered if he'd been invited to the wedding. She hoped not. It was a business arrangement, not a celebration.

Her eyes snapped open. A horrible thought had occurred to her: that Max had been asked to be best man; that he would be standing right behind her during the ceremony, handing over the ring when the time came. That would be pure torture.

~

Agatha was one of the last people to get off the train. She had to pass the compartment belonging to the girl on her way out. The door blind was pulled down. Agatha paused for a moment and listened. Not a sound from inside. Short of knocking, there was no way of knowing whether she had disembarked.

As Agatha walked out of the station into the late afternoon sunshine, she tried to put Ann Nelson out of her mind. This was the beginning of her big adventure—the kind of journey people might dream of making, if only they had the means—and she must not let fear spoil it.

But what are you actually afraid of?

That question had been popping in and out of her head ever since she left London. Being alone, missing home—the fears had been simple ones at first. But on the Orient Express they had taken on a new dimension. Now she was afraid that the past had climbed on board with her, that heartache would consume her.

Walking along the cobbled streets, she breathed in the mingled scent of cigarettes and coffee and dust. It was a continental smell, very different from London, and despite her gloomy thoughts, it set off a tingle of excitement. She joined a throng of people queuing for the vaporetto.

The arrival of the Orient Express in Venice had unfortunately coincided with the end of the school day, and it felt as if half the population of the city was heading home. The sight of a group of girls about the same age as Rosalind, smiling and laughing as they waited for the boat, brought a lump to her throat.

When the boat pulled into the quayside, a crush of uniformed bodies propelled her toward the gate. She was lucky to get a seat. Scores of people, including several women, were standing up, clinging to whatever they could as the boat lurched away from its mooring. The young men seemed to have no qualms about sitting down while a woman stood. It was everyone for him- or herself.

She was beginning to think she'd made a big mistake, choosing this way of seeing the city, but as the boat chugged along the Grand Canal, her mouth opened in silent wonder at the moving tableau: ornate facades of carved stone and gilded wood, flowers spilling from balconies, music drifting from floating restaurants, gondolas slipping out of hidden ribbons of green water.

Agatha's plan was to disembark at the Rialto Bridge and browse the souvenir stalls before heading toward Saint Mark's Square. But seeing a sign indicating the fish market, she decided to get off earlier. She soon found herself in a labyrinth of twisting, narrow streets punctuated by small, rickety bridges of weed-strewn wood. The signs had petered out and she had no idea which way to go.

Cut off from the bustling heart of the city by the high, dank walls of old houses, these streets had an eerie silence. She could hear her footsteps echo as she quickened her pace. The cobbled street was heading for what looked like a gateway. But when she reached the gate, she found that it was locked.

Turning round, she caught sight of a man at a window, watching her. The look on his face turned her stomach. For a moment she stood absolutely still, paralyzed by the sinister grin spreading across his face. Then she saw his hand move to the front of his trousers.

She put her head down and ran as fast as she could, back down the alley, the smack of her feet on the cobbles matching each beat of her heart. When she reached the bridge, she doubled over, panting, against the wooden railings. There was a gondola gliding toward her. What should have been a pleasing sight felt suddenly tainted, as if everything in this city would be forever colored by that seedy encounter in its backstreets.

As the boat drew closer, she could see a couple sitting behind the gondolier. They were kissing. He was stroking her hair, whispering something in her ear. They were about to pass beneath her when he glanced up at the bridge. It was Archie's face she saw. Archie's face framed with impossible black hair. Of course it wasn't him. She knew that. The couple looked Spanish or Italian, not English. But still she saw that face.

She whipped her head round, her eyes fixed on the gondola as it slipped away. Agatha knew at that moment what she was really afraid of: she was afraid she was losing her mind.

She stumbled through the streets, hoping at every turn for a glimpse of the Grand Canal. Her plan to see Saint Mark's Square abandoned, she just wanted to find a way of getting back to the comforting familiarity of the Orient Express. But to her surprise, she suddenly turned into a street with an arrow-shaped sign bearing the words "Piazza San Marco." She thought she might as well follow it, as it offered a better chance of finding the way back to the main thoroughfare than continuing to wander aimlessly.

Nothing could have prepared Agatha for the sight that met her eyes when she reached the end of the street. She emerged from a stone tunnel through an ancient building that straddled the cobbles. And there she was, in a vast open space bustling with people and pigeons. The last rays of the setting sun fell on the gilded facade of Saint Mark's Basilica. The ancient wood and stone glowed like the entrance to some heavenly city guarded by a winged lion gleaming in a starry sky.

People appeared to be coming in and out of the central archway. She glanced at her watch. The recital would have already started. She hesitated, nervous about going in. She no longer felt at home in churches. She had stopped taking communion. It wasn't that she no longer believed in God, more a case of him not believing in her. In divorcing Archie, she felt she had let God down, broken a sacred promise. Although she still went to church occasionally, she felt like an unwelcome guest.

Despite her misgivings, Agatha found herself drawn across the square, as if invisible hands were pulling her along. She passed under the golden-framed mosaic above the west door and stepped into the cool, dark interior.

She hesitated again as her eyes adjusted to the change of light. Fumbling in her bag, she pulled out a silk headscarf. *Yet another disguise?* Archie's voice mocked her as she knotted it under her chin. The sense of not belonging intensified as she saw shadowy figures lighting candles, crossing themselves, and kneeling at prayer. It was the music that persuaded her to take the next few steps. The melancholy strain of a violin. It sounded exactly how she felt.

As she walked further into the cathedral, it was almost impossible not to look up. Acres of gilded mosaics covered the vaults and cupolas.

It was like stepping into a cavern of hidden treasure. Silver lamps threw back a bewildering array of glittering images. Twisting birds and horned demons, wild-eyed disciples on a storm-tossed sea, John the Baptist plucking Jesus from what looked like a river of snakes.

Stumbling slightly, she made her way toward the music, which was coming from a side chapel to the left of the nave. But as she reached it, a uniformed attendant stepped in front of her, barring the way.

"Mi dispiace, non ci sono posti a sedere." Agatha frowned, uncomprehending.

"No seats left, I'm afraid." The young man from the train appeared from the shadows. "But there's a place over here: you can see through the screen."

She followed him round a stone pillar and, sure enough, she could see the soloist through the gaps between a frieze of carved wooden dragons and lions guarding the side entrance to the chapel.

"Please, have a seat." He gestured to the single chair beside the screen door.

"Oh, but it's . . ."

"No, really—I'm happy to stand after all that time on the train." He flashed a smile, a gleam of white from beneath the dark mustache.

The chair, although ancient and high-backed, was quite comfortable. She rested her head against the wood and let her eyes range across the gilded ceiling of the chapel as the music filled her head. She had a sense of almost drifting out of her body, of soaring up to join the impossible creatures depicted overhead. And for the first time since leaving London, she felt safe, out of reach of the tormenting voices and haunting faces that had followed her onto the train.

If there is a God, she thought, music must be his language. She closed her eyes to shut out all other distractions, breathing in the ancient, comforting scent of old churches, of polished wood, melting wax, and lingering incense. She had fallen into a sort of sleep when a voice behind her startled her back to the present.

"Are you all right?"

His eyes were upside down, his mustache like a black arrow piercing his nose. It took her a couple of seconds to register that her head was tipped backward and he was leaning over the top of the chair.

"Did you enjoy it?" His eyes crinkled at the edges. As dark as sloe berries, they had an oriental look from this angle.

"Oh yes, very much!" Agatha jumped up from the seat, hoping he didn't think she'd slept through the whole thing.

"I don't know about you, but I'm terrifically thirsty. Would you like something to drink or eat? We've got an hour or so before we need to get back."

She hesitated for only a fraction of a second. If the suggestion had come from a man of her own age or older, she might have suspected the motive. But because he was young and came out with it in such an unselfconscious way, she felt quite safe in accepting. And she was in a foreign city where nobody knew her. Where was the harm in it?

"I'm so sorry, I haven't introduced myself properly, have I?" He held out his hand. "Max Mallowan."

"Ag . . . Mary," she stuttered. "Mary Miller." He made a little bow as he released her hand. "Where would you like to go? A bar or a restaurant?"

"Well . . . I'm not sure. I'm not really hungry, but I'm not all that keen on bars . . ." She paused, aware of sounding ungrateful and rather pathetic.

"Do you like ice cream?"

At this she nodded enthusiastically.

"There's a very good place not far from here."

It was dark when they stepped outside. He led her across the square and down a narrow street lined with shops selling everything from carnival masks to cigars. They crossed a bridge that led to the Canale della Giudecca and came to a waterside café with candles on the tables whose menu featured the largest selection of ice creams Agatha had ever seen.

"Have you tried pistachio? It's very good. Or, if you like liqueur, you can get Amaretto flavor."

She admitted her inability to tolerate alcohol, and his mouth turned down in sympathy. "I'm afraid I developed the opposite problem at Oxford. Too much claret and not enough concentration, my tutors would probably tell you."

Agatha blinked. Her nephew, Jack, had gone to Oxford. They had very likely been there at the same time. She opened her mouth to ask when he had graduated, but closed it before the words came out. To mention Jack would be to risk giving herself away. Instead, she told him about the time she and her mother had ordered half pints of cream as an alternative to wine on holiday in Cornwall.

"Did you drink it?"

"Every drop. I've become rather a fan since. It's my favorite thing to drink."

He laughed. "Do they serve it on the Orient Express?"

"I'm sure they would if I asked, but I daren't—there's so much food, people would think me an absolute glutton."

"Well, I think that when you're on holiday, you should do exactly as you please." He grinned. "And as they probably don't serve half pints of cream here, I'm going to insist on you having two ice creams as compensation. So what will you have?"

It was strange, being treated like an indulged child by someone younger than herself. But she was beginning to see that Max's youthful face masked what her mother would have called a wise soul. Despite the age difference, he somehow seemed years ahead of her.

After much agonizing, Agatha settled on *cioccolato fondente* accompanied by *dulce de leche*—a wicked but heavenly combination for a cream addict. Max chose something called *crema dei Dogi*, whose flavor he described as treacle tart with a dash of marsala. Between mouthfuls, he asked her how far she was traveling.

"To Damascus by train, then on to Baghdad," she said. "And you?"

"I'm getting off at Trieste," he replied. "I'm heading in the same direction as you, but I have to take a boat to Beirut to pick up some supplies there." He scooped up another spoonful of ice cream. "Do you have family in Baghdad?"

She told him the same story she had given Katharine, adding that she hoped to visit the dig at Ur at some stage during her stay. At this, his eyes lit up.

"That's where I'm going—I'm working on the dig."

To Agatha, this was a most extraordinary coincidence. But when she told him she was sharing a compartment with one of his colleagues, his expression suddenly changed. It was only a fleeting look, and he covered it instantly with a smile, but he was a poor actor. It was as if a fly had landed in his ice cream.

"Oh, you're sharing with Mrs. Keeling, are you? I didn't realize she was on the train—I thought she was coming by sea." He scraped with his spoon at the sticky residue in the bottom of his glass. "How are you getting on with her?"

Agatha took a breath. "She's quite charming." She couldn't see his expression. His eyes were still on his spoon. "She seems to have led a most interesting life."

"Quite right." Max raised his head slowly. "A most interesting woman. And soon to be changing her name again. I must remember to call her Mrs. Woolley in the future."

"Mrs. *Woolley*? You mean she's . . ."

"Oh yes." He nodded. "She's marrying our esteemed boss. Next Tuesday, I believe, at the Anglican church in Haifa Street."

Agatha shook her head, perplexed. "I wonder why she didn't mention it? She told me so much about herself—all about the dig and the things she'd worked on—but she never hinted that she was about to be married to the very man we were discussing." She looked at him expectantly, but he simply shrugged. Either he didn't know or was too discreet to disclose the reason for Katharine's reticence. Glancing at his watch, he artfully changed the subject.

"I think we'd better get our skates on—it's five past eight."

"Oh!" She scraped back her chair in alarm. "Do you know the way back? I got terribly lost this afternoon."

"Don't worry. We can get a water taxi from down there." He pointed to a jetty about a hundred yards from the café.

A boat arrived just as they reached the water's edge. This time, there was no crush of people waiting to embark and they found seats easily. As the rope slipped into the water, Agatha turned to look at the softly lit facades of the buildings on the opposite bank. A gondola glided past, just a few feet from their boat. Another couple, holding hands, smiled up at the passengers in the water taxi. The man raised his hand in an awkward sort of wave. Agatha made herself look at them, at him, half-afraid of what she would see but daring herself nonetheless. To her relief, the man's face stayed just as it should be. There was no trace of Archie about the eyes, the cheekbones, or the mouth.

She realized that she had the young man sitting next to her to thank for that. With music and ice cream, he had transformed her sinister experience of Venice into something joyful. He had saved her from herself. As the gondola disappeared into the night, she felt an inexplicable sense of peace.

In the darkness, the journey down the Grand Canal had an extra dose of magic. Lanterns spilled colors onto the black water, and peeling plaster glowed in the moonlight. There were fleeting glimpses of elegant diners and costumed street performers. Apart from the occasional observation, Max said little, as if he, too, was wrapped up in his own thoughts. But as they boarded the Orient Express, he said something that intrigued Agatha.

"Would you mind not telling Mrs. Keeling that I'm on the train?" He glanced left and right, as if afraid she might emerge from one of the carriages. "I hope you won't think me rude. It's just that I'd rather our paths didn't cross until I'm back at the dig house."

"Am I allowed to ask why?"

He gave her a sheepish smile. "Of course—but I can't promise to be completely honest. I don't want to color your opinion of her with my own particular prejudices."

"You don't have to tell me anything if you don't want to," Agatha said. "I've heard enough to guess what life must be like for you all, cooped up together for months on end in that heat."

He gave a small shake of his head. "She's a fine artist and a great publicist. If it wasn't for her, the dig would have run out of backers long ago. But she has this need to . . ." He trailed off, rubbing his chin. "She likes to control people, I think. She casts a spell on you, and before you know it, you've become her slave." With a wry smile, he said, "Be careful of that, won't you?"

Before she could make any response, he tipped his hat and turned toward his carriage. "Thank you for your company, Mrs. Miller. I look forward to our meeting again in the not-too-distant future." And with that he was gone.

CHAPTER 6

Venice to Trieste

Nancy sent the steward away when he came to offer supper. She hadn't eaten since breakfast, and that had only been a piece of toast. She knew she ought to have something, but she couldn't face it. In a bid to distract herself, she rifled through her bag for Delia's letter.

If her cousin had been surprised at Nancy's sudden decision to pay her a visit, she hadn't hinted at it. The letter was full of plans for outings to exotic-sounding restaurants, trips to the theater, and afternoons at the tennis club.

Delia's large, bold handwriting was just what you would expect of a woman who had defied convention to take a man's job in a foreign city. As a child, Nancy had been in awe of her. Delia was twelve years older and the brightest girl in her school. At eighteen, she had won a place at Cambridge to study classics and had taught herself Persian in her spare time.

When war came, Delia was recruited by the Foreign Office for work so secret she wasn't even allowed to tell her parents where she was based.

Then, in peacetime, came the posting to Baghdad. Nancy wasn't sure exactly what she did. Something to do with keeping an eye on the local tribesmen, Uncle Rowland had said.

Nancy's biggest fear was that Delia would throw her out if she discovered the real reason for the visit. Laying the letter aside, her fingers came to rest on the soft fabric of her dress. She let them trace the pattern of diamonds and zigzag lines, finding the place where her stomach swelled. She couldn't really believe it herself. But in the past few weeks she had been feeling a fluttering inside, a sensation that reminded her of a robin she had tried to rescue when it flew down the chimney. Trying to open the window with her elbow, she had felt its tiny wings beating, trapped inside her hands as she struggled to set it free.

Thank goodness for jersey dresses and loose-fitting jackets with big pockets. Nancy hated the idea of lying to her cousin. But it wasn't fair to confront her with the scandalous truth. She was going to have to pretend to have fled England to escape a violent husband. It was a shabby thing to do, but Nancy's very survival depended on it. Delia was the only family she had left. She had to make her an ally, make her see that, with a baby on the way, there had been no other choice but to get as far away as possible.

The hoot of the engine scattered the images inside her head. The train was beginning to move. She was glad to be leaving Venice. Relieved that night had fallen outside the window, preventing her from catching any further, torturing glimpses of the place where she had spent the happiest and most wretched days of her life.

As the train picked up speed, there was a knock at the door.

"Madame?"

The steward again. He was so attentive, trying so hard to look after her. Why couldn't he just leave her alone?

"It's all right, thank you," she called out. "I really don't need anything."

"But, madame." His voice was louder now, with a note of urgency. "I have something for you. A telegram."

She jumped off the bed, her heart lurching. He must have changed his mind. Decided to come with her after all. He must have wired as soon as he got off the train.

"Oh, thank you!" She took the telegram from the steward with trembling hands. Flashing a grateful smile, she shut the door and unfolded the stiff paper.

The words swam before her eyes.

```
DEEPLY   REGRET   TO   INFORM   YOU   DELIA
GRANDFIELD DEAD.
```

~

Katharine had taken supper on a tray—a dish of deviled eggs and a bowl of Waldorf salad, the remains of which lay beside her on the banquette.

"How did you like Venice?"

"It's breathtaking." Agatha took off her hat and hooked it over the end of the luggage rack. "Quite exhausting, though. Do you mind if I go to bed?"

The steward had already effected the nightly transformation of the compartment, pulling down the bunk and hooking the little ladder over the side. Katharine had not consulted Agatha about the sleeping arrangements. The banquette was clearly marked as her own territory. But Agatha didn't mind. She liked the privacy the top bunk afforded. She planned to get undressed lying down if she could manage it, to save having to peel off her clothes in front of Katharine.

"Aren't you hungry?" Katharine pushed the tray to the far end of the banquette and picked up her book. "The steward will be back in a minute—shall I order you something?"

"No, thank you." Agatha opened the cupboard that contained the washbasin and took her toothbrush from the glass. "I had the most delicious ice cream, and I couldn't eat another thing."

"Do you mind if I carry on reading for a while? I'm wide awake now: worst luck!"

Agatha didn't mind that either. She had always been able to fall asleep quickly, almost anywhere. And once she was unconscious, she rarely woke up. Last night had been an exception, which she put down to the excitement of sleeping on a train for the first time in her life.

As she put away her toothbrush, she caught a glimpse of Katharine in the mirror. Her book was propped up on her knees, obscuring most of her face. Agatha could see that she was more than halfway through *The Murder of Roger Ackroyd*. It was unnerving to think of her reading the story with no notion that its creator was lying fast asleep above her head.

She climbed the ladder and lay down, trying not to bang her elbow on the wall as she undid the buttons of her blouse. She was wriggling into her nightdress when Katharine's voice rang out from below.

"Do you think she *really* lost her memory?"

Agatha's stomach contracted.

"Agatha Christie," Katharine persisted. "Do you think it was all an act?"

The bed creaked as Agatha breathed out. "I . . . er . . . I . . . don't know much about it," she mumbled.

"Really? It was all over the papers—of course, you can't believe half of what they say—but it was a fascinating case. I think the business with the abandoned car was a cry for help, don't you?"

Agatha felt as if her tongue were glued to her gums. She lay absolutely still, praying that Katharine would think she'd fallen asleep.

"I imagine the amnesia thing was her husband's idea. A very convenient smoke screen for whatever sparked the whole thing off, I'd say."

Agatha heard the rustle of sheets as Katharine shifted her position. Perhaps she didn't expect a response. Perhaps the remarks were nothing more than throwaway observations, a brief interlude in her reading. Still, Agatha didn't move. She lay on her back, her nightdress rucked up around her middle, terrified of advertising the fact that she was still awake.

It was only later—what seemed like hours later—that Katharine reached across to put out the light. Agatha fell into a sort of doze after that. She woke up suddenly and sat bolt upright, grazing her head on the roof of the compartment. She felt a desperate urge to relieve herself and wondered why. Then she remembered. In her haste to get into bed she had forgotten to visit the lavatory.

She eased her legs over the side of the bunk, feeling for the ladder with her toes. It squeaked as she put her weight on it and she paused, listening. There was no change in the rhythm of Katharine's breathing. Agatha's left foot made contact with the carpet. Then she felt for the handle of the door.

She would not normally have ventured into the corridor without her dressing gown, but there was no hope of locating it in the dark. And her spectacles—where were they? With a silent groan she remembered that she had tucked them under the pillow. She prayed she wouldn't encounter anyone outside the compartment. She had no idea what time it was. Hopefully the steward had finished his rounds and was tucked up for the night.

The lamps in the corridor had been turned down low—just enough light for passengers to find their way to the lavatory in the middle of the night without dazzling the other occupants of the compartments when they opened the doors. As Agatha made her way toward the end of the carriage, she saw that every compartment was in darkness. It must be very late, she decided. But as she drew nearer to the engine, she caught a flicker of movement. Her heart sank. Someone else had got to the lavatory before her.

She hesitated, wondering whether to hide in the shadows for a while. But a sudden blast of cold air caught her face, taking her breath away. The person she had seen must have pulled down the window in the top half of the door at the end of the carriage. She shivered. Why on earth would they do such a thing? Wrapping her arms round her billowing nightdress, she marched indignantly toward the source of the icy draft. But as she drew level with the last compartment, she stopped dead. It was the girl. Ann Nelson. She was leaning out of the window, her hair plastered against her face with the force of the freezing air. And her fingers were on the handle of the door, her knuckles white as she grasped it. In a moment of horrible clarity, Agatha saw that she was about to throw herself from the train.

In the split second before she acted, a single word seared Agatha's brain.

Good.

Nancy was going to die and Archie would be free of her.

As it shot through her mind, she batted the thought away, her body already hurtling toward the end of the carriage. She saw the door fly open, heard metal crash against metal as it swung against the side of the train. The girl was silhouetted against moonlit clouds, clinging onto the handrail.

"Nancy!" Agatha's voice was drowned by the rush of air. "Nancy! Don't jump!" she yelled.

The girl twisted round just as Agatha reached her. Agatha grabbed her round the waist, trying to pull her away from the open door. But a gust of air knocked her off balance. She felt herself falling, saw the ground below, rocks glinting where the moon caught them. Her hands flailed, searching for something, anything to grab hold of. Suddenly her body jerked sideways, as if some invisible hand had hooked itself under her waist and scooped her up. The last thing Agatha remembered was her head hitting the handrail. Then everything went black.

CHAPTER 7

Zagreb to Sofia

Agatha was dreaming of Torquay, of sitting in the garden at her mother's house, surrounded by daffodils. She and Archie were all dressed up for a day at the races. Suddenly he reached out and swapped their hats. The brim of his came down over her eyes and when she pushed it back, she saw him grinning at her from beneath a confection of net and silk daisies. They looked at each other and laughed and he said, "Good Lord, I do love you!" But before she could reply, his hat fell back across her face, smothering her as she tried to open her mouth. And then she was falling, through the daffodils, into the cold, dark earth. Past the bones of Tony, her Yorkshire terrier. Past worms the size of fire hoses and earwigs with fangs like kitchen knives. Falling, falling . . .

It was the smell that brought her back to life. A sharp metallic scent of iodine. She opened her eyes to blue sky beyond the window. And Katharine's face hovering over her, the blonde halo of hair giving her the look of a ministering angel.

She dabbed the wound and Agatha flinched, her hand flying to her head.

"No, you mustn't touch it." Katharine's voice was different. Gentler than before.

"I . . . She . . ." Agatha tried to sit up, a jumble of images crowding her brain.

"It's all right—you don't have to explain." Katharine put her arms around Agatha's shoulders, easing her back onto the pillow. "I saw what happened. There was a terrific bang, and I ran out into the corridor to see you rugby-tackle that girl. You were very lucky not to fall out of the train, you know. You saved her life."

"She's . . . ?"

"Yes, she's fine. Just a few bruises. Do you know who she is?"

Agatha looked away. Did she? Was Ann Nelson really Archie's lover? She had no proof.

"The Honorable Ann Grandfield, as was." Katharine took a dressing from a green tin box and applied it to Agatha's forehead. "Voted Debutante of the Year by *Tatler* a few seasons ago—and made the front cover of *Vogue*. She married Viscount Nelson earlier this year: April or May, I think it was." She ran her fingers around the edge of the dressing, sealing it to the skin. "I wonder what's gone wrong."

As Katharine's hand withdrew, Agatha screwed her eyes shut. It wasn't the sting of the iodine. She could bear that. Katharine's revelation was like a punch in the stomach. She felt stupid, confused. This was not her husband's lover, then, but some other Nancy: a society beauty whose face had become public property. That, at least, explained why Agatha had thought she knew her.

But if she was not the girl Archie had gone off with, who was the man Agatha had seen on the train? She could almost have sworn it was her ex-husband. Could Archie possibly be involved with the newly married wife of a viscount? Was that why he had been so desperate to keep her name out of the divorce proceedings? And if it *was* him, why had this Nancy tried to kill herself hours after waving him good-bye?

When she opened her eyes, the sunlight dazzled her. It occurred to her that she had no idea what time it was or what country she was in.

"Don't try to sit up," Katharine said as Agatha raised her head from the pillow.

"I just . . ." Agatha sank back again. "Where are we?"

"Yugoslavia. We've just crossed the border." She looked at her watch. "You weren't unconscious for very long. They brought a doctor on board when we stopped at Trieste, but you probably don't remember."

Agatha frowned. "No . . . I . . . What did he say?"

"That you might be concussed and I was to keep a careful eye on you. How do you feel now? Not sick, I hope? You must tell me if you get a headache."

Agatha's hand went to her temple. Did she have a headache? Her head was certainly sore where she had caught it on the handrail. As her fingers made contact with the skin above her ear, she gasped.

"What's the matter? Are you in pain?"

"I . . . No. My glasses . . . Do you know where they are?"

Katharine reached across to the table. "Here you are," she said. "The steward found them when he dismantled the bed."

Agatha stared, dismayed at the tortoiseshell frames folded in Katharine's hand. As she took them, Katharine's eyes locked on hers. There was a hint of a smile, which could have meant something or nothing. Had Katharine seen her photograph in the back of *Roger Ackroyd*? Did she know?

"I'm going to sit here and read while you rest, if you don't mind," Katharine said, with no trace of irony in her voice. "I want you to close your eyes and try to go back to sleep. In an hour or two, if you feel up to it, I'll order us something to eat."

Agatha felt a sudden wave of exhaustion wash over her, as if Katharine's words had a hypnotic power. There was nothing she could do. If her cover was blown, she would just have to face the consequences later. Right now all she wanted was oblivion.

~

Nancy pulled the sheets up over her eyes. She longed to be left alone, but there was no chance of that. A fearsome Italian woman in the tight-fitting navy uniform of the Wagons-Lits company had come onto the train with the doctor and installed herself in the compartment.

Nancy's Italian was no better than this woman's English, so their conversation had been limited. But no explanation was necessary. Signorina Tedaldi was clearly on suicide watch.

"You sleep, no?" No doubt the words were kindly meant, but the gruff manner in which they were delivered made it sound like an order. And Nancy was beyond sleep. Her head felt as if it were on fire.

What would have happened if she had gone through with it? If that woman hadn't grabbed her? Now that she was safe, she wasn't sure. All she knew was that she was glad to be alive, whatever the consequences. Standing on the edge of the train in the moonlight with the wind snatching the breath from her body, she had suddenly felt that familiar fluttering in her belly, as if the half-formed being inside were rattling the bars, begging to be heard. In that moment she realized she had no right to do what despair had driven her to. Because it was not just *her* life she was about to destroy.

She closed her eyes, thinking of the woman who had risked her life to save her. Her memory was hazy. She remembered white cotton billowing out like a ship's sail in the moonlight. A woman in a nightgown, on her way to the lavatory. If she had not woken up, not needed to leave her compartment . . .

Nancy sucked in her breath. Wondered what she herself would have done in a similar situation. Would she have been brave enough to try to stop a complete stranger from throwing herself off a speeding train? And yet . . . Nancy searched the jumbled images of the night before. No, not a stranger: she distinctly remembered someone calling her name.

Whoever the woman was, she had hurt herself. Nancy dug her nails into the back of her hand as she remembered. Her head was gashed, and there were drops of blood on her nightgown. She must find her as soon as possible. Beg her forgiveness and thank her for what she had done. Yes, thank her. For in spite of the fear, the panic that bubbled up every time she allowed herself to think about the future, there *was* something to live for. She felt an overwhelming urge to tell this Good Samaritan that she had saved not just one life but two.

Nancy opened her eyes a fraction of an inch, glancing sideways at her Italian minder, who was writing something in a notebook. She wondered if she would have to ask permission to leave the compartment and go in search of the lady in the nightgown. Signorina Tedaldi was probably under orders to escort her all the way to Damascus. It was understandable, she supposed, that the company would want to avoid the taint of passengers taking their own lives while on the train. But once she disembarked, she would be on her own. No Delia waiting in Baghdad to take her home.

Nancy's throat constricted at the thought of her cousin. The last time she had seen Delia was at Victoria station two years ago, at the end of a spell on leave. They had laughed together over a couple of sailors who had been leaning out of one of the carriages, blowing kisses as their train pulled away.

"Come and visit!" Delia had called as she climbed aboard. "We'll have a blast!"

Nancy had smiled and waved furiously until the smoke drove her away from the platform's edge. Baghdad had sounded so strange, so alien. Delia's stories of her life there—of the heat, the insects, the tribesmen with their gaggle of wives—made Nancy think it was the last place on earth she would choose to go for a holiday.

It seemed impossible that Delia was dead. She had been so passionate about her work, so in love with life. The telegram had given no clue as to what had happened. Nancy wondered who had sent it. Probably someone at the British Consulate's office, where Delia had worked. She wondered fleetingly if she might be able to appeal to someone there for a place to stay while she worked out what to do. They were supposed to help British citizens in extremis, weren't they? And there couldn't be many worse predicaments than the one Nancy was in now.

~

Katharine studied Agatha as she slept. In the bright sunshine it was possible to see that her hair, swept back from the wound, was a different color at the roots. It was only a fraction of an inch of new growth—no more than a week, Katharine guessed—but enough to betray the fact that Mary Miller was not a natural redhead.

Katharine opened her novel at the inside back cover, holding the book as close to her traveling companion's face as possible without disturbing her. Yes, she thought, the nose was the same: a strong Roman nose—but not unattractive. A wide mouth with the upper lip a little less full than the lower one. And the eyebrows: if Katharine had been drawing this face, she would have enjoyed doing those. They were striking but not startling. There was no artifice about them—no plucking or cosmetic enhancement. They sat above the eyes like gull's wings, the outer edges sweeping out a good half inch beyond the lashes.

Hard to tell for sure, of course—especially with the eyes closed. To Katharine, it was like watching something emerge, half-hidden by sand, from the desert. She was used to piecing things together, seeing what was not yet there. And as she gazed at the woman lying on the banquette, the photographic image from the novel floated through space, superimposing itself on flesh and bone.

"This is you, isn't it?" she whispered.

~

Agatha slept through the whole of Yugoslavia, waking only when the train stopped at the border with Bulgaria. Through the window she could see a sign written in an unfamiliar alphabet. There was a stall on the platform with black-and-white sausages piled alongside a smoking charcoal brazier. A woman wandered past the window with a tray of what looked like chunks of baked pumpkin topped with walnuts and icing sugar. Agatha glanced at her watch. It was half past three, and she was ravenous.

Katharine had anticipated this. She summoned the steward, who instantly brought a plate of elegantly arranged sandwiches and a ramekin of chocolate mousse.

"It's good that you feel like eating," she said, as Agatha tucked in. "What about this evening? Do you think you'll be up to walking as far as the dining car?"

"I think so." Agatha nodded. "But can I get away with it?" She raised her hand to her head, fingering the dressing. "I must look an awful sight."

"We could cover it up. Do you have a headband?"

"No—only hats. I can't wear a hat to dinner, though, can I?"

Katharine shook her head. "Not to worry—I have one. It's mauve with black and silver sequins. Do you have anything that would go with it?"

"I have a black flapper in crepe de chine—would that do?"

"Perfect," Katharine replied. "Now, do you have a different pair of spectacles? Those really don't suit you at all."

"Oh . . . I . . . ." Heat rose up Agatha's throat to her face.

"You have lovely eyes. It's a shame to hide them." Katharine was giving her that Mona Lisa smile again. Agatha felt horribly self-conscious, utterly tongue-tied. Was Katharine being deliberately provocative, trying to get her to confess? Or was it just her way to be so blunt?

The steward saved Agatha from having to make any response, knocking on the door to deliver a bouquet of white roses and sweet-scented French lavender.

"For you, madame." The steward handed Agatha a small card along with the flowers.

"From her?" Katharine pursed her lips.

"Yes." Agatha read the note aloud: "With profound gratitude and good wishes for your recovery. I hope to thank you in person when you are well enough. Nancy Nelson."

"I don't suppose she'll want to show her face at dinner." Katharine took a cigarette and inserted it in the silver-tipped holder. "She'll probably ask you to go to her compartment. I wonder what she'll have to say for herself."

~

Katharine seized her chance when Agatha left the compartment to visit the lavatory. She had been itching to look while Agatha was asleep, but that would have been too great a risk. The slightest movement might have woken her.

It was a shabby thing to do, rummaging through another woman's handbag, but Katharine told herself it was for Agatha's own good. If she wanted to visit the dig at Ur—to do it properly—she was going to have to win Leonard's approval. He detested tourists. Resented their presence for even a few hours. The idea of having one around for several days and nights would be anathema to him—particularly if it was a woman.

Leonard was a man's man through and through. But one thing he always respected, regardless of gender, was a clever mind. The other thing guaranteed to get his attention was money. If Mary Miller really *was* Agatha Christie, Leonard would welcome her to the dig house with open arms.

It was a matter of seconds before she found what she was looking for. Her fingers made contact with something flat and hard, wrapped in a lace-edged handkerchief. As she pulled it out, she saw a corner of matte black. Beneath the lace was a glint of gold—the lion and unicorn crest of a British passport. She glanced at the door before flicking through the pages. There was her proof: Agatha Mary Clarissa Christie. Maiden name: Miller.

~

Agatha hesitated as she passed Nancy's compartment. *I hope to thank you in person when you are well enough.* It sounded like an open invitation to knock on the door. But the blind was drawn. Agatha wondered if Nancy was asleep. She glanced up and down the corridor before putting her ear to the glass.

She heard a cough, then a creaking sound, like someone getting on or off the banquette. Would Nancy be alone? It seemed unlikely that a person in a state of such distress would be left unattended. The proper thing to do would be to use the steward as an intermediary. Send a message asking if it was convenient to visit. But that seemed absurdly formal in the circumstances.

As she lifted her hand to knock, the door suddenly opened. The view of the compartment beyond was blocked by a very large, crosslooking woman in the uniform of the Wagons-Lits company.

"Who is it?" The voice, tremulous and very English, came from someone else.

The woman in uniform looked over her shoulder, creating a sliver of space between her body and the door frame through which Agatha could see Nancy Nelson. She was sitting on the edge of the banquette, pushing her bare feet into slippers that matched her dressing gown of turquoise silk.

"May I come in?" Agatha gave the guard a tentative smile.

The woman frowned. "She sleep."

"But I can see that she's awake."

The woman shifted her weight, obstructing the view of the compartment again. *"Non capisco,"* she replied.

Agatha was not going to be fobbed off. *"Parlez-vous français?"*

This question elicited a wary look. *"Un petit peu."* Agatha spoke fluent French—something she had picked up while living in Paris with her mother as a child. She explained that she was the person who had stopped Mrs. Nelson from harming herself and that she wished only to speak to her for a short while.

The guard glared at her, then looked at her watch. *"Dix minutes,"* she muttered, marching off in the direction of the lavatory.

"Mrs. Miller!" Nancy was smiling, but her jaw trembled, as if it took every ounce of strength she possessed. "I'm so terribly sorry . . . I . . . Your head . . ." She trailed off, pulling a handkerchief from the pocket of her dressing gown.

"It's nothing, really—just a graze." Agatha saw that Nancy's brown eyes were red-rimmed and puffy. She looked as if she'd been crying all night. She took a step closer. "I haven't come to pry. Just send me away if you'd rather be alone."

Nancy closed her eyes and took in a long breath. "Thank you for coming. It's awful, having that woman in here with me. I feel like a prisoner."

Agatha sat down on the chair that had been brought in for the guard. There was a host of questions clamoring in her head but she kept silent, waiting for Nancy to speak.

"You knew my name." The eyes were still closed. "You called out to me, didn't you?" The lids parted. "How did you know me?"

"I . . . I recognized your face. I must have seen your picture somewhere—in a magazine, I think."

"Ah." The sigh caught in her throat, halfway to a sob. "I suppose you're wondering what on earth can be the matter with me."

"Well, I . . . ," Agatha faltered, aware that any response was likely to sound insensitive.

Nancy's eyes ranged over the carpet, as if the answer were concealed in its pattern. "It's the old story, I'm afraid: I married a man who doesn't care for me."

Her words hung in the air. Agatha held her breath, waiting for her to go on.

"I thought running away was the answer." Another long pause and then: "I was going to my cousin in Baghdad. I was going to stay with her until I worked out what to do." Nancy opened the hand that contained the handkerchief, screwed into a tight ball. "But last night there was a telegram." She stared at the handkerchief, her eyes brimming with tears. "Delia, my cousin, is dead."

"Oh . . . I'm so sorry."

Nancy's grief was like the pull of a magnet. Agatha wanted to lean across the space between them, put an arm around those trembling shoulders. But something made her resist. It was the memory of the face reflected in the train window. Those eyes, so like Archie's. If there was even a chance that he was part of this . . .

"I felt so . . . alone." Nancy's voice was barely more than a whisper. "I lay here in the dark, listening to the wheels going round and round. And it occurred to me that the simple answer was to jump out of the train." She raked her hair with her fingers. "I've let everyone down. My father would turn in his grave if he knew what a mess I was in. He thought Felix would be the perfect husband." Nancy's whole body shuddered as she said this, as if her dislike of her husband bordered on dread. "But I couldn't stay—I couldn't stand it."

"Does anyone know where you are?" The way Agatha said it sounded innocent enough.

Nancy blinked, as if the question was incomprehensible. "There's no one to go back to, if that's what you mean. Delia was the only family I have left."

No one to go back to. So who was the man on the train?

Agatha suddenly wondered if she had got it all wrong. Put two and two together and made five. She had seen a face reflected in a window and assumed it was the person Nancy had seen. But what if the reflection had come from the opposite end of the carriage, confusing the eye the way a mirror would? What if Nancy had merely been trying to attract the attention of one of the waiters, visible to her but unseen by Agatha?

If that was the case, the man who so resembled Archie could have been anyone: just a passenger who had boarded the train at Paris and got off a few stops later. Agatha silently cursed herself for being such a fool.

"I've been married for less than a year, but it felt like a lifetime." Nancy turned her head to the window. There were mountains in the distance, their peaks blue and purple in the fading light. "Forgive me for asking—have you been married long?"

"Thirteen years." Agatha felt heat surge into her face.

"Did you ever—" Nancy broke off, her eyes searching the carpet again. "What I mean is . . . have you ever reached a point when you felt you couldn't go on?"

Her words transported Agatha back in time. The fourteenth of December 1926. Ten days before their twelfth wedding anniversary. She saw Archie's face as he came up the stairs of the hotel in Harrogate, marching toward her with a look of cold fury. She had felt more alone at that moment than at any time in her life.

"I loved him very much." The words came out unbidden, as if someone else had spoken them. Agatha's throat tightened. "We . . . I . . ." She swallowed hard. She had never confided in anyone. Not Charlotte, not even her sister. What she felt about Archie, why she had wanted him to think she might have killed herself, was too humiliating, too painful to confess. But here was a woman who was running away, just as she had done, a woman who had *really* tried to kill herself.

Agatha suddenly felt an overwhelming urge to protect her, to tell as much of the truth as she could bear.

"He fell in love with someone else and I thought my life was over." Her voice sounded even stranger to her now, like a distant echo. But Nancy was looking at her, wide-eyed. She had to go on. "It was a Friday evening and I'd been waiting for him to come home. But he didn't. So I got into my car and drove to the house where I knew he'd be staying. They were friends of his, and her car was there—the girl he'd been seeing. I don't know what went through my head. I parked outside for a while, just watching the house, the shapes of people moving behind the curtains. Then I drove off into the night, not really caring where I was going. I remember just wanting to die. I got to an old quarry and I thought about driving right over the edge."

"What stopped you?"

Agatha's eyes went to the darkening mountains beyond the window. She knew what the answer should be. And yes, Rosalind had been there in her head as she drove to the place where she abandoned the car. But it was Archie she was thinking about as she switched off the engine. How she could make things look. How she could turn his world upside down.

"I couldn't leave my daughter. That would have been   " Agatha left the rest unsaid, her breath misting the window.

Nancy's head moved a fraction of an inch. A barely perceptible nod.

"And something else went through my mind as I was sitting there in the dark," Agatha said. "Something a teacher came out with in the middle of a math lesson when I was about twelve years old." Remembering the words, she hesitated. What had once seemed so profound was something she was no longer sure she believed in. The teacher had spoken of love and suffering and Christ in the garden of Gethsemane. She had told them that they would all, at some time in their lives, feel as he had, utterly alone and forsaken by everyone—even by God. When that time came, Miss Johnston said, they must hold on to the belief that this was not the end, that God *was* there and would help them if they put their trust in him. For some reason, those words had stayed with her more than any sermon she had ever heard in church. But she couldn't repeat them to Nancy. Not now.

"What did she say?" Nancy leaned closer.

Agatha took a breath. "She said: 'All of you, every *one* of you, will pass through a time when you will face despair.'" That much was faithful to the original. "She told us that it was impossible to love without suffering—but if we never loved, we would never know the true meaning of life. Then she said, 'When everything goes against you and you get to a point when it seems you can't hang on a minute longer, never, never give up—for that is just the place and time that the tide will turn.'"

Agatha glanced at her hands. At her mother's ring on her wedding finger. "And so I wrapped myself up in my coat and closed my eyes. I must have fallen asleep. And when I woke up, it was morning. The sun was coming up through the mist and there was a blackbird singing. And I was glad I was alive."

"Thank you." Nancy's hand moved a few inches into the space between them, freezing in midair, as if she wanted to touch Agatha on the arm or the shoulder but was afraid of the intimacy of such an action. A footfall outside the door made her snatch it back.

"If you need to escape, come and find me," Agatha said quickly. "I'm in compartment number sixteen."

CHAPTER 8

Sofia to Simeonovgrad

Katharine looked up from her novel, wondering what was taking Agatha so long. She glanced at her watch. Twenty minutes, at least, since she'd left the compartment. What if she'd had a fainting fit and was lying, unconscious, on the floor? Katharine sprang to her feet. She shouldn't have allowed herself to get so wrapped up in the damned book with its cryptic scenario of a body behind a door locked from the inside. It was a lot of nonsense, of course: what her father would have called *chewing gum for the brain*. But clever nonsense, all the same.

As her fingers made contact with the door, she felt it move.

"You took your time," she said, as Agatha appeared. "I nearly sent out a search party!"

"I called in on Nancy Nelson," Agatha replied.

"Oh, it's *Nancy* now, is it?" Katharine cocked her head. "And?"

"We didn't have much chance to talk." She sank down onto the banquette, rubbing the place beneath the broken skin on her forehead. "She has a woman with her: someone from the Wagons-Lits company."

"I suppose they're worried she'll try again." Katharine nodded. "Did she say why she did it?"

"She was running away from her husband." Agatha hesitated, looking away from Katharine into the darkness beyond the window. "She said she couldn't stand it any longer because he doesn't love her. She was going to stay with a relative in Baghdad. Delia somebody. But there was a telegram yesterday saying she'd died. That's what pushed her over the edge."

"Delia?" Katharine frowned. "Delia Grandfield?"

"I don't know. I don't think she mentioned a surname."

"It *must* be her," Katharine said. "I met her a couple of times. Sharp as a pin and spoke fluent Persian as well as Arabic. She was a spy, I think."

"A *spy*?"

"Yes. She worked for the British Consulate. Got to know the wives of the local tribesmen and monitored activity in the Kurdish area to the north. She came to the dig once. Leonard showed her round."

"I wonder how she died," Agatha said.

"Well, she was doing a pretty dangerous job. It's not hard to imagine someone like that—a woman, especially—getting herself murdered."

"Poor Nancy. As if she didn't have enough to contend with."

Katharine took a cigarette from the case on the table. "What will she do now? Did she say?"

"I don't know. If I was her, I'd catch the next train back to London. If she's planning to go it alone, she'll have a better chance there than in a foreign city where she knows no one." Agatha shrugged. "But she says she can't go back."

Katharine lit the cigarette and blew out a plume of smoke. "Is the husband really such a brute?"

"I suppose he must be." Katharine saw Agatha's eyes go hard and smooth, like pebbles in a river. Thinking about her own marriage, perhaps. There had been much speculation in the newspapers, when she ran off to Harrogate, about Archie Christie having a mistress.

She took the cigarette from her mouth, thought about saying those five simple words: *I know who you are*. But something stopped her. She could pretend to herself that it was concern for Agatha's physical and mental state after the traumatic events of last night, or respect for her clear desire to hide her identity. But it wasn't that. The truth was that she relished the power this knowledge gave her. She would play her hand when the time was right.

"I suppose we should think about getting ready for dinner," Katharine said. "I should change that dressing first, though: the bleeding should have stopped by now."

Agatha made no sound as the blood-encrusted lint came away from her skin. She seemed to have retreated to a place inside her head where the outside world no longer registered. The place, Katharine imagined, that she went to when she was writing her books. It was something Katharine could easily understand. She experienced a similar escapism when she was reconstructing an ancient object. The concentration—the mental effort required in visualizing something as yet unformed—was the best therapy, the surest way of banishing memories that still had the power to overwhelm her.

She thought fleetingly of the images she had seen in *Tatler* of Nancy Nelson's wedding day. She wondered if Nancy had felt as she had when she walked down the aisle: so excited, so in love, so naïvely optimistic. How long had it been before Nancy's dreams were shattered? That marriage, it appeared, had crashed to earth even faster than her own.

And Agatha. What had *really* happened there? She knew from bitter experience not to believe most of what was reported in the newspapers. Why was she traveling to Baghdad, of all places? And what had made her want to pretend to be a widow? Did she hate her husband so much? Or did she herself feel guilty about the failure of the marriage—to the extent that she couldn't bear to admit being divorced? Katharine grimaced as she applied a plaster to the cut below Agatha's hairline. If guilt was the name of the game, she could beat this woman hands down.

~

As the Orient Express rolled through Bulgaria, rain began to speckle the windows. By the time Agatha and Katharine reached the dining car, hailstones were clattering against the glass. All eyes were on the windows, for which Agatha, conscious of the lumpy dressing beneath her borrowed headband, was profoundly grateful. No sooner had the two women taken their seats than a huge bolt of lightning split the night sky, followed almost immediately by a terrific thunderclap. This produced awed sounds from the passengers. The waiter smiled as he arrived with the menus.

"Don't be alarmed, ladies," he said. "We often get storms like this when we are going through the Rhodope Mountains—it should pass quickly."

But another lightning flash, with more thunder, came as they gave their order. The woman at the table across from theirs jumped to her feet, upsetting a glass of wine that narrowly missed her gown of sequin-studded *eau de nil* silk. As a second waiter arrived to change the tablecloth, Agatha saw that Katharine was scanning the diners, casting her head this way and that as if she was looking for someone. When she turned her eyes back to the table, she caught Agatha's curious face.

"I saw someone yesterday when we got to Venice," she said. "One of the chaps from the dig. He must have been on the train, but there's no sign of him now." She reached inside her bag and pulled out a cigarette. "Probably doing this leg of the journey by boat. His name's Max. You'll meet him when you come to visit."

Agatha nodded. She wondered if it would be all right to admit to her encounter with Max now that he was safely off the train. On balance, she decided, it was probably better to keep quiet.

"He's what you'd call the strong, silent type." Katharine inserted the cigarette in its holder. "He was a real mouse when he first came to

Mesopotamia. Straight down from Oxford and not much clue about anything."

"How old is he?"

Katharine had the holder between her lips now. "Twenty-five," she mumbled, flipping up the top of a lighter inlaid with mother-of-pearl. A plume of smoke drifted across the table. "He looks older, though. Had a fairly bad time of it just before he came to us." She tapped her cigarette against the ashtray. "He told me he had a friend at Oxford he was very close to: Esme Howard—son of Lord Howard of Penrith. He was unwell for most of the final year, and in the end, they diagnosed Hodgkin's disease. Max was actually with him when he died."

"How tragic." Agatha blinked. The words sounded trite.

"It had quite a profound effect on him, I think. It took a while for him to open up, but he told me all about it one night." Katharine inhaled, turning her head sideways as she blew the smoke out. The woman across the aisle cast her a black look, which Katharine returned with a tight smile. "He told me he made a deathbed promise to his friend to convert to Catholicism. Apparently, Esme was very religious, and the way he dealt with the business of dying made a huge impression on Max. At the dig he goes to Mass every Sunday even though it's a twenty-mile round trip by mule across the desert."

Agatha found it difficult to square this description with the warm, funny person who had treated her to ice cream in Venice. Perhaps, like her, grief had made him careful how much of himself he gave away.

"Leonard won't let him have the car because he's not keen on Catholics," Katharine went on. "Len's father was an Anglican priest, and he was going to go into the church himself. He's very hot on the Old Testament: looks for names from Genesis on every tablet we dig up." She shrugged. "He's convinced that Ur is the site of the Great Flood."

Agatha had read about this theory in a newspaper report. From the look on Katharine's face, Agatha gathered that Katharine thought her soon-to-be husband was barking up the wrong tree. There had been a photograph of Leonard Woolley alongside the article. He stared out from beneath thick, bushy eyebrows with a stern, uncompromising look—a zealous intensity in his eyes. His hair was thinning on top and gray around the ears. Agatha guessed he must be a good ten years older than Katharine. They would make an unusual couple. A shared passion for archaeology had, apparently, bridged the gulf that age and physical appearance might have put between them. Perhaps it had been an unflattering photograph: perhaps Leonard Woolley was not the ogre he appeared to be.

"Your *terrine aux fruits de mer*, madame." The waiter broke into her thoughts, depositing a small work of art on the table in front of her: a pink jellied mousse molded into the shape of a starfish, with radishes and carrots expertly carved to resemble sea anemones. She felt a trickle of saliva under her tongue.

"You'll like Max." Katharine crushed her cigarette against the ash-tray. "He's a darling."

~

In the saloon after dinner Katharine wanted to order White Russians.

"Oh, not for me," Agatha said. "Just a glass of water, please."

"Is your head hurting?"

"No—it's not that. Alcohol doesn't really agree with me."

"You poor thing!" Katharine shook her head, making the bugle bead trim on her chiffon dress dance like the raindrops on the window. "I'm going to make the most of it, I'm afraid. Not much of the hard stuff to be had in the desert—and Leonard's a teetotaler."

At the other end of the carriage the pianist struck up the opening bars of George Gershwin's *Rhapsody in Blue*. Agatha drew in a breath. The air tasted smoky. It wasn't just Katharine's cigarette. There were a number of men smoking cigars. Agatha longed to open a window, but the storm raging outside made that impossible.

When the waiter brought Katharine's cocktail, a man came in his wake and asked if they would mind if he joined them. He was a tall, sad-eyed Frenchman who said he was an engineer traveling to Syria.

Agatha saw straight away that Jean-Claude, as he insisted on being called, was entranced by Katharine. Her French was not particularly good, and his English was halting. Agatha could have joined in the conversation quite effectively, but from the moment he sat down, she felt like an unwanted extra. Watching Katharine with this man was like watching a beautiful bird of prey hovering over a rabbit. She was not flirting, exactly—it wasn't as blatant as that. It was the way she looked at him from under her eyelashes, her head tilted to one side and her lips parted in a half smile, as if everything he said was clever and funny. He was talking about the dam he was in charge of building. It wasn't the least bit funny, nothing but dry facts and figures. But Katharine seemed to be enjoying it.

Jean-Claude called for more cocktails and turned to Agatha for the first time, looking at her glass of water. This was her cue to exit.

"You don't mind if I turn in, do you?" she said to Katharine.

"Oh no—of course not." Katharine barely turned her head. Her eyes were locked on those of her new companion.

As Agatha made her way back to the compartment, she wondered what Leonard Woolley would say if he could see his bride-to-be knocking back cocktails with a complete stranger. The photograph in the newspaper, together with the glimpses Katharine had given, suggested a stern, high-principled, remote sort of man for whom work came before everything else. Hard to imagine him having fun of any kind. Was this evening a last fling for Katharine? And if she really was the party-loving, flirtatious type, what on earth was she doing marrying a man like Woolley?

CHAPTER 9

Lyubimets to Istanbul

Agatha didn't hear Katharine come to bed. In the restless minutes between closing her eyes and drifting off to sleep, she thought of Nancy, wondering if she was lying awake in the storm. It seemed an eternity since last night. The memory of the door flying open, the blast of the wind, and the sight of the ground falling away made her head throb. She hoped that Nancy was not awake, that she was not reliving the events of the night before, that she was not secretly planning a repeat performance.

The thunder and lightning had stopped by the time Agatha fell asleep. But something else woke her in the middle of the night. She blinked in the darkness, her eyes adjusting to the gloom. Suddenly she realized what was wrong. There was no movement. No sound from the engine. The train had stopped.

The ladder creaked as she climbed down to look out of the window.

"What time is it?" Katharine's voice, croaky and a little slurred, drifted up to her.

"I don't know." Agatha could smell the ripe fumes of vodka. She wondered how many White Russians had been downed after she left.

Lifting a corner of the blind, she gasped. The storm clouds had vanished, leaving a clear sky with a huge full moon. And down below, glittering as the wind rippled its surface, was water: right up to the wheels of the train.

Agatha pulled the window down a couple of inches. Cool, pine-scented air set her skin tingling.

"Aargh! It's cold!" Katharine grunted.

There was a shout from somewhere outside. Then Agatha saw two figures wading knee-deep through the water. "I think the line's flooded."

"What?" Katharine was wide awake now, fumbling for the lamp. At the same moment there was a knock on the door. The steward appeared, bearing a steaming jug and two cups.

"Please do not worry, ladies—we are having a little trouble." He laid the tray down on the table. "I have to go and see, so please excuse me for some time. There is fruit and some pastries in the dining car if you become hungry."

"Thank you." Katharine leaned across to sniff the jug as the door closed. "Hot chocolate—ugh!" She made a face. "I need the bathroom." As she stood up, there was another knock on the door.

"Oh! I'm so sorry—I thought . . ." Nancy Nelson shivered in the draft from the window as the door opened.

"You're looking for Mrs. Miller?" Katharine gestured behind her. "Please excuse me." She clapped her hand to her mouth, pushing past Nancy, who stood, bewildered, pulling up the collar of her turquoise silk dressing gown to cover her neck.

"I do apologize, Mrs. Miller—I didn't realize you were sharing. Is your friend all right?"

"I'm sure she'll be fine." Agatha smiled. "Just a gippy tummy, I think."

"She's gone to see what's happening—the woman who's been sitting with me, I mean," Nancy said. "I thought I might . . ." She paused.

"Yes, please do come in." Agatha pulled the single chair out from the table. "Would you like some hot chocolate?"

Nancy sat down. Taking the proffered cup, she raised it to her mouth, inhaling the aroma but not drinking. "How's your head now?"

"Healing nicely, thank you." Agatha settled herself on the edge of the bed that Katharine had vacated. "I don't think I'll need the dressing on it much longer."

"That's good." A pause and then: "It feels like an omen, the train getting stuck. A sign I shouldn't go on." She took a sip of her drink, staring into the cup. "I was thinking, at Istanbul I could catch a train back to England."

"But you said you couldn't go back," Agatha replied. "Have you changed your mind?"

"I feel as if I'm caught between the devil and the deep blue sea. I don't want to go back, but I'm afraid of going somewhere I don't know. Now that Delia's . . ." She couldn't finish the sentence.

Agatha opened her mouth, then closed it again. It was a delicate situation. She didn't know this woman, not really. And yet she reminded her so much of herself: of the desperate person she had been on that cold December night almost two years ago. Nancy clearly needed help. But would it be sensible to offer to look after someone in such emotional turmoil? After all, she had come on this trip to discover places on her own, not to hook up with a fellow traveler.

Don't be so selfish. Her mother's voice rang out loud and clear.

"If it's any comfort," she began, "I'm going to Baghdad, too. I've no idea how I'm going to like it, but I intend to stick it out for a couple of months at least."

"Really?"

Agatha nodded. "We can explore the place together, if you'd like to." She waited for a moment. It was the first time she'd seen anything like a smile on Nancy's face. "I've booked a room at a hotel for a few nights until I find my way round the place. I'm sure they'll have other rooms available at this time of year."

"Thank you." Nancy blinked. "That's such a kind offer." She was smiling still, but she looked close to tears. "Are you sure you'd want me with you? Don't you have things already arranged?"

"Not really." Agatha shrugged. "I've deliberately avoided making plans because it's quite exciting not knowing where each day might take me."

"That sounds really . . . But . . ." Nancy twisted her wedding ring. "I don't know how to put this: it's awfully embarrassing to admit to . . . What I mean is, there won't be much time for exploring: I'm going to have to find some sort of job." She glanced up, shaking her head. "You see, there isn't much money. I don't have any of my own. I had to sell my jewelry to get this far."

Agatha reached for the jug of hot chocolate, topping up Nancy's cup. "What kind of work would you look for?"

"I don't know. Something in an office, I suppose. I've never had an actual job. I helped my father run his estate before it was broken up. I'm quite good with figures. And I can type."

Agatha paused at this, her cup halfway between the saucer and her lips. "I might be able to offer you something temporary," she said. "I need a secretary."

Agatha didn't need a secretary. She was perfectly capable of typing her work herself. But as the words came out, she felt something bordering on relief. The divorce had changed her overnight from an amateur writer to a professional. The stories she had composed as a hobby were now her only source of income. And she had been dreading sitting at the typewriter with a blank sheet of paper. Perhaps with an assistant, she would feel more like a real author.

"Oh!" Nancy's face brightened. "What would you want me to do?"

"It would mainly be typing up handwritten notes. Nothing too onerous." Agatha wasn't ready to reveal herself completely. Not yet. "I hope to rent a house for a couple of months, so you could work in return for bed and board if that suits. And while you're with me, you could look for something more permanent."

Before Nancy could respond, the door opened.

"Gracious, it's like the trenches out there!" Katharine bustled in, her face betraying no sign of the hangover that had sent her scurrying to the bathroom. Her cheeks were glowing and her eyes sparkled with the drama she had just witnessed. "Men up to their waists in mud! Goodness knows how long we're going to be stuck here." She sat down on the lower bunk, next to Agatha, bending low to avoid knocking her head on the bed above. "I've brought us a midnight feast." She unfolded a linen napkin that contained bananas, pears, and a selection of muffins and pastries. Holding out her hand to Nancy, she said, "Sorry: I didn't introduce myself properly earlier. Katharine Keeling."

"Nancy Nelson." Nancy stood up as she released Katharine's hand. "I must leave you both to enjoy your food."

"Nonsense!" Katharine laughed. "The more the merrier." She offered Nancy an apple strudel. "You were on the cover of *Vogue*, weren't you? I remember the dress you wore—Dior, wasn't it? I did the drawings for it at their Paris show."

Nancy looked startled. For a moment Agatha thought she was going to run out of the compartment. But she took the pastry and sat down, examining it as if it were the clue to some abiding mystery. Then she said, "Yes, I loved that dress. Do you work in fashion?"

"Not anymore. I'm at the British Museum now, with a team of archaeologists in Mesopotamia." Katharine reached to the end of the bed, pulling her bag out from underneath a cushion. Delving into it she produced a small shiny object, creamy white and shaped like a pebble. "This is the kind of thing I draw nowadays." She set it on the table next to the bananas.

"What is it?" Agatha asked.

"An amulet of the moon god," Katharine replied. "Pick it up if you like. It's not the real thing—just a replica. I found the original in one of the death pits. Hamoudi, our foreman, copied it for me."

"Is this a hare?" Agatha said, examining its carved surface.

"Yes. Turn it over. Can you see what's on the other side?"

"It looks like a pair of feet with something in between them. A snake, I think." Agatha passed the amulet to Nancy.

"Quite right," Katharine said. "It was a magical symbol in ancient Mesopotamia. Very potent. It was supposed to protect the dead person in the afterlife."

"What's it made of?" Nancy asked.

"Ivory: a boar's tusk."

"It's beautiful." Nancy passed it back.

"Thank you." Katharine tucked it inside her bag. "I carry it with me always. Silly, really—but I won't be parted from it." She laughed. "I expect you've both got something of that kind with you—something you couldn't leave behind, even when you're traveling." She looked at Agatha.

"Well, I don't have anything as interesting as that, I'm afraid. I have my daughter's photograph, of course . . . Nothing else really." This was a lie. Agatha had a letter hidden inside the inner zip compartment of her handbag: the letter that her publisher, John Lane, had written to her nine years earlier, making an offer for her first manuscript, *The Mysterious Affair at Styles*.

"What about you?" Katharine was looking at Nancy now.

Agatha glanced from one to the other, fearing the effect this thinly disguised nosiness might have on Nancy. But the reply came with only a moment's hesitation.

"I have a scarf," Nancy said. "It's rather moth-eaten, with a pattern of peacock feathers. It reminds me of living in Ceylon as a child. I used to wake up in the morning and watch the peacocks in the trees outside the window."

"How marvelous!" Katharine took a pear and bit into it. "I've always wanted to go to Ceylon. How long were you there?"

"About ten years. My father had a tea plantation near Trincomalee. I was born there."

"It must have been quite a shock, coming back to England at that age," Agatha said.

"Yes, it was. The cold was something I've never really got used to—and it took me a long time to stop looking out for snakes every time I went for a walk."

"Well, you'll be right at home in Baghdad." Katharine smiled. "It's absolutely roasting in summer: in fact, it's never cold at all, not even at Christmas."

"I've tried to imagine it." Nancy blinked and bent her head, brushing away a flake of apple strudel that had attached itself to the lapel of her dressing gown.

"It's quite beautiful," Katharine said. "Imagine the Garden of Eden: that's what it's like. Flowers everywhere. And on a hot summer night, the mist hangs in long white ribbons over the river. When the light fades and the lamps are lit in the houses on either side, it's full of mysterious reflections and it glitters like gold."

With a few well-chosen words, Katharine had Nancy on the edge of her seat. Her anxious, preoccupied expression had turned into one of eager anticipation. Nancy wanted to know more about Mesopotamia and all about life at the dig. As Katharine regaled her with stories of Arab sheikhs and hidden treasure, Agatha remembered the words Max had spoken on the platform at Venice. *She casts a spell on you, and before you know it, you've become her slave. Be careful of that, won't you . . .*

Almost imperceptibly, Katharine was steering the conversation away from her own experiences in Mesopotamia to probe Nancy's future plans. Lost in thought, Agatha didn't realize what was happening until she caught the tail end of one of Nancy's sentences:

". . . and Mrs. Miller has very kindly offered me some temporary secretarial work."

"Really?" Katharine's head swiveled. "You didn't tell me you were traveling to Baghdad on business, Mary. What line of work are you in?"

"Well, I . . ." Agatha felt herself go hot. "I write a little—for magazines. I'm hoping to do some travel pieces."

Katharine's lips slid into the Mona Lisa smile. "How very interesting! Which magazines do you write for? I wonder if I've—"

A sudden screech of the train's whistle brought Katharine to an abrupt halt. "Oh!" She jumped up. "What's happening?" She peered out of the window at a landscape turned gray by the first hint of dawn. "I can see something. Looks like another locomotive. It must have come to pull us out." There was another whistle, more distant this time.

"I'd better be getting back." Nancy's anxious look returned as she got to her feet, wrapping her dressing gown tightly round her body. "Thank you—you've both been awfully kind."

~

By sunrise they were on their way again. Breakfast was served as they crossed the border into Turkey, and by lunchtime they were close to Istanbul.

Nancy was not in evidence for either meal and neither was Katharine's French companion, Jean-Claude.

"I managed to get rid of him eventually," Katharine said when Agatha inquired how the evening had gone. "He's a frightful bore. How anyone can be so obsessed with things like stress fractures and water pressure, I can't imagine!"

Agatha felt a twinge of sympathy for the sad-eyed Frenchman, written off for no worse crime than being passionate about his chosen profession. She wondered why Katharine had bothered staying on in the saloon if that was how she felt, when she could so easily have left earlier.

"Oh, look!" Katharine gesticulated with a forkful of salmon.

The train had begun to wind in and out through strange wooden houses with slatted walls. As they entered the outskirts of Istanbul, they slipped past great stone bastions—a legacy of the city's ancient and bloody past—which gave fleeting glimpses of the sea.

"You don't get much of an impression on this side," Katharine said, taking a sip of Chablis. "Once we cross the Bosphorus to the Asian coast, you'll really see Istanbul."

"I'm very disappointed that we're not stopping," Agatha replied.

"Can't be helped, I suppose. We lost too much time last night. Never mind—you'll be able to see it all on the way back, won't you? How long are you staying in Baghdad?"

"I'm not sure." Agatha spread butter onto a fragment of melba toast. "It depends on how I like it, I suppose. I'll want to be home for Christmas, of course."

"Christmas, yes." Katharine gave a wry smile. "I can hardly remember Christmases in England."

"How do you celebrate it in Mesopotamia?"

"With a day off—our *only* day off all season."

"Goodness, that sounds rather harsh!"

Katharine nodded. "Leonard's a real slave driver. As far as he's concerned, you're out there to work, and work is what you must do, day and night. I remember the first season Max came to us, he produced a pack of cards one evening and started playing gin rummy with Michael, the draftsman. Leonard was beavering away in the Antiquities Room— as he does every night until two or three in the morning—and when he came out and saw what they were doing, he hit the roof. He said to Max, 'If you're not capable of working, you'd better go to bed.'"

Katharine grinned as she finished this story. Agatha was perplexed. According to Max, the wedding was due to take place in just three days' time. How could Katharine talk about Leonard Woolley as frequently as she did without mentioning the big event? There was no shame in a widow marrying for a second time—but perhaps there was some sort of scandal on his side. Agatha couldn't remember reading anything in the papers about a previous wife, but that didn't mean there wasn't one. Maybe Katharine had reduced this high-minded vicar's son to a quivering heap of lust. After witnessing her performance in the saloon the previous night, it wasn't difficult to cast her in the role of temptress.

As the train slowed to a crawl on the approach to its final destination in Europe, Max's voice echoed through Agatha's head again. *Would you mind not telling Mrs. Keeling that I'm on the train . . . I'd rather our paths didn't cross until I'm back at the dig house.* What was that all about, she wondered? Had Max fallen for her hypnotic charms like the Frenchman, Jean-Claude? Was this some sort of addiction for her, leading men on and then casting them aside? If so, Leonard Woolley must be an exceptional sort of man to have snared her.

CHAPTER 10

Istanbul to Ulukisla

The crossing from Europe into Asia was chaotic. On the other side of the narrow stretch of water separating the two continents, a connecting train was due to depart in less than two hours. There was precious little time to get the passengers and their luggage off the Orient Express and onto the ferry. In the mad scramble of people and suitcases, Agatha lost sight of Katharine.

Boarding the boat, Agatha's main concern was avoiding a recurrence of the seasickness that had made the crossing from Dover to Calais so miserable. She decided that the best strategy would be to remain in the open, close to the side. She climbed out onto the upper deck and found a place to stand, next to the rail. As she peered over the edge, she saw that the gangplank had already been hoisted. With a honk of its foghorn, the ferry slipped away from its mooring.

To Agatha's relief, the Bosphorus was as calm as a millpond. There was none of the pitching and rolling that had made her so queasy in the Channel. She watched the quayside recede, gazing in wonder at the mosques and minarets standing out against an azure sky.

"It's very beautiful, isn't it?"

It was Nancy, not Katharine who had found her.

"I've never seen anything like it." Agatha stepped sideways, making room for Nancy to stand beside her. "It seems incredible that in a few minutes' time we'll be stepping onto a different continent."

"I can't wait." Nancy smiled. "By the way, I'm free at last: Signorina Tedaldi's responsibilities ended when we reached Istanbul. I couldn't understand most of what she said, but I got the gist of it. Apparently, the Wagons-Lits company has no jurisdiction on the Asian side."

"Well, there's a whole new world waiting for you over there." Agatha swept her hand toward the opposite bank, where countless wooden fishing boats bobbed at anchor. As the words came out, she knew that she was really saying them to herself.

"I was dreading it until last night." Nancy grimaced. "Did you mean what you said about needing a secretary?"

Agatha nodded. In the cold light of day it seemed even more reckless, inviting a total stranger to share her life for the next two months. But there was no going back now. To withdraw the offer would be downright cruel. "I did mean it," she said, "as long as you're sure that's what you want—don't feel you have to accept out of politeness. If something better turns up when we get to Baghdad, you must feel free to take it."

"It's perfect—more than I dared hope for. But you must promise me something."

"What?"

"You've come on this trip to see new places, and you mustn't let me cramp your style. As long as I have a roof over my head, I'll be quite happy to stay put while you go exploring and to type it all up when you get back."

"Won't that be a bit dull?"

Nancy gave a wry smile. "Believe me, it'll be an absolute pleasure after the life I've had lately." She glanced over her shoulder, as if she were afraid her husband might be in hot pursuit. "Oh, there's Mrs. Keeling! Doesn't she look lovely?"

Striding toward them in the dazzling sunshine, Katharine looked more striking than ever. She was wearing a white linen outfit with navy polka dots. The wide-legged trousers would have made Agatha look distinctly dumpy, but on a woman of Katharine's stature, they were very elegant. The matching blouse was trimmed with navy at the neck, echoed by a ribbon of the same color below the bust. A short-sleeved navy cardigan draped over her shoulders completed the ensemble.

"I thought you'd been left behind!" She squeezed into the space between Agatha and Nancy.

"We were just admiring the view, Mrs. Keeling," Nancy said. "But I suppose you've seen it many times?"

"Please, call me Katharine. And yes, I have seen it before—but it never loses its impact. The last time I made the crossing, it was early in the morning. The sky was a wonderful pale blue—like forget-me-nots—and there was mist rising up from the water, making the domes and minarets look all ghostly, like a mirage." She turned to look at the fast-approaching coastline of the eastern side of Istanbul. "A word of advice: stock up with food from the market stalls when we get to the other side. The meals on the next train will be ghastly."

"How long will it take us to get to Damascus?" Nancy asked.

"Well, barring any further mishaps, we should be there by tomorrow afternoon. We usually have a couple hours for shopping in the bazaar, then it's off into the desert." Katharine lifted the sleeve of her blouse, twisting her head to examine the skin at her elbow. "Damn! I thought so: blasted bugs have been at me again!"

Agatha saw a row of angry red bites on the pale underside of Katharine's forearm.

"It must have been last night." Katharine winced as she rubbed her skin.

"Try not to scratch," Agatha said. "They look as if they might be infected."

"Yes: I think my arm looks a bit swollen." She held out both arms for the others to inspect.

"I've got some calamine lotion in my suitcase," Agatha said. "I won't be able to get at it until we're on the other side, though."

"Thank you. I usually bring some myself—can't think why I didn't remember it." Katharine reached for the rail of the boat, swaying slightly.

"Are you all right?" Nancy caught her arm as she staggered sideways.

"I . . . I'm . . ." The color drained from Katharine's face.

"You need to sit down." Agatha took her other arm. "That's it—lean on us. There's a seat over there."

When the ferry reached the Asian side of Istanbul, Katharine said she felt better. She refused the help of a Turkish sailor who offered her his hand as she stepped off the gangplank. But she still looked very pale. Agatha persuaded her to take a cab to the train rather than wait in line in the hot sun for one of the coaches.

Inside Haidar Pasha station, it was bedlam. The Taurus Express was waiting, but no one could board until the customs officials had cleared every item of luggage destined for the journey to Syria. The air was full of shouting and screaming, and passengers thumped their suitcases, trying to get attention.

"You have to bribe them," Katharine whispered in Agatha's ear. "Do you have a pound note?"

"I think so." Agatha delved in her purse.

"Wave it in the air."

With a dubious look, Agatha did as she was told. A customs man dripping with gold braid bustled up and chalked cryptic symbols on their baggage. The ripe odor of sweat oozed from his body as he worked. It was such a male smell, and so long since Agatha had encountered it.

It made her think of Archie. Of running from the railway station in Torquay the night they were married, racing each other to the Grand Hotel. They had collapsed onto the bed, pulling each other's clothes off, laughing like children at the way his shirt stuck to his body. And as they lay together, sleepless, listening to the bell of All Saints' Church chime away their precious night, she breathed him in.

"Have you got another pound?" Katharine's voice tugged her back to the present. She had already dispatched Nancy to a row of stalls at the far end of the station to gather supplies for the journey, and now she began instructing Agatha in the fine art of bribing a porter to get them into one of the better carriages. Sitting regally on her largest suitcase, she paused for breath, fanning herself with a magazine.

"Are you sure you're well enough to travel?" Agatha asked.

As Katharine nodded, a bead of perspiration trickled down the side of her face. "I'll be fine once we get out of this hellhole."

~

The Taurus Express was comfortable but not luxurious. Nancy was alone again, but there was a connecting door from her compartment to the one occupied by Agatha and Katharine. As soon as Nancy had stowed her luggage, there was a tap on the wooden panel.

"Katharine's asleep," Agatha whispered as the door opened. "I think it's the best thing for her—she looked as if she was going to pass out on the ferry, didn't she?"

"She looked feverish to me." Nancy arranged the food she had bought on the table by the window. Peaches, grapes, bananas, and half a dozen squares of baklava. The bag containing the pastries gave way as she set it down, the paper translucent with oozing honey.

"I think she might be." Agatha nodded. "Those bites on her arm looked horrible."

A muffled sound came from the other side of the wall. It was high-pitched and frantic, like a cry for help. Nancy jumped to her feet and opened the door, Agatha right behind her. Katharine was lying on her side, her face wet with perspiration, the sheet pulled from the bed and tangled around her middle. As the door closed behind them, she lashed out with her arm.

"Get away! Leave me alone!" Katharine lurched onto her other side, pulling the sheets with her.

"Katharine . . ." Agatha bent over her. "Can you hear me?"

"He's got a gun!"

Nancy caught her breath. "She's delirious, isn't she?"

Agatha nodded. "Can you get some cold water and a face flannel?"

Nancy opened the cupboard containing the washbasin while Agatha cradled Katharine's head.

"That fool should never have told him!" Katharine's voice was getting louder. "Might as well have pulled the trigger himself!"

"It's all right, Katharine—just lie back, now."

Nancy's eyes met Agatha's as she handed her the wet flannel. "What's she talking about?" Agatha put her fingers to her lips.

"Such a shock . . . No one could take a thing like . . ." Katharine tossed her head, sending the flannel flying off.

"She needs a doctor, doesn't she?" Nancy whispered. "Shall I ring for the steward?"

Agatha shook her head. "There's nothing much a doctor could do. I nursed men with infected wounds during the war, and this is just the same. The fever has to run its course. All we can do is watch her and try to keep her cool."

"We'll take turns, then," Nancy said.

"Don't you see?" Katharine suddenly sat up, her eyes wide open. "They said your husband's dead." She grasped the collar of Agatha's blouse, twisting the fabric between her fingers. "He did it at the foot of the pyramid. Like a sacrifice . . ."

~

Nancy and Agatha spent the next few hours creeping between the two compartments like nuns from a silent order. Nancy gave instructions to the steward not to knock on either door until morning. He had brought them bowls of stew for supper—a thin, grease-blobbed soup with some unidentifiable lumps of meat floating in it. Katharine had been right about the quality of the food.

Thank goodness for the baklava, Nancy thought. Misshapen and crumbling though they were, the little squares of pastry tasted heavenly. As Nancy ate hers on the other side of the door, she watched the sun set over the Sea of Marmara. Little islands dotted the coastline. The fading light turned them into humps of gray, like a school of whales basking in the water. As the sun sank into the ocean, the train veered to the left, away from the coast, and began winding its way up a gorge. She listened for sounds from next door. She could hear nothing but the distant chug of the engine and the rhythmic rumble of the wheels on the track. Katharine must be sleeping.

Snatches of her fevered speech spilled through Nancy's head like beads from a broken necklace. *He's got a gun . . . That fool should never have told him . . . They said your husband's dead . . . He did it at the foot of the pyramid.* What had happened? Had Katharine's husband killed himself? The reality of someone actually doing what she had only contemplated hit her with such suddenness, she felt paralyzed. What on earth had he been told, to push him over the edge? She wondered how much Agatha knew about the woman whose compartment she was sharing. Had Katharine confided in Agatha the way she herself had done?

As darkness enveloped the train, Nancy went to take her turn at Katharine's bedside.

"She's been a little better this past half an hour," Agatha whispered. "Still very restless, but quieter."

Nancy took the chair that Agatha had vacated, feeling the warmth her body had left behind. They had agreed to sit with Katharine for three hours at a time, taking a nap in Nancy's compartment between shifts. But seeing how exhausted Agatha looked, Nancy decided she would try to sit it out until morning. If Agatha didn't wake, she wouldn't disturb her.

It was a long night. Nancy lost count of the number of times she got up to refresh the flannel with cold water and a few drops of cologne. Katharine felt very hot to the touch. The flannel sucked up the heat, wafting the scent of lavender through the compartment. It made Nancy feel drowsy, but she battled to stay awake. She had brought a copy of *Vogue* with her to read. As she gazed at the pouting faces of the models, it was hard to believe she had ever been part of that world. It seemed like another life entirely.

The thought of what lay ahead was too intimidating to contemplate. A life in a foreign city, with a baby. Nancy knew that in accepting her new friend's offer, she was clutching at straws. How long would she be able to cover up what was happening to her body? What would this kind woman say if she knew the truth? Nancy put down the magazine, running her hands over her stomach. She could feel the difference, especially sitting down. Her clothes still fitted, just about. But when they got to Baghdad, she was going to have to find a way of dressing differently, find things that concealed her condition for as long as possible. No one in their right mind would take on a secretary who admitted to being nearly six months pregnant. With luck, Nancy would find some other work: earn enough to rent a place of her own and hire a nanny when the baby came. But until that happened, she must go on pretending, playing the part of the unloved runaway.

She tried not to think about what her baby's father was doing as the train took her farther and farther away from him. He would be back in London by now. She knew the street where he lived, had walked past the house, torturing herself with the little she knew of his life there. The wife, the little girl. She had hurried past, afraid of catching a glimpse of the child through the window. She knew even then—before her own child had made its presence felt inside her—that if she had seen his daughter, she would never have been able to write that letter, begging him to come with her to Baghdad.

"I'm most frightfully thirsty." Katharine was suddenly sitting up in bed, sending the flannel slithering to the floor. "Could I have a glass of water?"

"Yes, of course!" Nancy jumped up. "Are you feeling better? We were so worried . . ." She turned to fill the glass.

"Really?" Katharine shivered, pulling the sheet up to cover the ivory silk straps of her lace-edged nightgown.

"We've been taking turns to sit with you."

"You darlings! Was I really that bad?"

"You've had a fever. It must have been the insect bites."

"Wretched things!" Katharine examined her arm. "Have I been asleep long? What time is it?"

Nancy looked at her watch. "Ten to six."

Katharine blinked. She leaned across to pull up the blind. "My God, it's getting light! What day is it? Where are we?"

"Still in Turkey, I think. We haven't stopped anywhere for ages. And it's Sunday, by the way."

Katharine put her hand to her head. "I feel quite peculiar. Dizzy. I need food, I think, but I couldn't face it."

"Could you manage some grapes?"

Katharine nodded slowly. "I could try one."

Nancy took one from the bunch and cut it in half, removing the pips. "Try just holding it to your lips at first if you're feeling queasy."

Katharine did as she was told, closing her eyes as she held the fruit up to her mouth. After a few seconds, she swallowed it down. "Mmm . . . that's lovely. Can I have another?"

As Nancy cut one open, Agatha appeared in the doorway. "Oh, you look so much better," she said. "I'm sorry, Nancy—I must have slept through the alarm."

"No need to apologize. I thought you needed a good long sleep after what I put you through the other night."

With a wry smile, Agatha perched on the end of the bed. "Grapes: what a good idea."

"They're delicious," Katharine said. "Just what the doctor ordered."

"I remember getting very ill with a fever when we lived in Ceylon." Nancy moved the bowl of fruit onto the bedside table where Katharine could reach it. "I had a nanny—a native woman called Amanthi—who looked after me. I was refusing to eat or drink, and my parents were going frantic. She asked them for grapes, and she sat by my bed day and night, popping one into my mouth whenever I opened my eyes. I can't eat them nowadays without thinking of her."

"I do envy you, growing up in a place like that." Katharine broke off half the bunch and began eating them, pips and all. "My childhood was spent in London, and I absolutely hated it: the cold, the smog, the whole vast sprawl of it. I love going to Mesopotamia because it's the exact opposite."

"Well, I envy *you*, having a profession," Nancy said. "I wanted to be a teacher in Ceylon, but . . . well, things turned out differently."

"What happened?" Katharine asked.

"My uncle was killed in the last war, and suddenly we were back in England. My father became the heir to a title and land in the Cotswolds—which sounds like a blessing but turned out to be a curse." Nancy paused, wondering if she'd said too much. The two women were looking at her expectantly. It couldn't hurt her father to tell them, could it? Not now. "The inheritance tax was crippling," she went on. "My mother had died when we lived in Ceylon, and being the only child, I tried to help him keep things going. But we had to sell one thing after another—fields, outbuildings, paintings, furniture—until there was nothing left but the house itself. And every time it rained, we'd be running around with buckets because the roof leaked like a sieve."

She turned her face to the window, ashamed to tell them the rest: that a good marriage had been the only means of saving the place; that she had accepted Felix's proposal for her father's sake, only to lose him to a heart attack a month after the wedding.

She was saved from further interrogation by a hoot from the engine and the sudden slowing down of the train.

"Oh, look!" Katharine knelt up in bed, her nose against the glass. "It's the Cilician Gates!"

Nancy craned her neck, expecting to see the entrance to an ancient walled city or ruined castle. But all she could see were towering pillars of natural sandstone, great cliffs of rock turned coral pink by the first rays of dawn.

"What is it? What are you looking at?"

"You'll see in a minute," Katharine replied. "It's the pass through the Taurus Mountains. Alexander the Great brought his army through here in 333 BC, and Saint Paul passed through on his way to visit the Galatians. The train always stops to let people get out and admire the view."

With a second long whistle, the Taurus Express juddered to a halt.

"Go on, you two." Katharine waved toward the door.

"You go, Nancy," Agatha said. "I'll stay here."

"Nonsense!" Katharine rolled her eyes. "Don't worry about me."

"Are you sure?" Agatha frowned.

"Quite sure. Better get a move on—we won't be stopping for long. Believe me, it's a sight not to be missed."

The sun was just rising over the eastern ridge of the mountains as Nancy and Agatha climbed out. They couldn't see much at first, but as they joined the group of passengers who were gathering a few yards away, both women caught their breath.

"It's like standing on the rim of the world!" Nancy took Agatha's arm. The rock beneath their feet dropped almost vertically. They were looking out at a vast plain, hazy with mist in the early sunshine.

"It's incredible!" Agatha's voice was an awed whisper. "Like looking down on the promised land."

The words triggered a feeling in Nancy that she couldn't describe. A feeling that transcended all the fear, despair, and loneliness of the past few days. A feeling of . . . well, she would almost call it joy. She felt the warmth of the sun on her body as it climbed higher. The scent of cedar, juniper, and wild iris filled the air. As she gazed at the vast plain below, the colors changed before her eyes, from a milky violet blue to smoky gray to a pale yellow green.

"It makes you glad to be . . ." Agatha checked herself with an apologetic sideways glance.

"It's all right." Nancy squeezed her arm. She wanted to say that yes, she did feel thankful to be alive. But the memory of her lover's face slipped between her eyes and the horizon, like a cloud over the sun.

CHAPTER 11

Adana to Damascus

At the next station a gaggle of hawkers crowded the platform. Agatha's stomach rumbled as she leaned out of the window. The aroma of spiced meat competed with the sulfurous smell of the engine. A wild-looking man ran toward her, bearing a tray of stuffed leaves, marinated meat on skewers, and a bowl of brightly painted eggs.

"Are you hungry?" Agatha looked over her shoulder at the others.

"Not me," Katharine called. "I can't face anything but grapes."

"What is there?" Nancy sounded doubtful.

"Come and see!" Agatha laughed. "I've no idea what it is, but it smells delicious!"

Katharine made them eat their Turkish breakfast in Nancy's compartment, saying the smell made her feel sick.

"Is it lamb, do you think?" Nancy slid a chunk of meat off the skewer with her teeth.

"Mutton, more likely," Agatha said. "And I think these must be vine leaves."

"I'd forgotten how good spicy food can be." Nancy smiled. "I used to love the curry we had in Ceylon."

"Well, this is a hundred times better than that stew they came round with last night." Agatha nodded. "There's not much I can't eat, but that was nothing but lumps of gristle swimming in grease."

"This should keep us going until we get to Damascus, shouldn't it?" Nancy picked up one of the cigar-shaped vine leaves and bit into it. "Do you think we should save some for Katharine in case she's hungry later?"

Agatha nodded. "It's a relief to see her looking so much better. I was beginning to wonder how on earth she was going to make it across the desert."

"Those things she said last night . . ." Nancy stared at the food still left on the brown paper bag that served as a plate. "I know it's none of my business, but . . ." She picked at a corner of the paper, twisting it between her finger and thumb. "Did her husband . . . Did he commit suicide?"

"I don't know," Agatha said. "She told me they met during the war, when she was nursing in France, and that they'd only been married six months when he died. I assumed he'd been killed in action."

"She was talking about a pyramid, wasn't she?" Nancy glanced up, her fingers still working away at the paper. "Was that delirium, do you think?"

"She did tell me she lived in Egypt after the war," Agatha said. "Perhaps she went there with her husband. She didn't say."

"If it's true—if he really *did* take his life—I . . . well, I feel awful. She's been so friendly toward me and I . . . What I did . . . It must have been a horrible reminder."

"You mustn't think like that. We don't know if it's true—and even if you did trigger memories she prefers to suppress, well, I'm certain she won't remember anything she said last night."

Nancy nodded, looking out of the window. The train was taking them through a mountain gorge. Stunted bushes clung to steep-sided cliffs with a river glinting far below.

"What you're doing is very brave, you know," Agatha said. "It takes guts to strike out on your own, to make a new life halfway across the world."

Nancy blinked as the sun caught her eyes. *Brave*. How she wished that was true.

~

The Taurus Express wound its way southeast through Turkey and into Syria at Aleppo, and from Aleppo to Beirut, where the Mediterranean lapped along a curving bay. Agatha found it strange to think that this was the same stretch of water she had looked out on in Venice. It was even lovelier than the coast of northern Italy, an endless chain of sandy coves with a backdrop of hazy blue mountains.

Nancy was catching up on her sleep in the next-door compartment, and Katharine had dozed off after managing to eat a hard-boiled egg and a couple of peaches. Agatha was sitting by the window, too captivated by the changing landscape to want to close her eyes. After an hour or so, the open view of the ocean gave way to large flat-roofed houses with lush gardens full of tumbling white jasmine and scarlet poinsettia. They were on the outskirts of Damascus—the final destination for the train.

"You'd think it'd be a bit more civilized, wouldn't you?" Katharine rolled her eyes as she emerged, a little unsteadily, onto the platform. "It's supposed to be the oldest capital city in the world."

The women's baggage was seized by a gang of porters, all screaming and yelling at each other. Others ran up behind them, trying to grab the cases off them. What looked like a wrestling match ensued, until a representative of the travel agent, Cook's, intervened. Once the baggage had been satisfactorily dispatched to the coach depot, he offered to organize a sightseeing tour, but Katharine shooed him away.

"They never take you to the best places," she said. "I'll be your tour guide this afternoon."

"But you've only just left your sickbed," Agatha protested. "You mustn't overtax yourself."

"I don't plan to." Katharine smiled. "The first port of call is the most relaxing place on earth—and we can get a lift all the way."

When Agatha and Nancy saw the transport she had in mind, their mouths fell open. A row of camels, saddled up with pommel seats, stood outside the station. Katharine went up to one of the men standing next to them and addressed him in Arabic. A short conversation followed, during which she placed her hands on her hips and shook her head several times before dipping her hand into her bag and pulling out a five-franc note.

"Daylight robbery," she huffed as she returned to the others. "Never mind—it's an experience not to be missed!"

Agatha watched, aghast, as Katharine demonstrated the art of mounting a camel in a ladylike fashion. The beast was first brought to its knees by its master. Katharine then stood sideways to its flank and eased herself onto the saddle. As the camel raised itself back up, it lurched forward. For a moment it looked as though Katharine would be catapulted over its head. But she clung on, laughing as the animal righted itself.

"Come on," she called from on high, "you'll love it once you're on—and it's the best way to see the city!"

Agatha and Nancy exchanged glances. "I don't know if I can do it," Agatha said. "Did you see how it swayed when it got up? It looked just like being on a boat on a stormy ocean—and I get terribly seasick . . ."

"I'm not keen either." Nancy shook her head. "I've never been much of a rider: I was thrown by a horse once and it really put me off."

"What are you waiting for?" Katharine shouted over her shoulder. "We haven't got all day!"

"I suppose if Katharine can do it after being laid up in bed for twenty-four hours, we shouldn't be so lily-livered." Agatha gave a wry smile. "I'll try it if you will."

"Well, I . . . er . . ." Nancy's face had gone very pale. But before she could say another word, the camel driver scooped her up in his arms and set her on the saddle of the smallest animal, which knelt as he approached.

"Hold on tight and lean back!" Katharine shouted.

Nancy shut her eyes as it rose up from the ground. More graceful than its stablemate, it managed to stand up without tipping her forward. She opened her eyes with a look of wonder. "Oh! I'm still on!"

"Of course you are!" Katharine laughed. "It's only a camel—not an elephant! Come on, Mary: your turn now!"

As Agatha got close to her camel, it made a guttural groaning sound and spat at her. "Ugh!" She dodged sideways to avoid its dribbling mouth. "I don't think it likes me!"

"Pat his flank firmly," Katharine called. "Show him who's boss!"

"I'm not sure I want to touch him." Agatha raised her hand tentatively, just as the camel twisted its neck, snakelike, to spit at her a second time. She felt a pair of hands grasp her from behind, and suddenly she was up on the animal's back, protected from any further liquid bombardment by the front of the saddle, which looked like the upturned leg of a stool.

She held on for dear life as the camel staggered to its feet. It reminded her of a fairground ride on the promenade at Torquay. A wooden horse on a pole that had lurched in time to the music. Her mother had made the mistake of buying her an ice cream a few minutes earlier. She wasn't sure who had been most angry: the owner of the ride, who'd had to clean up the resulting mess, or her sister, who was sitting in front of her on the horse and had to walk home with vomit in her hair.

To her relief, when the camel began walking, the motion was slow and steady—nothing like a rocky boat—and she could see right down the street, over the tops of the market stalls, to an ancient-looking stone archway.

"That's the Bab Sharqi," Katharine said as her camel came alongside Agatha's. "The Eastern Gate: it's the one Saint Paul came through when he entered Damascus. The Romans built it. They dedicated it to the sun." She turned to look over her shoulder. "Are you all right, Nancy?"

The driver took the reins of Nancy's camel, bringing it level with the others. "It's not as bad as I thought it would be," she said. "It's quite pleasant, isn't it, when you get used to it?"

"This is Straight Street," Katharine said. "Remember it from the Bible? The Arabs call it Midhat Pasha Souk. In a minute you'll smell the spice stalls. We're going to the hammam on the other side of the city."

"What's that?" Agatha grabbed the front of the saddle as her camel lowered its head to investigate a tomato squashed on the cobbles.

"It's a bathhouse," Katharine replied. "Just what we need after five days on a train: an attendant will scrub you cleaner than you've ever been in your life and then massage you with scented oil. It's absolute heaven! When we're done there, we'll walk back through the Khan Al-Harir—the silk souk—and do some shopping if you like. There'll just be time for something to eat then, before we board the coach."

"That sounds wonderful." Nancy smiled. "Oh, what's that smell? It's really lovely. Like . . . some sort of perfume. What is it?"

"Rose petals." Katharine swept her arm toward a huddle of stalls farther up the street. "Can you see the sacks? They're full of dried petals and rosebuds. They use them to flavor the food here as well as for perfume. You can get rose-tasting water and ice cream if you fancy it."

As the camels ambled through the spice souk, the air filled with more exotic scents. Sacks of cardamom, turmeric, and cinnamon were stacked on the cobblestones alongside baskets of nuts and juniper berries. Bunches of garlic and fresh mint hung from hooks, above bowls of frankincense and dried lemons. The walls on either side of the street echoed with the sound of Arab voices calling out their wares, haggling over sales and greeting passersby.

Agatha's mouth watered as they passed a stall on which meat roasted on a spit above a charcoal fire. The vendor was cutting off chunks and placing them on little triangles of bread, then pouring on a thick dark-red sauce. "What's that?" she asked Katharine.

"Cherry kebabs," she replied. "Damascus is famous for black cherries: they grow all over Syria. They make a savory sauce with cinnamon and pistachio nuts: it's delicious. We can have some later if you like."

The route to the bathhouse took them through streets selling carpets, copper pots, brass plates, and wooden furniture inlaid with intricate marquetry. Veiled women with laden baskets bustled past huddles of ragged beggars squatting on the cobbles.

"We couldn't come this way last year," Katharine said. "Syria was a battleground. There was an uprising against the French. It left thousands homeless—that's why there are so many beggars."

A little boy, half-naked, ran up to them, reaching up to where Agatha's feet dangled from the saddle. He looked about the same age as Rosalind. His dark eyes, framed with thick lashes, had a look of desperate defiance. Agatha fumbled in her pocket for the change from the food she had bought on the train. Would Turkish lira be any good? She wasn't sure. But she had to give him something.

"Oh! Don't do that!" Katharine saw her drop the coins into the boy's outstretched hand. "They'll all be after us!" She kicked her camel so it lurched forward. "Hurry up," she called over her shoulder.

The bathhouse was at the end of a long narrow alley. Katharine reached it first and had already dismounted when the others got there.

"How do we get down?" Nancy gripped the saddle with both hands.

"Don't worry—he'll do it." Katharine jerked her head at the camel driver, who was sauntering up the street in their wake.

With a single word and a flick of his stick, the camel driver brought the camels to their knees. Getting down was much easier than getting up, Agatha thought as she stepped sideways onto the ground. She glanced at Nancy, whose face showed obvious relief at being back on terra firma.

"Well done, you two!" Katharine beamed. "Now, let's go and indulge ourselves!" She led the way into the dark, cool interior, whose roof was pierced with beams of sunlight. "It's women only, in case you're wondering," she said. "The men's is on another street. This is the only place you'll see the women without their veils."

The three women were shown to individual cubicles, where they undressed and left their clothes.

"Are you ready?" Katharine's voice floated over the dividing wall.

"What happens now?" Nancy sounded nervous.

"You lie on a table while they soap you and scrub you down," Katharine called back. "Then you get the massage."

"Where is it? The table, I mean?"

"In the main room. You're not shy, are you? It's all just women together."

Agatha emerged still wearing a silk camisole and knickers. Nancy had managed to just about cover the middle part of her body with a strip of towel she found hanging in the changing room.

"I felt like you the first time." Katharine pinned up her hair, her breasts shifting as she raised her arms. "The Arab women have a different attitude to nudity: they're far less prudish than us Brits when they're away from men."

Agatha tried not to stare. Katharine stood, unabashed, a feather of pale brown pubic hair standing out against the milky skin of her belly. She beckoned the others to follow her. Bare feet padded on rush mats as they made their way to the shampooing room. There was a sharp, fresh scent of lemons and rosemary, and they could hear the distant, echoing chatter of voices.

Attendants greeted them as they entered a room full of naked Arab women, all of whom stared with unbridled curiosity at the pale-skinned newcomers. Katharine said something in Arabic, waving her hand toward Agatha and Nancy as she did so. The attendants nodded. One of them opened a cupboard and produced a towel the size of a bedsheet, which she pegged up on a sort of washing line hanging over a table. She repeated the process with a second towel, creating a tent around the table.

"There!" Katharine smiled at Nancy. "No need to be embarrassed, now—you'll be out of sight of prying eyes." She turned to Agatha. "Would you like one, too?"

Agatha nodded. In her time as a nurse she had seen plenty of naked men, but there were never any female patients. Apart from her sister, she had never seen a woman without clothes on. She felt uncomfortably self-conscious, well aware that her stomach and breasts, after childbirth, bore no comparison to Katharine's taut, voluptuous body.

Out of the corner of her eye she saw Nancy duck behind the hanging towels. Agatha wondered why she was so self-conscious. Nancy was at least ten years younger than she and Katharine, and there was hardly an ounce of fat on her. Perhaps growing up as an only child had made her inhibited. Then it occurred to Agatha that there might be another reason. How long did Nancy say she'd been married? Was it five months or six? Long enough, at any rate, for her to be pregnant and know it. This possibility cast a new, cold light on the events of Thursday night. How desperate Nancy would have felt, receiving that telegram, if she had also just discovered she was pregnant.

Putting herself in Nancy's shoes was a sharp reminder of the day she had broken the news of her own pregnancy to Archie. They had been in a taxi, coming home after a night out at the Palais de Danse in Hammersmith. She had felt queasy and Archie had shouted at the driver for going too fast. "No, it's not that," she said. His face had frozen as she whispered in his ear. For what seemed like an eternity he sat there in silence, the yellow beams of street lamps glancing off his skin like arrows. When he spoke, the words cut her to the heart. *I don't want a baby. You'll think of it all the time and not of me.*

Agatha felt a hand on her arm. The attendant gestured toward the table, and Agatha obediently lay down. She felt very tense as she waited to be washed. The concept of a complete stranger soaping every crevice was not her idea of relaxation. She closed her eyes, bracing herself for an ordeal. But to her surprise, the moment when the warm, fragrant flannel made contact with her skin was intensely pleasurable. The attendant worked methodically up her body with deft, firm strokes, beginning with her feet. By the time she reached her knees, Agatha had fallen into a delicious state of drowsiness. It was almost a shame to be bundled into a steaming bath to soak after that, but the massage that followed was even more soporific. Lying on her front this time, she felt warm oil being poured onto the small of her back. Then the strong, purposeful hands were at work again, kneading away all the tension in her body. She was barely conscious when it came to an end.

"Time to go!" The voice came into her dream. She was in the garden at Sunningdale, playing French cricket with Rosalind and Archie. Someone was calling from the house, but it wasn't her they wanted. Suddenly, she saw her mother coming across the grass. She looked very angry. She was mouthing words that Agatha couldn't hear.

"Wake up!"

Agatha opened her eyes, struggling to make sense of what she saw. It was a pair of legs. Katharine's legs. She sat up, rubbing her eyes, aware that she was naked. Somehow it no longer mattered.

"We need to get a move on if we're going to go shopping." Katharine smiled. "Did you enjoy that?"

Agatha nodded. "I feel like a new woman." The truth of the words struck her as they came out. It was as if all the pain of the last two years had been scrubbed away with the grime and sweat. Not gone forever, of course. It would come back as surely as dirt under her fingernails. But she would savor this feeling while it lasted. She couldn't remember when she had felt so tranquil, so liberated.

CHAPTER 12

Damascus to Baghdad

At the Souk Al-Harir, Agatha bought a length of white silk embroidered in dark blue to send home to her sister and a pair of leather slippers, embellished with gold, for Charlotte. Then, for Rosalind, she spotted a doll in the scarlet robe and sequinned headdress of a Syrian bride. She caught up with Nancy and Katharine at a stall selling ready-made women's clothes.

"I quite envy them," Nancy was saying. "I think I should quite like to go about in a veil. Think how much time it would save: you wouldn't have to bother about your hair or makeup."

"I suppose you *could* look at it like that," Katharine said. "But it's fundamentally wrong, isn't it, making women cover themselves while men dress exactly as they please?"

"Well, yes, you're right of course. If a woman was to do it out of choice, though, there could be advantages, couldn't there?"

"You're not thinking of buying one, are you?" Agatha said as she ran her fingers over a shawl of lilac cashmere.

"Not a veil," Nancy replied. "But I'm rather taken with that dress." She pointed out a long robe of *eau de nil* silk with silver frogging at the neck.

"I think it would look charming on you," Katharine said. "Why don't you get it?"

"No. I mustn't." Nancy glanced at Agatha. "But I might buy a length of fabric and have a go at making something similar when we get to Baghdad."

Katharine looked at her watch. "You'd better not spend too long deciding—we've only got an hour until the coach leaves."

"I saw something that color over there." Agatha pointed to the stall where she'd bought the bolt of silk. "Shall we go and have a quick look?"

Fifteen minutes later they joined Katharine at an open-air café on the edge of the souk. She had ordered for them, and within moments of their sitting down, a huge plate of food arrived.

"It's for us all to share," Katharine said. "There's falafel, tabbouleh, and baba ghanoush—oh, and that's the meat dish we saw on that stall on the way to the hammam." Agatha had never heard of such things. Katharine reeled off the ingredients of the meal as they helped themselves. Chickpeas, mint, tomatoes, aubergines, cracked wheat, pine nuts, black cherries, and minced lamb. When they'd polished almost everything off, she beckoned the waiter over and spoke to him in Arabic.

"I've just ordered the speciality of the house for dessert." She smiled. "Rosewater and almond-flavored ice cream topped with fresh pistachio nuts."

Agatha thought that nothing could surpass the Venetian ice cream experience, but this was sublime. She had a sudden vivid image of Max licking a blob of *crema dei Dogi* from the corner of his mouth. What would he make of this flavor, she wondered? She tried to work out where he would be now. Somewhere in the Mediterranean: probably nearer to Asia than Europe by now.

His words of warning floated back into her head again as she savored the last spoonful. *She casts a spell on you, and before you know it, you've become her slave . . .* She glanced at Katharine, who was trying to catch the waiter's attention to settle the bill. Everything they had done in Damascus had been directed by her, and they had fallen in with her plans without question. So yes, she *had* cast a spell, but it was a wonderful kind of enchantment. The camels, the massage, the souk, the food . . . Agatha smiled to herself, knowing that she would always remember this day.

~

A fleet of six-wheeler buses awaited the passengers from the Taurus Express who were traveling on to Baghdad. The operation was run by a pair of Australian brothers, the Nairns, one of whom looked Katharine up and down appraisingly when she went to ask about seats. His frank blue eyes had white cat's-whisker creases at the corners where the desert sun had not penetrated.

"We have to be near the front." Katharine held his gaze. "My friend doesn't travel well—she'll be ill if she sits at the back." She glanced over her shoulder at Agatha, who was out of earshot, frowning at something Nancy was saying.

"The seats are already allocated," the Australian replied.

"Well, *un*-allocate them!" Katharine thrust the tickets at him. "Otherwise, you'll have an extremely unpleasant mess to deal with."

He bent his head, examining the tickets. "I'll see what I can do. Miss—"

"It's Mrs." She nodded slowly. "Thank you, Mr. Nairn." Her lips parted, revealing her perfect teeth. As she turned away, she could feel his eyes following her.

"Call me Jim!"

She saw Agatha and Nancy look up from their conversation with curious faces.

"It's all sorted out," she said to them. "No need to worry about getting travel-sick."

"That's a relief." Agatha glanced at the steps up to the nearest coach. "But we saw one of the drivers carry a pair of rifles on board. They were half-hidden in a blanket, but the barrels were sticking out."

"Oh, that's quite normal," Katharine said. "We're unlikely to run into trouble, but I wouldn't care to cross the desert without guns. Come on—let's get ourselves settled, shall we?"

Three veiled Arab women were being shooed to the back of the bus as they boarded. One had live chickens in a basket, which joined in with squawks of protest as the women remonstrated with the driver.

"I feel awful, taking their seats," Agatha said.

"Well, you mustn't." Katharine plopped down on a seat by the window. "They're used to it, and you're not. And they wouldn't be very happy if you were to be violently sick in the middle of a nineteen-hour journey—particularly in this heat."

Ten minutes later the coach rolled out of Damascus, past orchards of fruit trees and date palms, which gradually gave way to the barren wilderness of the desert. Soon there was nothing to be seen but sand dunes and rocks. The sameness of the surroundings had a hypnotic effect, and before long, both Agatha and Nancy had nodded off.

Katharine glanced at their sleeping faces, wishing that she, too, could lose herself in sleep. She looked at her watch. Six thirty. She counted the hours in her head. Less than forty to go until she was standing at the altar of the Anglican church in Baghdad. The thought of Leonard waiting for her, turning to smile at her, to kiss her, made her blood freeze.

She felt a desperate urge to unburden herself, to pour out the fears she had been bottling up ever since she stepped onto the train in London. She looked again at the dozing women, realizing that they were both probably worn out from staying up most of last night looking after her.

Something had changed on that journey down through Turkey. It had begun on the night of the flood, when they were all together in the compartment into the small hours. But Katharine's fever had turned them into more than just fellow travelers. There was a tangible bond between them now. And Katharine longed to confide in these . . . She stopped short of the word that was nudging its way from the back of her mind.

Friends.

She didn't think of herself as a woman who had friends. Not women friends, anyway. If someone had asked her to list those closest to her, she would have reeled off the names of the men at the dig. There was her sister in Norfolk, of course. But they had never been what Katharine would describe as close. Not close enough to confide in when Bertram died. And not close enough to know about the . . . what? There was no word to describe it. The doctor had come up with some gobbledygook about a congenital insensitivity to hormones, but even he had been unable to put a name to the thing that had driven Bertram to an early grave.

She glanced out of the window. Nothing but sand and sky as far as the eye could see. There was something rather sinister about this bright landscape. You could get lost in it despite the openness. At noon it was impossible to tell if you were going north, southeast, or west, and these buses sometimes took the wrong way in the maze of tracks.

Is that what you're doing?

The voice in her head was Bertram's. She carried him with her still. If he had only told her what the doctor had said, talked to her instead of marching out into the night with a gun.

You don't have to go through with this, you know.

"Oh, but I do," she whispered at her reflection in the window. If she pulled out of this marriage to Leonard, she would be on her way back to London on the next train. Not back to the British Museum—there would be no job for her there once she was off the dig team. She would be reduced to touting for business around the fashion houses. But the world of haute couture, once so glamorous, held no appeal now. She couldn't go back to hemlines and handbags and hats. Not when she was making her mark in a man's world. A world of lost kingdoms and buried treasure. Living like a man was what she loved, what she craved.

She had mastered them all—all the young men she worked with—and she could master Leonard, too, if she was clever about it. For all his gravitas, he was a novice in matters of the heart. His lack of protest about what *wasn't* going to happen on the wedding night had made that plain. She would have to tantalize him, as she had tantalized Max. Give him glimpses of her, like a painting in an art gallery—something that could be gazed upon but not touched.

In the seat beside her, Nancy stirred in her sleep, her body twitching as if she was in the middle of a nightmare. Which, in reality, Katharine thought, she *was*. And Agatha was not much better off. According to the newspapers, the ink was barely dry on her divorce from a husband whose infidelity had driven her to a nervous breakdown. How could either of these women bear to hear Katharine talking about her wedding? Confronted with the news, they would have to muster fake enthusiasm, pretend to be pleased for her. Then there would be questions about how the romance had evolved. That would be excruciating. And yet she found herself wanting to invite them to the church. Why? For moral support? Now that the time was almost upon her, she felt unaccountably terrified.

As the bus veered to the right, a towering sand dune came into view. This stretch of desert was very much like the landscape outside Cairo. And it had been around this time, just as the sun was setting, that her husband had climbed onto the Great Pyramid at Giza and shot himself.

She had never seen Bertram's body. His commanding officer had come to find her, to break the awful news. She had asked to go to the mortuary, but he had advised her against it. In shock, she had acqui-esced. Later, she wished she hadn't. She tortured herself, imagining what had happened. And the nightmares made her afraid to fall asleep.

The thought of what she was about to do, of repeating the very same vows she had made to Bertram, set off a wave of panic. Pain and guilt rushed in, threatening to overwhelm her.

I'm getting married the day after tomorrow.

She tried to picture herself telling them. Perhaps if she left it until they were actually in Baghdad, at the moment they parted. *Oh, by the way, I'm getting married tomorrow—will you come?*

No time for questions then.

~

The only real landmark on the whole journey between Damascus and Baghdad was the desert fortress of Rutbah. The fleet of coaches arrived there at just after midnight. Agatha woke up as the driver applied the brakes. The one sign of life was a flickering light looming out of the darkness. As they came to a stop, she saw huge wooden gates. The thud as they were unbarred could be heard through the window. Standing on each side, their rifles raised, were a pair of guards in pith helmets and long leather boots. They boarded each coach in turn and walked the length of it, eyeing each passenger with fierce expressions.

"The Camel Corps," Katharine whispered. "They're on the lookout for bandits masquerading as bona fide travelers."

When the inspection was over, the coaches were allowed to drive into the fort and the gates were shut behind them. Then Jim Nairn climbed aboard with a megaphone.

"We're taking a short rest here," he announced. "It'll be three hours until we get moving again. They don't have many rooms, but if you don't mind sharing, there are some beds."

It was even more cramped than he had suggested. Katharine, Agatha, and Nancy were herded into a windowless room with dark mud-brick walls. The only furniture was a pair of double beds. Before they could decide who would sleep where, another three women—all veiled—were shown into the room.

"Well, it's a good thing none of us is fat!" Katharine patted the mattress, sending a little shower of sand onto the floor. "Who's going to be piggy in the middle?"

"Do you think we should lie on our coats?" Nancy edged gingerly onto the bed. "Ugh! Is that a cockroach?" She pointed to a dark shape moving on the wall.

"There's another one!" Agatha was looking at the ceiling, where a naked lightbulb gave out a dim glow.

There was a rustle from the other side of the room. One of the veiled women stepped forward, holding a small tin in her hand. "No frighten," she said. "I have fire."

"What's she doing?" Nancy craned her neck as the woman struck a match.

"She's lighting *ajwain* seeds," Katharine said. "Can you smell it?"

A curl of smoke rose from the tin and wafted across the room. "Oh," Agatha said, "it's like . . . rosemary or thyme or something."

"They use it out here to drive away insects." Katharine nodded, beaming at the woman with the tin, who set it down on the floor between the two beds. "It's very effective—I wish I'd had some on the train."

As the smoke rose toward the ceiling, the cockroaches came scuttling down, disappearing into a hole in the skirting board, which one of the other Arab women proceeded to block with her suitcase. Then everyone settled down for what remained of the night.

Katharine closed her eyes, but sleep refused to come. She could feel the warmth of Nancy's body through the coat she had wrapped herself up in. From the sound of their breathing, both the others were asleep.

Across the room one of the Arab women was snoring. She couldn't see her watch in the dark, but she knew it must be getting on for one o'clock in the morning. Monday morning. She had just one more night of freedom.

She tried to imagine how she would feel if it was Leonard, not Nancy, lying beside her now. The thought made her insides curl. It wasn't that she didn't like him. He was not handsome, like Bertram, who had swept her away the first time she set eyes on him. But even if Leonard had been the most gorgeous creature ever to walk God's earth, it wouldn't have helped. She would still be afraid.

She felt the bed shift as Nancy turned over. "Are you awake, Katharine?" she whispered.

"Yes. Can't seem to nod off."

"Me neither. I wish it was morning. I don't like this place. If I fell asleep, I'd have nightmares—would you?"

Katharine longed to spill it all out then. Her secret clung to her like the scent of the burning seeds beside the bed. If she whispered it now, in the dark, would it matter? Would it help? There was nothing Nancy or anyone else could do to change things. Better to keep it to herself, to maintain the image of the confident career woman who did exactly as she liked and feared no one.

"I'm not worried about nightmares," she said. "It's the snoring that's keeping me awake. She sounds just like Mary's camel, doesn't she—when it kept spitting."

Nancy giggled in the darkness. "I'm glad you're not asleep," she said. "It's horrible when you're lying awake on your own, isn't it?"

~

It was still dark when Jim Nairn came banging on doors to wake everybody up. People trudged out into the courtyard and onto the waiting coaches like sleepwalkers. An hour into the onward journey, the first hint of light appeared in the eastern sky. As the horizon turned from gray to apricot, the coaches juddered to a halt. Agatha peered through the window, her eyes bleary with sleep. A group of men in traditional Arab robes were setting up primus stoves and unpacking copper pans from large wicker baskets. Then—to her amazement—they produced large tins of what looked like sausages.

The passengers were summoned from their seats by Jim Nairn, who looked annoyingly bright-eyed and lively for a man who had probably had no sleep at all.

"Breakfast!" he barked through the megaphone. "Line up in front of the bus, please!"

Agatha could smell the sausages as she stepped onto the sand. Steam was rising from the row of saucepans, all perched on the stoves held steady by rocks arranged around the base of each one. She lined up with the others and was soon handed an Arab flatbread with a fat sausage nestled inside. To wash it down, there was a tin mug full of hot, sweet black tea.

Agatha sat cross-legged on the sand to eat. As she bit into her breakfast, it tasted like the most delicious thing she had ever eaten. There was something about being in the desert, at daybreak, with the colors of the dawn—pale pinks, corals, and blues—and the pure, cool air that gave everything a sense of wonder. Suddenly, her old life in England seemed very small, very insignificant. This was what she had dreamed of. Here, in this barren landscape, she was truly away from everything—with the silent morning air, the rising sun, the sand for a seat, and the taste of sausages and tea.

When the time came to move on, the men who had cooked breakfast disappeared over the ridge of a sand dune, their baskets loaded onto the backs of camels.

"They're Bedouin tribesmen," Katharine said. "You'll see more like them when you come to the dig." She turned to Nancy, who was sitting across the aisle. "You'll come and visit, too, won't you?"

"Well, I . . . er . . ." Nancy looked from Katharine to Agatha, as if seeking permission.

"We can travel together, can't we?" Agatha said. "How far is it from Baghdad?"

"Quite a way: about twelve hours by train. But there are interesting places to see along the way. You could take your time. Stop off for a day or two at Karbala and Ukhaidir. Then we can put you up in the annex for a few days. It's quite basic, but I think you'll enjoy it. The boys will love to have you, I'm sure."

"That's awfully kind of you," Nancy said. "It sounds absolutely fascinating."

A shout from the front of the coach made them all turn their heads. The driver suddenly swerved to the left. Through the window they saw what had caused the diversion. A truck was parked right in the middle of the track, with rifles pointing out of the windows.

"Bandits!" Katharine hissed. "Don't worry. They won't come after us. They'll be waiting for the caravans."

"Those men on camels?" Nancy frowned.

"Not the ones who made our breakfast—they'll be well away by now. But there'll be others coming through—merchants on their way back from trading their wares in Damascus—that's who they're waiting for."

After bumping along on a detour of several miles, the coach picked up the track again. At just after ten o'clock, Agatha spotted a dome and minarets shimmering in the heat rising from the sand.

"That's Fallujah," Katharine said. "You can just about see the river running past the mosque. It's the Euphrates."

To enter the city, the coach had to drive over a bridge made of boats. It swayed alarmingly and Agatha felt a wave of nausea, which thankfully passed as soon as they were back on dry land. They drove through palm groves on a rutted track of a road. Then, on the left, were the golden domes of another, bigger mosque, which Katharine told them was in a city called Kadhimain.

"We'll come to the Tigris soon," Katharine said. "It's only a few miles to Baghdad."

They were on a proper road now, with rows of palms on either side and herds of black buffaloes wading in pools of water. Then they passed houses and gardens full of flowers. Agatha glimpsed tennis courts with European people—young men and women—darting around in white.

"Welcome to memsahib land." Katharine smiled. "This is Alwiyah—the smart suburb. I'd avoid it if I were you."

The tennis courts and manicured gardens eventually gave way to what looked like a shantytown. Shacks made of petrol cans surrounded a vast, muddy enclosure full of buffaloes. The stench of manure penetrated the coach and had everyone holding their noses.

"This is Buffalo Town." Katharine pointed out of the window at a pair of women squelching about in the mud, smiling as they threw feed into a trough for the animals. "It looks like a slum, doesn't it—but these people are actually quite wealthy by Arab standards. A buffalo is worth a hundred pounds or more. Can you see those bracelets on their legs?" Agatha watched the women as they staggered back through the mud. Sure enough, there was a glint of silver around their ankles. Each woman had a clutch of bracelets: silver chains laced with beads of lapis, jade, and amber.

Buffalo Town was on the banks of the river Tigris. This was crossed by another bridge of boats—not as long as the first—and then they were in Baghdad, driving up a street full of rickety buildings, heading toward an imposing mosque with domes of turquoise. Then the coach stopped, and Agatha realized that this was it: after five days of traveling, she was finally there—in front of the Tigris Palace Hotel.

Katharine got out to say good-bye as the driver unloaded Agatha's and Nancy's luggage. "Some words of advice," she said. "When you go shopping, remember that nothing in the Middle East is what it appears to be. If you see a man gesticulating at you violently to go away, he is actually inviting you to approach. On the other hand, if he beckons to you, he is telling you to go away. And if you want someone to listen to you, you have to shout. That's how they do things here. If you speak in an ordinary voice, they'll ignore you: they'll think you're talking to yourself."

"Where are you staying?" Nancy asked.

"On the other side of town, at the Maude. It's a guesthouse, not a hotel. Leonard hates to spend money on accommodation." She rolled her eyes. "Sorry: that probably sounds rather disloyal." She paused for no more than a heartbeat. "Actually, we're getting married tomorrow. Leonard and me, that is. Will you come?"

CHAPTER 13

Baghdad

Nancy wondered if there were any other guests staying at the Tigris Palace Hotel. There was no one to be seen in the marble-floored reception area when they came downstairs that afternoon after unpacking. Tea was served in the cool interior courtyard by a uniformed waiter who wouldn't have looked out of place at Claridge's.

"Why didn't she tell us before?" Nancy said, spreading a napkin on her lap.

"Perhaps she didn't want a fuss." Agatha paused while the waiter poured tea into her cup. "It's her second marriage, after all."

"But you'd think she'd have mentioned it, all the same. Do you think she's been having second thoughts?"

"I suppose she might have been mulling it over on the journey: trying to decide if it was what she really wanted."

"I remember feeling like that the morning after Felix proposed." Nancy reached for a cucumber sandwich. "I'd told my father—who was absolutely thrilled—but I remember looking out of the window at the buds coming out on the horse chestnut trees and thinking that getting married would be like those leaves unfurling. They looked so pale and tender and—I don't know—*exposed*. They were coming out, and there was no going back. And who knew if a gale or a frost might suddenly come along?"

"Had you known Felix long?"

"Not really. I'd seen him at a few social occasions around Christmas. And then he was at a party thrown by a girl I was at school with. It was fancy dress—very wild—and a lot of people were already very drunk when I arrived. Felix had come as Zorro. He looked just like Douglas Fairbanks, in a red cape and a black sombrero hat. I found out later that he'd proposed to several other girls at the party before he got to me." Nancy shook her head. "I think he'd have called it off if he could when he realized what he'd done. But my father had already put a notice in the *Times*. It was too late to back out. So we were married six weeks later."

Agatha picked up the teapot, topping up Nancy's cup, then her own. "Marriage is always a leap into the unknown, even if you think you know the other person inside out. It works for some people. But I doubt there are many truly happy marriages."

Nancy glanced at a butterfly—striped red, white, and black like a flag—that had landed on the wall above Agatha's head. "When we were talking on the train, you said your husband had been in love with someone else. Did he give her up?"

Agatha stared into her cup. "He . . . We . . . we're no longer married."

"I'm sorry—I shouldn't have asked."

Agatha let out a long breath. "It's a terribly hard thing for me to talk about—even now. When I first met Katharine, I was too ashamed to tell her. I'm afraid I let her think my husband had been killed in the war."

"Well, I don't blame you. And from what you told me the other night, it wasn't your fault that things didn't work out." Nancy took a bite of her sandwich.

"The trouble is people always think it *must* be your fault when men have had enough of you. That you didn't try hard enough. And when you have a child that makes you feel even more of a failure."

Nancy felt the bread turn into sawdust in her mouth. What was she going to tell this child when it was old enough to understand, if its father didn't make good on his promise?

If you can just lie low out there for a few months . . .

The memory of his words taunted her. Here she was, in this foreign city halfway across the world, dependent on a woman she barely knew. A woman who would no doubt recoil in disgust if she knew Nancy's secret. How on earth was she going to get through the next few weeks—let alone months?

~

Agatha woke early the next morning. It took her a few seconds to remember where she was. She had fallen into bed exhausted at just after six the previous evening, and now, looking at her travel clock on the bedside table, she saw that she had slept for more than twelve solid hours.

For a while she lay there, luxuriating in the feeling of being in a proper bed, in a room of her own, for the first time in almost a week. Then she climbed out and went to the window, which opened onto a small balcony. Below her was Al Rasheed Street, the busy main thoroughfare of Baghdad. It was full of people. They were nearly all men in Arab dress, though there were a few in Western-style suits. Most were on foot, but some were in carriages drawn by mules or horses. As she watched, an ancient-looking bus trundled past, pulled by a team of mules. It had a spindly staircase spiraling up the back end and was stuffed with dozens of people. This, Agatha thought, must be the morning rush hour.

In the shade of an awning across the street, a man in an Indian-style turban was serving food from a makeshift stall. She could see another man behind him, flipping slices of what looked like eggplant on a griddle over a charcoal fire. Yet another was inserting lettuce and some sort of white sauce into flatbreads. Arab men were queuing for the food, chatting and spitting on the pavement as they waited. The smell of the cooking wafted up to where Agatha stood watching, making her feel very hungry.

She and Nancy had arranged to meet for breakfast at eight thirty. The wedding was at ten, and when it was over, they planned to set about the business of the day. Agatha was to go house hunting, while Nancy wanted to go to the British Consulate to find out exactly what had happened to her cousin.

Agatha couldn't help wondering how Katharine would be feeling, waking up on what was to be her wedding day. She herself had mixed feelings about attending the service. It was going to be a painful reminder of what she had traveled all this way to avoid. Archie and his fiancée were due to marry in just four days' time.

She shut the image out of her mind by sorting through her clothes, deciding what would be appropriate for a wedding in a city where the temperature was predicted to reach around ninety degrees Fahrenheit by the time they stepped outside the church. She settled on a dress of lilac silk with a trim of cream rosebuds at the neck. She would wear it with the new straw cloche she had bought in Harrods' hat department. She grimaced as she lifted it out of the box, remembering her embarrassment as an assistant had explained the significance of the different styles of ribbon trim on offer for this type of hat.

"It's the latest thing," the girl had said, sweeping her hand toward the blank-eyed china heads. "The ribbon you choose sends out a message: a sort of code." She pointed to an arrowlike pink grosgrain ribbon.

"This shape indicates that the wearer is single but has already given her heart to someone." She glanced at Agatha, seeing from her expression that this was not going down well.

"Or there's this one." She indicated a complicated-looking knot of mauve silk ribbon. "This means that you are already married." Her smile was met with an even deeper frown.

"Perhaps this would be more appropriate?" She picked up a hat with a flamboyant bow of cerise with white polka dots. "This one says that you are single and interested in mingling."

"I just want something plain, actually." Red in the face by now, Agatha had plucked a hat from the nearest mannequin. It had a narrow cream ribbon trimmed with a single button of mother-of-pearl—and if this carried a cryptic message, she didn't want to know.

As Agatha laid the hat on the bed, there was a sharp rap on the door of the bedroom. She glanced at the clock. She had ordered tea for seven thirty, but it was only just after seven. Thinking that perhaps it was Nancy, she went to open the door. To her surprise, Katharine was standing there.

"Sorry to disturb you so early." She looked agitated, the smooth skin of her forehead puckered. "It's Max and Michael. They've been held up. They wired from Beirut last night: some problem with the ship carrying our supplies." She huffed out a breath. "Anyway, it means we haven't any witnesses for the wedding. I was wondering if you and Nancy would do the honors."

"Oh . . . I . . ." Agatha stalled. "You mean . . . sign the register?" The full significance of it struck her. This would blow her cover completely. To use an alias on a certificate of marriage would render it invalid. It would make a mockery of the whole wedding: Katharine and Leonard Woolley would, effectively, be living in sin. "I . . . I'm not sure if I . . ." She was at a loss for an excuse. How could she refuse such a request without appearing downright rude?

"You don't need to pretend anymore, you know." Katharine took a step closer, put her hand on Agatha's arm. "I know who you are."

Agatha felt herself wither in the beam of Katharine's eyes. *She knew.* She had very likely guessed within hours of their first meeting.

Moments from the train journey flashed in rapid succession through Agatha's mind. The times she had caught Katharine looking at her with that Mona Lisa smile. *Do you have a different pair of spectacles? Those really don't suit you at all* . . . She was probably laughing up her sleeve the whole of the journey.

"You're not on the train now." Katharine's voice fell to a gentle whisper. "You don't have to worry about people pointing the finger. In Baghdad you can hide yourself away if you want to."

Agatha took a breath. She felt as if her lips were glued together. "When did you realize?"

"When I saw you without your glasses, after you hurt your head. You were lying fast asleep and I held my book up to your face, comparing it to the photograph on the back page. I'd had my suspicions before that. I was dying to ask, but I didn't want to make things awkward for you on the train."

Agatha turned away, shaking her head. "I was stupid, thinking I could get away with it. It's just—"

"You don't have to explain. It's completely understandable." A pause and then: "I read all about it in the papers, of course, like everybody else. If it's any comfort, I know how that feels—having your private life hung out like so much dirty washing."

"You do?"

Katharine nodded. "I wasn't quite truthful on the train. When you said you were a war widow, I let you believe that my husband met the same fate. He didn't. He committed suicide six months after we were married."

"Oh, Katharine—I'm so sorry . . . I . . ."

Katharine held up her hand. "You don't have to say anything. But please, just support me now, will you?"

"Yes, of course I will."

~

Saint George's Church on Haifa Street was dwarfed by the towering minarets of the Abu Hanifa Mosque. But despite its relatively small size and unimposing architecture, Agatha felt a soothing sense of peace as she and Nancy followed Katharine inside.

"There's no need to tell her—not yet," Katharine had said as she left Agatha's bedroom to get ready for the ceremony. "I'll ask her to sign the register first. That way she won't see your name."

Agatha had felt very guilty and hypocritical when Nancy greeted her with "Good morning, Mary," at breakfast. But there wasn't time to go into it now, to explain why she had wanted to conceal her identity and how, once begun, the tangled web of deception had enveloped her. And so, once she had imparted the news about their acting as witnesses, she had deliberately steered the conversation away from talk of the wedding, chatting about the business of renting a house until the eggs, bacon, and toast were eaten.

Katharine had arrived by horse-drawn carriage to collect them. Her outfit was stunning: a Chanel suit in cream wool, edged with black braid, a double string of pearls, and a cream broad-brimmed cloche with matching trim of folded silk embellished with a single flower of white tulle. A small bouquet of lily of the valley lay on the seat beside her.

It had taken no more than ten minutes to reach the church, despite their way being blocked at one point by a man leading two buffaloes across the road. Katharine had laughed when this happened.

"Oh dear," Nancy said. "Aren't you worried we'll be late?"

"It's a bride's prerogative, isn't it?" Katharine replied. "And anyway, Leonard can't go anywhere without me: I've got the keys to our new expedition truck."

As the carriage drew up outside the church, Katharine had fallen silent. Agatha noticed that her fingers were shaking slightly as she handed down her bouquet before stepping onto the pavement.

"Are you all right?" Agatha whispered as they went inside. "Not too nervous?"

Before Katharine could reply, a man with ginger whiskers emerged from the shadows. "Hullo, Katharine, old girl!"

"Michael! You made it after all!"

"What?" He gave her a crooked smile that revealed a gold tooth. "Didn't think we'd let you down, did you?"

"Is Max here?"

"Up front." He jerked his head toward the altar. "Ready to do his duty with the ring."

"Well, that's . . . wonderful." Katharine glanced over her shoulder at Agatha and Nancy. "Looks like you two will be able to relax after all." She gave a tight smile. "Michael, let me introduce you to my friends." At that moment the organ struck up the opening chords of "The Arrival of the Queen of Sheba."

"Oops! No time for that, I'm afraid!" Taking Katharine's arm, he steered her toward the aisle.

Agatha and Nancy waited until the bride and her escort were almost at the altar before following in their wake. As they made their way up the aisle, Agatha wondered what to make of the sudden change in the proceedings. The look on the face of the man giving Katharine away had been one of amused puzzlement, as if her remark about his turning up after all was a joke. Had the men really been held up? Could it have been a ruse cooked up by Katharine to get her to reveal herself? She brushed the idea away. It was pure conceit to imagine that a woman could wake up on the morning of her wedding with thoughts of anyone but herself and her future husband.

Agatha stopped at a pew a few rows back from the front on the bride's side of the church. As she did so, Max looked round and smiled, raising his hand in a discreet wave.

Katharine was at the altar rail now. Leonard turned to her as she drew level with him. Even in profile, Agatha would have recognized him. There was something very distinctive about the high, sloping forehead, the bushy eyebrows and the long, rather wild-looking beard. From this distance he looked old enough to be Katharine's father.

The music stopped and the vicar stepped forward, making the sign of the cross over their heads. "Dearly beloved, we are gathered here this morning for the sacrament of marriage." It might have been an Anglican church, but his lilting accent was straight out of the Welsh valleys. He made the word "marriage" sound as if it had three syllables.

"Leonard and Katharine—" He looked at each of them in turn. "The vows you are about to take are to be made in the presence of God, who is judge of all and knows the secrets of our hearts. Therefore, if either of you knows a reason why you may not lawfully marry, you must declare it now."

There was a moment's silence. Out of the corner of her eye, Agatha saw Max drop his head. She wondered what he was thinking. If there had ever been something between him and Katharine, this must be excruciating for him.

The secrets of our hearts . . . The phrase echoed in her head. Yes, she thought, the chances are that every one of the six other people standing in this church—including the vicar—has at least one secret they will never, ever tell.

There were some secrets that could be let go without too many repercussions. Others, though, might shatter lives. This morning two secrets had been exposed: that of her own identity—which was annoying, but not the end of the world—and the truth about the way Katharine's first husband had died. She wondered why Katharine had chosen to reveal it on this day of all days. On the face of it, the secret had been delivered up in response to Agatha's embarrassment at being found out. But perhaps there was more to it than that.

Why did he kill himself?

That was the unspoken question. Was there something else Katharine had wanted to say? Had she been seeking some sort of reassurance before entering into this second marriage?

That fool should never have told him . . . Such a shock . . .

The night of delirium on the train seemed to hold the key to whatever was locked up inside Katharine's heart. But something had held her back this morning. If she had come to the hotel intending to confide in her new friend, something had made her change her mind.

"Leonard, will you take Katharine to be your wife?" The vicar's melodic voice broke the silence. "Will you love her, comfort her, honor and protect her, and, forsaking all others, be faithful to her as long as you both shall live?"

Agatha's insides crumpled like burnt paper. Archie had broken all those promises within a few years of making them. He had only really loved her at the very beginning—before life had intervened to spoil his impossible image of what married life was supposed to be like. But when she had really needed him—when she was pregnant with Rosalind and feeling frightened and vulnerable, when she was knocked sideways by the death of her mother—he had not been there for her. He had neither loved her nor comforted her. And he had never protected her: he had wanted *her* to protect him. He couldn't bear it if anyone was ill or unhappy because it disturbed his equilibrium. And as for honoring her, any vestige of that had vanished when he fell for another woman.

As Agatha listened to Leonard Woolley make his marriage vows, she wondered if Archie would feel even a glimmer of shame when he said those same words in four days' time.

She glanced at Nancy, who must be finding all this just as demoralizing as she was—probably even more so, as she had been a bride just a few months ago. Nancy was gazing straight ahead—not at the couple themselves but at the stained glass window behind the altar. Her expression was unreadable.

The vicar turned to Katharine and began the vows a second time. "I, Katharine . . ."

"I, Katharine, take you, Leonard, to be my husband." Katharine's voice was low and husky, as if she had just come out of a deep sleep. The brim of her hat cast her face into shadow, so there was no indication of how she felt. As she completed her vows, Max stepped forward with the ring. The vicar took it from him and placed it on a red velvet cushion.

"Heavenly Father, by your blessing, let these rings be to Leonard and Katharine a symbol of unending love and faithfulness, to remind them of the vow and covenant which they have made this day through Jesus Christ our Lord." He held out the cushion to Leonard, who took the ring. For a long few seconds he seemed to be struggling to get it onto her finger. In the end she pulled her hand away and did it herself.

"Katharine, I give you this ring as a sign of our marriage." With an awkward smile, Leonard took her hand again. "With my body I honor you; all that I have I share with you . . ."

Agatha couldn't help imagining the two of them in bed together, as they would be in just a few hours' time. It was a strange, rather distasteful thought. Her own inner voice berated her for being so superficial. Just because Leonard was older and less physically attractive than his new wife didn't make him an unsuitable husband. What if Katharine had been marrying the much younger and undeniably handsome Max? Would that have been more acceptable? To her surprise, that image was even more disturbing. Why should that be?

Her train of thought was derailed by the vicar's proclamation. "Katharine and Leonard have made their vows to each other and declared their marriage by the giving and receiving of a ring. I therefore proclaim that they are husband and wife. Those whom God has joined together let no man put asunder." A pause and then: "You may kiss the bride."

It wasn't so much a kiss as a bob of his head toward her upturned face. It was as if Leonard was afraid his lips would mar her perfect skin. Then he hooked his arm through hers and led her down the aisle. Neither of them was smiling. He looked embarrassed and she looked . . . Agatha struggled to pinpoint the expression on Katharine's face. Resignation, determination, and anxiety were the words that sprang to mind. It reminded Agatha of the way she had felt during her divorce proceedings, when she was called to hear the evidence of Archie's fake adultery at the Grosvenor Hotel. Yes, she thought, Katharine looked like a woman about to face an ordeal.

Max and Michael followed the bride and groom down the aisle, and Nancy slipped out of the pew behind them. Agatha hung back. She felt an overwhelming urge to be alone in this place, just for a few moments. She sat down, her eyes on the stained glass image of Saint George slaying the dragon.

I'm sorry.

She wasn't sure if she'd whispered the words aloud or just heard them inside her head.

Sorry for not being a good enough wife, for depriving Rosalind of her daddy.

Would Archie have strayed if she hadn't left him alone in London while she went to nurse her mother? Would he have fallen for a younger, prettier woman if she had tried harder with her own appearance after Rosalind was born?

She was apologizing for these things to someone who she was no longer sure was listening, or was even there. But saying it made her feel better, all the same.

When she got outside, Nancy was standing by the horse-drawn carriage with the men and Katharine was chatting with the vicar.

"Oh, there you are!" Katharine gave the ghost of a smile. "I'm afraid there isn't time for any kind of reception." She made a sweeping gesture with her hands, one still clutching the bouquet of lily of the valley. "We have to leave for Ur in an hour's time and get the dig house open for the rest of the team. Max is staying here for a couple of days to organize the supplies." She looked over her shoulder to where the others were standing. "I haven't introduced you to them yet, have I?" Taking Agatha's arm she led her down the steps. "Leonard, Michael, Max—this is my friend Agatha: Agatha *Christie*."

CHAPTER 14

Jebel Sinjar

The day after the wedding, Agatha was breakfasting alone on the terrace overlooking the river Tigris. Nancy was spending the morning in bed, still recovering from her sleepless night on the Taurus Express and the long coach ride through the desert.

The view across the river reminded her of Venice. The Arab boats with their high-scrolled prows and faded paintwork were not so very different from gondolas. As Agatha glanced upstream, she saw a procession of the more primitive, raftlike vessels that Katharine called *gufas* coming toward her. They were loaded with melons and chickens and sacks of grain. As she watched them glide by on the muddy brown water below, she mulled over the events of the day before.

She had almost died of embarrassment outside the church when her deception was exposed so publicly. On the way back to the hotel, Nancy had been very good about it, reassuring her that no one would blame her for wanting to travel incognito. In a way it was a relief to have it out in the open. But there had been no chance to explain it to Max—he had gone off with Katharine and Leonard as soon as the service was over.

So it was a surprise when the waiter brought a note on the tray with her coffee. Max had come to the hotel. He was waiting for her in the lobby.

"Could you ask him to join me—out here?"

Agatha wasn't sure if the waiter had understood. She was spreading marmalade onto a piece of toast when she spotted Max walking through the French doors, shading his eyes against the sun.

"Good morning!" He beamed as he strode across the terrace, waving away the broken branch of a large potted palm that caught at his hat as he passed it.

"Hello." Agatha tried to read his face. He was still smiling, but he looked rather nervous, as if he had something unpleasant to say. "Please, do sit down. Would you like some coffee—or would you rather have tea?"

"Coffee would be lovely."

She poured some into the empty cup that had been put out for Nancy. "Milk and sugar?"

"Just black, thanks."

"I'm awfully sorry to have misled you in Venice," she began. "It's just that I—"

Max raised his hand. "Please—don't worry about that. I absolutely understand that a successful writer would want to travel incognito. It must be an awful bore to have complete strangers accost you when you're trying to relax."

"That's very gracious of you." Agatha felt all the tension in her body melt away. "Do help yourself to toast, by the way—they've brought far too much for one person."

"Thank you, Mrs. Christie—I am a bit peckish, actually. The food over at the Maude isn't much to write home about."

"Well, dig in. And do call me Agatha." How she wished she could revert to her maiden name. *Mrs. Christie*. It was a constant reminder of what she was not. But it was how the world knew her. She was stuck with it.

"Thank you, Agatha." His cheeks went slightly pink as he said her name. He covered his self-consciousness by helping himself to a piece of toast, to which he applied liberal quantities of butter and marmalade. "You're probably wondering why I'm here," he said, as he laid down the knife. "I'm going to be in Baghdad for the next few days, organizing supplies for the dig, and I wanted to invite you and your companion on a sightseeing trip, if you're interested."

"Oh? That's very thoughtful." It occurred to Agatha that Nancy might be the reason for the invitation. She and Max were about the same age, and Nancy was very attractive. She wondered if Katharine had filled him in on the disastrous marriage. "The thing is," she went on, "I'm not sure if Nancy's up to doing any more traveling at the moment. She hasn't managed to get much sleep these past few days, and she's trying to catch up."

She watched Max's face. If he was disappointed, he was too much of a gentleman to show it.

"Never mind," he said. "What about you?"

"Well, where were you thinking of going?"

"I thought you might like to see the Yezidi shrine at Jebel Sinjar, in the Kurdish hills near Mosul. It's called Sheikh 'Adi. Have you heard of it?"

"Well, I've heard of the Yezidis—aren't they devil worshippers?"

"That's what people say, but it's not strictly true. Their religion is based on a spirit called Shaitan—very similar to Satan in the Bible—but they don't worship him: they're just afraid of him. They believe he was put in charge of the world by God and that he will be succeeded one day by Jesus, who they recognize as a prophet, but one not yet come to power. Their beliefs are all about appeasing Shaitan while he's in charge." Max took a bite of toast and swallowed it down. "They're a very peaceable lot, and their shrine is one of the loveliest, most tranquil places I've ever seen."

Max had cleared the table of toast by the time Agatha had finished quizzing him about the Yezidi tribe and their mountaintop home. The prospect of a trip to this remote region of northern Mesopotamia seemed far more exciting than her original plan to spend the morning house hunting. That could wait until tomorrow. She wondered if Nancy would change her mind about staying in bed when she heard about Max's offer.

"You don't mind walking, do you?" Max asked.

"What? All the way to Mosul?"

"No." He grinned. "Just the last couple of miles to the shrine. You can only do it on foot or by horse. It's quite cool, even in the afternoon, because of the altitude."

"No, I won't mind that," she replied. "I think it'll probably be too much for Nancy, though. I'd better pop up to her room and let her know what we're doing. What about lunch? Shall I ask the housekeeper if they could give us something for a picnic?"

"No need—we can pick up stuffed flatbreads from a stall along the way. You could ask them if they'd fill a flask with tea, though."

Half an hour later they were on their way. Max had the use of a car while he was in Baghdad—a battered black Austin 7 with a dusty windscreen, whose suspension had been severely compromised by years of motoring over bumpy desert tracks.

Halfway through the journey they stopped for lunch. Max spread a moth-eaten tartan rug on the sand while Agatha fished out the flask and two tin mugs. A few yards farther up the road was a party of women working by the roadside, digging up roots and picking leaves. They wore turbans of bright orange and robes of green and purple.

"They're Kurdish women," Max said.

"They're very tall, aren't they?" Agatha looked up from pouring the tea. She saw that the women had spotted them. They began walking toward them, their bodies very erect, their heads held high. Agatha saw that their faces were bronzed, with rosy cheeks. As they drew nearer, she noticed that they all had blue eyes.

They called out some sort of greeting, then one of them said something to Max, whose reply made them laugh. Another took a fold of Agatha's skirt, examining it with interest. They chatted to each other, nodding and smiling. Then, as quickly as they had come, they turned away, swaying like a bunch of exotic flowers as they walked off toward the blue mountains on the horizon.

"What did they say?" Agatha asked.

"Oh, they were just being friendly." Max brushed away a fly that had landed on the rim of his cup.

"I suppose they thought my clothes were very strange?"

"Oh no—it wasn't that." He had that sheepish expression again. The same look he'd given her when he asked her not to tell Katharine he was on the train.

"What, then?" she persisted.

"If you really want to know, they asked if you were my woman."

"Ah!" Now it was Agatha's turn to feel embarrassed.

"I told them that we were friends," he went on. "And they said they knew you couldn't be my wife because, if you were, you wouldn't have been the one pouring the tea."

"Really?" Agatha gave him a puzzled glance.

"They're a rum lot, these Kurdish women." Max made a gruff sound in his throat—something between a grunt and a laugh. "The Arab workmen on the dig tease the Kurdish men because their wives bully them. They're all Muslims—but you'd never mistake a Kurdish woman for an Arab one." He spread his hands, palms up. "It's not just the way they dress. The Arab women are shy and modest and will always look away when you speak to them—whereas a Kurdish woman has no doubt that she's the equal of any man. They'll talk to anyone—even strangers—and when they marry, the woman is always boss."

"Splendid!" Agatha smiled. "Where do I sign up?"

Max grinned. "What would *Mister* Christie say about that, I wonder?"

Agatha's face clouded.

"Oh dear—have I put my foot in it?"

Agatha couldn't look at him. Did he really not know? Didn't he read the newspapers? "I'm . . . ," she faltered. "We're . . . no longer married."

"Oh, I'm so sorry—I didn't mean to put you on the spot."

"It's all right. It was all over the papers a few weeks ago. I tend to assume people know."

"That must be miserable for you."

"It's not pleasant." She poured the last of the tea into the tin mugs. "I've had all kinds of hurtful things written about me. If the press don't know the facts, they speculate, and their readers take it as gospel."

Max nodded. "I suppose I was vaguely aware of some sort of incident attached to your name. But I've never come across anything specific in the papers."

"Well, that's something of a relief. At one time I was splashed all over the front pages. I thought the world and his wife knew everything about me." She paused, wondering how much she should reveal. "Things had got on top of me, and I took off without telling anyone where I was going. It never occurred to me that it would cause such a sensation. People thought it was a publicity stunt."

"When did that happen?"

"Nearly two years ago. Just before Christmas of 1926."

"Ah, that explains it. I was away from England then." He picked up his mug, took a gulp of tea, and set it down again. "I had a friend—a close friend—who was very ill. His family had taken him to the Mediterranean in the hope that the climate would help his condition. I went out to be with him, but . . ." His finger found one of the moth holes in the blanket, tracing its edges. "A few days after I got there, he died."

It was on the tip of Agatha's tongue to tell him that she already knew about Esme Howard, that Katharine had told her all about it on the train. But she sensed that Max would be just as sensitive about having his private life picked over as she was. Instead, she reached out to touch his hand. It was a brief touch—no more than a heartbeat. "That must have been devastating," she said.

"It was." His eyes met hers, then darted back to the blanket. "I never thought it was possible to feel such loss. He was my best friend."

For a moment they sat in silence. The only sound was the wind tugging at the brown paper wrappings containing the remains of their lunch. "I know it's not quite the same thing," Agatha said, "but I felt that way when my marriage ended. I always thought we'd be together for life. It was like a bereavement."

"I'm sorry to have raked it all up again for you—you've probably come on holiday to forget all that."

"Yes, I have." She went to get up, groaning at the stiffness in her legs. "Goodness—my foot's gone to sleep!"

"Here—let me help you." Max was on his feet, offering her his arm. "You'll enjoy this next part of the journey—the scenery gets much more interesting as you get higher."

After a few miles, the car began to climb. They wound far up into the hills they had seen on the horizon, through oak and pomegranate trees, following a mountain stream.

"This is Jebel Sinjar—the Yezidis' mountain." Max wound the window down as far as it would go and took in a long breath. "Ah! That's better! Not too cold for you, is it?"

"No." Agatha stuck her head out of the window. The air was fresh and clear with a tang of citrus and wild thyme. They passed a couple of men who turned to wave as they went past. They had pale skin and bright-blue eyes and a gentle, almost melancholy, look about them.

"There's something very innocent about them, don't you think?" Max said. "Human nature is said to be so pure in these parts that the Christian women can bathe naked in the streams without any fear."

"And do they?"

"I don't know. *I've* never come across anyone doing it—male or female. It's probably one of those apocryphal stories." He pulled in at the roadside and switched off the engine. Lifting his hand from the wheel, he pointed at something in the distance. "Look—there's Sheikh 'Adi."

Agatha saw white spires rising from a grove of trees. She climbed out of the car and wrapped a shawl round her shoulders. Soon they were walking past low wooden houses with pale-eyed blond children playing outside them. When she turned to smile at them, they giggled and pointed.

Then they came to the gates of the shrine itself. Stepping inside, she had difficulty believing that this place was on a mountaintop surrounded by desert. Peaches, figs, and lemons hung from trees growing in the courtyard. The sound of running water gave a calm, tranquil feel. As they entered, a group of the gentle-faced Yezidis came to greet them. Soon they were sitting on rugs piled with embroidered cushions, sipping tea from earthenware cups.

"It's incredibly peaceful here, isn't it?" Agatha whispered as the men left them alone in the courtyard.

"I've never experienced anything like it." Max nodded. "We'll go into the temple in a minute. It's quite different from any church or mosque you'll ever see. Quite sinister if you analyze the imagery, but it does something to you. You feel as if you could stay there forever."

They finished their tea and walked over to the entrance of the temple. Agatha immediately saw what Max had meant about the imagery. Guarding the entrance was a great black serpent, carved into the stone of one of the columns.

"The snake is sacred to them," Max said. "The Yezidis believe that Noah's ark was grounded on Jebel Sinjar and that a hole was made in the side of it. The story goes that the serpent formed itself into a coil and stopped up the hole. So it saved all the people and animals on the ark." Max bent down, untying his shoelaces. "We have to take our shoes off now," he said. "And when we go inside, be careful not to step on the threshold; it's forbidden to touch it, so you have to step over it. The other thing you have to remember is not to show the soles of your feet—it's considered the worst kind of insult."

As she unbuckled her shoes, Agatha thought of the amulet Katharine had shown them on the train, of a snake coiled around a pair of feet. Strange that these things featured so prominently in a different religion, thousands of years after the moon worshippers of ancient Mesopotamia. Stranger still, she thought, that in both these religions the snake was revered as a protector, not vilified as an incarnation of evil.

The interior of the temple was dark and cool. To Agatha's surprise, she could still hear the sound of running water. She asked Max where it was coming from.

"It's a sacred spring," he whispered. "It's supposed to run all the way to Mecca. Can you see that statue—over there?"

As Agatha's eyes grew accustomed to the dimness, she saw what he was looking at. An enormous image of a peacock stood by an altar lit with a single candle. The peacock statue glinted in the light. It appeared to be made of silver, with jeweled feathers. Beads of emerald, amethyst, and lapis lazuli cast a shower of colors on the stone walls.

"They bring it into the temple at festival times," Max went on. "It's the Peacock Angel—otherwise known as Lucifer, Son of the Morning."

As Agatha stared at it in wonder, a group of men in white robes appeared through a door to the right of the altar. They wore silver bells around their wrists, which made a tinkling sound as they walked. Combined with the trickling of the spring, it made Agatha feel as if she were in a meadow in the Swiss Alps.

"We have to sit down when they do," Max whispered. "Just over there, on those cushions."

Agatha soon discovered that sitting cross-legged on the floor was not an easy thing to do without exposing the soles of one's feet. In the end she gave up, bending her legs to the side instead and tucking her toes under her bottom. She couldn't help wondering why the Yezidis found feet so unacceptable yet—according to Max—were totally unmoved by the sight of the naked female form.

She wasn't sure why, but this brought Katharine to mind. She thought of her stepping out of the cubicle at the hammam in Damascus, totally at ease with her nakedness, proud of her voluptuous body.

She glanced at Max, whose eyes were closed, as if he was praying or meditating. Katharine's words came back to her. *At the dig he goes to Mass every Sunday even though it's a twenty-mile round trip by mule across the desert . . .* It seemed unlikely that someone with such devout beliefs would be susceptible to a woman like Katharine. But, she reminded herself, Leonard Woolley was a religious man and *he* had fallen for her.

She closed her eyes and leaned back against the cool stone wall. She felt herself falling into a semiconscious state in which images drifted into her head like a flurry of snowflakes. Then her mind seemed to take flight. It was as if she were hovering somewhere above her body, looking down at herself. Suddenly, she heard Hercule Poirot's voice. The words were as clear as if they had been spoken by a living person: *Why does it disturb you so much,* ma chérie, *the idea of this man and that woman having a . . . tendresse?*

She was startled out of her trancelike state by the sound of a gong. One of the white-robed men walked past them swinging a censer from which pungent smoke billowed.

Max opened his eyes and smiled. "That's the signal for us to go," he whispered.

With some difficulty Agatha got to her feet. She had pins and needles again and hobbled the first few steps like an old woman. Max was in front of her, having sprung up off his cushion, agile as a cat.

"What did you think of it?" he asked when they were back in the courtyard.

"It's surprisingly lovely, isn't it? Not at all what you'd expect of a religion based on Lucifer. It feels like one of those special spots you sometimes come across on a walk in a wild place, a grove of trees with the sunlight shining through them or a waterfall in a hidden valley. They have an almost magical feeling—ancient and good and somehow *right*, despite any past associations with pagan worship."

"Yes," Max said. "They're sanctuaries, I suppose, just like this place." They walked back through the gates onto the mountain track. "Actually, the shrine became more than that during the war," he added. "Hundreds of Armenian refugees fled to Jebel Sinjar to escape the Turks. If the Yezidis hadn't taken them in, they'd have been massacred."

When they reached the car, Agatha climbed inside in silence. She was thinking that despite the serenity of Sheikh 'Adi—or maybe because of it—she now felt less composed, less certain of herself, than when she'd entered that dark, cool space with its jewel-speckled walls. The trouble with still, peaceful places was that they allowed all manner of uninvited thoughts to push their way inside your head.

Why does it disturb you so much, ma chérie, *the idea of this man and that woman having a . . . tendresse?*

It was a question she didn't want to answer.

CHAPTER 15

Baghdad—Three days later

Nancy had left the hotel early for an appointment at the British Consulate, so Agatha was having coffee on her own. The waiter brought a letter out to her on the terrace. Her heart leapt at the sight of the large, careful writing on the envelope. It was from Rosalind.

> *Dear Mummy,*
> *Thank you very much for the letter you sent me, although it was very long. I am sorry to hear that you were sick on the boat to France. Flora Peterson was sick in Geography yesterday. It went all over my drawing of an oxbow lake . . .*

Agatha smiled to herself as she read on. But her smile vanished when Rosalind began describing how Flora Peterson had made a swift recovery when her mother came to collect her for a day out the next afternoon, and how nice she had looked in the new hat her mother had bought her. The stab of guilt intensified as the letter came to an abrupt end:

*I am getting a bit tired of writing to you, so I will
now write a short letter to Daddy . . .*

At nine years old, Rosalind could be brutally honest. Just like her father. She had far more of Archie in her than Agatha, in appearance as well as temperament. Looking at Rosalind was like seeing Archie's face superimposed on a china doll. Sometimes Agatha wondered if Rosalind could possibly love her as much as she loved her daddy, because they were so alike.

She tucked the letter inside her bag, realizing that Archie, being in London, would have already received his. Thinking of him turned her stomach to ice. Today was the day he would become another woman's husband. She wondered if Rosalind had included good wishes for his wedding.

She glanced down at her wrist, an automatic movement. But she averted her eyes before they could register the position of the hands on her wristwatch. She didn't want to know how many hours remained until her daughter acquired a new stepmother.

~

Nancy made her way past the coppersmiths' souk, on her way to the British Consulate. In the dark alcoves she caught glimpses of Arab men with blowlamps, melting metal into fantastic shapes. Outside, on the street, the finished wares were stacked up for sale. Kettles, cooking pots, and plates glinted in the morning sunshine. And a little farther on, the metal goods gave way to piles of rugs and striped horse blankets. A young boy leading a mule pushed past her. The animal was laden with bales of brightly colored cotton, the load so high it was a wonder it could move. She stepped aside to let it get ahead of her, only to be pinned to the wall by more little boys, all with trays suspended from their necks.

"See, lady, I have pins—good English pins—and buttons!" The child looked no more than five years old, the hem of his tunic torn and dirty.

"Look, lady! Nice elastic—good for knickers!"

This produced gales of laughter. Nancy couldn't help smiling, too. Katharine had warned her about buying from hawkers. Do it once, and you'll have them swarming round you like flies. But how could she resist these impish faces with their huge dark eyes? They looked so thin and their clothes were little more than rags. She fished in her pocket for what little money she had. She had changed twenty pounds into dinars yesterday morning, most of it set aside for the hotel bill. Agatha had been very generous, paying for all the food they had had since they arrived in the city, but Nancy's pride wouldn't allow her to pay for the room as well.

She divided a handful of coins among the children, taking a packet of pins and a length of elastic in return. They would come in useful when she started making her own clothes. She had found a pattern for the length of fabric she had bought in the silk souk in Damascus. As soon as they moved out of the hotel, she would be able to unpack her sewing machine and get started. Agatha had already seen a house she liked. With a bit of luck they would be moving into it tomorrow.

The children followed Nancy as she crossed a bridge over a canal that ran parallel with the Tigris and turned into Banks Street. She walked faster, turning twice to shoo them away. Eventually, they were distracted by the sight of a gleaming car, which stopped outside one of the banks to drop off a Western woman with a little dog tucked under her arm.

Nancy glanced up and down the street, anxious to avoid being caught a second time. It was full of people and very noisy. Along with the cries of stallholders and the braying of donkeys and mules was the guttural sound of men coughing up spittle as they walked along the pavement. This seemed commonplace in Baghdad—no one looked the least bit embarrassed to be caught doing it—and she was learning to walk with her eyes down to avoid catching any of the slimy gobbets on her shoes.

She hurried on, past an alley of tailors sewing cross-legged on the floor, pictures of smart Western-style suits propped up beside them. Then she came to stalls piled high with bales of velvet and embroidered brocade. This route was familiar to her now. It was her third visit to the British Consulate, her last-ditch attempt to get some answers about Delia's death. On each of her previous visits, she had been fobbed off by officials who were unfailingly polite and respectful but absolutely unmovable. She had been given no more than the date of her cousin's death, the location of her grave in the English cemetery, and the fact that she had died at her apartment in Baghdad.

It was Agatha who had suggested she should demand an appointment with the top man—the Consul-General. She had offered to come along, but Nancy felt that this was something she needed to do by herself. Now that the time had come, she wondered if it had been the right decision. Agatha was so much more confident than she was and had such a quick brain. She was not the sort of person who would allow herself to be cowed by any government official, however high-ranking.

Nancy was at the gates of the building now. She rang the bell and waited for someone to come and let her in. She was led in silence across the inner courtyard to a door with a polished brass plate inscribed with the words "Consul-General." Her mouth went dry as the door opened. She caught a glimpse of a tall man with a shock of white hair standing with his back to her, looking out of the window. As she entered the room, he turned to face her. He had the look of a bird of prey about to swoop from the sky. Cold blue eyes and an aquiline nose.

"Lady Nelson?" He reached across his desk to shake her hand with a grip so strong it crushed her bones. "Please sit down. My sincere condolences on the loss of your cousin. Miss Grandfield was an outstanding member of the team here in Baghdad and her absence is keenly felt by everyone who worked with her."

"Thank you." Nancy felt a lump in her throat. She must not cry. Not now. "I . . . I just wanted to know what happened. No one seems to be able to tell me anything."

He clasped his hands together, resting them on a piece of paper on the desk. "I'm afraid that the circumstances of Miss Grandfield's death are subject to the Official Secrets Act. I'm not at liberty to disclose any details."

"But surely you can tell me how she died? Was it natural causes or . . . ," she faltered, unable to voice her worst fears. He was staring at her, unblinking, saying nothing in response. The silence was unnerving. The only sound was the ticking of the clock on the mantelpiece. Her instinct was to get up and run from the room, away from his penetrating gaze. But she remembered Agatha's instructions: *Don't let him intimidate you. You must insist on an explanation.*

Nancy swallowed hard. "I'm sorry: that's simply not acceptable. There *must* be something more you can tell me. What about Delia's personal effects? The things she had in her apartment—where are they?"

She saw the muscles in his jaw tighten. "There was a fire at Miss Grandfield's apartment. There's nothing left, I'm afraid."

"A fire? Is that how she died? Was it an accident, then?"

"I really can't go into that." His eyes dropped to the piece of paper on the desk. "As I said, her death is subject to the Official Secrets Act. Now, if you'll excuse me." He stood up, clearly eager to get rid of her. As if by magic, a door opened behind her. The same man who had led her into the building escorted her back through the courtyard. Two minutes later she was out in the street.

As she walked back to the hotel, she cursed herself for not pressing him further. Perhaps if she had made a scene, started shouting or crying, he would have caved in. She felt like crying now, right here in the street, at the thought of Delia dying in that way. But the shock of hearing him come out with it had numbed her. It wasn't until she was standing on the pavement with the gates closing behind her that the full significance of his words had hit her. *There was a fire at Miss Grandfield's apartment . . .* If it had been an accident, surely he would have been able to say so. What had happened, then? A wave of nausea swept over Nancy. She pictured her cousin waking up in a smoke-filled room, terrified and unable to escape. Then another equally horrible possibility occurred to her: that someone had murdered Delia, then set fire to her apartment to cover their tracks.

She pushed her way through the knots of people on Banks Street, desperate to get back. She needed to talk to Agatha. Agatha, she felt sure, would know what to do. They had arranged to meet for lunch on the terrace overlooking the river. Nancy couldn't face the thought of food. Not now. But she could sit and talk while Agatha ate.

By the time she reached the Tigris Palace, it was five past one. No time to go up to her room. Walking through the lobby, she spotted Agatha through the French doors. She was sitting at one of the tables, gazing out over the river.

"Hello." Nancy pulled out a chair. "Have you already ordered?"

Agatha looked startled, as if she'd been in some far-off land of her imagination. Her face was paler than usual and her eyes were puffy and red-rimmed. It looked very much as if she'd been crying. As Nancy opened her mouth to ask what was the matter, she caught sight of one of the men from the wedding striding across the terrace toward them.

"Oh, it's Max." Agatha's hand went to her hair, tucking a wind-blown wisp behind her ear.

He smiled as he reached them, resting his hands on the back of a chair. "Sorry to barge in, ladies—were you about to have lunch?"

"We were—but you're welcome to join us," Agatha replied.

"I'd love to, but I'm afraid I haven't time: I'm setting off for Ur this afternoon. And I'm under strict instructions from Mrs. Woolley not to leave without setting a firm date for you both to visit." He looked expectantly from Agatha to Nancy, waiting for one of them to speak. When neither did, he said: "Oh dear: you both look rather glum—has something happened?"

Nancy sensed that whatever had upset Agatha, she wasn't likely to want to talk about it—not in front of Max, at least. She hadn't intended to broadcast what had happened at the Consulate, but she launched into it as a way of protecting Agatha.

"That's appalling." Max blew out a breath. "But I'm afraid it's typical of the way things work around here."

"There must be something more we could find out?" Agatha had lost some of her pallor. She had a determined frown on her face. "What if we mounted a private investigation?"

"I wouldn't advise it." Max rubbed his chin. "What you have to realize is that this place is on a knife-edge at the moment. The British are in control—in theory—but there are constant plots to get us out." He turned to Nancy then, meeting her eye for a fraction of a second before gazing out over the river. "To be in the job your cousin did was to live with danger. I met her once—only briefly—when she came to the dig. I was impressed by her strength of character and her resolve. But when I became aware of what she was doing, I have to admit that I was greatly concerned for her safety, knowing the strength of feeling against the British Mandate."

"So you think we should just do nothing?" Agatha bristled.

"Unfortunately, yes. As I said, these are dangerous times. We could be facing a political maelstrom, and I think it would be very unwise to get mixed up in it." He paused, looking from one to the other. "Look, I'm sorry: I'm giving you a terrible impression of the place. It's wonderful here as long as you don't try to tread on anyone's toes. It's a country in transition, with all the uncertainties that brings. But it's a country that you must see. So tell me, when will you come to us at Ur? We'll take good care of you, I promise."

~

Max left them with a railway timetable and a tin of foul-smelling yellow powder, which he said they would need to sprinkle all over the seats of the carriage on the train to Ur Junction as a precaution against fleas. If he had given this last gift *before* they'd settled on a date for their visit, they might have changed their minds. But Agatha had already promised to make the trip in early December. It was the place she most wanted to visit on her holiday in Mesopotamia and, as she told Max, she wanted to save the best until last.

Lunch arrived as soon as Max disappeared. Nancy had ordered a salad, and to her surprise Agatha asked for it, too.

"I thought you'd want the roast lamb," Nancy said.

"Oh dear, you're getting to know me too well." Agatha reached for the vinaigrette dressing. "I do like my food, as a rule."

"But not today?"

There was the slightest hesitation. "I . . . I'm not very hungry."

Nancy saw Agatha's eyes glisten, as if tears were not far away. She bent over her plate, jabbing her knife into a pat of butter, which she spread onto a roll with the concentration of an artist applying paint to canvas.

"I could see when I sat down that something was wrong," Nancy began. "Would it help to talk about it?"

Agatha laid down the knife, staring at it as if it were about to leap up and stab her. "It's nothing, honestly. Not compared to what you've been through, anyway."

"It didn't look like nothing." Nancy reached across the table to take hold of her hand. "Something's upset you enough to make you cry."

Agatha nodded, bringing her napkin up to her face as a single tear slid down her cheek. "I'm sorry," she mumbled. "It's just that Archie— my husband—is getting married today."

"Oh, Agatha! Why didn't you tell me? No wonder you're upset!"

"I thought I could cope with it. I thought that by coming here, thousands of miles away, it wouldn't seem so bad. But it . . ." She trailed off with a sharp indrawn breath. "I came down to lunch early. I left my watch in the bedroom so I wouldn't know the time, wouldn't know the exact moment when they . . ." She pressed her lips into her teeth, turning their pinkness to white. "He's marrying the girl he was with that night when I drove to the quarry. I wouldn't have known—but my daughter told me. She wanted to be a bridesmaid."

Nancy went cold inside. It was as if Agatha was telling her own story, from the other side. The intensity of her grief cast a harsh light on the letter Nancy had written to her lover, begging him to come with her, to leave his wife and daughter for a new life in Baghdad. She felt an overwhelming sense of shame: never for a moment had she put that other woman before herself, or thought about what her life would be like if her husband left her. She suddenly saw that being alone with a young child would be just as devastating as being alone and pregnant. How could she have imagined that her predicament entitled her to ruin another woman's life?

CHAPTER 16

Baghdad—Five weeks later

On the first day of December, Agatha was awake and dressed before sunrise. There was no sound from Nancy's room as she tiptoed to the kitchen to make tea. While she waited for the kettle to boil, she spread apricot jam onto a flap of Arab bread. There was just time before the boat arrived to take her downriver to the ruined city of Seleucia.

In the weeks since her arrival in Baghdad, Agatha had experienced a surge of creativity. Up to the day of Archie's marriage—the whole time she was traveling—she had been unable to write a thing. But that night at the Tigris Palace, once she knew that the wedding was over and done with, it was as if a dam had burst inside her head. Ideas suddenly flooded in. Things she had seen, fragments of conversation she had overheard, suddenly began to form patterns. And as she began taking day trips to the towns and cities beyond Baghdad, fresh ideas came to her. She had already filled three notebooks with material for Nancy to type up. The outlines of two novels were there: one set on the Orient Express and the other here in Baghdad.

Today she was going to visit the last ancient capital of Babylonia, built by Alexander the Great, and on the way back she planned to observe Baghdad's expatriate community without actually having to set foot in the district where they lived. By taking a boat, she would pass right through Alwiyah—past the gardens and tennis courts—close enough to watch without anyone realizing what she was doing.

Finishing her breakfast, she grabbed her bag and a shawl to cover her head. Then, very quietly, she opened the door onto the veranda. It was not fully light yet, and she took care as she climbed down the steps that led straight to the water's edge. The steps stopped abruptly—and if you weren't paying attention, you would end up falling into the river.

She didn't have long to wait. Within a couple of minutes she spotted the gufa coming toward her. It wasn't exactly going to be a luxury cruise: she was sharing the boat with a consignment of fruit boxes and a tethered goat, which had already marked out its territory with a peppering of droppings. Stepping sideways as she climbed aboard, she just managed to avoid getting any of it on her shoes.

"Please—you sit!" The wizened-looking Arab in charge of the boat gestured to a rug on top of what looked like a sack of grain.

Agatha settled herself down, smiling. This was what she wanted. To be part of the life of the river, blending in as inconspicuously as possible. As the boat pulled away, she looked across to the east bank of the Tigris, where the sky was turning coral with the sunrise. It felt good to be out on the water early with a day of new discoveries awaiting her. These past few weeks she had been happier than she had been for years. The thought of going back to London stirred up mixed feelings. She was longing to see Rosalind, but she knew how miserable she would feel when her daughter went back to school and the flat in Chelsea was empty. Agatha told herself she must not think about it. Not today. She still had three weeks left—and in a few days' time, the excitement of traveling to Ur.

She turned her mind to what Katharine would be doing at this moment. Her letters described how everyone at the dig was up and working by dawn. She was out each day with the men, digging alongside them and drawing the finds in the evenings. She wrote that Leonard rarely went to bed before two or three in the morning. He seemed to be able to function on just a couple of hours' sleep a night. Not exactly a recipe for a happy married life, Agatha thought when she read it.

She wondered what it was like in the evenings for Katharine, sitting down to dinner with Leonard and four other men. She could imagine what might be going through their heads as they watched her go off to bed alone, knowing that her husband was holed up in his office, oblivious of everything but the fragments of long-dead lives that surrounded him. And Katharine—lovely Katharine—what would she be thinking as she undressed, brushed her hair, and climbed into an empty bed?

Agatha couldn't help imagining the worst: that Max, for all his apparent straightforwardness and devotion to the Catholic faith, was madly in love with his boss's new wife. What other explanation could there be for his caginess on the train? If Katharine had been grumpy, irritable, or offensive in some way, his attitude might have been understandable. But she had been a wonderful traveling companion—a little too dominating at times, perhaps, but not unbearably so.

Why are you even thinking about him?

This time it was not Hercule Poirot's voice but her mother's. Her mother had always had an unerring instinct when it came to men. She hadn't liked Archie, although she'd made a good job of hiding it when she realized the relationship was heading toward marriage. Agatha could still remember her remarks after Archie's first visit. *He's not very considerate, is he? He seems quite ruthless.* How right she had been about that.

She pushed thoughts of Archie out of her mind by pulling her notebook from her bag and jotting down a description of what she could see: the way the water was changing color with the sunrise, the milky wreaths of mist clinging to the banks, the group of women walking through the palm groves with bundles of washing balanced on their heads.

As she looked up from her writing, it occurred to her that, had she still been married to Archie, she would not have seen any of this. He said that flying during the war had put him off traveling abroad. He was far happier to be in London or driving down for a weekend in the country at Sunningdale. The thought of a day trip to an ancient ruin in Mesopotamia would not have excited him in the least. He would probably have spent the whole time thinking about the golf he could have been playing back home in England.

Yes, she thought, tucking her notebook back into her bag, there was something to be said for being single.

~

As the first rays of sun penetrated the slatted blinds at her bedroom window, Nancy was woken by a sharp kick under her ribs. She had become used to her unborn baby's gymnastics, but they usually came after a meal, not while she was still asleep. She eased herself out of bed, pulling on the dressing gown she had made from the leftover silk bought at the souk in Damascus. It was a simple pattern—shaped like a kimono and baggy enough to conceal her expanding waistline. She had made three dresses as well—all in the Arab style—which did the same job during the day.

If Agatha wondered why she had adopted this mode of dress, she didn't comment on it. She herself had taken to wearing long, loose clothes and covering her head when she went shopping or sightseeing. Nancy suspected that it was partly about not wanting to be recognized. If the cocktail party set got wind of the fact that a famous British author was in town, the invitations would no doubt come flooding through the letter box. But Agatha had chosen to rent a house away from the garden suburb where most of the expatriates lived.

It was in the heart of the city, just off Al Rasheed Street, right on the banks of the Tigris. A perfect place to watch the comings and goings on the river. On most evenings the two women would sit out on the veranda in companionable silence, reading or sewing, looking up if a boat chugged past or stopping to wave at children splashing about on the opposite bank.

The sight of the children always had an unsettling effect on Nancy. At times she could almost forget what lay ahead, pretend that she could go on living in this bubble of tranquillity. But the shouts and laughter of the Arab boys and girls brought her sharply back to reality. Agatha was leaving Baghdad the week before Christmas. What would happen to her then? She had tried in vain to find a secretarial job in the city, but the only place with vacancies for an English typist with no Arabic was the British Consulate, where she was apparently on some sort of blacklist after the confrontation over her cousin's death. The feeling of panic, never far beneath the surface, threatened to overwhelm her again.

With trembling hands, she opened the blinds and peered outside. There was a thin blanket of mist over the water. On the far bank she could see the masts of sailing boats sticking up like needles in a white velvet pincushion. She thought about Delia, who would have had a view very much like this one, a mile or so downriver. She wondered if her cousin had had any inkling when she looked out over the Tigris that she would never see England again.

It was hard to think about Delia, hard to get over the feeling that she had failed her. She had visited her grave half a dozen times in the past few weeks, talked to her as if she were standing nearby, just out of sight. The graveyard was a beautiful place, with almond trees in blossom. But the peace she sought never came to her there. All she felt was anger and frustration.

Nancy made herself go to the kitchen to make breakfast. Anything to pull herself out of this whirlpool of fear and tension. Agatha had hired a cook to prepare their evening meal, but they saw to themselves the rest of the time. Before coming to Baghdad, Nancy had never cooked anything in her life—not even a boiled egg—but within a week or so, Agatha had taught her how to make all manner of things.

This morning she would make a cheese omelet. Something that required concentration. And if she was still hungry afterward, she would have bread and jam. This baby was going to be a whopper.

After breakfast, she settled down in the room they were using as an office and spent the morning typing up Agatha's notes. She was fascinated by the account of her visit to the Yezidi shrine and the way she had taken the statue of the Peacock Angel as the starting point for the plot of a novel. Agatha had simply written the word *Lucifer* at the top of the page and jotted down a whole series of ideas based on this word being part of a coded message uttered by a dying man who has stumbled into the bedroom of a young English woman newly arrived in Baghdad. She smiled as she typed it out, wondering if the heroine would in any way resemble her.

At one o'clock she warmed up some *keema*, a stew of minced meat, tomatoes, and chickpeas left over from the night before. She ate it on the veranda, then returned to the typewriter. She needed to write a letter, and she wanted to type it rather than write it by hand. It was a letter to him, to make him think she had secured a job in an office.

Darling,

Thank you for your last letter and the lovely brooch. It arrived safely at the post office here, and I'm afraid I made a fool of myself by opening it there and then and bursting into tears when I saw what was inside. I wish I could send you something. I often see things that I think you would like, but I know that any kind of present would probably stir up trouble.

As you can see, I've managed to find work as a short-hand typist. It's only temporary at the moment but hope-fully will turn into a permanent job by the end of the year.

I miss you terribly and I long to have you in my arms again. I realize, however, how difficult things must be for you at home. You say that your marriage is dead, but I feel dreadful when I think of your wife and how she would cope if you were to leave her. At the same time, I can't help the way I feel about you. I know that I'm being selfish when I . . .

Nancy stopped typing. She had caught a flicker of movement out of the corner of her eye. Over by the window. She turned her head and froze. A snake. The color of sand, with emerald eyes and a pair of scaly spikes on the top of its head. She had been warned about this kind of snake by the staff at the Tigris Palace. *Looks like a devil, miss.* A horned viper. Absolutely deadly. Its body was as thick as her wrist. And it was slithering across the floor toward the desk.

Somehow, she managed to jump up and kick the chair sideways at the same time. It landed near the snake's head, making it rear backward, away from her legs. And then she ran, slamming the door behind her, out into the hall, through the back door and onto the veranda, where she almost collided with Agatha, just back from her boat trip down the river.

"Goodness! You're as white as a sheet! Whatever's the matter?"

When Nancy told her about the snake, Agatha called to the Arab boatman whose gufa was still moored at the bottom of the steps. He came to their rescue with a rifle. Less than a minute after he had entered the house, a shot rang out. He emerged with the snake draped round his neck like a scarf.

"The size of it!" Agatha blew out a breath. "You had a very lucky escape. Now, I think we both need a strong cup of tea—will you make it while I go and get an extra big tip for our friend?"

It wasn't until Nancy was pouring hot water into the teapot that she realized what she had done. The money was in the office—Agatha kept it in a locked drawer—and the letter was still in the typewriter. If Agatha saw it . . .

She dashed out of the kitchen into the hall. Too late. Through the open door of the office she heard the paper rip as Agatha pulled it from the rollers.

CHAPTER 17

Agatha was so angry she could barely look at Nancy. Marching past her in stony silence, she went to pay the boatman. When she climbed back up the steps, Nancy was pacing the veranda, white-faced.

"I . . . I owe you an explanation," Nancy faltered. "I know what it must look like—but if you would just hear me out . . ."

"What it *looks* like is that you've taken me for a fool." Agatha sank down onto a wicker chair, her eyes following the gufa as it glided away. "I've housed you, fed you, bent over backwards to help you—all for a pack of lies! And to add insult to injury, you've been using *my* typewriter to write love letters to a married man!"

"I didn't mean to deceive you—honestly, I didn't." Nancy's voice rose higher, on the verge of breaking. "That night on the train I was at my wits' end—and you were so kind, so understanding. Don't you see? I couldn't tell you the whole story—not after what you'd told me about your husband."

"So you pretended to be a sad little wife running away from a brute of a husband—when what you actually are is . . . an *adulteress*." Agatha spat the word out like a fish bone. In the silence that followed, the only sounds were the cries of wading birds picking about in the mud on the far bank of the river.

Nancy was holding on to the rail of the veranda, looking down into the water. "I'm not proud of what I've done, if that's what you're thinking." She turned to face Agatha. "But there's a reason why it happened: please, let me explain."

Agatha met Nancy's eyes with a cold glare. "Listen to me, young lady: you might have fooled me once, but don't you dare try telling any more lies." She folded her arms across her chest. "Give me one good reason why I shouldn't kick you out this minute."

"The reason I fell in love with . . . with someone else . . . is this"— Nancy swallowed, blinking back tears—"my husband brought his mistress on our honeymoon. I found them in bed together."

"What?"

"The man I was writing to . . ." Nancy glanced at the torn letter on the table. "He was there, at the villa in Venice, and he . . ." She turned away. A tear trickled down her cheek.

Agatha was on her feet in an instant. "I'm going to get that pot of tea," she said. "And then you're going to tell me the whole story."

~

Nancy regained some of her color as the tea went down. She spoke haltingly about the whirlwind romance with Felix, the wedding in Westminster Abbey, and her excitement at the prospect of a honeymoon in Venice.

"He told me he was renting a villa near the Lido," she went on. "There would be other people there—friends of his—but that would make it even more fun, he said. There would be cocktail parties and picnics on the beach, dancing, and boat trips. He made it sound so alluring. I had no idea who any of these people were because I hadn't known him very long." Nancy stared into her cup. "There was a woman there—a married woman—who was very attractive. She and Felix seemed very friendly, but I never thought anything of it because her husband was there, too. And then, when I was lying awake on the second night wondering why he hadn't come to me, I decided to go to his room. And I opened the door to find him . . ." Her hand shook as she put her cup back on the saucer.

Agatha was watching Nancy intently. Clearly, the memory of what she was describing was still raw. There was no way she was making this up.

"I . . . I just ran out of the house," Nancy mumbled. "I didn't know what to do, where to go. And one of the men from the house party was sitting outside, on his own, smoking a cigarette. He could see that I was crying, and he sat me down and just listened as it all came pouring out. Then he fetched a bottle of brandy. We must have stayed there for hours because I remember how the stars moved across the sky and the moon sank into the sea. The next morning he came knocking on my door with coffee and some peaches he'd picked from the garden. He told me about the film he'd come out to Venice to work on, made me laugh with stories of the other actors and the goings-on behind the scenes. Then, next morning, we met for a swim." She raised her cup to her lips again. "I was so unhappy, so desperate for a friend . . . I had no idea he was married. He didn't tell me until the last day of the holiday. And by that time it was too late."

Agatha waited for a moment, seeing it all in her mind's eye. "And your husband—did he know?"

"I don't think so. We were very discreet. Felix and I had a showdown, of course, over his mistress. I wanted to know why he had been so keen to marry me when all the while he was in love with someone else. After all, I wasn't exactly a catch: my father's estate was on its knees."

"What did he say?"

"Oh, he gave it to me straight—said he'd had to marry in order to inherit and thought I would do as well as any of the five other girls he'd already proposed to at the party where we met."

Agatha let out a sharp breath. "And what was he expecting you to do when you found out about the other woman? Just go along with it?"

Nancy nodded. "He said that once I'd produced a child, my job would be over. It wouldn't matter if it was a boy or a girl—as long as there was a baby. That was another condition of his inheriting the earldom, apparently—I think perhaps his father feared he might never marry. Once I'd done my duty, he said, I could take a lover of my own, if I wanted, and we'd lead separate lives under the same roof."

"What a dreadful situation." Agatha shook her head. "I suppose you were in love with him, though, at the beginning?"

"I was. He swept me off my feet that first night, when he proposed. I think he was probably very drunk, but I didn't realize it. I'd been leading a very quiet life in the country with my father. I was too busy trying to keep things going on the estate to be part of the London crowd. It was the first party I'd been to in ages—and when Felix proposed, I suddenly saw that this was the answer to all our problems. My father wouldn't have to worry about money ever again." Her eyes were brimming again, but she swallowed back the tears. "He was so delighted about the wedding. But he died two weeks after I came back from Venice."

"Oh, Nancy." Agatha leaned across the space between them, taking her hand and squeezing it. "No wonder you were in such a state on the train. Where is he now—your . . . friend?"

"Back in London. With his wife and daughter." Agatha flinched. A wife and daughter. This was so horribly familiar. Her mind flipped back to the December night two years ago, when she had sat in her car outside the cottage in Godalming that belonged to Archie's friends, the Jameses, watching shadows on the curtains, knowing that he was inside with . . . She looked up suddenly. "Who is he, this man you were writing to? What's his name?"

It had suddenly fallen into place—like the missing piece of a jigsaw. She had *seen* him. On the train. Spotted him on the platform in Paris, then again, the next morning. That reflection in the glass *was* the face of Nancy's lover: she must have been waving good-bye to him as tears streamed down her face . . . waving good-bye to a man with an uncanny resemblance to Archie. But *not* Archie; it *couldn't* be. She had said he was an actor. In films.

"I . . . I can't tell you." Nancy dropped her head. "He made me promise not to tell a living soul. He's worried that if it got into the papers . . . Not that I'm suggesting you'd ever do anything like that, of course . . ." She gripped Agatha's hand as if it were a lifeline.

"I think there's something else you need to tell me though, isn't there?" Agatha paused. This was a shot in the dark. "You're expecting a baby, aren't you?"

Nancy closed her eyes. "Yes," she whispered.

"Is it his or your husband's?"

"His."

"Are you sure?"

"Absolutely sure." She opened her eyes, blinking as the sun caught them. "Felix and I . . . after those first few days of the honeymoon, I couldn't bear to have him anywhere near me. To keep him away, I told him I'd fallen pregnant the very first night we'd made love. I'm ashamed to say I let him go on thinking that until I left him. I wrote a letter for him to find after I'd gone, telling him it was a pack of lies."

"Is that what made you decide to run away? Finding out that you were expecting the other man's child?"

"Yes. I didn't have much of a plan. I just needed to escape. Felix is not the kind of man you'd want to get on the wrong side of. He can be very frightening when he's angry."

"And the . . . other man. Does he know?"

Nancy gave a small, almost imperceptible shake of her head. "I wanted him to leave his wife—I admit that—but I couldn't resort to emotional blackmail."

Agatha fell silent then. How could she give an opinion, or any advice? How could she be impartial? She had a sudden, vivid image of the wife of Nancy's lover going about her daily routine in a house somewhere in London. In her mind's eye it was a place like the one she and Archie had lived in as newlyweds. This woman would be looking after her home and her child, spending the evenings with her husband, having no idea that he was in love with someone else. Not just in love, but soon to be the father of another woman's baby. What a nightmare.

She thought about how she had pleaded with Archie to stay when he told her about his affair. How she had begged him to give their marriage another chance, to stay for three more months before making a decision. She remembered how awful that had been, how cold he was toward her and the rows they had had. Things had become so bad that if she entered a room, he would get up and leave.

Eventually, she saw that by trying to cling to him, all she had done was prolong the agony. There were no half measures with Archie. *I can't stand not having what I want, and I can't stand not being happy. Everybody can't be happy—somebody has got to be unhappy.* He'd said it time and again during those three months. And as the weeks went by, she felt his hatred, his sense of being trapped, and it scared her. She feared he wanted her dead.

It was unnerving, seeing an almost identical scenario through Nancy's eyes. She ought to despise her for what she was trying to do, but deep down that wasn't what she felt. Why not? Perhaps it was because she had glimpsed something she had never accepted up to now: that living with a husband who doesn't love you is far worse than living alone.

"I suppose you're wondering what I'll do—when the baby's born." Nancy's voice cut across her thoughts. "If I find a job, I'll be able to rent an apartment and hire a nanny."

"How far along are you?" Agatha glanced at the voluminous aba Nancy had made for herself. It really was impossible to tell what shape her body was under that.

Nancy's hand went to her stomach. "I'm not completely sure. About six months, I think."

"Six!" Agatha gasped. "You can't possibly go looking for a job at six months' pregnant. We're going to have to think of something else."

Nancy looked up. "We?"

"You don't think I'm going to leave you to face this on your own, do you? Listen, if the worst comes to the worst, you'll have to come back on the train with me: come and stay at my house in London—at least until the baby's born."

Nancy shook her head. "That's awfully kind of you—but I couldn't possibly. You've been so good to me already. And besides, Felix would play merry hell if he found out. I'd be afraid of what he might do. I think I'd rather take my chances in Baghdad."

"Do you think your baby's father will leave his wife, eventually? Come and join you out here?"

Nancy looked past Agatha, her eyes following a solitary pelican skimming the water. "I wish I knew," she murmured.

CHAPTER 18

Baghdad to Ur—Five days later

"Are you sure you want to come?" Agatha was in the kitchen, wrapping hard-boiled eggs in a cloth. She put them in a basket alongside a pile of flatbreads and a jar of damson jam.

"Yes, I do." Nancy added four peaches in twists of brown paper to the basket. "I don't think I could have faced it when we first arrived, but it's much cooler now. I don't think it'll be too bad on the train."

"I hope not," Agatha replied. "It's a long way. But hopefully we'll be asleep for part of it."

"Have you packed the bug powder that Max gave us?"

"In here." Agatha patted her jacket pocket.

They traveled to the railway station in a cart drawn by mules. On the way they stopped at the coppersmiths' souk, where Agatha climbed down and spent a few minutes haggling with one of the stallholders. She returned to the cart followed by a young Arab boy carrying a large wooden box.

"I'm getting better at this," she said, smiling as it was loaded on top of their suitcases. "I hope Katharine will like it." She turned in her seat, lifting the lid of the box to reveal a coffee set nestled in straw. The pot had a swan neck and an intricate pattern of silver wire inlaid in the copper. The same pattern was repeated on the cups and saucers.

"She'll love it," Nancy replied. "It'll be nice for her to have something elegant. From what she said in her letters, life at the dig is pretty basic."

"It does seem strange to think of her in that environment." Agatha settled back as the mules set off again. "She's the last person you'd imagine wanting to spend their time bent over a burial pit in the burning sun."

"And very different from what she did before. I wonder how she came to it."

"I think she came out here as a nurse at first. That's what she told me on the train. She said that after her husband died, she stayed out in the Middle East, and nursing was how she made her living. I think she must have started drawing some of the finds at the dig—and when they saw how talented she was, they offered her a job."

"She's got guts, hasn't she?" Nancy said. "After what happened in Egypt, most people would have turned tail and run home."

Agatha nodded. "I think she found it easier to be away from England, though. She must have realized that the papers would get hold of it. It's unbearable, knowing that the world and his wife are devouring every detail of your private life with their toast and marmalade."

"I don't know how you got through all that. It must have been sheer hell." Nancy clicked her tongue against the roof of her mouth. "The press would have an absolute field day with my life, wouldn't they?"

"Well, let's just hope they never get wind of it. I think you're pretty safe out here." The cart drew to a halt outside the station, and the driver jumped off to unload their bags. Ten minutes later they were on the train, which had comfortable Pullman-style carriages not unlike those of the Orient Express.

"It's much better than I was expecting," Nancy said as they stowed their luggage. "I can't believe there would be fleas."

"We'd better do the seats, just in case." Agatha opened the tin of powder and began sprinkling it over the plush upholstery. "Ugh! It smells awful!"

"Shall I let in some fresh air?" With some difficulty, Nancy pulled the window open a couple of inches. As she sat down, the train began to move.

"That's better. I . . . Oh! What's that?" Agatha's mouth fell open as a cloud of insects squeezed through the gap in the window.

Nancy jumped to her feet. "Oh! Look at their tails! I think they're hornets!"

The women clung to each other as the insects zoomed round the carriage like fighter planes.

"Quick!" Agatha made a grab for the door, pulling Nancy out into the corridor before slamming it shut. Luckily, the next-door compartment was unoccupied. As they sank onto the seats, Agatha glanced at the tin of bug powder, still clutched in her left hand. "I think, on balance, fleas are the less dangerous option, don't you?"

"I do," Nancy giggled. "Death by hornets—sounds like the title of one of your novels, doesn't it? Or how about *The Sting of Death*?"

"Are you sure you don't want to come back to England with me?" Agatha smiled.

~

Half an hour into the journey, there was nothing much to be seen out of the window but featureless scrubland or sandy desert. As the sun sank below the horizon, a steward came with tea and a plate of hard, inedible biscuits. When Agatha explained that their luggage was in the hornet-infested compartment next door, he went retrieve it. Five minutes later he returned, apparently unharmed, to stow the cases and pull down the bed.

Nancy hadn't realized there would be beds on the train. She thought they would be sleeping in their seats. She was worried about getting undressed in front of Agatha, having deliberately underestimated the length of her pregnancy. She wasn't sure exactly how far along she was because her monthly cycles had never been very regular. The baby might have been conceived in the last few days of the holiday in Venice, or it might have been six weeks later, when he took her to a flat in Pimlico owned by an army friend who was serving abroad. So it could be seven months or eight. To tell Agatha this would have probably sent her into a panic. It would have upset all her plans, which wouldn't be fair. Nancy had done her best to convince her friend that she could cope perfectly well on her own, that by the time the baby arrived, she would have everything sorted out.

Yesterday afternoon, when she had visited Delia's grave in the blossom-filled churchyard, something almost like a miracle had occurred. While she was kneeling by the stone, wiping it clean of the red desert sand that clung to its surface, an elderly man had appeared from behind one of the almond trees. He had called her by name and introduced himself as a former colleague of Delia's. They had walked around the churchyard together, and he had told her what he knew about her cousin's death: that she was probably murdered by an assassin sent by one of the local tribal leaders she had been keeping under surveillance.

"Why did you come to find me?" Nancy asked as they returned to the grave.

"Because Delia left this for you." He reached into his pocket and handed her an envelope. "Your cousin was a very brave woman. She always knew that what she was doing was dangerous. She didn't trust the banks here, so she asked me to keep this for her. Don't open it here—wait until you get home."

The envelope contained three hundred pounds. Nancy and Agatha had stared at one another in wonder as the notes slid out onto her lap. They had spent the evening planning exactly how to spend the money. As soon as they got back from Ur, they would go to see Agatha's landlord and renegotiate the lease on the house so that Nancy could stay on there. There would be enough left for her to employ help for the baby when it arrived and to live on for three or four months, by which time she would, hopefully, have found a job of some kind.

"Are you hungry, Nancy?" Agatha's voice brought her back to the present. "We could have the eggs if you like—or would you rather save them for breakfast?"

"Could I have one egg? And some bread and jam?" Nancy felt hungry enough to devour everything in the basket there and then. Hopefully, there would be something more to eat when they arrived at the dig house in the morning.

"I'll get myself ready for bed now, I think," Agatha said when they had finished eating. "I'll take the top bunk, shall I?"

"Would you mind?" Nancy shot her a grateful smile.

"Not a bit. I quite like the idea of climbing up a ladder to go to bed. It reminds me of when I was a child: my sister and brother and I had a den in the barn—we were allowed to sleep there sometimes."

"That sounds like fun." Nancy glanced at her stomach. Would her baby ever have a brother or a sister? She didn't want it to grow up an only child, as she had done. Her thoughts drifted back to London as she lay down on the bed. What time would it be there now? What would he be doing? It was Saturday afternoon there. He might be Christmas shopping with his daughter or taking her to the park. And then he would go home, perhaps read the little girl a story after supper. And then . . . She hated the thought of him climbing into bed with his wife. Now, when she imagined this woman, she could only see Agatha's face.

The train arrived at Ur Junction a little after dawn. Agatha and Nancy were woken by the steward knocking on the door. Agatha put one foot on the ladder and eased herself down. Nancy was lying on her side, on top of the sheets, with her back toward the ladder. *Poor thing*, Agatha thought, she must have been too tired to get undressed.

"What . . . what time is it?" Nancy mumbled, pulling her shawl over her eyes.

"Ten past six." Agatha peered out of the window. "Oh, there's a little church—right next to the station." This must be the place where Max went to Mass.

As she watched, the door of the church opened and two nuns in black tunics and billowing white veils emerged. They were young, small in stature and dark-skinned. Their features were more Indian than Arabian. She had seen Indian Christians going into the Anglican church in Baghdad and had recognized some of them as shopkeepers whose stores she had visited in the area around the coppersmiths' souk. But she hadn't expected to find an Indian community in a place as remote as this.

She tried to imagine Max among them, arriving hot and dusty after trekking across the desert. She remembered the peaceful, almost beatific expression that had come over him at the Yezidi shrine. Yes, she thought, he would be at home here, among people whose spirituality had a flavor of the East.

"Are we there?" Nancy was sitting up now, rubbing her eyes. "I'm terribly thirsty. Do you think they'll bring more tea?"

"I doubt it." Agatha smiled. "But hopefully someone will be here to meet us. You won't have long to wait."

Sure enough, transport was waiting for them when they made their way out of the station. It looked like a railway carriage, cut in half and mounted on rubber tires. It had been painted an attractive shade of lavender blue but was full of dents and scratches and covered in dust. The man who jumped out to greet them was Michael Cruft-Deacon, the draftsman at the dig, who had walked Katharine up the aisle at the wedding.

"Good morning, ladies!" He grinned broadly as he swung their bags into the back. "Sorry about the transport—I think the chap Leonard bought her from picked her up in a ditch sometime after the First World War and set her in motion for the princely sum of about a tenner. We had to get the chassis raised to cope with the rough ground: makes her look rather majestic, don't you think?" He opened the door, ushering them in with a sweep of his hands. "It's rather impertinent, but we call her Queen Mary."

Although only a short distance in miles, the road to the dig was rutted and uneven. "You're lucky," Michael said as the truck bounced over yet another pothole. "It rained here at the end of last month and the wadi flooded. We couldn't get out for a week."

"What did you do?" Agatha had to raise her voice to be heard above the noise of the engine. "About food, I mean."

"Oh, we just about survived on the supplies we had. We were getting a bit fed up of eating beans and rice every night, but then the local sheikh came to the rescue with a couple of goats."

Agatha and Nancy exchanged glances.

"The cook we have at the dig this season isn't bad," Michael went on. "His puddings aren't up to much, but he makes the most marvelous stews and curries. I expect he'll have breakfast waiting for you. You'll have the place to yourselves because the others are all out on the mound. Once you've settled in, I'll get someone to bring you up to where we're working and you'll get the guided tour."

As the car rounded a bend, Agatha caught sight of a distant building surrounded by a high barbed-wire fence.

"There's the expedition house." Michael jerked his head toward the open window. "It's called *Sahra' Alqamar*—Desert Moon in Arabic. Doesn't look very inviting, I'm afraid, from this angle. The fence is to protect us from marauders. We've dug up so much gold, we're running out of places to store it: we're literally stuffing it under our beds." He changed gear as they took another bend. "You can see the mound now—over there. The Arabs call it a *tell*."

Agatha and Nancy looked to the left, where he was pointing. Silhouetted against the pale-yellow morning sky was something like a small volcano—a cone-shaped pile of earth protruding from the flat scrubland surrounding it. There was something moving over its surface. Men, who from this distance looked no bigger than ants.

"How many people do you have working on the dig?" Nancy asked.

"We employ around a hundred men most of the time," he replied. "It varies from one week to the next. They come from the villages round about. Sometimes, when you pay them, they disappear for a while. Then, when the money runs out, they're back again. Max is in charge of all that side of things because he speaks such good Arabic. It's not an easy task, keeping them all in order. A bit like being a headmaster, really."

He slowed down as they approached the entrance to the compound. A pair of tall Arab guards with rifles and bandoliers of cartridges slung over their shoulders leapt up at the sound of the car. Michael waved at them as he drove into the walled courtyard. As he cut the engine, they heard barking. "Guard dogs," he explained. "They won't bother you once they get used to your smell."

Another Arab—a young boy in a white robe who looked no more than twelve or thirteen—emerged from inside the building with a mongrel puppy chasing behind him. "That's Saleem. He'll take your bags and unpack for you. I'll show you round, and then you can have a bite to eat."

He led them through a veranda into the main building, which, he explained, was constructed of mud bricks gathered from the surface of the mound they were excavating. "The youngest brick is twenty-five centuries old, but they're incredibly sturdy."

Agatha was surprised by how attractive it was inside. The rough walls were painted a pale terra-cotta color and the floor was covered in rush matting. The living room—although minimally furnished—had a welcoming feel to it.

"This is my office." Michael swept his hand toward a cubicle off the living room that was just big enough for a desk and chair. "And down the hall is the Antiquities Room. We keep it locked during the day, but I'm sure Katharine will give you a proper look this evening."

He led them to an annex across the courtyard. "The Woolleys' bedrooms are back in the main building," he said. "The rest of us are in here."

Agatha glanced over her shoulder at a pair of small curtained windows. Katharine hadn't said anything in her letters about sleeping in separate rooms. Perhaps it was because her husband worked such long hours, didn't want to disturb her when he came to bed. Not for the first time, Agatha found herself wondering how a newly married couple would fare in a situation like that.

"These are your rooms." Michael ushered them to the end of a passageway, where the young boy who had taken their bags was taking towels from a linen cupboard. "There's only the one bathroom, I'm afraid, but Saleem will bring you jugs of hot water morning and evening."

The bedrooms were small and basic but had a rustic charm, with iron-framed single beds, goatskin rugs on the floor, and ceramic jars of what looked like wild tulips on the windowsills. Michael left them then, and when they had freshened themselves up, they went to find out what was for breakfast.

As they entered the main building, they could smell something frying. It turned out to be goat's cheese and tomato omelets, which Ibrahim, the cook, served with a great flourish, giving each of them a courtly bow as he set their plates in front of them. This was followed by toast, neatly sliced into triangles and arranged in a wire rack. Butter and marmalade were already laid out on the table.

"Goodness," Nancy laughed. "Not exactly roughing it, are we?"

"It's much nicer than I expected," Agatha agreed. "I thought we'd be eating round a campfire and sleeping on the floor."

"I thought Katharine might be here to greet us, though, didn't you?"

"I suppose she has to start work when the others do. Perhaps she thought the train might be late and didn't want to waste time hanging around the house."

Nancy nodded. "Are you ready for the guided tour?"

"Are you?" Agatha wondered if it was wise for Nancy to be climbing the mound. It was only half past seven, but the temperature was rising rapidly.

"I'll be fine." Nancy smiled. Leaning across the table, she whispered: "I'm only pregnant—not ill!"

CHAPTER 19

Ur

Climbing the tell was not as strenuous as Agatha had feared. The sun was pleasantly warm—not unbearably hot as it had been the first few weeks in Baghdad—and a proper path had been hewn into the side of the mound. They found Katharine halfway up, squatting on the dusty ground, deep in conversation with a man in an Arab kaffiyeh and a striped robe. She was dressed in a khaki shirt and skirt, brown brogue shoes, and a broad-brimmed hat. Despite the fact that she was clearly hard at work in the middle of the desert, she still managed to look effortlessly stylish.

When Agatha called her name, she jumped up.

"Oh! You're here!" She kissed each of them on both cheeks, French-style, her lips barely grazing the skin. "You both look very well: Baghdad obviously agrees with you. And you look like a Bedouin woman, Nancy, with that tan and those clothes!"

She inclined her head toward the man she had been talking to, whose headdress had fallen back as he stood upright to reveal a very handsome face. "This is Hamoudi," she said. "He's the one who made

the ivory talisman I showed you on the train. He's our site foreman."
She said something in Arabic to him and he smiled, stepping forward
with his right hand extended.

"He doesn't have many words of English," she explained as they
shook hands. "He and Max are great friends: Max is the best Arabic
speaker of any of us."

"Where is Max?" Agatha asked.

"Digging with Leonard on the other side," Katharine replied. "We'll
go and find them."

Nancy and Agatha attracted curious glances from the men and boys
who were sorting through the piles of rubble being excavated from the
mound. "They don't often see Western women," Katharine said. "They
probably think you're here as wives to one of the men in the dig team."
Seeing her friends' faces, she added: "Don't worry—Max will put them
right!"

The path wound round up and around the tell, and as they veered
toward the other side, Agatha caught sight of a huge, stepped building of a rich red color off to the left. She stopped short. "Oh! Is that a
ziggurat?"

Katharine nodded. "We excavated it last season. It was built as a
temple to the moon god. Can you see the tower at the top? That was the
shrine, where all kinds of mysterious ceremonies took place."

"Like what?" Agatha shaded her eyes against the sun.

"Well, there was a couch inside that the king would lie on to imper-
sonate the god. There was a fertility rite in which he had to have sexual
congress with a woman representing the goddess: usually his daughter
or his sister. And afterwards they would sing hymns in praise of the
woman's private parts." She glanced from Agatha to Nancy. "Sorry—I
hope I haven't shocked you."

"I did read something about it in the papers," Agatha replied. "I
didn't know about the incest, though—or the vulgar songs. Not very
pleasant but rather fascinating, all the same."

"I'm sure I read something about human sacrifice," Nancy said.

Katharine nodded. "That happened over there." She pointed to a line of columns to the right of the ziggurat. "It's the royal cemetery. Whenever the ruler died, all his wives, concubines, and servants would die with him. Animals were slaughtered, too, and all manner of precious objects were buried at the same time. The idea was that the king would have everything he needed in the afterlife. It was terribly wasteful, of course—especially of female lives—and eventually they abandoned it."

"So all that treasure—the things you've been digging up—came from the cemetery, did it?" Nancy asked.

"Mostly, yes. I have to say, though, the rumors of what we've found far exceed the truth. Someone put it about that we'd unearthed a solid gold sphinx, which is absolute rubbish. We do have gold objects, but nothing on that scale. It makes us very nervous when stories like that go around. You can imagine what might happen. That's why we have to have armed guards at the expedition house."

"Hello!"

The shout came from somewhere above their heads. They looked up to see Max scrambling down the mound, setting off little trickles of grit and sand.

"What are you doing up there?" Katharine shouted back. "Found anything?"

"A statue," he yelled back. "Looks like Ningal."

"The moon goddess," Katharine said over her shoulder.

Max was almost level with them now. His shorts were muddy round the edges, and his black hair had gone a rusty shade of red from the dust. His face—what Agatha could see of it—was even more sun-tanned than before.

"Good to see you both." He looked at his hands. "Sorry I can't give you a proper greeting—it's a mucky business, as you can see!"

"Is Leonard coming?" Katharine raised her hand to the brim of her hat, peering upward.

"He's on his way," Max replied. "He just wants to make sure the statue's properly wrapped before he lets it out of his sight. He said he'd meet us by the baker's."

"The baker's?" Agatha echoed. "Surely there can't be?"

"Not these days." Max smiled. "But there was, three thousand years ago. It's down there." He pointed to an area of low ruined walls punctuated by round stumps. "That's where the shops and houses were in the time of Nebuchadnezzar."

"As in the Bible?" Nancy asked.

Max nodded. "This place is straight out of the Old Testament: Ur of the Chaldeans is mentioned in the book of Genesis. We think Abraham lived here before migrating to Palestine. That's part of what we're doing—looking for physical proof of things written about in the Bible."

"Would you take them down there, Max?" Katharine tilted her head, a rather imperious look on her face. It reminded Agatha that by virtue of her marriage, Katharine had gone from being Max's equal to his de facto superior.

"Of course." If Max found this change in her status difficult, he didn't show it.

"I'll see you all back at the house for lunch." Katharine went back over to where Hamoudi was waiting.

"This way, ladies." Max led them to a different path from the one they'd come up by. When they were out of earshot of Katharine, he said: "You're in for a treat. Leonard Woolley's quite a showman. He's literally rewriting the history books, and he loves telling visitors what we've found here."

While they waited for the great man to arrive, they wandered around the ruined buildings. Max explained that when the city was built, the river Euphrates ran much closer, its course having deviated by ten miles in the past three millennia. "It was a great trading city," he said. "We know from the stone tablets that there were goldsmiths and jewelers as well as butchers and bakers. Ships came in from the Persian Gulf, bringing emeralds from Egypt, sapphires from Kashmir, lapis lazuli from Afghanistan . . ." He stopped by a flight of steps that led down to a mud-brick floor. "I'll never forget the day we unearthed the first of the royal tombs: there were seventy-four bodies—all buried alive at the bottom of a deep shaft—but when we exposed it, we thought at first that what we were looking at was a golden carpet. It turned out to be the headdresses of the ladies of the court—made from gold beech leaves—and the gold harps and lyres on which they'd played the funeral dirge to the end."

"It's almost impossible to imagine, isn't it?" Agatha said. "To be sacrificed like that."

"It reminds me of the Titanic." Nancy nodded. "The band playing on, knowing they were going to drown."

"Who's been talking about drowning?" A voice boomed out behind them. "I hope this young man hasn't been stealing my thunder!"

Leonard Woolley's mouth curved up at the edges in what was probably his version of a smile, but his eyes had an intensity that made Agatha feel like a naughty child about to be admonished by the headmaster.

His handshake was firm and brief. "Follow me now," he said. "And Max, you bring up the rear: we don't want any accidents."

He took them past the ruined buildings to a vast pit whose sides were striped with the sedimentary deposits of thousands of years. "It's sixty feet deep." He stood at the edge, one hand outstretched. "There are steps built into the walls. When we reach the bottom, we get beyond recorded history." He moved forward, beckoning the others to follow, and disappeared over the edge.

Agatha cast a worried glance at Nancy. "What do you think? It's very steep."

"You go," Nancy said. "I'll wait over there." She pointed to a low wall of mud bricks, which was just the right height to sit on.

"Are you feeling unwell?" Max was by her side in an instant. "I have some water if that would help."

"No, thank you," she said, smiling. "I'm just a little tired after the journey. I'll be fine—really. You take Agatha down."

"Well, if you're sure . . ." He turned to Agatha, offering her his hand as she stepped over the side of the pit.

They walked in single file down the steps, gradually descending into semidarkness. When they caught up with Leonard, he appeared not to notice. He was staring intently at something halfway down the side of one of the walls. "Do you see the layer of reddish sand over there?" He spoke without shifting his gaze.

Agatha peered down into the pit, her eyes gradually adjusting to the gloom. "Yes," she said, "I see it."

"That's the period when writing was invented." He paused for a moment, and when he spoke again, his voice had a different intonation, as if he was delivering a well-rehearsed lecture. "Here in the southern valley of the Euphrates, between 3500 and 3200 BC, ancient scribes devised a system of making wedge-shaped, triangular marks in clay— the cuneiform script which eventually led to the first alphabet."

That's more than five thousand years ago, Agatha thought. She scanned the layers of earth between this one and the top of the pit, trying to work out how many generations had come and gone in that time. She wondered if there had been some distant ancestor of hers, writing stories on tablets of clay.

"Now," Leonard said, "look further down and you'll see a broad brown layer of alluvial clay."

Agatha looked where he was pointing.

"That kind of clay could only have been deposited by floodwater," he went on. "It dates back to the time of the book of Genesis. We found prehistoric graves in that layer—the remains of people drowned in the Great Flood."

"Really?" Agatha gazed in awe at the thin line of brown earth sandwiched between two dirty yellow layers. "I didn't realize Noah was from Mesopotamia."

Leonard nodded. "His story is recorded in the eleventh tablet of Gilgamesh—the earliest-surviving written record in the world. He has a different name, of course—he's Utnapishtim in the Sumerian language—but many of the details of the story, such as the sending out of birds from the ark, are sufficiently close to what's written in the Bible to prove that it happened here." He forked the air with his hands, looking to the top of the pit as he did so, as if seeking approval from on high.

"Of course, what you see at ground level now came thousands of years after the flood," he went on. "Most people don't realize that the period of time between Noah and Nebuchadnezzar is just as long as the one that separates *us* from Nebuchadnezzar." He pointed to the bottom of the pit. "Come and stand on the last step."

As they made their way deeper into the pit, Agatha caught her foot on a loose stone. She felt herself slip sideways and flailed out for the wall, disorientated by the lack of light. She felt a hand on her shoulder, steadying her from behind.

"Careful—it gets a bit tricky down here."

She felt Max's breath, warm on the back of her neck.

"Thank you," she whispered.

When they reached the last step, Leonard stood in silence for a moment. It felt rather like standing in church, waiting for the service to begin. "You've just walked through ten thousand years of human existence," he said at last. "What we're standing on now is virgin soil. And in the layer above it, we found fragments of the reed huts built by the very first inhabitants, when this place was just an island in the middle of a marsh."

Agatha felt a shiver run down her spine. "How marvelous to be the one to have discovered all this."

"There's more still to be found, of course." His face was in shadow, but the tone of his voice—softer but with an edge of excitement—betrayed his obvious sense of pride. "We'll go back up now—to where Abraham lived."

As they wound their way through the ruins aboveground, he brought everything to life in vivid detail. He became quite animated, leading them through the narrow streets, miming knocking on doors and explaining that, thanks to the cuneiform tablets found at the site, they knew the name of every occupant. A merchant, a tailor, a jeweler, or a schoolmaster—he knew whether they had failed or prospered in their line of business, how many children they had had, and how old they were when they died. He was showing them the site of an inn when Michael pulled up in Queen Mary, offering a lift back to the expedition house.

Nancy—who had tagged along when they came up from the pit—turned to Agatha. "Do you mind if I go back? I could do with a lie-down."

"Of course not—would you like me to come with you?"

"No—stay and hear the rest. This is what you've come for. I'll be fine."

Leonard Woolley cleared his throat in a rather theatrical way. Clearly, he didn't like his show being interrupted. The door slammed and Nancy was off in a trail of dust.

"Now for the moon temple." Leonard cocked his head toward the ziggurat, whose stepped walls cast a monstrous shadow on the sand.

He led Agatha and Max up an outside staircase flanked by two parallel rows of steps. "Abraham was a moon worshipper before he was told to leave Ur and worship Jehovah instead," he said as they climbed high over the desert. "The moon god was the principal deity all over Arabia—his legacy still exists in the crescent moon symbol of Islam." He made his way inside the ziggurat, into what he told Agatha was a sort of antechamber to the shrine. "We have to go through there." He pointed to a narrow archway no more than five feet high. "There's a spiral staircase beyond it—rather claustrophobic, I'm afraid: the ancient Sumerians were quite a bit shorter than we are." He took an oil lamp from a shelf cut into the wall and lit it. "Just follow me," he said.

Leonard, who had hardly an ounce of fat, disappeared through the arch with no trouble, but Agatha found that her hips were too wide for the aperture, so she had to go in sideways.

A short passageway brought her to the foot of a twisting row of mud-brick steps, which were just visible in the leaping beam of light cast by the lamp up ahead. She had to bend her head to avoid knocking it on the roof as she climbed up. After the first turn of the staircase, she was in almost total darkness, feeling her way along the rough walls. She could hear the distant echo of Leonard's footsteps. He hadn't said how many stairs there were or how long it would take to reach the shrine. She felt sweat trickle down her back. The air was dry and full of dust. Suddenly she panicked. Unable to go on, she took a step backward, trying in vain to turn around in the tight space.

"Oh!"

She had forgotten that Max was right behind her. She felt the firmness of his chest against her back, his thighs against her buttocks. In that split second her panic was eclipsed by a very different feeling: the erotic sensation of this man's body pressed against hers. It set off something deep inside, a fizzing, tingling sensation, shocking in its familiarity.

She broke away, stumbling back onto the step she had just vacated. "I'm so sorry . . . I—"

"Are you all right?" Max reached out to her in the darkness. "Here's my arm. Hold on: I'm just going to light a match." His face appeared in a halo of light. "There we are: Can you see where you're going now? It's only a few more steps to the top."

Agatha groaned when she saw how close she was to the end of the staircase. "Oh dear," she said. "You must think me very pathetic."

"Not at all," he said, and then smiled. "I don't blame you for panicking. Leonard's always haring off at a hundred miles an hour. Doesn't consider what it's like for people who are not used to it." The match went out so he lit another. "I'll ask him to let you have the lamp on the way down."

When they caught up with Leonard, he was sitting on a sort of throne carved into the far wall of a bare, low-ceilinged room.

"Is this the shrine?" Agatha tried to keep the disappointment out of her voice.

"You have to imagine it as it was in Abraham's time," Leonard replied. "It was the last word in luxury: glazed with sky-blue bricks, silk carpets on the floor, huge sofas for the king and his handmaidens to lie on, gold plates and goblets for the food and wine. And over there," he said, "was an enormous statue of Nannar, the moon god. He was represented as an old man in a turban with a beard the color of lapis lazuli. Every evening he got into his bark—which to mortals appeared in the form of a brilliant crescent moon—and set sail across the night sky."

The flickering light of the lamp gave the room a rather sinister look. Agatha remembered what Katharine had said about the bizarre ceremonies that had taken place here.

"This place was steeped in magic," Leonard went on. And then, as if he'd heard what she was thinking, he said: "What went on in this room was the most immoral kind of pagan ritual—quite shocking to the modern mind."

"Yes: Katharine told me," Agatha said.

"Did she?" Leonard looked at her directly for the first time. Something in his eyes told her that this was dangerous territory, that to reiterate the words Katharine had used to describe the ancient fertility rite would provoke acute embarrassment in her host.

"She told me about the death ritual, too," she said, as a way of changing the subject. "Quite terrifying, I imagine, if you were a wife or servant of the king. You'd be watching him all the time, wouldn't you—if he was ill or anything, I mean: wondering if he was going to die."

Leonard nodded. His eyes were still on her. She felt uncomfortable under that piercing gaze. "Hard to countenance, isn't it?" he said. "But there are remnants of that kind of practice to this day. The suttee ritual in India, for example, where the widow throws herself on her husband's funeral pyre: it was outlawed a century ago, but it's still regarded by some Hindus as the ultimate form of womanly devotion."

There was a slight inflection on those last two words. Was it her imagination or was there a harsh edge to the way he said them? There was a bad feeling in this room, an almost tangible sense of menace. Was it the legacy of those unnatural acts of long ago—or the rivalry between the two men who stood here now?

CHAPTER 20

Max and Agatha rode back to the expedition house on a pair of mules. The other members of the dig team had already gone home for lunch, but Agatha said she wasn't really hungry, so Max suggested taking her back by the scenic route.

It was only four miles, but the terrain made the going slow for the animals. This was a relief to Agatha, who found mules only slightly less intimidating than camels.

"We have to cross the wadi in a minute," Max said as he drew level with her. "It's quite shallow at the moment—you won't get your feet wet."

As they came down the side of a sand dune, Agatha saw a ribbon of sparkling water, its banks peppered with wildflowers. The delicate red tulips she had seen in the vase on her windowsill grew alongside purple irises and feathery white tufts of what looked like cow parsley.

"That's the Bedouin village—over there." Max was looking out toward the western horizon. Agatha could just make out a wooden palisade, above which were the domed ceilings of tents, identical in color to the sand that surrounded them. "We'll be visiting them later in the week," Max went on. "They've invited us all to a feast."

"Really? How exciting!" Agatha shaded her eyes. "They're not a threat, then? Katharine said you'd had trouble with rumors spreading about the finds at the dig."

"We pay the local tribe to protect us," he replied. "The chieftain has a small army of men who patrol the area, keeping a lookout for bandits. He has the most wonderful title: Sheikh Munshid of the Ghazi." He smiled, eyes twinkling from a dust-covered face. "I think I'd like to come back as a Bedouin sheikh—they all seem to have at least ten wives."

Agatha gave him a dubious look.

"Only joking! It's the nomadic element of their lives that appeals to me: that ability to up sticks and travel whenever and wherever it suits them. I wouldn't mind it at all—wandering about the desert, living in a tent, always finding new places to explore . . ." He trailed off with a shrug. "We lived in tents when we first came here. It wasn't practical for long, though, given the stuff we were unearthing. Have you seen the Antiquities Room?"

"Not yet."

"I expect Katharine will want to show it to you herself. If Leonard doesn't lock himself in there for the afternoon, that is."

"He's very passionate, isn't he?" Agatha glanced at Max, watching his face. She had deliberately not said *about his work*.

Max raised his hand to wipe away a trickle of perspiration that had made a path through the dust on the left side of his face. The movement screened his eyes from her view. "Yes," he said. "He's probably the most dedicated man I've ever met. Works all the hours God sends. And he's brilliant at remembering facts: even the ones he's made up."

"Oh?" This threw her.

"All that stuff about Abraham and Noah—you mustn't take it as gospel." He was looking directly at her now. "We've searched high and low for a tablet that mentions Abraham by name, but nothing's emerged so far. And that layer of alluvial clay he pointed out: yes, it indicates a flood. But there's no proof of it being the Great Flood—the one in Genesis."

"But he seemed so sure . . ."

"It's all part of the show." Max huffed out a breath. "For the benefit of people who might have the wherewithal to keep the expedition going for as long as it takes him to find the evidence to back it all up." He paused. "I hope you won't think me impolite for drawing your attention to it. I just wanted to warn you, that's all. The Woolleys are quite a team: they know how to charm people. But you mustn't feel you have to give in to them."

He moved away then, steering his mule down the bank toward the streambed. As Agatha followed behind, his words echoed in her head. Had *he* given in to them? Allowed Katharine to steal his heart only to cast him aside when a better prospect presented itself? The thought of it wormed away at her as they splashed through the wadi and urged their animals up the other side. Max was so attentive, so patient, always mindful of the needs of other people. In that sense, he was the polar opposite of Katharine, who, for all her charm, clearly had her own interests uppermost.

Opposites attract.

Her mother had said that the day she announced her engagement to Archie. *He's not like your other young men, is he, dear?* She had said it with a bright, brittle smile and a film of tears in her eyes. Agatha had been too much in love to see that these were not tears of joy. She had taken her mother's observation as a compliment to Archie: no, he wasn't like the others—he was impetuous, mercurial, and very, very handsome . . .

In that moment she sensed that Max felt just as she had: captivated, dazzled, and hopelessly out of his depth.

~

Saleem was clearing away the remains of lunch when they got back to Sahra' Alqamar. Max grabbed a plate of flatbreads before the boy had a chance to take it back to the kitchen.

"Are you hungry now?" He offered the plate to Agatha. "There's some goat's cheese left, too, if you like it."

Katharine's face appeared round the door. "Oh—you're back at last! I thought you'd been kidnapped!" She stepped into the room, taking Agatha's arm. "You must see the Antiquities Room—there's just time while Leonard's with Duncan in the darkroom. You haven't met Duncan, yet, have you? Or Pierre?"

Agatha shook her head.

"Pierre's our epigraphist—he translates the cuneiform tablets—and Duncan's our ceramics expert. You'll meet them both at dinner tonight. Anyway, come with me: Nancy's already in there."

She led the way down the passageway to a room at the heart of the expedition house. "It has no windows," she explained. "There's no way of getting to it from the outside. We still keep it locked at all times, though."

As Agatha stepped over the threshold, she could see why. Lit by two oil lamps, the room glittered like an Aladdin's cave. Nancy was standing next to a golden statue with the head of what looked like a pharaoh and the body of a lion. In her hand was a goblet of the same color with a design of rams' heads around the rim.

"Look at this!" Nancy held it out to Agatha. "It's really heavy—is it solid gold?"

Katharine nodded. "The statue isn't though—it's gilded ivory. That's the one that sparked the rumors I was telling you about. If it *was* solid gold, it'd be worth a king's ransom."

"It looks almost Egyptian," Agatha said.

"There are similarities between the Sumerians and the Egyptians," Katharine replied. "That striped headdress is almost identical. And look at this . . ." She took down a box from the top shelf, lifting the lid to reveal a beautiful gold dagger with dark-blue stones in the handle. "This came from a prince's grave, and we think the sapphires came from Egypt. We had to pay the workman who found it its weight in gold— very expensive, but we have to do it to discourage stealing. We found other royal graves, but most of them had already been plundered." She gestured to the goblet in Nancy's hand. "This cup is our best find. Early Akkadian. Unique."

"What's this?" Nancy was looking at a life-sized bust of a man's head. It looked very different in style to the other heads in the room. The headdress was more Arabic than Egyptian. And it was a different color—not golden, but a darker, tawny shade.

"Oh," Katharine laughed. "That's one of mine, I'm afraid. It's Hamoudi—our foreman at the dig—do you recognize him?"

"You did this?" Agatha reached out to touch the sculpted features.

"Last season, yes: I got it cast in bronze back in London and gave it to Leonard as a wedding present."

"It's frightfully good," Nancy said. "So very lifelike."

"Well, it took a long time to get it right. Poor Hamoudi: he must have been bored rigid, posing for me night after night, when all the other workmen had gone home." A wistful look crossed Katharine's face, which she quickly covered with a smile. "We'd better make ourselves scarce now: Leonard will want to get to work on today's finds." She ushered them out of the room and locked the door. "We usually have a nap in the afternoons—apart from Leonard, that is, who doesn't actually sleep at all . . ." She pulled a face. "I expect you're both worn out after the train journey—I'll see you in a couple of hours, shall I?"

～

Katharine lay down and closed her eyes but sleep wouldn't come. She could feel the beginnings of a migraine pulsing behind her eyes. She wasn't sure what had triggered it. Maybe it was spending too long hunched over the new trench on the east side of the mound, with the morning sun shining right at her. Or perhaps it was the arrival of Agatha and Nancy, bringing the realization that there would be questions, questions she wasn't sure she would be able to deflect.

Sliding off the bed, she slipped on a robe and unlocked her bedroom door. She stood in the passageway for a moment, listening. She could hear a distant clatter from the kitchen: Ibrahim and Saleem preparing the evening meal. She heard the scrape of clay on wood as Leonard took something from a shelf in the Antiquities Room. He wouldn't hear her tiptoe past the door on her way to find Max, wouldn't have any idea how she was going to spend what was left of the afternoon.

The sleeping dogs didn't stir as she crossed the courtyard. The door to the annex was slightly ajar, left that way deliberately to allow some air into the low-roofed mud-brick dormitory whose six bedrooms were now all occupied. Max's room was the one nearest to the entrance, so she didn't have to creep past anyone else's room to get to him.

She hesitated for a moment, her fingers on the latch of his door. There was no sound but the muffled grunts of someone snoring. Michael probably, or Pierre. Noiselessly she lifted the latch. There was a bolt on the inside, but Max never used it. She pushed the door open.

Max was lying on top of the bed, fully clothed. An open book had slithered, facedown, onto the counterpane. With his eyes closed, he looked serene, almost regal, like a young pharaoh about to be laid in a sarcophagus.

"Max," she whispered. He didn't stir. She went closer, bending over him. When she spoke again, her mouth was inches from his ear. "Max, are you awake?"

His eyes snapped open. "What?" He sat up quickly, knocking his book to the floor, where it fell onto a goatskin rug with a soft thud. "What's the matter?" He blinked and rubbed his eyes.

"I've got a headache." She raised a hand to her temple, rubbing the skin. "Could you give me one of your massages? You're so good at it."

Max hesitated, a frown creasing his forehead. "Yes, I suppose I could. I'll have to wash first, though."

Katharine sat on the bed as he went to pour water into the tin bowl on the dressing table. She saw that his legs were still dusty from the dig. He wetted a flannel and rubbed it across his face, then washed his arms up to the elbows.

"Do you want to sit in the chair?" he said, toweling himself dry.

"I'd rather lie down," she replied. "If I put the pillow at the other end of the bed, you could sit in the chair. I expect it'll be more comfortable for you like that."

"All right." Max gave her a doubtful look. "I'll try it." He moved the chair from its place under the window while she positioned herself on the bed, pulling her silk robe over her bare legs. She closed her eyes, waiting for the delicious moment when his fingers made contact with her skin.

~

Agatha woke up with a jolt, wondering for a moment where she was. She had fallen asleep naked, on top of the covers, having left the window open in a bid to get some air into the stuffy little room. She wondered what had woken her. A noise from outside, perhaps.

Pulling on her dressing gown, she went over to the window. It was difficult to see much through the heavy metal bars. Not that there was much out there: just bare scrubland punctuated with the odd boulder. She couldn't hear anything much, either, just the low rumble of somebody snoring in another room.

She decided to get dressed and take her notebook to the sitting room. It would be more pleasant than staying here. There might be something to eat, too. It was another couple of hours until supper, and she regretted turning down what had been left of lunch.

A few minutes later she lifted the latch on her bedroom door, taking care not to let it drop as she let herself out. She didn't want to disturb Nancy next door. As she made her way along the narrow passageway, she noticed that one of the other doors was slightly ajar. She didn't know whose room it was. Apparently, one of the men had abandoned his afternoon nap in favor of something else. She wondered if she would run into whomever it was in the sitting room. Rather awkward, she thought, if it was one of the two she had yet to be introduced to. And not in the least conducive to writing up her observations of the dig.

What she saw as she drew level with the door stopped her dead. Through a gap no more than an inch wide, she caught a glimpse of Katharine sprawled on the bed upside down, one bare leg protruding from a dressing gown of crimson silk. And bending over her, his hands buried in her hair, was Max.

As she stood there, rooted to the spot, his head whipped round. In the split second before she darted out into the courtyard, his eyes flashed with the shock of seeing her. When she reached the sitting room, she sank into one of the rickety armchairs, panting for breath. There was no one else around. For that, at least, she was thankful. When she had recovered a little, she went and helped herself to a glass of water from the jug on the table. She sipped it slowly, feeling the beat of the pulse in her throat as the liquid slipped down.

She tried to distance herself from what she had just witnessed. Tried to view it dispassionately, like a scene from a movie. What business was it of hers, what these people got up to?

But there was no denying the familiar stab in her stomach—the same physical pain she had experienced that night in the car outside the home of Archie's friends.

This was jealousy, pure and simple.

How can you be jealous? Why are you chasing after a man more than ten years younger than you are?

"I don't know, Mama," she whispered to the empty room.

~

At just before six Agatha went back to the annex. The door of Max's bedroom was shut now. She hurried past, not wanting to hear whatever might be going on inside. She had agreed to wake Nancy in time for supper—otherwise, she would have stayed in the living room until the meal was served.

Nancy didn't hear the first, tentative knock. When Agatha did manage to rouse her, she came to the door looking bewildered.

"Sorry—I was in such a deep sleep," she said, stifling a yawn. "Did you manage to drop off?"

Agatha nodded. "Just for half an hour or so. Then I made some notes about what we saw this morning." Part of her wanted to tell Nancy what she had seen on the way to the living room. But as the words took shape on her tongue, she bit them back. Telling Nancy would make it real. And the atmosphere at supper was going to be uncomfortable enough without dragging her into it. "How are you feeling now?" she said instead. "I was worried about you earlier."

"Much better, thank you." Nancy glanced down. Her dressing gown was hanging open, revealing the curve of her belly. She pulled one side over the other and knotted the belt. "You won't tell Katharine and the others, will you? I couldn't bear it if everyone knew."

"Of course I won't, if you don't want me to. But what will you say if Katharine notices?"

"Do you think she will? Is it that obvious?"

"Not when you're wearing an aba," Agatha replied. "I don't think anyone would guess. But what if she starts quizzing you? She's bound to ask what you're planning to do when I go back to London."

"I'll tell her the truth—that Delia left me enough money to be going on with and that I'll start looking for a job in the spring."

"But . . . ," Agatha hesitated, searching Nancy's face. The thought of her going through the ordeal of giving birth with no one but strangers to help was very worrying. Katharine ought to be told. But what Agatha had just witnessed felt like a betrayal, and made her unwilling to let Katharine in on the secret.

"But what?" Nancy frowned.

She had to say it. Whatever Katharine was up to in her private life, she could still be a friend to Nancy. "Well, it's just that . . . ," Agatha faltered. "I know you're going to get a nanny when the time comes—but Katharine might be able to help. In an emergency, I mean."

"I don't see how," Nancy said. "Ur's a long way from Baghdad."

"But she's bound to know people. It wouldn't hurt, would it, to tell her about the baby—as long as she kept it to herself?"

~

Katharine was alone in the sitting room when they got there. There was no hint of embarrassment in her eyes as she greeted them. Had Max said anything, Agatha wondered? It seemed unlikely that he would keep something like that from her, given their obvious closeness. Perhaps her plan was to just brazen it out: act as if nothing had happened in the hope that Agatha would think she had imagined seeing her in Max's bedroom.

"Come up to the top," Katharine said. "You get a wonderful view of the sunset from up there."

They followed her up an open staircase on the far wall of the courtyard to the flat expanse of whitewashed bricks that formed the roof of the expedition house. The sun was already low in the sky, a red ball hanging over the distant mound of the dig. Agatha could see the tiny figures of the workmen scrambling down the sides.

"This is where we keep all the ceramic ware we excavate." Katharine gestured toward the piles of terra-cotta shards dotted all over the roof. "I've got jobs for you both this evening, if you're willing. Do you like jigsaw puzzles?" Her eyes went from Agatha to Nancy. "We have a room downstairs where we take the pieces and try to fit them together to find out what we've got. It's like doing a jigsaw in three dimensions. There could be bowls, pitchers, drinking vessels, storage jars—it's quite good fun when you get into it. And it'll give us all a chance to catch up—I'm dying to hear how you've been getting on in Baghdad."

Nancy and Agatha exchanged glances. As they examined some of the broken pieces, a face appeared at the top of the staircase. A man of about fifty with curly gray hair and a bushy beard greeted them with a little bow.

"Good evening." He spoke with a French accent.

"This is Pierre," Katharine said. "He's from the Sorbonne." She put her hand on Agatha's shoulder, ushering her forward with gentle pressure. "Agatha speaks very good French, Pierre. I'm sure you two will get on like a house on fire."

By the time the sun sank below the horizon, Agatha was deep in conversation with the epigraphist. He was telling her about the cuneiform tablets found in the houses at Ur, offering to draw an alphabet in her notebook so that she could understand the basics of the ancient language.

When the gong rang for supper, he took her arm and helped her down the staircase. "Sit by me," he said in French as they made their way to the table. "It's nice to have someone new to talk to. Max is the only person on the dig who speaks my language with any degree of fluency."

Agatha saw that Max was already sitting on the opposite side of the table, next to Michael. She looked down as she took her seat, avoiding his eyes. She glanced sideways at Katharine, who was seating Nancy next to a young man she guessed must be Duncan. Katharine had mentioned him in her letters. He was an archaeologist from Scotland—the newest member of the team—who had only just graduated from Saint Andrews University. He looked very young. If she hadn't known he was a graduate, Agatha would have guessed he was no more than a teenager.

Leonard was the last member of the household to come in to supper. He took his place between Katharine and Michael with an abstracted air. Agatha sensed that for him, food was an unwelcome but necessary interruption, not something to be anticipated and enjoyed. She wondered what he would say if he knew what had been going on just yards away from where he had been working this afternoon, if he had seen what she had seen.

She watched Katharine as a steaming bowl of lamb stew was set on the table. She was leaning across Leonard, saying something to Michael. There was no tension in her expression, no indication that, less than two hours ago, she had been in another man's bed.

For Agatha, the meal was an uncomfortable experience. She spent the whole time trying not to look at Max, which proved very difficult with the nature of the meal, which involved a central platter of torn flatbreads to be dipped in the stew. Each time she reached for a piece, she lowered her eyes. There was a tense moment when Max's hand went to the plate at the same time as hers and their hands almost touched.

Leonard looked at her across the table as this happened, a quizzical expression on his face. She wondered if he had some inkling of what had been going on, and her heart missed a beat.

"I've just finished reading one of your novels," he said. "It was very good."

"Oh?" She felt a wave of relief. "Which one was it?"

"*The Murder of Roger Ackroyd*. Katharine lent it to me." He glanced at his wife with the ghost of a smile. "I've read some of your others, too. I do like detective stories."

Agatha was pleasantly surprised. She'd had him down as too intellectual to bother with her kind of fiction.

"As it happens," he went on, "I have an idea for a murder mystery."

"Really?" Agatha was even more surprised.

"Set in ancient Egypt." He nodded. "I know that's not your period, but I'm sure you could pull it off, with enough research."

"Poor Agatha!" Katharine turned to him with a little shake of her head. "She's come here for a rest!"

"It's all right." Agatha smiled. "I'm always on the lookout for new ideas. Perhaps I could jot down a few notes later."

When the meal was over, coffee was served in the courtyard, which had been transformed into a magical-looking space with hurricane lamps hanging from hooks on the walls. Leonard and Katharine were the first to go outside. Agatha hung back in the dining room until Max had left the table. Then Pierre asked her if she would like to see the cuneiform tablet he was working on at the moment.

"Oh yes," she said, grateful for the chance to escape.

"Reste là," he said when she jumped up. *"Je vais l'amener à vous."* He would bring it out to the courtyard. So she had no choice but to join the others.

Max was waiting on the other side of the door.

"I must talk to you," he whispered.

She went to pass him, pretending she hadn't heard.

"Please!" She felt his hand on her arm. "I need to explain. Come with me, will you? Just for a second."

"You don't need to explain your personal affairs to me, Max," she said sharply. "It's none of my business."

"But I do." He glanced over his shoulder at the others, who were helping themselves to coffee. "I don't want you thinking there's something going on between me and . . ." His voice died as the Frenchman reappeared with the cuneiform tablet. Taking Agatha's arm, Max propelled her back into the room. "Excuse me, Pierre," he said, "there's something I've got to show our guest—she'll be back in two ticks."

He took her to a cubicle off the sitting room, which contained a trestle table covered in broken pottery. He closed the door behind them. "Sorry," he said. "I just had to put things straight. What you saw—I know what it must have looked like, but it's not as it seems." His eyes met hers, and he held them. "It might sound a peculiar thing, but she gets these terrible headaches. Severe migraines. And it falls to me to treat them." He glanced down at his hands. "I have no relish for the task, but she says that massage is the only thing that relieves the pain."

Agatha paused for a moment, considering this. "Why on earth can't Leonard do it? It seems a strange thing to ask a colleague to do."

"He's far too busy for that."

"Well, why doesn't she go to a doctor, then?"

"The nearest doctor is in Nasiriyah, thirty miles away, and as there's no telephone here, we have to survive without him." He clicked his tongue. "Katharine often wakes up in the night feeling unwell. She's tried rousing Leonard, but no amount of calling seems to wake him— which is hardly surprising given how little sleep he allows himself. A few days after they were married, she resorted to tying a piece of string round his toe and tugging it violently when she needed him—but to no avail. So now she comes to me in emergencies."

The thought of the great archaeologist being tethered by the toe made Agatha want to smile in spite of herself.

"I sometimes have to apply leeches to her forehead as well." Max mirrored her expression with a wry look. "A doctor who visited the dig last season said bloodletting would be beneficial."

"Oh, that sounds a bit grim!" She saw the look of relief on his face at the lightness in her voice. "I suppose I did rather jump to conclusions when I saw her lying on your bed." She went on, "After what you'd said on the train about not wanting her to know you were there, well . . ."

He nodded. "I can see why you might put two and two together. She's a very difficult woman to be around—if you're a man, that is. She's what my mother would call an *allumeuse.*"

Despite her fluent French, this was a word Agatha hadn't heard before. "Oh . . . ," she hesitated. "Like a match, you mean?"

"Exactly," Max replied. "She draws men to her like moths to a flame. Except a flame doesn't do it on purpose and she does. Even if you're not interested, she makes it very hard to resist. It's like a game to her." He picked up a piece of pottery from the table, examining its rough edges. "When I first came here, three years ago, she used to ask me to brush her hair. It was in the evenings, when Leonard was holed up in the Antiquities Room. He'd have gone mad if he'd known what I was doing: not because he was jealous, or anything, but because he can't stand people being idle. I tried to tell her that, but she wouldn't have it. She has this way of making you do what she wants. She can be absolutely entrancing—but if you cross her, she creates this poisonous, charged atmosphere."

His face was still in shadow. Apparently, he was afraid of betraying his feelings. How far had things gone, Agatha wondered? Had she rebuffed him or had it been the other way round? She wanted desperately to know but sensed that to probe any further would be more than he could bear. "What about her husband," she asked instead. "Does he know about all this?"

She heard him sigh before he spoke. "It's because of it that he married her. Word of her behavior got back to the trustees at the British Museum. A lot of the money comes from the Presbyterian Church in America, and if they got wind of it, there'd be a good chance of them pulling out—so the trustees made it clear she couldn't go on living here as a single woman."

"But why him?"

"Because he's the boss." Max looked up, his eyes wary, as if he was afraid of being overheard. "She likes people to think that she's very independent—but what she really wants is security, someone who can protect her."

Agatha found this difficult to square with the confident, self-assured persona Katharine had projected on the train. But she reminded herself that she had already glimpsed what lay beneath the surface. The night Katharine had been delirious: the anguish in her voice when she had spoken of her first husband's suicide; and the morning of the wedding, when she had said she knew what it felt like to have your private life picked over by the press. Perhaps it wasn't so very hard to believe that she craved the solid respectability a man like Leonard could provide.

"But does she love him?" At the risk of sounding nosy, Agatha had to ask. Because if Katharine *didn't* love her husband—if it was just a marriage of convenience—then maybe she still had Max in her sights.

Max opened his mouth to reply but was cut short by a knock at the door.

"As tu fini?" Pierre sounded impatient.

"We'd better go," Max said. "Otherwise, you'll be the one they're whispering about."

CHAPTER 21

"I can't tell you how good it is to have you here." Katharine was holding her cigarette in one hand and the handle of an ancient terra-cotta urn in the other. "I didn't want to leave you in Baghdad. I'd have packed you both into Queen Mary if I could."

"I'm not sure Leonard would have been keen on that." Nancy shot a sly glance at Agatha. "I expect he wanted you all to himself while he had the chance."

Katharine put the cigarette to her lips, inhaling deeply. The smoke she blew out hung like a cloud in the confined space of the cubicle. "Would you like to know how I spent my honeymoon night?" She paused, looking from one to the other. "Supervising the digging of the latrines. When we arrived, the workmen hadn't finished preparing the new dig site. So I had to stand over them all night, to make sure they got it done before the others arrived."

"Oh, poor you—how miserable!" Nancy said. "I hope things have improved since."

"Not exactly." There was a warning note in Katharine's voice.

"Well, if it's any consolation," Nancy went on, "I had what probably ranks as the worst honeymoon in history."

There was a curious intensity in Katharine's eyes as she listened to Nancy's description of her husband's blatant infidelity. "I think I would have wanted to kill him," she said. "What on earth did you do, stuck there with the two of them?"

Nancy looked at Agatha before replying. "I'm afraid I jumped out of the frying pan into the fire."

Agatha watched Katharine's face as Nancy gave a faltering account of her affair with the married actor. Katharine's expression was unreadable. Agatha wondered if there were echoes of her own past in this story. Had she been unfaithful to her first husband? Was *that* why he had committed suicide?

She scoured her memory for the exact words Katharine had uttered while she was delirious. *That fool should never have told him . . . Such a shock . . . No one could take a thing like that.* Yes, she thought. That could easily be what had happened. Katharine had taken a lover out in Egypt. Possibly a friend or a close colleague of her husband's. And then someone had told him.

"The thing is . . ." Nancy fell silent. Agatha watched a wisp of cigarette smoke float across the table, eddying around the pile of pottery that lay abandoned now. "I . . . I'm expecting a baby."

Katharine made a small whispered sound, like a dry leaf crushed underfoot. She had gone very pale. Even her eyes seemed to have lost some of their color. Their vivid violet blue had a ghostly opalescence. "A baby?"

"I'm sorry." Nancy's face flushed. "I've offended you. It's an awful thing to admit to. I wouldn't blame you if you threw me out."

"No, I . . ."

Agatha sensed that Katharine was at a total loss for words. She had never seen her like this. All of her confidence seemed to have evaporated. Nancy's news had delivered a body blow. Why?

"I'm just surprised, that's all." Katharine stubbed out her cigarette and reached for another one. "I mean, you don't *look* pregnant . . ."

"I've still got a while to go." Nancy patted her stomach. "I've been trying to hide it. I'd be grateful if you didn't mention it to the others."

"Of course I won't. I'd better tell them you're getting over some bug, though—just in case any of them tries dragging you off on some jaunt across the desert." She flipped her lighter open and held it to the end of her cigarette. "Try not to be offended if they flirt with you. Max and Duncan, especially. It's hard for them, stuck out here for months on end. And you're a very pretty girl."

Agatha flinched. In Katharine's mind, Max and Nancy were potential mates. Would she have said that if she was still interested in him herself?

~

That night, when all the others had gone off to their beds, Katharine asked Saleem to bring hot water for a bath. The bathroom in the main building wasn't much bigger than the one in the annex. It housed a small copper tub, just big enough to sit in with knees bent. It took five journeys to and from the kitchen for Saleem to fill it, but it was a nightly ritual Katharine insisted on—the one luxury of life at the dig.

When the bath was ready and the oil lamp set on the floor, she sent Saleem away and slipped out of her robe. Then she poured in a splash of emerald liquid from a bottle purchased in Harrods' beauty department the week before her wedding. The water bubbled up when she agitated it with her fingers.

Climbing into the tub, she drew the foam up around her breasts so that only her neck and face were visible above the water. There was a window in the bathroom—just a square no more than a foot across—and she had left the blind up, deliberately.

She began to soap herself, drawing her hands slowly and seductively over her body, knowing that *he* was watching.

~

Agatha wasn't sure how long she had been asleep. She had left the shutters open when she blew out her candle. The sky beyond the window was a smudge of gray in the black of the mud-brick wall.

A single star came into view as she propped herself up on her elbows. Perhaps it was the sight of it that gave her the idea of going onto the roof. Or it might have been the claustrophobic feel of the little room. No need to light the candle. She would find her way across the courtyard by starlight.

She felt her way along the corridor, hearing the now-familiar rise and fall of snoring from the room at the far end. Michael or Pierre? She wasn't sure whose room this was. Not Duncan's, she guessed. He was too young, surely, to have developed such a habit. And as for Max, well, she knew which room was his, and there was no sound coming from inside as she groped her way past the door.

Stepping into the courtyard, she turned her face to the sky, dazzled at the sight of all the stars. In Baghdad she had often sat out on the veranda at night, looking at the sky. But it had never looked quite as spectacular as this. The stars looked close enough to touch.

Carefully, she climbed the steps up to the roof. She picked her way past the heaps of broken pottery until she found a place to sit. The roof was still a little warm—from the stored heat of the sun or the fire Saleem had made after supper? She wasn't sure. She made her shawl into a pillow and lay down flat, wishing she knew the names of the constellations scattered overhead like raindrops in a web of indigo silk.

There was a patch of a different color low in the sky. An apricot haze, like the dying rays of the sun. She wondered what it could be. Not the sun—far too late for that. As she stared at it, it changed shape. Its edges became sharper, with a curve like a slice of melon. With a little gasp, she saw what it was. The moon. A crescent, on its back, rising up from the horizon like a golden boat gliding into an inky ocean.

As she watched it rise higher, she thought of Nannar, the Sumerian moon god, an old man guiding his boat across the night sky. She might not know the names of the constellations, but she had enough awareness of the moon to know that a crescent rising late at night meant that it was waning, not new. An old moon. With an old man steering it. Strange that it was a man, not a woman, when in so many other cultures the moon was perceived as a female deity, with its changing shape echoing the rhythms of a woman's body.

The maiden, the mother, and the crone.

She had been a maiden and a mother. Was this all that was left to her now, then? To be like the ever-shrinking slice of moon overhead, growing paler and more insignificant with every passing hour?

I'm thirty-eight years old.

She was not ready to relinquish the full-moon phase of her life. Not ready to give up on . . . what? Possibilities. That was all.

She thought of her mother, who by the age of thirty-eight was already a widow. Had it ever crossed her mind that she was too young to live out the rest of her life alone? In Paris, or in Egypt, had there been men who noticed her, alone with a young daughter, and looked for an encouraging word or glance?

As far as Agatha had been aware, there had never been even a hint of interest in anyone else. It was unlikely that her mother would choose to be anywhere now but in the place where she had been buried, next to her husband. But Agatha felt her spirit so strongly sometimes. Here. Now. Whispering in her ear.

Was that possible?

She focused on one star, brighter than the others, not far from the crescent moon. Scientists said that it took light from a star like that thousands, millions of years to reach people on earth. That seemed incredible. Unbelievable. But it was true. Looking at the stars, anything seemed possible. And sensing that, a strange sort of peace came over her. She was utterly alone. Just her and the moon and the stars. And it didn't matter. It was enough.

A small sound, like a pebble thrown against a window, pulled her back. She listened. Someone was climbing the stairs to the roof. Leonard? Come to gather more material for inspection? What would he say if he saw her lying there? She sat up quickly, the stars swirling in a giddy haze.

"Agatha?"

It was Katharine who emerged at the top of the staircase, silhouetted against the sky.

"What are you doing up here?" There was a smile in her voice. "Couldn't you sleep?" She slipped through the pottery shards with the grace and speed of a cat. "It's wonderful, isn't it?" She settled herself down, cross-legged, next to Agatha and tilted her head back. "Do you see that very bright star, right above us? That's Sirius. And to the left of it—that constellation is Aquarius."

Agatha craned her neck. "I never knew it looked like that. Oh yes—I can see it now: like a woman sitting on the ground, clutching a jar. Amazing!"

"I know. You can imagine people doing this thousands of years ago, can't you? Sitting round a campfire, gazing at the sky, night after night, watching all the patterns come and go. The sheer scale of it. So beautiful and so empty. I come up here often, just to escape."

"I'm sorry—I've spoiled it for you."

"Not at all. It's the men I want to get away from—not you."

"I suppose it must get oppressive sometimes." Agatha paused. She wanted to ask if things had changed—for better or worse—since Katharine's marriage. But she was afraid to stray into what she sensed was forbidden territory.

"It's not as tense now as it used to be." Katharine stretched out her legs, propping herself up on her elbows. "Now that Len and I are married, it's . . . well . . . like a line drawn in the sand, I suppose. We all know where we are."

Len. She hadn't ever called him that before. It seemed to signal a loosening up, a willingness to confide. If Agatha was quiet, if she made herself almost invisible, Katharine might just reveal a little more.

"I understand, now, why you're here." Katharine was still looking at the stars. Her words took Agatha by surprise. "I wrote to my sister in England, telling her you were coming, and she sent me a newspaper cutting. About your husband's marriage." A pause and then: "I don't blame you, wanting to get away. If I'd known, I wouldn't have inflicted my own wedding on you. It must have been miserable, being reminded like that."

Agatha felt a numbing tightness in her throat. She fixed her gaze on that very bright star, watching it blur as tears pricked the back of her eyes. *Sirius.* She said the name over and over in her head, like counting to ten when you stub your toe. She didn't want to talk about Archie. But Katharine was trying to make amends, trying to compensate for something she clearly felt embarrassed about. And was there any point in keeping silent when her life was public property anyway?

"I don't think I'll ever get over losing my first husband." Katharine sat upright, pulling her cigarette case from her dressing gown pocket. "He was the first man I ever truly loved—and I don't think you ever do get over that." She flipped up the top of her lighter, cupping it with her hands. The flame cast a yellow glow over her face. "There was an inquest into Bertram's death and a journalist phoned me, asking questions. It was absolutely ghastly—as if I wasn't feeling wretched enough, without the papers raking over it." She sucked in smoke and blew it out. "It must have been ten times worse for you—that business in Harrogate."

"Yes, it was." Agatha felt as if someone else was controlling her mouth, as if her voice was coming from some parallel universe. She had never spoken about those ten days in Harrogate. It was exactly two years ago—December 1926—that she had left her car at the edge of the quarry and walked through a winter dawn to the nearest railway station.

"I'd had a breakdown." Up here, in the darkness of the Arabian desert, it somehow felt safe to let it out. Like whispering a secret in the confessional. "I'd been away from Archie for a few weeks, nursing my mother at her house in Devon. We were very close, and I was devastated when she died. Then, the weekend after, Archie came down from London and told me he was in love with another woman. In those few days my whole world came tumbling down."

In the silence, all Agatha could hear was the sound of Katharine inhaling.

"I wanted to ask you about it on the train—when I first suspected who you were." Katharine's voice was softer, lower. "I'm sorry. It was crass of me. Pretending I didn't know and then posing that question about whether it was really amnesia."

"I can hardly blame you for that. It's only what the entire population of the British Isles seemed to want to know at the time." Agatha shifted her weight from one elbow to the other. "You were right, as a matter of fact: it *was* Archie's idea to say I'd lost my memory. He thought it was the only way to salvage both our reputations. He told the papers I'd had a mental collapse brought on by overwork. I even booked sessions with a psychiatrist to make it look convincing. One journalist was actually following me—every day for a couple of weeks—after I got back home. I felt like a criminal."

"I felt just the same when Bertram died." Katharine lay back, blowing a plume of smoke into the night sky. "I felt absolutely to blame—even though I'd done nothing wrong."

Nothing wrong? So, Agatha thought, the theory about the lover in Egypt was a white elephant. "Have you ever talked about it to anyone?" she asked. "I got the feeling that when you let it out—the morning of your wedding—there was something preying on your mind. Something you needed to get out in the open before you got married to Leonard."

"You're very perceptive." Katharine leaned across to tap ash over the side of the roof. "But no. It's too . . . private. I can't bring myself to put it into words. It's too painful." A pause and then: "I'm sorry. Do you understand?"

Agatha suddenly saw what Max had meant. *She draws you in.* Katharine had done exactly that. Drawn Agatha into revealing things about the darkest time in her life, then clammed up the moment the tables were turned. And in doing so, she had gained a psychological advantage. Now she knew things that no one else knew.

"Agatha?"

Something in the timbre of her voice gave her away. There was fear in that husky whisper. Once again it occurred to Agatha that she had got Katharine all wrong. That this was not some game. There was something about the circumstances of her husband's death that she really couldn't bear to talk about. A fragment of remembered conversation floated into Agatha's mind. Nancy's announcement of her pregnancy. And Katharine's reaction. Had there been a baby, out in Egypt? A stillbirth or a miscarriage?

"Of course," Agatha said softly. "Some things *are* too painful to talk about. I do understand."

CHAPTER 22

Ur to Ukhaidir

Agatha was in a deep sleep when Nancy came knocking at her door. She peered at her watch. Half past eight. She jumped out of bed, pulling her shawl round her shoulders.

"I thought I'd better wake you up," Nancy said. "I don't feel like breakfast—but the others have already had theirs."

Agatha dressed quickly. By the time she reached the main house, Saleem was clearing away the breakfast things. She grabbed a piece of toast and asked if she could have a cup of tea. As she was drinking it, Max popped his head round the door.

"Hello. Do you fancy a trip into the desert? I've got to go and collect the wages for the men from Najaf. We could go and see the palace at Ukhaidir."

"Oh." Agatha put down her cup. "I read about that. It's more than a thousand years old, isn't it?"

"That's right. It was built in 775 AD. It's a ruin now, of course—but spectacular, all the same. I'm setting off in about half an hour if you want to come."

"I'd better go and ask Nancy." Agatha drained her cup and stood up.

"I can't take both of you, I'm afraid." Max shrugged. "We have to pick up supplies and a Bedouin guard in Najaf." He cocked his head toward the courtyard. "Katharine's got plans for Nancy, I think. She said something about her not having been well. She's going to get her cataloguing photographs."

Agatha nodded. "How far is it to Najaf?"

"About fifty miles. There's a huge lake nearby." He smiled. "We can stop off for a picnic on the way home if you like. Can't expect you to travel all that way on a piece of toast."

Agatha smiled back. Clearly, Max loved his food as much as she did. Not at all like his boss, who only seemed to eat out of necessity.

As she went to get ready, she spotted Katharine and Nancy disappearing through a door on the other side of the courtyard. She felt grateful and rather surprised that Katharine had orchestrated things to make this trip possible. It seemed to confirm what had occurred to her last night: that she'd completely misread Katharine. Why would she want to send Agatha off with Max into the desert if she wanted him for herself?

~

On the way to Najaf, Agatha mentioned to Max how surprised she'd been to learn that Leonard liked detective stories.

"He's not as buttoned-up as he looks, is he?" Max chuckled. "I'm dying to hear about this ancient Egyptian murder idea of his—has he told you about it yet?"

Agatha shook her head. "To be honest, I'm awash with ideas at the moment—all set in the present day. I've never really thought about writing a historical crime novel." She told him about the plots she was developing for two new books.

"How clever." He smiled when she explained the idea of using symbols from the Yezidi shrine as a murderer's code. "I'm delighted to have taken you somewhere that inspired you." He slowed down as they approached a big pothole in the road. "Perhaps you should think about setting one of your novels in an expedition house." He cast a wry sideways glance. "Plenty of motives for murder there!"

"Are there?"

Max grunted a laugh. "With the possible exception of Duncan—who's only been with us five minutes—I don't think there's a single member of the team I wouldn't have cheerfully strangled at some point over the past three years. You wouldn't believe how tense it gets sometimes. A bunch of people thrown together twenty-four hours a day. We've never actually come to blows—but it's been a near thing on more than one occasion."

"What sort of thing do you fall out about?" Agatha was thinking of Katharine. She seemed the most likely source of tension. It wasn't difficult to imagine men fighting over her.

"All kinds of things. Anything from who's not pulling their weight on the dig to who's snaffled the last packet of cigarettes. The day before you came, there was a terrible atmosphere at breakfast because Katharine said no one had passed her the toast rack."

"Really? That sounds awfully petty."

"It is!" Max shook his head. "Out here things somehow get magnified out of all proportion. And Katharine, I'm afraid, is the worst offender. Living with her is like walking on a tightrope."

"I got a sense of that last night," Agatha said. She told him about going up to the roof to look at the stars and Katharine's sudden appearance. "She won't talk much about the past, but I get the impression that whatever caused her first husband's suicide still haunts her. I wonder if that's what makes her so edgy?"

"Very likely," Max replied. "I've often wondered about it myself. Did she tell you she won't allow Leonard in her bed? All he's allowed to do is watch her taking a bath each night."

Agatha turned to him, openmouthed.

"It's common knowledge among the team, so I don't suppose she'd mind me telling you. I don't know how he stands it, poor devil."

"That does seem very bizarre. Has she ever told you why?"

"Not really." His hands tightened on the steering wheel, his knuckles showing white through the tanned skin. "Like you say, she won't talk much about the past. But there's certainly something: some psychological thing, possibly, that makes her chew men up and spit them out. She gets away with it because of her looks and her magnetism. I feel sorry for Leonard. It must be wretched for him."

He turned the car sharply to the left, and Agatha was vaguely aware of the minarets of a mosque in the distance. But she was looking without really seeing, her mind spinning with images of Katharine. She felt quite certain, now, that something *had* happened between her and Max. It was there in his voice, in the way he tensed up when he was talking about her. Katharine must have led him on, then left him dangling, just as she was now doing with Leonard—the difference being that Leonard was her husband. He had rights. Reasonable expectations. How was it that a man who was so forceful in other areas of his life could accept a situation like that?

Soon they were passing roadside stalls and women leading mules laden with baskets of fruit. Max pulled up beside a market in the shadow of the mosque, and Agatha followed him from stall to stall, helping him to select the best onions, oranges, tomatoes, and cucumbers. Then they went across to the police station to pick up the Bedouin guard who accompanied them to the bank. Once the money was collected and stowed in the back of the truck, they set off for Ukhaidir.

~

The palace was the closest thing to a mirage Agatha had ever seen. It seemed to appear from nowhere after miles of featureless sand and scrubland. Its coral-colored walls rose like a cliff out of the plain, vultures circling the turreted towers at its four corners.

"It's amazing!" Agatha leaned forward, shading her eyes. "How on earth did they build something so enormous all those years ago?"

"Impressive, isn't it?" Max nodded. "Those walls are over sixty feet tall. I hope you've got a head for heights."

Inside the battlements was a vast empty space. The only remnants of the pleasure palace it had once been were fallen stone columns decorated with acanthus leaves. Max explained that the main attraction for visitors was climbing to the parapets to see the panoramic views of the desert. It was only when they emerged from a spiral staircase that she appreciated just how high the walls were.

"Oh!" She steadied herself on the remains of a stone archway. The precipitous drop made her feel dizzy. "It's quite terrifying, isn't it?"

"Take my hand if you like." Max reached out to her. "We'll take it nice and slowly."

His hand felt warm and firm in hers. He led her along the battlements to one of the towers, whose narrow window revealed an amazing sight. The dusty yellow of the desert gave way to a sparkling expanse of turquoise water.

"That's *Bahr al Milh,*" he said. "It means Sea of Salt in Arabic."

"It's breathtaking." She stood very still, wondering if he would release her hand now that they were no longer moving. But he didn't. "Is that where we're going for our picnic?"

"Yes. There's a lovely spot on the south side. It's very peaceful—no one around but the odd fisherman. We can kick off our shoes and dip our toes in the water if you like."

He was close enough for her to breathe in the scent of him. Sun-warmed skin with a hint of something sharp and aromatic, like thyme or eucalyptus. Agatha felt that fizzing sensation in her belly—the same feeling as when their bodies had accidentally touched in the darkness at the shrine of the moon god. She was aware of perspiration beading her forehead and hoped that her hand didn't feel clammy in his.

He kept hold of it. All the way round the parapet, not letting go until they reached the bottom of the staircase.

The Bedouin guard was waiting for them beside the truck, which Max had parked in the shade of the walls. His rifle was laid beside him, on top of a sack of onions. Max said something to him in Arabic, and he hitched up his robe, jumping nimbly into the back, where he perched on one of the other sacks of produce destined for the kitchen at Sahra' Alqamar.

Agatha was surprised at how quickly they reached the lake. From the palace walls it had looked a long way away, but they were there in less than half an hour.

"Are you hungry?" Max jumped out and came round to open the door for her, taking her hand again as she stepped down onto the sand.

"I am quite hungry," she admitted. "But I'm very warm. Could we go for a paddle first, do you think?" She would have liked to do more than just paddle. The lake looked so inviting. It reminded her of the seaside at Torquay. Long days spent on the beach as a child. Swimming was a passion she hadn't had the chance to indulge very often while married to Archie.

"Do you fancy a proper swim?" Max must have seen it in her face.

"That would be heavenly—but I didn't think to bring a swimsuit. What a pity."

"I wonder if we could . . ." Max looked at his feet. "Could you . . . improvise, perhaps?" He glanced back at the truck. "I'll get our friend to turn his back. And I promise to swim with my eyes closed."

Agatha's heart missed a beat. Could she? Should she? All she had on under her dress was a silk vest and knickers. It was too hot, out here, for any more underwear than that. She could just about preserve her modesty going into the lake—but she knew very well that her garments would become completely transparent once they got wet. She might as well be naked, coming out.

"Well, I . . . ," she faltered. The lake looked so tempting. "What would we dry ourselves on?"

"We can drip-dry in this heat." Max grinned. "But I can offer you a couple of sacks to wrap yourself in when you come out: not very luxurious, I'm afraid—but better than nothing . . ."

"And you promise you won't look?" She was smiling, too, now.

"Scout's honor." He touched his fingers to the side of his head.

Max was already in the water when she stepped out of the truck. She glanced down at her body, painfully aware of her lily-white legs and the little mound of baby fat that she had never quite managed to lose since giving birth to Rosalind. She took a deep breath, trying to flatten it, just in case Max or the guard were looking. It was just a few yards to the water's edge. She decided to take it at a run, plunging into the glorious coolness.

"Bravo!"

Max appeared suddenly from under the water. He was a couple of feet away from her, and his eyes were tightly shut.

"You can open them now if you like," she said. "I'm quite decent from the neck up."

She watched his eyelids part to reveal the irises. In the light reflected off the water, they were the color of melting chocolate.

"It's lovely, isn't it?" He tilted his head back and floated on the surface, his shorts rippling over his thighs. "I can't tell you how good it feels after weeks and weeks in an excavation pit."

"I can imagine." Agatha was trying not to look at his legs. Golden brown and muscular, with a peppering of dark hairs glistening in the sun. She glanced across the lake, afraid that he might catch her staring. "Is that a jetty over there? Could we swim to it?"

"Yes, if you're feeling energetic." Max slid back into an upright position.

She launched into a powerful crawl. "I'll race you!" she shouted over her shoulder.

She heard him laughing as he came up behind her. Their hands grasped the wood of the jetty at the same moment.

"Whoa! Where did you learn to swim like that?" He took a lungful of air and heaved himself onto the platform, offering her both hands as she went to pull herself out.

"I grew up by the sea. I can't remember actually learning. My sister taught me, I think." She realized, too late, that she was sitting next to him, dripping wet. And his eyes were open. Her hands went to her breasts. Then she remembered the knickers and tried to cover that part of her body as well.

"I'm awfully sorry," he said. "I . . . I forgot to close my eyes."

Seeing his face, she couldn't help giggling. Beneath the tan he was actually blushing. She gave up trying to cover herself and put a hand over his face instead. His skin felt as cool and smooth as wet clay.

He put his hand up to hers, tracing the outline of her fingers. "You're very beautiful."

The words hung in the air like a peal of thunder. Had he really said that? She felt suddenly tongue-tied, paralyzed. The water lapped against the struts of the jetty. Somewhere behind them a bird gave a piping call from its nest in the reeds.

Gently, he moved her hand from his eyes to his lips. The kiss was barely perceptible, as light as a butterfly brushing her skin. But its effect was electric. Her whole body pulsed with it.

"Oh, Max . . ." She looked deep into those melting eyes, wondering what her mother would say if she could see her now, sitting at the edge of a lake, as good as naked, with this young man.

But for once her mother remained absolutely silent.

"We should go back." He let go of her hand, looking away from her, across the lake. He meant to the truck, to the picnic packed in baskets—no doubt getting warmer and less appetizing with every passing hour. But she wondered if he now regretted that kiss. Those words.

With hardly a splash, he slid into the water. She followed him back to the shore, keeping her distance, treading water as he climbed up the bank. She waited for him to fetch the sacks from the truck. Saw him turn his back and walk away. Was he being a gentleman or had he lost interest in her already?

They ate their lunch in uncomfortable silence. She wanted to ask him what he was thinking. But she didn't. The intensity of what he had stirred up frightened her. He made some remark about a fishing boat that appeared out on the lake, about the chances of buying fresh fish to take back to the dig house—a rare treat, he said, for people living for months on end in the desert. Did he mean to pretend that kiss had never happened? Perhaps he was as afraid of his feelings as she was. She picked at the food, too churned up inside to feel like eating.

He wandered off when the meal was over, leaving her to put away the remains of the food. She covered the baskets with cloth to keep the flies off and packed them into the truck, wondering where he could have gone. She walked to the water's edge and back, pacing like a caged lion, her mind in turmoil. In a bid to still her thoughts, she went to the truck and got her notebook from her bag, scribbling down everything she had seen since leaving the expedition house. But all she could think of as she formed the words was the look in Max's eyes when he kissed her. Tossing the notebook back into her bag, she hurried back down to the lake, scanning the horizon. Suddenly he appeared. He was carrying something. The color was vivid orange against his khaki clothes. As he drew nearer, she saw what it was. An armful of flowers. Wild marigolds. Threaded through each other like a daisy chain.

"For you." He lifted the garland over her head, placing it round her neck. "There's a great patch of them—just beyond those bushes."

"How lovely of you!" She wanted to kiss him. Properly this time. But she was aware of curious glances from the Bedouin guard, who had followed her down to the lake when she went to look for Max.

"We'd better be getting back." Max's eyes were full of promise. "They'll be wondering where we've got to."

They all climbed into the truck, and he started the engine. It made a whining, jarring sound as it turned over. Muttering under his breath, he jumped out. Soon he and the guard were shoveling sand from under the wheels. But no amount of digging solved the problem.

"I'm sorry to say we're well and truly stuck." Max leaned in through the open window, perspiration trickling from his temples. "My fault for stopping here. The sand's still damp from the downpour we had a couple of weeks ago. I should have realized."

"Is there anything I can do? I could start the engine while you two push?"

"No—thank you for offering—the sand's up over the wheel arches. We're going to have to find someone to pull us out."

After praying to Allah, the guard set off on foot for the twenty-mile journey to get help. "We're in for a very long wait, I'm afraid." Max's face was grave. "I shouldn't have put you through this. I feel awful."

"It's all right." Agatha jumped out of the truck and walked round to the driver's side, which was in the shade. She spread out the sacks she had dried herself on and lay down on them. "Don't worry about me. I'll just go to sleep for a while."

He knelt down beside her with a wry smile. "You really are a most remarkable woman, Mrs. Christie. If Katharine Woolley had been with me instead of you, I'd never have heard the last of it. She'd have spent the next however-many hours berating me for my incompetence, getting us stuck in the middle of nowhere."

"Really?"

"Really." Max scooped up a handful of sand, making a pillow-shaped mound next to her head. "Would it be very forward of me to ask if I could lie down next to you?"

Agatha sat up, fingering her necklace of marigolds. "It was lovely of you to give me these. Forgive me for being wary, but"—she took a breath—"you know that I've been badly hurt and . . . What I'm trying to say is . . . it's hard to understand why someone like you would be interested in someone like me."

There was a moment of silence. Max made a spiral pattern in the sand with his finger. "Because you *are* interesting." He whispered the words as if he was afraid of being overheard. "You're talented, you're good company, and you have the most wonderful eyes. There. I've said it."

Now she fell silent. She felt blood surging up from her neck into her face. How long was it since anyone had said anything like this to her? Archie used to say romantic things. Many years ago. Before Rosalind was born. "Thank you," she murmured. "That's . . . very flattering. But . . . well, for one thing, I'm a good deal older than you. I've been married. And I have a child." She paused. He was drawing in the sand again: her name this time. "What could possibly come of it?"

"Well, if we can see a bit more of each other, perhaps we could find out." He rubbed the sand from his fingers and took her hand. "Listen, I've got to go back to London before Christmas. Please don't repeat this: we dug up a solid gold death mask earlier this month, and Leonard doesn't want to risk sending it back through the usual channels. He wants me to take it in person. I was wondering . . . When are you thinking of going home? Perhaps we could travel together?"

"That would be . . ."

He kissed her before she could finish the sentence. Cupping her head in his hand, he eased her gently down, his mouth exploring hers. Her tongue traced the edges of his lips, tasting salt from the lake mixed with his own perspiration. She felt the hardness of his body as he wrapped his arms around her. Felt the sand in her hair as they rolled off the sacks. She should stop. But it felt so . . . Words exploded into colors in her head. *Why not*, she thought? *Why shouldn't we?*

His lips were tracing a path down her neck when two shots rang out somewhere in the distance. Max leapt up.

"Stay down! Get under the truck if you can." He got in front of her, shielding her with his body. Reaching backward, he grabbed a pair of field glasses from inside the vehicle. "Well, I'll be blowed! It's Mahmoud—he's found somebody!"

She jumped up. Max was waving at what looked like a moving dot on the horizon. As they watched, they saw that it was a car—an old Model T Ford. By an amazing stroke of luck, the guard had run into it—a car crammed full of passengers on their way from Najaf to Basra. There were fourteen of them—all men—and they got out and lifted the truck bodily out of the sand.

The journey back to Ur was a silent one. Agatha felt overwhelmed by what had happened. Her brain was on fire, reliving each sensual moment, but she couldn't shut out the voices—her mother's, and Archie's—telling her she should be ashamed of herself, that no lady would ever allow herself to get into such a situation.

Once or twice she glanced at Max, wondering what he was thinking. His expression was unreadable.

When they reached the expedition house, he jumped out of the truck and came to open the door for her. "I've got to unload the supplies, then get over to the dig site to give out the wages," he said. "Will you be all right here on your own for a while?"

She nodded. "Max . . . I . . . ," she stammered. What had seemed so natural and right out there in the desert now seemed horribly embarrassing.

"I hope you don't think I was taking advantage this afternoon," he said. "I meant what I said—about wanting to get to know you better. Will you consider what we talked about? About traveling back together?"

She leaned forward and kissed his nose.

CHAPTER 23

The next morning, Agatha woke up knowing something was different. Her senses registered the scuttle of a bird on the roof, the scent of the wilting flowers on the bedside table, the creak of a door opening farther along the corridor. Everything was sharper, crisper, as if she had been living life behind a veil until yesterday. Something had happened to her in the desert. Something important. When Max had hung the marigold garland around her neck, she had glimpsed the person she used to be. Before Archie.

She reached for the chain of flowers, burying her face in the limp petals. If it wasn't for this tangible proof, she would have been asking herself if it had really happened.

She wondered what Max was thinking as he woke up this morning. They had skirted round each other last evening, casting shy glances across the table at suppertime. Then he had been summoned by Leonard to look at a collection of tools unearthed at the dig that afternoon. They had still been holed up together when she went to bed.

After dinner she and Nancy had continued with the task Katharine had set them, of piecing together shards of pottery. They were working alone, as Katharine had gone to help Leonard and Max.

Agatha had found it hard to keep quiet about what had happened at the lake. She was burning to talk about this sudden, unexpected chance of romance, but it seemed unfair even to mention it, given Nancy's predicament. And so they had talked about pretty much everyone else in the expedition team apart from Max.

Nancy was concerned about Katharine's marriage, having overheard the Woolleys talking together in the courtyard when she was sent to the darkroom to collect some photographs. "Katharine gave him such a tongue-lashing," she said. "All over some problem with the quality of the last crate of oranges they'd bought, which didn't seem the least bit important. And he was so patient with her. Never raised his voice once." Agatha didn't repeat what Max had told her about the physical side of the Woolleys' marriage. It would be disloyal, she thought, to sit in the home of their host and hostess, discussing their sex life—or lack of it.

"They're an odd couple," Nancy went on. "He's very distant, isn't he? Not the type of man you'd imagine being interested in marriage. I get the impression that a fragment of antique pottery is always more exciting to him than a mere human being born somewhere in the twentieth century AD."

Agatha nodded.

"Do you think it's a marriage of convenience? I mean, they sleep in separate rooms . . ." There was a look of recognition on Nancy's face, a look of bitter experience.

Agatha tried to change the subject then, not wanting to drag up memories that would do Nancy no good. A minute later Katharine appeared with a tray of coffee—the set that Agatha had bought as a wedding present. She was in very good spirits, full of praise for their efforts with the pottery. What she had brought them, she said, was what the Arabs called wild-colored coffee, ground with green cardamom, cinnamon sticks, and saffron. Then she taught them the etiquette that went with it.

"You'll need to know this tomorrow, when we go to the feast at the Bedouin village," she said. "Don't be offended when the person with the coffeepot passes you by to serve a man first. That's their custom—and they always begin with the eldest." She held up the swan-necked pot. "This is called a *dallah*, and cups like these—with no handles—are called *finjan*. At official functions they pour it from a distance of about a foot, because it's considered disrespectful to get any closer to the guest than that." She demonstrated, pouring a cup for each of them. "The cup will only be a quarter full, so it's not too hot and easy to savor the taste. The person offering it to you will say *samm*, which is an invitation to say the name of God."

"Do we have to say Allah, then?" Nancy asked.

Katharine nodded. "They don't mind if you're not a Muslim—they don't think it's hypocritical or anything. They believe our God and theirs is just the same, only with a different name." She lifted her cup and breathed in the aroma. "Once you've drunk it, there are two choices: shaking the cup indicates that you'd like some more, or tipping it upside down shows that you've had enough."

"Mmm—that's delicious!" Agatha drained her cup and shook it. "Where did you get it from? I must buy some to take home."

"You can get it from any of the stalls in the spice souk in Baghdad," Katharine replied. "You just have to know what to ask for, and they'll mix it for you."

Watching Katharine during that hour before bedtime, Agatha saw no hint of the angst Max had described. Agatha wondered if she would be taking a bath when they had all gone off to their rooms. The thought of Leonard sitting there, watching her, not allowed to touch, was almost unimaginable. How could any man be expected to restrain himself in a situation like that? It would be pure torture.

When Agatha went for breakfast, Katharine was sitting alone in the courtyard. She looked up from the book she was reading. "Will you come for a walk with me? Just a short one before we go and eat." She was smiling, but her voice betrayed her. Agatha sensed the tension in it. She wondered what was coming.

Katharine led her past the snoozing dogs, out of the gates of the compound, toward a place where the ground dipped slightly. There was a dried-up streambed with stunted bushes growing alongside it and the odd patch of dwarf tulips—same as the ones in the vase in Agatha's room.

"Did you enjoy your outing with Max yesterday?"

Ah, so this was what it was about. Agatha wondered how much Max had told her. "Yes," she replied, trying to keep her voice neutral. "It was very interesting—and very pleasant."

"You went to the lake?"

"Yes—it's lovely, isn't it?

"And Max went for a swim."

This took Agatha by surprise. She couldn't imagine him revealing that to Katharine. Not after everything he'd said about her.

"Don't try to cover up for him," Katharine said. "I saw his shorts hanging on the washing line this morning. He only ever washes them once a week—always on Saturdays. It's a dead giveaway." She took off her hat, swishing it at the cloud of flies that had formed around them. "I hope he behaved himself. He knows what an important guest you are. I wouldn't want him taking liberties . . ." She trailed off with a violent swipe a couple of inches from Agatha's left ear.

"Why would you think that?" Agatha wondered if Katharine had spotted her underwear on the line yesterday. It had never occurred to her, as she pegged it out, that anyone would guess she'd been swimming in it. Washing out one's underwear after a hot day in the desert seemed an entirely natural thing to do.

"Because I know him." Katharine turned to her, fire in her eyes. "He's a red-blooded young man, and you're an attractive, clever, successful woman. You have to be careful, Agatha. Face facts. Men will want you—not always for the right reasons."

Her words made Agatha's stomach flip over. Suddenly she saw yesterday in a harsh new light. Max holding her hand on the palace walls, the swim in the lake, the clinch in the sand: had it all been a ploy to sweeten her up for the Woolleys? She could almost hear Katharine giving him his orders: *Make her feel good, flatter her a little. Then she might give us some money* . . . Clearly, he had gone too far for Katharine's liking. Above and beyond the call of duty. And like a fool Agatha had lapped it up. It occurred to her that he had even stage-managed the car getting stuck in the sand, so he could send the guard off and be alone with her.

The flies buzzed round her ears, drowning out the voices in her head. Her mother, gentle but firm, telling her she should have known better. And Archie. In the cold, hateful tone she had first heard at Harrogate. Deriding her for thinking any man would find her desirable now—let alone a man as young as Max.

But then Max's voice broke through the others. The memory of him asking her to travel back with him to London. Why would he have pressed her to spend the best part of a week cooped up on a train with him if it was all a sham?

Katharine was still looking at her, waiting for her to respond. Agatha surged with indignation at this calculated attempt to warn her off. Clearly, Katharine was jealous. She had once had Max in her thrall, but he had broken free of her. And she couldn't stand to see him drawn to someone else.

"We swam together." Agatha tried not to betray any emotion in her voice. "It was a hot day, and we decided to go in. Max was a perfect gentleman about it. He kept his eyes closed the whole time we were in the water."

Katharine said nothing for a moment. Then: "Oh. I'm surprised at you, Agatha. I didn't have you down as such a . . . a *free* spirit."

Agatha's jaw clenched. "Let me remind you, Katharine," she said, struggling now, to keep her voice level. "You're married. Max isn't. And neither am I. What does it matter to you if we enjoy each other's company?"

"Oh! Please don't tell me you're in love with him!"

"Don't be ridiculous!" Agatha felt herself blushing. "I can't think why you're getting so het up about it: perhaps you should be asking *yourself* that question!"

It was as if she had fired a gun. Katharine suddenly dropped to the ground. She sat in the sand with her head in her hands.

"Katharine!" Agatha knelt down beside her. "What is it?"

Katharine lifted her head a little. Her eyes brimmed with tears. "I . . . I'm sorry. I hate myself!"

"Hate yourself?" Agatha's heart hammered against her ribs. Was she right, then? Was Katharine in love with Max?

"I . . . It isn't . . ." Katharine mumbled.

"Isn't what?"

"I . . . It . . . isn't him." Her mouth trembled as she spoke. "M . . . Max. I try to . . . control people, you see. I know it's wrong, but I . . . It's my . . ." She pressed her lips together as if she was afraid of what she might say.

Agatha took her hand. "What's this about? Can you tell me?"

"I . . . I c . . . can't." Katharine's teeth rattled with each syllable. "I . . . th . . . thought I could do it . . . b . . . but I can't."

"Take deep breaths." Agatha wiped a tear from Katharine's face. "There. That's better. Don't try to talk if you don't want to."

When Katharine spoke again, her voice was steadier. "I've . . . relied too much on Max," she said. "He's been a friend. A comforter."

"But you've got Leonard now, haven't you?" Agatha held her breath, wondering what was coming.

"I haven't, though." The sound she made was something between a sob and a sigh. "I can't be a wife to him, Agatha. Not to Leonard or anyone else."

"What? Why not?" Agatha thought, fleetingly, that Katharine was about to confess to a preference for her own sex. But that couldn't be so, could it? According to Max, she was a man-eater.

"I wanted to tell you the day of the wedding, but I was afraid to. You see, I've never told anyone." Katharine's eyes dropped to the patch of sand between them.

"What?" Agatha whispered. "What did you want to say?"

Katharine glanced up at her, then looked away, toward the horizon. "When Bertram died—the day he killed himself—he'd sent for a doctor. To see me." She fumbled in her pocket, pulling out a handkerchief to wipe her nose. "We'd been having . . . problems, you see."

She fell silent again. Agatha held her breath, afraid that anything she asked now would sound like prying.

"I . . . We . . . found it difficult. Impossible . . . to . . . ," Katharine faltered, searching Agatha's face. "Do you understand what I'm saying?"

Agatha nodded. She didn't. Not really. She wasn't certain if Katharine was talking about her sex life with her first husband or their inability to conceive a child. But she sensed that to ask outright would be like prodding a snail emerging from its shell.

"I wanted to, of course," Katharine went on. "I adored Bertram from the moment I set eyes on him. But on our wedding night . . . we . . . I . . . I mean, they tell you it's going to be painful, the first time, don't they? But I never dreamed it could hurt as much as that. And it never got any easier. Every time he . . ." She brought the handkerchief up to her nose. "After six months we decided to call in a doctor. We were in Egypt at the time, and it wasn't long after the war, so it wasn't easy to find one. He . . . examined me. I'll never forget the look on his face as he told me to get dressed. I asked him what was wrong with me, but he wouldn't tell me. He said he had to see my husband first."

Agatha saw another tear trickle down Katharine's face and land without a sound in the sand.

"I only found out later what he'd said." Katharine closed her eyes, a residue of tears seeping out at the corners. "It might have been the language. He spoke Arabic, of course, and his English was limited. But the way he put it was utterly blunt. He told Bertram that he had married a man, not a woman."

"What?" Agatha's mouth fell open. This was unbelievable. She had seen Katharine, naked, at the hammam in Damascus. She had the kind of body women envied and men dreamed of. A more perfect specimen of womanliness was hard to imagine. What wickedness had been in this doctor's mind?

"He had discovered that I had no . . . female parts. Not inside, anyway. No womb, no ovaries. And only a very tiny . . ." Katharine's voice died away, her face ghostly. "That's why it was so painful, you see."

"Oh, Katharine . . ." Agatha gathered her up, feeling her shoulders heave with sobs. Now she understood it all. The suicide. The look in Katharine's eyes when she came down the aisle at the church in Baghdad. The nightly bathing ritual designed to keep Leonard at arm's length. And the way she toyed with men like Max—even that was comprehensible, seen through this new lens. How wretched, to be attracted to a man, to sense that he was attracted to you, knowing all the while that mutual desire could never be consummated.

"There's no . . . name for it." Katharine raised her head, dabbing at her face with her handkerchief. "I tried to find out, of course, when I got back to England. I'm a freak of nature, is about all the medical books say. One in a hundred thousand is born like me. The curse of it is we look like real women—on the outside. And we *feel* like real women, too."

"Katharine, forgive me—I have to ask you this." Agatha paused. It wasn't prying. If she was going to be of any help to Katharine, she needed to know. "Why did you marry Leonard?"

A look of resignation crossed Katharine's face. "I thought you'd ask me that. And you're not going to like the answer. The fact is I had no choice. The trustees didn't approve of me being out here as a single woman. If I hadn't married him, I'd have lost my job. He proposed and I accepted."

"Does he know?"

"God, no!" Katharine gave a little shudder. "Do you think he'd have married me if he had? He might come across as a cold fish, but it turns out he's as keen on . . . that side of things . . . as any man."

"But you must have realized what you were letting yourself in for?"

"Not really," Katharine said with a shrug. "I thought he was marrying me as much for his own convenience as mine. He'd never betrayed any interest in women. I actually wondered if he might be homosexual. When I realized that he wasn't, I . . . well, I convinced myself that I could do just what I've done with other men: let him do . . . certain things . . . but not come too close, keep him at arm's length. But it's . . ." She broke off, shaking her head. "He was very patient at first, but now he keeps asking me when I'm going to let him into my bed."

"Do you love him?"

"What a question!" Katharine clicked her tongue. "I like him. I respect him. But . . . I don't know if I could ever love anyone again. Not after Bertram."

"That's understandable." Agatha nodded. "But is it really fair to string him along like this? Couldn't you come to some sort of . . . compromise?" She wondered how to say what she was thinking without making things even more excruciatingly embarrassing for Katharine.

"What do you mean?"

Agatha hesitated. "It's not my place to tell you how to behave within your own marriage, Katharine. But wouldn't it be better to have it out in the open? I can't believe a man as intelligent as Leonard wouldn't show some understanding if he knew the facts."

"What if he went the other way? Had the marriage annulled?"

"Does he love you?"

"He says he does."

"Then he'll remember the vows he made, won't he?" Agatha said. "For better, for worse. Till death us do part."

"I can't imagine anything much worse than being told your wife is incapable of the one thing that makes marriage different from every other kind of relationship."

"But there *are* worse things," Agatha said. "Sickness. Disability. People marry and stay together despite things like that." She paused. "You say he's very patient. Can't you give him the benefit of the doubt? Give him the chance to find a way through this? Because if you *don't* tell him, you're condemning yourself to a life of misery, aren't you? No job can be worth that."

Katharine said nothing. There was a distant look in her eyes.

"You're living a lie, just as I was with Archie in the end," Agatha said. "I know what that feels like. It's an intolerable burden. That's why I had a breakdown—and the same thing could happen to you if you don't open up to Leonard."

Katharine nodded. It was the slightest movement, almost imperceptible. "I know you're right. But I'm not sure I'm brave enough. How could I tell him?"

"Well, you told me. That's a start, isn't it?"

"I suppose so." She nodded again, with a little more conviction this time. "You won't tell anyone, though, will you? Not Max or Nancy. I couldn't bear it if everyone was whispering about me."

"Of course I won't." Agatha squeezed her hand. "I promise you, your secret's safe with me."

CHAPTER 24

It was several hours before Agatha saw Katharine again. They got back to the expedition house to discover that an official from the British Consulate in Baghdad had arrived at Ur Junction and was on his way to see them. The news sent everyone into a flurry of activity. Breakfast was cleared hurriedly away, and each member of the household—including Agatha and Nancy—was assigned part of the house to tidy up at top speed.

"Why is he coming?" Nancy called over her shoulder as she plumped up the cushions on the sofa.

"I don't know," Agatha called back. Her job was to empty the ash-trays, which were dotted all over the house and were always overflowing with cigarette butts in the mornings. "I suppose they have to keep an eye on things, with all the valuable goods being unearthed here."

"I expect he's coming about the trouble in Basra." Michael's face, with its frame of ginger whiskers, appeared round the door. "There's been an uprising near the border. Nothing for us to worry about—but they might want us to keep our eyes open."

Max had been dispatched to collect the visitor. By the time he drove through the gates, the house was looking fairly respectable. Agatha and Nancy watched through the living room window as Leonard and Katharine went to greet the new arrival.

"I've seen him before," Nancy said. "He's the assistant to the High Commissioner. His name is Hugh Carrington. Not very nice, I'm afraid."

"About Delia?"

Nancy nodded. "He tried to fob me off. Said there was no point pursuing the matter because it came under the Official Secrets Act. When I insisted on seeing his boss, he got very nasty. He didn't *say* anything unpleasant, but his manner was glacial. He made me feel like a nuisance, an intruder."

Agatha and Nancy didn't actually see Hugh Carrington face-to-face until later that day. Max drove them to the dig site so that Leonard and Katharine could be left alone with him.

There was a tent pitched in the shade of the ziggurat, where Nancy sat reading while Agatha went to one of the new trenches. Max gave her a trowel and a brush and showed her what to do.

"If you find anything—anything at all—just shout," he said.

It was thrilling, kneeling there in the sand like a real archaeologist. Before long, Agatha's trowel made contact with something hard. She brushed away the sand to reveal the tip of something blue and glassy. She called out to Max, who came running.

"A shard of a goblet, by the look of it," he said. "Don't worry too much about getting it out intact—it's much later than the period we're interested in: only a thousand years old at the most."

"Oh! What a shame."

Max smiled at Agatha's crestfallen expression.

"You can keep it if you like. Take it home as a souvenir of your visit."

By the time they went back to the house, Agatha had a bag full. The colored shards reminded her of the fragments of sea glass she sometimes used to find washed up on the beach as a child. Tiny pieces of blue, green, and amber, their edges worn smooth by the waves. She laid her new finds out on the bed of her room in the annex, angling them to the sun so that they glowed like jewels.

Only a thousand years old at the most.

It made her smile, remembering Max's words. She lay down next to her treasure trove, closing her eyes as images of the day before flooded in. Was it dangerous to let her mind run on? To imagine some kind of future with this man? Was it even remotely possible, with the kind of life he led?

She had fallen into a doze when his voice woke her up. He was on the other side of the door, telling her it was time to go to the Bedouin village for the sheikh's feast.

"I'll take you first, if you don't mind," Max said when she opened the door. His tone was businesslike. She wondered why. Then she saw that Duncan was coming along the corridor toward him. "Pierre and Michael and Duncan will go with you. Then I'll come back for Katharine and Leonard and our other visitor."

Max took them in the truck, the men in the back on sacks, and Agatha and Nancy in the front. Agatha was in the middle, her leg against the gear stick. There was a moment when Max's hand slipped. She felt the heat of his skin through the fabric of her skirt.

"Oh—sorry!" He jerked his hand away, glancing sideways. She could see that he was trying not to smile. She smiled back, knowing that Nancy wouldn't see. Images of the day before slid into her mind's eye again. His body glistening with water, his face hovering over hers as she lay in the sand, the look in his eyes when he kissed her.

"Is that Hamoudi?" Nancy's voice broke into her reverie. She was peering through the window, shading her eyes.

"Yes, it is." Max waved at the robed figure riding toward them on the back of a mule. When they drew level, he wound down the window and said something in Arabic. After a brief conversation, they were on their way again. "He went to tell them about our visitor," Max said. "It can be a little tricky if government officials turn up uninvited. It makes the tribesmen uneasy—and things are delicate enough as it is."

"Is it going to be all right?" Nancy sounded nervous.

"Oh yes—please don't worry," Max said. "It's just etiquette, you know—doing things by the book. Very important in this part of the world." He slowed down as the tented village came into view. "By the way, don't be offended if they seat you two in a different place from the rest of us. Their women aren't allowed at the feast, you see. Western women are admitted, but they're kept well away from the men."

He pulled up by the wooden palisade that encircled the village. As they stepped out, Agatha could smell the mouthwatering aroma of roasting meat. It was coming from a pit dug in the sand. Next to it, suspended over a fire, was a huge copper cauldron being stirred by two robed men.

"Come and meet the sheikh," Max said. "But don't try to shake his hand—they're not allowed to. Just nod your head."

Sheikh Munshid of the Ghazi was a striking individual with an emerald-green headdress and a henna-tinted beard. He greeted them with a bow under the wide brown canopy of his open tent. Once they had been introduced, Agatha and Nancy were ushered to the far end of the enormous space in which the feast was to be served. They sat on jewel-colored cushions laid on goatskin rugs, watching Max present Michael, Pierre, and Duncan to the sheikh.

When Max left to collect the others from the expedition house, Agatha heard the muffled sound of giggles coming from somewhere behind them.

"Who's that?" Nancy had heard it, too.

Agatha glanced over her shoulder. There was a partition screening off part of the tent, and she could see something moving through the fabric—an elbow or a shoulder made a lump that vanished as quickly as it had appeared.

It wasn't until Katharine arrived and took her place next to them that they found out what was going on. "Those are the sheikh's womenfolk," she said. "They're not allowed to sit with us, but they like to peep at the guests and listen to what's going on."

The tent was filling up with Bedouin men. Agatha lost count at thirty. When everyone was seated in a big circle, the sheikh gave an order and a man on his left went out, returning with a falcon perched on his wrist. He set the bird on a wooden perch in the middle of the tent. Max leaned across to the sheikh and said something in Arabic. Agatha and Nancy looked at Katharine.

"He's congratulating the sheikh on his magnificent bird," Katharine said. "It's all part of the ritual. Because we pay him to protect us, he has to show us his prize possession and we have to compliment him." She smiled. "Don't worry—it doesn't last long. The food will be here soon."

Sure enough the falcon was carried out and three men appeared, carrying the huge copper cauldron Agatha had seen when they arrived. They set it down in the middle of the circle, curls of smoke snaking out over the guests. The air was full of a delicious mix of spices and roast lamb.

"The pot is full of rice," Katharine said, "and the meat is cooked on a spit, then laid on the top. They'll come round with flaps of Arab bread in a minute. You have to help yourself from the cauldron and eat it with your fingers."

The men were served first. Agatha's stomach rumbled as she watched the sheikh and the elderly men of the village walk in procession to the cauldron, followed by Max and the others, and finally, the younger Bedouin men. Would there be anything left?

She needn't have worried. When everyone in the circle had had several helpings, the cauldron was still half-full. When the women had eaten their fill, it was lifted up and set down in a second circle where the lesser guests sat. Agatha noticed Hamoudi and Saleem among them.

Meanwhile, plates of sweetmeats were handed round the sheikh's circle, and coffee was served. Agatha bit into a square of something that was brown on top with a biscuit-colored base.

"Oh—this is delicious!" She took another from the proffered plate. "What is it?"

"It's called *holwah tamar*," Katharine said. "They make it with dates, walnuts, and sesame seeds."

"What's going on over there?" Nancy was looking toward the front of the tent. A crowd of ragged-looking men and woman had gathered just beyond the threshold. They all looked undernourished and were peering into the tent with anxious faces.

"They're waiting for the leftovers," Katharine replied. "They get anything that's still in the pot when the servants have finished. It'll be bones, mainly, and a bit of rice. But they're beggars. They'll take whatever's on offer."

The women watched what happened when the cauldron was taken outside. The waiting crowd flung themselves upon the food, and when the big copper pot was lifted, it was tipped toward the tent so that those inside could see that it was quite empty.

The sheikh got to his feet and nodded at the men sitting around him. It looked as if he was about to make a speech. Instead, he slid his hand inside the shawl draped over his shoulders and pulled out a pistol. There was a collective gasp as he pointed it at Leonard Woolley.

"Oh God," Katharine hissed. "What's he doing?"

Leonard glanced at Max, who said something in Arabic. The sheikh laughed and said something back. Katharine gasped, clutching Agatha's arm.

"What's happening?" Agatha whispered. "What did he say?"

"Max asked him if the gun's loaded." Katharine's grip tightened. "He said yes, what would be the point otherwise . . . and that he bought it with the money paid to him by our . . ."

The sight of Max rising from his cushion stopped her dead. He was saying something else to the sheikh. Pointing at something outside the tent. With a broad smile, the sheikh turned round and took aim. A bullet whizzed over the heads of his fellow tribesmen, swiftly followed by a terrific crack outside. All the Bedouin men roared with laughter as they flocked out to see what the sheikh had hit.

Max hurried over to where the women were sitting. "Don't be alarmed," he said. "It's just one of the urns they carry water in. I thought I'd better distract him with a bit of target practice!"

"The man's a lunatic!" Katharine huffed out a breath. "Poor Len: he's gone as white as a sheet!"

"Do you think you should go to him?" Nancy said.

"I can't." Katharine shrugged. "It would be considered very bad form for any of us to go to the men's end of the tent."

"But Max has come down to us."

"That's different, I'm afraid." Max grinned. "Terribly one-sided, I know, but that's how things are among these tribes." He turned to see the sheikh and his followers returning to finish their coffee. "Better get back," he said, "or he might point it down this end."

A few minutes later Max was back. "The sheikh has a special request." He looked at Katharine, then Agatha. "He wants you to take a look at some of his wives. They have various health complaints, apparently."

"*Some* of his wives?" Agatha raised her eyebrows. "How many does he have?" "About a dozen, I think. But he may have acquired a couple more since the last time I asked." Max looked as if he was trying very hard not to smile. "You were a nurse, too, weren't you? Do you think you could give Katharine a hand?"

"Well . . . yes, I suppose so." Agatha hesitated. "We don't have any medical equipment, though . . ."

"We do," Katharine said. "The first aid kit's in the back of Queen Mary."

Max and Nancy went to fetch it while the others made their way to the back of the tent through the partition. The sheikh's wives were all waiting there, sitting in line on cushions. The giggling rose to a crescendo when they caught sight of Katharine and Agatha.

"I wish Max could come in with us," Katharine said. "His Arabic is so much better than mine. We'll just have to make the best of it, I suppose."

The women appeared to range in age from midteens to late thirties. There were fifteen of them, and every one of them stepped forward when Katharine asked who was ill. The first one pointed to her eyes.

"Do we have any boric acid in the first aid kit?"

Agatha looked at Katharine, who smiled. "Oh—you don't think it's conjunctivitis?"

"Well, it could be . . ." Katharine chuckled. "I've just twigged what's going on. We were here last year—for this same feast—and I gave boric acid to one of the wives with instructions to bathe her eyes in it. But apparently she misunderstood me and drank it instead."

"Oh dear—what happened?"

"She gave birth to twins a few months later. Two boys. I guess the sheikh is hoping I'll give the stuff to all his wives!"

As if on cue, they heard the sheikh's voice through the partition. He was talking to Max. Katharine's lips twitched. She clapped her hand over her mouth.

"What's he saying?"

"That the *khatun*—that's me—is a miracle worker. He's asking if Max has some of the magic white powder in his box . . ."

It was good to see Katharine laughing. The wives joined in, and it was a while before she and Agatha were in a fit state to find out who was really ill. After giving out headache remedies, iodine, and demonstrating how to bathe sore eyes, they said their good-byes and went back to the truck.

They were the only ones left, Max having already ferried the others back to the compound. Katharine climbed into the middle, between Agatha and Max.

"Our visitor has asked to stay the night," Max said as he started the engine. "He said he didn't fancy sleeping on the train."

"Oh—that's a nuisance." Katharine clicked her tongue. "Trust him to turn up when we're full. He'll have to have Leonard's room, I suppose."

Agatha glanced sideways. Katharine's expression was unreadable. She had been very quick to offer up Leonard's bed. She could surely have asked Max to give up his room and sleep on the roof. Agatha sensed it was a calculated decision. Perhaps this was the night she would tell her husband the truth.

CHAPTER 25

Katharine wasn't asleep when Leonard came to bed, but she pretended to be. She had lain awake in the dark for what seemed like forever, rehearsing it in her head. But when she heard the click of the door latch, she knew she couldn't go through with it.

For the past six weeks she had given him one excuse after another. On their wedding night—the only night they had been alone together at the dig house—she had pretended she was having her monthly period. It was the first of many lies. She had never had a period—had only heard other women talk about them. Then, when more than a week had passed, she told him she had a stomach bug that had left her feeling weak. Then she had used the others as an excuse, saying she felt inhibited by the presence of so many other people in the compound.

It was a month into their marriage that he had resorted to watching her take her bath. Now it had become their nightly ritual. She would knock on the door of the Antiquities Room to tell him that she was going to hit the hay. That was his signal. And when she was standing there, naked, about to climb into the tub, she would hear the telltale scrape of the wooden stool he brought outside each evening to stand on.

Two nights ago he had knocked on the door and asked if he could come to her room when she went to bed. To her shame, she had used Bertram as an excuse, mumbling through the door that it was the anniversary of his death and she was feeling too sad for company. Another lie. Bertram had died in the spring. But Leonard didn't know that. There was so much that he didn't know. But now he was here. In her bedroom. And he had nowhere else to go.

She closed her eyes tight as he padded across the floor. She heard the rustle of his clothes coming off and a slight creak as he placed them on the chair back. Then she felt the bed shift as he climbed in. Her body stiffened. She was facing the wall. She felt his arm brush against hers. It was a gentle, tentative movement.

"Katharine, are you awake?" She lay absolutely still, afraid even to breathe in case the rhythm betrayed her. She heard Agatha's voice in her head. *Go on! Now's your chance! You can't go on like this . . .*

No. She couldn't. But the thought of opening her mouth, of uttering those incriminating words as he lay here beside her made her feel sick with fear.

After a minute or two she felt him shift onto his other side. He had given up. Still she lay there, paralyzed, until she heard the steady breaths of sleep.

What about tomorrow? And the next day . . . Agatha's voice again.

She must tell him. She had to. But not like this. Not in the bedroom, the source of all the trouble. And not face-to-face. Because she couldn't bear the reaction her confession was likely to unleash. Rage and pity and disbelief fused in a look of utter contempt. The same look she had seen in the mirror the day the doctor examined her.

I'll write him a letter. It came to her suddenly. Far better for him to read it than to hear her say it. She would leave it for him to find when she was somewhere else, somewhere well away, so he couldn't confront her until he'd had the chance to calm down. Agatha and Nancy would give her the excuse she needed. Tomorrow was their last day. She would suggest a picnic by the river. Just the three of them.

She took a long, deep breath, stretching just a little in an effort to release the tension in every muscle. She tried to turn her mind to trivial things, like what they would take to eat, whether Nancy would want to swim, how to arrange it all to get the truck back in time to pick up the others from the dig. She made a mental list for the picnic, hoping sleep would overtake her before she got to the end of it. When that didn't work, she tried an A-to-Z of all the food they had in the larder at the expedition house. Anything to shut out those other thoughts. She must sleep. She must.

~

Across the courtyard Nancy was awake, too. She wasn't sure what had brought her out of her usually deep slumber, but as she turned over in bed, she felt a griping pain in her belly.

Her hand went to the spot, rubbing the taut skin through her nightgown. Was it something she had eaten at the feast? She thought about the lamb, roasted in an open pit. What if flies had settled on it? Or perhaps it wasn't cooked all the way through.

She shifted onto her back and the pain subsided. But she was wide awake now. She wondered what time it was. There was no hint of dawn in the star-studded patch of sky beyond the window. She closed her eyes, knowing what she would see.

His face.

Lying here, alone, in the small hours of the night, she felt the lack of him more keenly than ever. The familiar questions crowded her mind. Where would he be at this moment? What would he be doing? Who was he with?

Will he come?

That question was always there, a disturbing whisper which, at times like this, grew loud enough to drown out every other thought in her head. She wondered if there would be a letter waiting when she got back to Baghdad. He hadn't said, in the last one, how things stood with his wife. Perhaps he had decided it would be too cruel to tell her until after Christmas. There was his daughter to consider, of course: not fair to ruin that time of year for her.

Should she tell him about the baby if it was born before he was able to come out to Baghdad? She had written that letter in her imagination countless times. She had promised herself never to use emotional blackmail. But from the moment of that first fluttering inside, the urge to tell him had become overpowering.

How would he react to such a letter? Would he jump on the next available train? Take her and the baby back to London? Where would they live? He was not exactly rich and would still have a wife and child to support. And all she had was the money Delia had left her, which wouldn't last long in London. But he had said he couldn't live in Baghdad . . .

She felt her stomach turn over—a different sensation to the cramping pain of before. This was a familiar churning borne of panic. What if he never came? What sort of life would she make for herself and this baby? Who could she turn to when Agatha went home?

Her mind reeled with too many questions. She must stop thinking. Get back to sleep. For the baby's sake as well as her own. In a bid to distract herself, she tried to think of what she would call the child when it was born. Would it be a son or a daughter? She had read in a magazine that some women had a sixth sense about the sex of the baby they were carrying, but this wasn't true for her. She tried to think of names that would suit both a boy and a girl. She began going through the alphabet.

Alex . . . Frances . . . Hilary . . . Kim . . .
Before she got any further, she was asleep.

~

Katharine wrote the letter before breakfast, while Leonard was in the Antiquities Room. It was the most difficult letter she had ever written in her life. She was baring her soul to the man who held her whole future in his hands. Knowing that it was the right thing to do didn't make it any less harrowing.

When it was finally done, she couldn't push it under his bedroom door because Hugh Carrington was in there. And she didn't want to leave it where someone else might find it. She would have to wait until their visitor had gone.

In the meantime, she busied herself with preparations for the picnic, instructing Ibrahim about food and gathering together blankets, cushions, and towels. She put her camera in the bag that contained her swimsuit. She had been meaning to take pictures all week but had not got round to it. It would be good to have a framed photo of herself and Agatha hanging on the living room wall. A nice conversation piece for future visitors.

If you're still here.

Her hand stopped in midair as she withdrew it from the bag. Would Leonard throw her out when he read that letter? Would she come back from the picnic to find her bags packed?

A sudden knocking pulled her back from a dark spiral of thoughts.

Max was on the other side of the door. "He wants to see the excavations before getting his train. Just thought I'd better warn you."

"He really doesn't like women, does he?" Katharine sighed. "He was quite rude to me yesterday. He said he was surprised to hear that I was working at the dig because he thought a man of Leonard's distinction wouldn't want to be distracted by having his wife on-site." She rolled her eyes. "The cheek of it!"

Max shook his head. "Yes—he's very old-school."

"Well, don't worry—I plan to keep my distance until he's gone back to Baghdad. I'm going to take Agatha and Nancy for a picnic. Will you come back when you've dropped the others off and give us a lift to the river? You can pick us up after lunch."

"Is that wise?" Max frowned. "Leaving you there on your own?"

"It's only for a couple of hours—and I'll take one of the rifles. I can't imagine we'd be of much interest to bandits, without a vehicle."

"Hmm." He looked unconvinced. "Well, if you're sure."

"It's all arranged." A cool smile ghosted onto Katharine's face. "Agatha will love it. She likes swimming, doesn't she?"

~

The place Katharine had chosen for the picnic was in a grove of trees bordering the river. Their boughs hung low, almost touching the emerald-green water, like weeping willows.

"They're Babylonian poplars, actually," Katharine said when Agatha commented on them, "but they do look like willows." She spread a blanket under one of the trees and laid cushions on it. "I thought Nancy might like to sit in the shade while we swim."

Agatha looked across to where Nancy was standing. She had found a patch of wildflowers—tiny blue-and-mauve spikes, like lupins—and was holding one up to her nose.

"It's a shame I haven't got a swimsuit to lend you," Katharine went on. "I only have this one."

"It doesn't matter." Agatha replied without looking round. If Katharine was fishing for details of the outing with Max, she was not going to oblige.

"I need a smoke first anyway."

Katharine went to get her bag, which was hanging from a branch of the tree. Agatha sat down on one of the cushions, watching the river slip lazily by, barely a ripple marring its glassy surface. Soon the pungent aroma of a Turkish cigarette came wafting across the blanket. She watched the smoke curl and rear like a ghostly snake as the warm desert wind took it down to the river.

The water looked very inviting. She couldn't help wishing that it was Max, not Katharine, who was about to go plunging in with her. There had been no chance to be alone with him since their trip to Ukhaidir. No chance even to talk without being overheard. And this was their last day. Tomorrow she and Nancy would be on the train back to Baghdad.

This morning, as they were getting into the truck, Max had given her a look that spoke volumes. It was the kind of look Archie had given her the first time he came to her mother's house in Torquay: a look that seemed to say *I want you so much it hurts.*

Last night, as she lay in bed, she had fantasized about the train ride back to England. Five whole days with Max. It seemed impossibly romantic, getting to know each other while traveling through some of the most breathtaking scenery in the world, stopping off to explore Istanbul and seeing more of Venice.

She hadn't breathed a word of it to Nancy or Katharine. She hadn't said or done anything to fuel Katharine's suspicions about what had happened at the lake. And to say anything to Nancy would be downright cruel, given the heartbreaking situation she was in. But Agatha longed to confide in someone, longed to be told that she was not being foolish to hope for some kind of future with a man like Max.

"Shall we go in?" Katharine's voice startled her. Agatha looked round to see that she was already in her swimsuit. "I changed behind the branches," she said, grinning. "Not that I'm prudish, as you know—but you sometimes get fishermen coming along the river."

Katharine looked so different this morning. It was hard to believe that, less than twenty-four hours ago, she had been so utterly miserable she could barely string two words together. Had she spoken to Leonard, Agatha wondered? Had they managed to work something out? She didn't dare ask.

"I won't be a minute." Agatha ducked under the dangling fronds of the tree. She kicked off her shoes and peeled down her stockings. Then she took off her skirt and blouse. In her bag she had another set of underwear. She pulled the camisole over her head—on top of the one she was already wearing—then stepped into the knickers. Hopefully two pairs, when wet, would preserve her modesty rather more effectively than one. When she emerged, Nancy was settling onto the rug, arranging the cushions to support her back.

"Come on—last one in's a lily-livered landlubber!" Katharine ran toward the river, her long, slim legs bending like saplings in a breeze. Agatha hurried after her, unable to keep up. She had never been particularly athletic. Swimming was the only thing she was reasonably good at. And it was a long time since she had taken any regular exercise. By the time she reached the water's edge, she was out of breath. Katharine was already yards out from the bank.

"Wait for me!" Agatha dived in, feeling the rush of adrenaline as the cold water enveloped her body.

"Let's swim to the other side!" Katharine bobbed up and down, treading water as she waited for Agatha to catch up. As the distance between them closed, Katharine disappeared beneath the surface.

"I'm over here!" Katharine emerged on the other side of the river. When Agatha reached her, Katharine began splashing her mercilessly. "That's . . . your . . . punishment!" She sent a shower of water with each word. "For . . . being . . . last!"

Agatha retaliated by creating a barrage of spray with her feet. Soon they were falling about, helpless with laughter.

"I'm absolutely starving, are you?" Katharine said when they'd both calmed down. "Shall we go and get something to eat?" With effortless strokes, she swam back across the river and scrambled up the bank to where Nancy lay dozing on the blanket. Grabbing a couple of towels, she threw one to Agatha, who was having trouble keeping her balance in the slippery mud at the water's edge.

Nancy sat up, rubbing her face where droplets of water had landed.

"Sorry," Katharine said. She rummaged in her bag and brought out a camera. "Will you take a photo of us?" Before Agatha had time to register what was going on, Katharine bounded over and draped one arm round her shoulder.

"Smile!"

The camera clicked.

"Oh!" Agatha glanced down, dismayed at the thought of being captured on film in this state.

"Don't worry—you can't see anything!" Katharine chuckled. "We'll get another one when we've dried off and got our clothes on. And when Max comes back, I'll get him to take one of the three of us." Agatha was behind the tree, fastening her stockings, when a cry from Nancy stopped her dead.

"What is it? Did something bite you?" Katharine's voice came through the branches of the tree.

They both ran out, fronds of leaves catching at their faces. Nancy was clutching her stomach, an agonized look in her eyes.

Oh no, not the baby . . . Agatha's hand flew to her mouth.

"Oh! Oh my God!" Nancy doubled over. "I . . . I . . ."

"I think her waters have broken." Agatha heard the sudden difference in her own voice. It was her nurse's voice. Forgotten for a decade, it had returned, unbidden, at the speed of light.

"What shall we do?" There was fear in Katharine's face. Like most wartime nurses, she had only ever treated men. This was unknown territory. She clearly wanted Agatha to take charge.

Agatha opened her mouth and closed it. No good telling her that she didn't know, that all she knew about giving birth was her own single experience. That wasn't something Nancy needed to hear right now. She had to calm her down, pretend that she knew what she was doing.

"It's all right, Nancy," she said. "No need to panic. It's just a sign that you're in the very early stages." As Agatha helped her out of the soaking-wet aba, she did a quick calculation. *About six months . . .* That's what Nancy had said a week ago. But was that six months from her last period or six months from the time she found out? Either way, it was too soon. If her baby came now, its chances of survival were slim.

"What time is Max coming back?" Agatha mouthed the words over Nancy's head.

Katharine held up three fingers.

Agatha glanced at her watch. Another two and a half hours. How were they going to cope for that long?

Nancy let out an agonized groan, digging her nails into Agatha's arm. "S . . . sorry," she gasped.

"No need to apologize." Agatha rubbed her back. "Now: we need to get you into a more comfortable position. If you could just lie back, I'm going to put this cushion under your head and these other ones under your knees. Katharine, is there some water in the picnic basket?"

Katharine blinked, as if she couldn't quite take in what was happening.

Nancy let out another yelp of pain.

"She's going to get very warm, so she'll want something to drink." Agatha was struggling to keep her voice calm. She glanced at her watch. She needed to time the contractions. But she already knew they were coming too fast. Rosalind had taken hours and hours to arrive, but Agatha had heard of women whose labor came on so quickly, their babies were born on the bathroom floor.

Katharine leapt into action, dragging the picnic basket from its place by the tree and pulling out a tin mug, which she filled with water from a flask.

"Do you have another towel?" Agatha looked up as Katharine passed the mug across the blanket. "We need a dry one."

"Yes, there's one in my bag." Katharine watched Agatha lift Nancy's head so she could take a sip of water. "Is it . . . ?" She completed the sentence with an agitated look.

Agatha nodded. "We'll need something warm and dry to wrap the baby in when it comes." Turning to Nancy, she said: "I know it's not very dignified, but I need to take a look down below. I think this baby's in an awful hurry to meet you."

Nancy's mouth gaped in horror. "I c . . . can't . . . not . . ." Her face contorted with pain.

"You're going to be fine." The words were for herself as much as Nancy.

"B . . . but . . . I . . ." Nancy's jaw clenched as another contraction came.

"Women are made to have babies." Agatha realized, too late, what a tactless thing this was to say within Katharine's hearing. She glanced up, apologizing with her eyes. Katharine gave the smallest shake of her head, a gesture that said *It doesn't matter*.

"Remember, I've done this before." Agatha murmured a silent prayer that Nancy wouldn't realize that her only experience of this was as a patient, not a nurse. She had to keep her calm. Make her believe everything was under control. Nancy's life and her baby's depended on her doing exactly as she was told until Max arrived with the truck.

"Do you feel the urge to push?"

Nancy nodded, her eyes snapping shut as the pain overtook her.

"You need to try to stop yourself from doing that—just until the baby's ready," Agatha said. "Can you breathe for me? Three quick pants and a long blow . . . that's it! Keep doing that each time it hurts." Turning to Katharine, she said: "Can you brace her against you? Raise her up and support her shoulders?"

Katharine dropped down onto the blanket, sliding her legs around Nancy and lifting her into a semisitting position.

"That's better . . . Oh! I can see the head!" Agatha swallowed hard, terrified of what was happening, of this little life about to emerge into the world with only her to help it. She heard the voice of the matron at the hospital in Torquay. *Come on, Nurse Miller: show some backbone!*

She grabbed the towel and held it ready. If only she'd paid more attention to what the midwife had done while she was giving birth to Rosalind. Was it right to push when the head crowned? She could barely remember anything through the fog of pain that had descended on that August day nine years ago. But she *must* remember.

"Nancy, you're doing really well." Agatha's voice came out louder and shriller than she meant it too, betraying her trepidation. "I need you to hold on just a tiny bit longer. Then, when I say the word, I want you to push as hard as you can."

"Please, God," Agatha whispered, "let it be all right."

Nancy gave a heartrending scream, and blood surged into her face. Katharine wiped away the beads of perspiration on Nancy's forehead with the sleeve of her blouse.

"Push now, Nancy! Push!" Agatha yelled.

The speed with which the little thing slithered out was a shock. Agatha just managed to catch it in the towel. She stared at it, paralyzed with wonder. A little boy. Almost as big as Rosalind when she was born. But not moving. And his skin was blue gray under the welts of blood.

"Is it . . . ?" Nancy gasped, collapsing into Katharine's lap.

Agatha rubbed the little body with the towel, willing him to be alive. The cord hung, bloody, from his belly. It had not been round his neck when he came out—so why wasn't he breathing?

"What is it?" Suddenly Katharine was there beside her. She took the baby and laid it on the blanket, bending low over its face. Agatha watched in horrified amazement as Katharine covered his nose and mouth with hers, as if she were kissing the tiny dead thing. She raised her head for a moment, took a breath, and did it again.

"Katharine! No!" Agatha grabbed her arm, but she wouldn't budge. Katharine kicked out at her, pushing her away like a woman possessed. *Oh God*, Agatha thought, *seeing this has tipped her over the edge*.

A sudden sharp wail cut through the air between them. Katharine threw her head back, panting for breath. "Look!" she gasped. "He's alive!"

CHAPTER 26

Nancy was in her bed at the expedition house, propped up on pillows with the baby nestled in the crook of her arm. She was very weak after her ordeal in the desert, but she had managed to give little James his first proper feed. He was to be James Frederick, after Katharine's father and Agatha's. If it had been a girl, Nancy said, she would have named her after the two of them.

"Is she asleep?" Katharine whispered.

"I think so," Agatha replied.

"Should we put him in his bed, do you think?" Katharine glanced at the makeshift cot—a drawer out of the chest in her bedroom, lined with a towel and square of the softest cashmere cut from one of her shawls.

"Yes," Agatha whispered back, "if we can do it without waking him up."

She watched Katharine gently lift the sleeping baby from his mother's arms. If James had been made of solid gold and unearthed from the sands of Ur, she couldn't have been more careful. Agatha had been amazed at the way she had taken control after the birth when all seemed hopeless. Somehow she had known just what to do.

When the baby was settled and they had crept out of Nancy's bedroom for a well-earned cup of coffee in the courtyard, Agatha asked Katharine where she had learned the resuscitation technique.

"It's what the Bedouin women do," she replied. "I saw one giving birth outside in the desert once. It was our second season here. She was the wife of one of the workmen on the dig, and she'd walked miles to bring him the news that his father was dying. She collapsed a few minutes after she arrived and went into labor. She was completely calm about it—refused any help—and delivered the baby herself. When she saw it wasn't breathing, she put her mouth over its face. I thought she was just grief-stricken, kissing it because it was dead, but then I saw that she was actually sucking away the fluid that was blocking its nose and mouth. Then she was taking breaths and breathing them into the baby."

"And it worked?"

Katharine nodded. "Half an hour later we took them back to her village in the truck and the baby yelled at the top of its lungs every time we hit a pothole."

"Well, thank goodness." Agatha smiled. "And because of it you saved James's life."

"I . . . ," Katharine hesitated, staring into her coffee cup. "I didn't know if it would work. I had this moment, when I saw him lying there in the towel, all blue and bloody, when I knew what I should do—but I thought I couldn't. He looked so . . ." She shook her head. "It sounds ridiculous now, but he reminded me of Bertram. I never saw him, of course: not after . . ." She trailed off, bringing the cup up to her lips, not drinking, just breathing in the smell. "I've seen so many dead people. Soldiers, during the war—and civilians: corpses the Germans left behind in the villages along the front. I've always prided myself on having a strong stomach. But somehow, when I saw James . . ." She closed her eyes with a sigh that sent coffee sloshing over the side of her cup. "Look at me! Clumsy idiot!" She dabbed at her skirt. "Fancy trusting me with a baby!"

In that moment, Agatha saw a glimmer of something she hadn't grasped before. That in making the decision to try to save James's life, Katharine had confronted something inside herself: something that must have haunted her since the day of her husband's suicide. When that doctor had delivered his brutal verdict on her body, it was not just her marriage he was annihilating. He was telling her that she was incapable of doing the one thing every woman expects to be able to do. She would never have a baby.

For years Katharine had lived with that knowledge, alongside the other wretched facts of her medical condition. And she had dealt with it by throwing herself into a new career. Agatha could just imagine Katharine saying to herself that if she was a man on the inside, she would damn well live like one. And no one would expect a woman—a widow—who was so devoted to her chosen profession to be interested in having babies.

But what had happened out there by the river had changed all that. Agatha could see it in Katharine's face. This baby of Nancy's seemed to have unleashed feelings that she found utterly bewildering.

~

Max appeared in the courtyard as they were finishing their coffee. After transporting Nancy and her baby back to the expedition house with Agatha and Katharine, he had had to go straight back to the dig site to take Hugh Carrington to Ur Junction in time for his train. He wiped his forehead with the back of his hand as he strode across to where the women were sitting.

"How is she now?" He pulled out a chair and sank onto it.

"She's sleeping," Katharine replied.

"And the baby? Is he all right?"

"I think so." Katharine glanced at Agatha, who nodded. "What about the doctor? Did you manage to contact him?"

"Yes. I used the telephone at the station. He should be here in an hour or so." He took the coffee that Katharine had poured for him. "You both did marvelously well." He smiled at Agatha over the rim of his cup. "I don't—"

"Katharine!" Leonard Woolley, calling across the courtyard, cut him short. "I need you in the Antiquities Room, please!"

Katharine's face changed in an instant, apprehension dissolving her smile. "I'd better go," she said, scraping her chair as she got up. "You'll look after Nancy, won't you, Agatha?"

"Yes, of course—but you'll be able to help later, won't you—after the doctor's seen her?"

Katharine didn't reply. She strode across the courtyard with her chin tucked against her chest.

Like Marie Antoinette on her way to the guillotine.

Agatha wondered why that image had jumped into her mind again. Something about the tone of Leonard's voice and the expression on Katharine's face made her think that a showdown was coming. But why now? If she had told him last night, the row would have happened then. And Katharine had had no chance to tell him this afternoon: she hadn't seen him since they got back from the river.

"You were very brave out there, you know." Max's voice broke into her thoughts. "Keeping calm in a situation like that—well, not many people could do it."

"I didn't really know what I was doing." Agatha shrugged. "I was terrified, actually."

"It all turned out all right in the end, though, didn't it? I was telling Hugh Carrington about it on the way to the station. Turns out he was at school with Nancy's husband."

"Really?"

Max nodded. "He was rather surprised, I think, that she was out here. Said the wedding was only about a year ago."

"Less than that, actually." In a few sentences Agatha told him as little as she possibly could to explain Nancy's presence in Mesopotamia. She'd made a promise to be discreet and she was not going to break it now. Little James was going to have a tough enough time without people knowing he was illegitimate.

"Poor girl. What on earth will she do now?"

"She wants to stay in Baghdad. She's going to keep on the house I've been renting. I think she hopes to get a job eventually."

"Well, I don't think she'll be going anywhere in a hurry, do you? Will you stay on, too?"

"I'd rather not go back until she's well enough to travel." Agatha looked into his eyes, returning his smile. "I hope I won't be a nuisance."

"How could you possibly be?" He glanced over his shoulder, then reached across the table for her hand, lifting it to his lips. "You're an angel. And I'm so glad you won't be on that train tomorrow."

~

Katharine's hand was shaking as she opened the door of the Antiquities Room.

Leonard was standing by the sculpture of Hamoudi she had given him as a wedding present. Her letter was in his hand.

"Oh—you found it," she said in a small voice.

"Why didn't you tell me before?" He sounded unnaturally calm, as if he was making a supreme effort to control himself.

"I'm sorry, Len, I . . . I was afraid of telling anyone."

"But I'm not just *anyone*, Katharine. I'm your husband. Don't you think I, of all people, had a right to know?"

"I thought . . . ," she faltered, unable to look him in the eyes. "I thought perhaps it wouldn't be an issue."

She heard him draw in a long breath. "Why would you have thought that?"

She swallowed hard. "Because unlike all the other men who have worked here over the past three years, you never showed me the slightest interest. In *that* way."

"Oh, I see." His feet shifted on the bare mud floor. "You had me down as a queer, did you? Someone who would leave you alone once the veneer of respectability had been established? Well, I'm sorry to disappoint you, but as you've obviously gathered by now, I'm as normal as most men in that regard."

"I suppose you'll want me to leave?" Her throat felt tight. The words came out as a croaky whisper.

"Did I say that?"

She raised her head, perplexed. His face had lost some of that imperiousness. He looked more sad, now, than anything.

"But how can I . . . How can we . . ."

"Come here a moment, will you?" He held out his hand. "Come closer. I won't try anything, I promise."

She took a step toward him. He caught the ends of her fingers. "It's all right," he said. "Don't be afraid." She took another step, and another, until her face was just a few inches from his. Now she could see the film of tears in his eyes.

He made a small noise in his throat, as if he was about to deliver a well-rehearsed speech. But what he said took her completely by surprise. "Listen, Katharine, it's not about . . ." He lowered his voice to a whisper. "It's not about the *act*. Not really. Not that I wouldn't have wanted to if you'd been able to, of course—but what I truly long for is something far simpler than that."

He turned her hand palm up, stroking her fingers. She held her breath, tried not to flinch. Despite his promise, she feared what might come next.

"Is this all right?"

She nodded slowly.

"You see, I've never done this before." His fingertips felt warm. Years of digging had roughened the skin and turned it dry.

"Never?"

He shook his head. "Barring handshakes and the odd tackle on the rugby field at school, I've never known what it feels like to touch another human being."

She blinked, uncomprehending. "That can't be true, surely? When you were a child . . . ?"

"My mother died when I was two years old, so I can't remember what it was like to have her arms around me." His voice was matter-of-fact. There was no hint of self-pity. "And my father was a fire-and-brimstone preacher. He never showed emotion unless he was giving a sermon. He thought little boys should be toughened up, so he packed me off to boarding school at the age of five." He took her other hand, looking into her eyes. "So you see, Katharine, if I come across as a cold fish, it's because I've never had the chance to be physically close to anyone. Until now."

"What are you saying, Len?" She searched his face.

His lips parted, then closed again, as if he was afraid to express what was in his mind. After a long moment, he said: "I just want to feel . . . loved. Could you do that? Is it too much to ask?"

CHAPTER 27

One week later

Agatha had baby James against her shoulder. She was patting his back to burp him. Nancy was in bed, her eyes closed. As Agatha tiptoed across the room, she heard footsteps in the corridor. Katharine's face appeared round the door.

"Are you all right?" she mouthed.

Agatha pointed to the drawer that served as a cot, jerking her thumb toward the door. Katharine cottoned on straight away. She crept into the room and lifted the drawer, tucking it under her arm. Agatha followed her out of Nancy's room, back to her own bedroom.

"Would you like to hold him before I put him down? He's nearly asleep, I think."

"I wouldn't want to disturb him. He looks so peaceful," Katharine replied.

Agatha nodded. She doubted that James would have minded being held by another pair of arms. He was still too young to know the difference between his mother and anybody else. But over the past few days, she had noticed how reticent Katharine was to handle him. She would do anything to help as long as it didn't involve any physical contact. There was ambivalence there, as if, having saved his life, she was afraid of what she had brought into the world.

Agatha sensed that she didn't want to talk about it, nor about the state of affairs with Leonard. Since the day James was born, she had undergone a subtle but noticeable change: she was quieter, less bossy, and . . . Agatha struggled to think of the right word to describe the difference in her friend. *Gentler.* That was it. Agatha no longer walked into the room wondering if she was going to give her the third degree.

"I'll leave you to it now, shall I?" Katharine set the drawer down on the rug. "I expect you'll want a nap, too, once he goes off?"

Agatha nodded. "Will you ask Saleem to get some milk ready in case he wakes up? I don't want to disturb Nancy until suppertime."

When she'd gone, Agatha laid James on the bed. Then she knelt on the floor, between him and the rug. Placing one hand under his head and the other round his body, she eased him off the bed and into the makeshift cot. She tucked in his blanket, anxious not to wake him. The slightest whimper, she knew, would bring Nancy hobbling down the corridor to fetch him.

She was worried about Nancy. She wasn't eating much, and she had developed an unhealthy pallor. She was trying her best to feed James, but every time it was a struggle. More than once Agatha had found her in tears, worn out with it. So they had been supplementing his diet with goat's milk. It was a painstaking process, with no bottle. You had to twist the end of a piece of muslin into a point, dip it in the bowl, then try to get it into James's mouth.

The doctor was due to make another visit tomorrow. The last time he had come, he had pronounced her absolutely fine. He had congratulated Agatha on the delivery, saying that Nancy couldn't be in better shape if her baby had been born in a hospital. But Agatha wasn't so sure. Each night, as she was falling asleep, she went over and over it in her mind, reliving each traumatic moment. It had all happened so quickly. She hadn't even been able to wash her hands before assisting Nancy. She had gone to her aid within minutes of coming out of the river—with goodness knows what potentially dangerous bacteria clinging to her skin. And then, when Katharine had saved James's life and he was lying on the blanket, yelling for all he was worth, they'd had to cut the cord. To do this, Agatha had sent Katharine to retrieve her shoes from under the tree. She had removed the shoelaces, tying one close to James's tummy and the other a couple of inches along the cord. Then she had cut it with the knife Katharine had used to peel the oranges for their picnic.

She ran the images through her head for the umpteenth time, thinking of how different things would have been if she hadn't brought Nancy to Ur, if she had stayed in Baghdad instead and got her to a hospital when she went into labor. And something else was preying on her mind. James was not a premature baby—she was certain of that. He might have been born a couple of weeks early—but no more. Which meant he must have been conceived at the end of April: the time Nancy was on her honeymoon. She had been so adamant that the baby was not her husband's—but could she really be so certain?

She closed her eyes. No point in worrying about that now. The most important thing was to get Nancy back on an even keel, get her back to Baghdad, and into some kind of normality.

Thinking about that, Agatha drifted off. She slipped into a dream where she was swimming—not in the river Euphrates but in the lake with Max. He was laughing and holding little James above the water, dipping his feet in, then throwing him into the air and catching him. But when Agatha swam up to them, she saw that the baby wasn't James: he had Max's face and her blonde hair . . .

"Agatha! Agatha!"

She woke to the sound of Max's voice, an urgent whisper on the other side of the door. She scrambled off the bed, careful to avoid the drawer where James lay, still fast asleep.

"What is it?" She opened the door, rubbing her eyes.

"Can I come in for a minute? I won't wake him, I promise."

They sat down on the bed together. She could see from the look on his face that this was not a social visit.

"It's about Nancy," he began. "I had a wire from a friend in Baghdad. Her husband's turned up there. He's on his way here now, apparently."

"What?" Agatha gasped. "But . . . how did he know?"

"Hugh Carrington must have told him," Max said with a shrug. "That was my fault, I'm afraid. It never occurred to me when I was telling him about it that he'd be straight on the phone to Felix Nelson."

Remembered words surged from some dark chamber of her mind with the force of a torpedo. They were Nancy's words—a fragment of the story of her doomed honeymoon in Venice: *He said that once I'd produced a child, my job would be over. It wouldn't matter if it was a boy or a girl—as long as there was a baby.*

Oh my God, Agatha thought, *he's coming to take James.*

"We've got to get them away from here." Katharine couldn't keep still. She was standing over Agatha as James sucked milk from the muslin rag. She reached out, her hand stopping a fraction away from the soft black down on his head, as if she was itching to touch him, to protect him.

"But how can we?" Agatha moved the bowl of milk so that Katharine wouldn't knock it over with her elbow. "Nancy's still very weak; I don't think she's well enough to go anywhere just yet."

"She's certainly not well enough for a train journey—I wasn't thinking of that—but there's somewhere else she could go."

"Where?"

"The Bedouin village. It's less than five miles away. They'd hide her for us."

Agatha's hand stopped midway between the bowl and James's mouth. "Are you serious? Leaving a tiny baby and a woman who's just given birth in a tent in the middle of the desert . . ."

"We wouldn't be *leaving* them. They'd be well looked after. The Bedouin women have been looking after babies in those conditions for thousands of years. They're far more experienced than we are."

Agatha glanced at the scrap of muslin dripping milk, most of which had missed James's mouth. "I suppose you're right. We'd have to ask them first, though, wouldn't we?"

"No time," Katharine said, shaking her head. "There's only one train coming in from Baghdad today, and if Max's friend is right, Felix Nelson will be on it. That gives us just under two hours to get Nancy and James out of here."

~

Max was asleep when Agatha knocked on his door. He opened it rubbing his eyes, his hair sticking up like a chimney sweep's brush.

"Didn't mean to doze off," he mumbled. Then, seeing her face, he said: "How did Nancy take the news?"

"Not well. She's terrified of him. Says he's not the sort of person you'd want to get on the wrong side of. We need to get her and the baby out of his way." She rattled off Katharine's plan. "Could you drive us? Katharine's going to stay here and deal with him when he arrives."

Max looked perplexed. "But James is his son. Surely he has a right to see him—even if they're no longer living as man and wife."

"But he's . . ." She'd promised not to tell. But this was an emergency. If Max was going to help them, he needed to know the truth. "James *isn't* his son." Even as she said it, she wondered if it was true. But Nancy was in no fit state to be interrogated about it. And a confrontation with

Felix could just about finish her off. What mattered most was to get her to a safe place. Somewhere she could recover in peace until she was ready to face the world.

"Not his son?" Max echoed.

Agatha took a deep breath. "I couldn't tell you before . . . I promised Nancy I wouldn't. I know it sounds awful, but there are"—she fumbled for the right words—"extenuating circumstances. I haven't got time to explain it all now. What Nancy's afraid of is that Felix will take James from her."

"Why would he do that if he's not the father?"

"Because he needs a child born in wedlock in order to inherit the earldom. And in law he *is* the father: he's still married to Nancy."

Max looked even more bewildered. "So . . . who's the real father?"

"I don't know. She wouldn't tell me."

"Does he know about the baby?"

"Not yet."

"Good grief! What a mess."

"You're right: it is a mess—but we have to help them, Max." Her eyes searched his. "We can't let Felix take James."

He stood there for what seemed like an eternity. She could almost hear the scales tipping this way and that inside his head. He had principles, faith in God. Nancy had committed adultery. But her baby was an innocent victim and surely she was more sinned against than sinner?

"I'll get the truck ready," he said at last. "I'm not doing this for her, though: I'm doing it for James. Because he needs his mother. And when it's over, I want you to promise me something."

"What?"

"That you'll talk to Nancy. Get her to write to the father and tell him the truth."

"I can't *make* her do it, Max," she said softly. "But I promise to try."

CHAPTER 28

A warm wind tugged at Agatha's hair as she followed Max outside. He was carrying the drawer that held James, who was fast asleep, oblivious to the drama unfolding around him. She and Katharine were supporting Nancy, who hadn't walked farther than the bathroom since giving birth.

"Oh!" Nancy brought her hand up to her eyes. "It's so bright!"

Agatha looked up at the sky. It wasn't really bright. Not today. There were big purple clouds bubbling up on the horizon, giving the sunlight a strange grayish tinge. But to Nancy, who had been cooped up inside for a week, it must have seemed dazzling.

"We'll put you in the middle, Nancy, I think," Katharine said, opening the passenger door of the truck. "You can hold on to the armrest if you feel unsteady. I think Agatha had better have James on her lap. We can't have him rolling around in that drawer."

"We'd better be quick." Max glanced at his watch. "The train's due in ten minutes."

When they were all settled, he turned the key in the ignition. The engine made a slow, whining noise, like an animal in pain. Max tried again. This time there was no sound at all. He jumped out and pulled something from underneath the front of the truck.

"What's he doing?" Nancy's face was etched with worry.

"He's just cranking the engine," Agatha said. "It's all right. I often have to do it to my car. We'll be off in a minute." She leaned out of the window, calling to Max. "Do you want me to rev her up?"

"Could you?" Max called back.

Agatha passed James to Nancy to hold while she got out of the truck.

Katharine saw what was happening as she came running out of the house with a basket of food. "Do you know what to do?" The look on her face mirrored Nancy's. "Oh yes, of course: you have a car . . ."

Agatha waited for the whir of the starting motor. As she heard the splutter of the engine, she pressed down hard on the accelerator pedal. The truck gave a heave as the engine burst into life.

Nancy clutched Agatha's arm. Feeling the sudden movement, James let out a whimper.

"Don't cry, sweetheart—we'll be on the way now." Agatha reached across to stroke James's cheek. With a puzzled frown, he closed his eyes.

"Well done!" Max gave her a big smile as she jumped down from the truck. "Thank goodness we've got someone who knows what they're doing!" He glanced up at the sky. "I don't like the look of this weather. I think there's a sandstorm brewing. Let's hope we make it to the village before it comes."

~

Katharine went into the Antiquities Room and set to work on a sand-encrusted Sumerian knife while she waited for Felix Nelson to arrive. It was painstaking work, performed with a delicate brush of badger hair, but it took her mind off what was about to happen.

She was the only member of the team left at the expedition house. Max had had to take the others to the dig site before returning to Sahra' Alqamar to make the mercy dash across the desert to the Bedouin village.

Katharine hadn't told Leonard about the imminent arrival of Felix Nelson. She could just imagine his reaction if she tried to explain the true nature of Nancy's predicament. Better to wait until after the fact, she decided. Once Nancy and James were out of harm's way, there would be time to try to make him understand.

She hoped it wouldn't demolish the fragile equilibrium of the past few days. Leonard had opened up like a flower. He was smiling at people—not just her—and chatting away at mealtimes. It was as if their confrontation had lifted a great dark cloud from the expedition house. To her amazement, he had readily accepted the presence of Nancy's baby—something that would surely have sent the old Leonard into a blind rage. But if he had known that James was illegitimate, that Nancy had been having an affair with a married man, his attitude would undoubtedly have been very different. For all the progress they had made, he was still very much a preacher's son. Those values ran through him like the grain in a plank of wood. They were never going to change.

"Khatun!"

A distant shout from Saleem jolted her back into the present. He was in the kitchen. He must have spotted Nancy's husband at the gates of the compound. She picked up the badger-hair brush and worked it furiously into the crevices of the bone handle of the knife. She would pretend she hadn't heard. Play for time.

"*Khatun!*"

Saleem was outside the door now. She replaced the knife on the shelf and smoothed down her skirt. Then she took a deep breath. Nancy's whole future depended on her ability to present a calm, unruffled front, to lie well enough to throw Felix Nelson off the scent.

She waited in the living room while Saleem went outside to tell the guards to let him in. When he introduced himself, she pretended to be surprised.

"Viscount Nelson? What an unexpected pleasure!" She held out her hand and flashed the smile that she had perfected in the mirror as a girl of sixteen—a smile that sent most men weak at the knees.

"Mrs. Woolley."

The photograph in *Tatler* had not done him justice. He had film-star looks, tall and slim with light-brown hair that flopped over his forehead. A well-trimmed pencil mustache outlined a petulant upper lip. He didn't return her smile.

"Would you like some coffee? It's thirsty work traveling in these parts." She tried another smile—the sympathetic one this time.

"Thank you, no." The mustache twitched as he glanced around the room. "I believe my wife is staying here as your guest. I've come to take her home."

"Nancy, yes. We've so enjoyed having her here. We met on the Orient Express—did she tell you?" If she could just stall him until Max got back . . . She did a quick calculation in her head. The train to Ur Junction went on as far as Basra, then turned round, returning a couple of hours later. If she could persuade him he'd come on a wild goose chase, they could get him back on that train, and then fetch Nancy out of hiding.

"I'm afraid she's put you to a lot of trouble." Felix gave her a penetrating look. "I . . . We . . . weren't expecting the baby to arrive when it did."

"Well, yes, that was rather a surprise—but a wonderful one. Mrs. Christie and I helped with the delivery. Luckily, we'd both been nurses during the war—not that I had the opportunity to learn much about midwifery in a field hospital in France, but—"

"Is he all right?" Felix cut her short. "The baby?"

"Yes. He's absolutely fine. Nancy was a little weak after the birth but—"

"Where is he?"

Clearly, he was not the least bit interested in Nancy's state of health. The baby was all he cared about. Seeing Katharine's expression, he looked away, conscious, perhaps, of how desperate he sounded. "I've been worried about both of them, of course," he said. "I want to take them back to England as soon as possible." He glanced out of the window. "I came here from the station in a cart pulled by a decrepit old mule. Quite unsuitable for a mother and baby. Anyway, I sent the fellow away. I wonder if you could spare one of those layabouts at the gate to drive us to Ur Junction?"

"We only have a truck," Katharine replied. "It's not here at the moment. We can certainly give you a lift when it comes back from the dig site—but I'm afraid you've had a wasted journey: Nancy and the baby left us yesterday."

"What?"

Blood surged to his face, turning his pale cheeks red. "Where have they gone?"

"To friends in Baghdad, I believe." Katharine's eyes didn't leave his. "She was talking about staying there for a night or two before traveling back to England."

"Back to England?" he echoed. His irises were green with flecks of yellow, like a fox. The lids squeezed together, turning them into slits. "These friends—who are they?"

"She didn't say." Katharine put on a concerned face. "I'm sorry not to be able to be of more help." She reached into the pocket of her jacket, pulling out her cigarette case. "You look as if you need one," she said, flipping it open.

"Thanks." He took a cigarette, along with the proffered lighter. He walked over to the window as he smoked it, looking out at the darkening sky and the billowing sheets on the washing line. "How long till your truck gets back?"

"Oh—any minute now," Katharine replied. "But you must let me organize something to eat while you're waiting. It's a long journey, and the food on the train is dire, I know."

"Very well. A sandwich would be most welcome. And a cold beer if you have one."

"No beer, I'm afraid." Katharine shrugged. "My husband doesn't allow alcohol in the house. We have lemonade or tea."

Felix muttered something incoherent under his breath.

"I'll bring both." Katharine hurried from the room, relieved to be out from under his piercing gaze. She poked her head round the door of the kitchen, where Saleem and Ibrahim were slicing eggplant for the evening meal. She took her time ordering the sandwich, going through possible fillings with Ibrahim until she settled on spiced lamb and tomato laced with a yogurt and cucumber dressing. She asked Saleem to prepare the drinks, and then she took them out on a tray.

"Food won't be long," she said as she stepped into the living room.

There was no reply. She set the tray down on the table, looking this way and that. Where had he gone? To find the bathroom, perhaps? Then she caught a flash of something beyond the window. He was out there, by the gates, which were open. He looked as if he was calling out to someone. She craned her neck. Two figures were approaching on mules. Duncan and Michael. The wind was tugging at their clothes. They had scarves wrapped around their faces to shield them from the blowing sand. Len must have sent them back because of the coming storm.

As she watched, they dismounted. Felix was talking to them now. She saw Michael point to the horizon over to the east. A horrible sense of foreboding gripped her. He was pointing in the direction of the Bedouin village. But they *couldn't* know, could they . . . ?

She ran to the door and felt the wind pull it as she twisted the handle. She reached the gates of the compound just in time to see Felix grab the reins of Duncan's mule and leap into the saddle. Before she could reach him, he kicked it in the ribs, making the animal lurch off at a fast trot that quickly turned into a canter.

"Where's he going?" she gasped. "What did he ask you?"

"He said he was Nancy's husband." Michael gave her a puzzled look. "He wanted to know if we'd seen her."

"We'd just passed her in the truck with Max," Duncan added. "They were stuck in the sand and we helped dig them out. We told him what Max told us: that they were going to the Bedouin village."

"You did what?" The wind whipped Katharine's words away.

"What's the matter? Why are you—"

Michael never got to complete the sentence. Katharine snatched the reins of his mule. Jumping onto the animal's back, she sped off in pursuit of Felix Nelson.

CHAPTER 29

The sand stung Agatha's face as she braced her body against the back of the truck. Max was beside her, his shirt soaked in perspiration. When the wheels had lost traction a second time, he tried in vain to free them from the encroaching sand while Agatha gunned the engine. All she could do now was try and help him push.

"You shouldn't be doing this!" Max had to shout to make himself heard above the hiss of the wind.

"Why not?" she called back. "Because . . . I'm . . . a woman?" Her words were punctuated with breathy grunts.

"I don't want you hurting yourself!"

"I won't—honestly!" She winced as the truck's bumper bit into her leg. But she didn't let go.

"Okay—if you're sure. When I say the word, heave like mad!"

For a moment it looked as if it was going to work. The truck inched up the ramp of sand. But the movement only made things worse at the front end. The wheels had sunk up to the metal.

"It's no good," Max called as he straightened up, shovel in hand. "I'm going to have to get help."

"Where from?" Agatha came round to where he was standing, tucking her scarf round her face.

"We're only about a mile and a half from the village. I could bring a whole gang of men back with me." He pressed his lips together, turning the flesh white. "But I don't like the idea of leaving you. I'd rather we all went."

Agatha glanced through the window at Nancy, who was half sitting, half lying on the seat. Her forehead was beaded with perspiration, and her cheeks were flushed. James lay fast asleep beside her. She looked much worse than when they had left the expedition house. The bumpy ride and the breakdowns had been too much for her. She looked incapable of walking a few yards, let alone a mile or more.

"We'll be fine," she said. "Don't worry."

"Are you sure?" He blinked as a gust of wind blew sand into his eyes.

"Yes!" She tried to smile. "I'm more worried about you, going across the desert in this weather."

"It won't be so bad: I'm heading east, so I'll have the wind behind me." Reaching out, he pulled her to him. She felt his lips on her forehead, setting her skin on fire. "I'll be as quick as I can," he said.

Agatha watched him from inside the truck. Despite the vicious wind, he was making good progress. In five minutes he was out of sight. Nancy opened her eyes and groaned, rubbing her neck and shoulders. She'd fallen asleep in a most awkward position, and Agatha decided to try to make her more comfortable. She rolled up her jacket to make a pillow and lifted Nancy's head and legs so that she was lying down properly.

"What's happening?" Nancy moaned. "Where's Max?"

"He's gone to get help. He won't be long—and we'll be just fine here. There's plenty to eat and drink. Would you like something?"

Nancy shook her head. She was feverish, and there was a strange, distracted look in her eyes. It scared Agatha. She had seen the same warning signs in men who'd died from septicemia after surgery.

"Try to get some sleep, then."

But the moment Nancy lay down again, James let out a cry. Agatha knew he was hungry.

"Don't get up: there's milk in the basket in the back—I can feed him."

She lifted him out and held him against her shoulder as she opened the door. It was a struggle to keep it open as the wind gusted around the truck, but she braced her back against it, shielding James's head with her hand. Getting the back door open was even worse. The wind took it, slamming it against her left hip as she climbed onto the sacks that lined the floor. The pain was eye watering, but all she cared about was getting James safely inside. She made a nest of the sacks and settled down, cradling him in her arms as she rummaged in the basket for the flask of milk wrapped in a clean strip of muslin.

At first he didn't want to take it. It was as if, young as he was, he could sense that something was wrong. Agatha stroked his cheek with her finger. It was a trick she had learned with Rosalind, and it always seemed to work. In a few minutes he had stopped grizzling and was sucking on the rag.

It wasn't long before he closed his eyes. When she was sure he was asleep, she laid him down in the nest of sacks. Her hip was throbbing, and she straightened up as best she could—although the roof was too low to stand up properly. As she rubbed her bruised skin, she caught sight of something through one of the high windows in the side of the truck. A dust trail. Someone was coming. She pressed her face to the glass, which was dusted with sand on the outside. Hard to see if it was a car or a camel. A frisson of fear ran through her body. Could it be bandits? As the dust cloud grew closer, she saw the head of a mule at the front of it. Just one animal. A wave of relief replaced the fear. Bandits didn't normally go round on their own. This was a lone traveler, perhaps coming to offer help.

As the rider approached, she saw that the clothes were European, not Arab. She was at the door in a moment, clinging to it with both hands to stop it swinging out of her grasp. She jumped out to the muffled thunder of hooves.

"Katharine!"

"Where . . . are they?" Katharine leapt off the mule, gasping for breath as she pulled down the shawl that covered her mouth. "He hasn't . . ."

Agatha's insides turned to ice as sand blasted her face. "What's happened?" She yelled the question into the wind.

"Felix . . . He knows . . . Got it out of Michael and Duncan." Katharine shook her head violently. "No time to explain. Are they in there?"

Agatha nodded. "Both asleep."

"Max?"

"Gone for help." Katharine made for the back door of the truck, wrenching it open. She cocked her head at the sleeping baby. "I think it's best if I take him. You're like sitting ducks here."

Agatha stared at her, horrified. "But—"

"Believe me: he's completely ruthless. I think he'd take James by force if he found you." She took off her shawl. "I can carry him in this, like the Bedouin women."

"But there's a storm coming! It's—"

"We'll be there in no time." Katharine waved away her protests. "And he'll be well protected." Before Agatha could say another word, she reached across the truck and plucked James from his bed of sacks. He murmured in his sleep but made no more sound as she held him to her.

Agatha watched, mesmerized by what was unfolding before her eyes. Katharine had never done this, never held him since the day she had brought him back to life. It was as if invisible fetters had suddenly fallen away. This was a new Katharine, the determination in her eyes softened by something that had not been there before.

In a couple of deft movements, Katharine tossed the end of her shawl over one shoulder and wrapped the other round her waist, knotting the ends together. "Look after Nancy!" She called as she climbed back onto the mule. "Get in and lock the doors!"

~

Katharine rode with one hand on the reins and the other under the bundle tied to her chest. She had watched the Bedouin women make slings for their babies, but she had never actually tried it herself. Terrified of dropping James, she kept the mule to a trot, constantly looking over her shoulder to check for Felix.

She knew she had an advantage because this part of the desert had been her backyard for the past three years. The weather made it more difficult, but she could probably have found her way to the village blindfolded. It was no surprise that she had beaten Felix to the truck. She guessed that he had followed one of the myriad tracks that crisscrossed the land between the expedition house and the dig site. With a bit of luck, he would be hopelessly lost by now. And with a sandstorm coming, that could prove fatal.

Divine retribution if that were to happen. To him, James was nothing more than a bargaining chip.

She hugged the sleeping baby closer, feeling his little fist unfurl and close around the fabric of her shirt. The movement sent a wave of protective tenderness surging through her. The ferocity of her feelings surprised her, shocked her. If Felix came anywhere near her now, she was ready to kill him with her bare hands.

The wind tugged at her hair, blowing it across her face. She had long since lost the pins that had held it up, and her hat had flown off within minutes of her leaving the expedition house. She tossed her head to see where she was going. Not much farther now. She could make out the wooden palisades of the village. The whirling air had turned them into smudges of brown against a slate-gray sky. There was just the wadi to cross now—still shallow, thankfully—though it would quickly become impassable once the storm broke.

She slowed the mule down as it approached the edge of the ditch. She would have to be extra-careful with James as they scrambled down and back up the other side. She was concentrating so hard on keeping the animal steady that she didn't see what was lying in wait for her.

"Stop right there!"

The voice came through the air like a whip. She froze. It was *him*. But where was he? The landscape dissolved into a treacherous jumble of sand and rock. She tugged on the reins, trying to turn the mule back up the slope.

"I said *stop*!"

Suddenly he was there, in front of her, emerging chameleonlike from the sand.

"Give the baby to me!" He took a step toward her, drawing something from inside his jacket. A gun.

"Put that away!" She screamed over the roar of the wind.

"Shut up! Get down!" He was just yards away now.

"He's not yours!" She wrapped both arms tightly round the baby, the reins still clutched in one hand.

"Do you think I care?" He spat the words like hailstones. "Give him to me!"

"You'll have to shoot me first!"

"Don't think I won't do it." He planted his feet, pointing the gun at her head. "I'll count to ten. One . . . two . . . three . . ."

She clung to James, paralyzed, as he counted down. Sand swirled around them, rising from the ground like a ghostly army. The storm was closing in, purple black, as if a giant fist had punched the clouds.

"Four . . . five . . . six . . ." The air was suddenly rent by a piercing shriek, as if the wind had summoned the demons of hell. She saw beating wings, yellow eyes. Felix's hand flailing as the creature landed on his head. The roar of the gun going off, the bullet blasting the bank of the ditch. And an echoing crack, away across the sand. Felix crumpling to the ground.

Only then did the shapes make sense. Wings spread wide, rising from the body like an avenging angel. A falcon, its plumage creamy white against the bruised sky. Turning east, toward the Bedouin village, toward its master, who emerged on the opposite bank, his robes flying out behind him, wisps of smoke scudding from the rifle over his arm.

CHAPTER 30

It was five days before Felix Nelson's body was found. The weather closed in soon after he died, whipping up a whirlwind of sand that left the corpse half buried. A goatherd from the Bedouin village stumbled across it early one morning. But the giant desert ants had got there first. By the time the police superintendent from Najaf arrived at the scene, there was not enough left of his body for anyone to say for sure how he had died.

Katharine hadn't breathed a word of what had happened: not to Agatha, nor to Leonard, not even to Max, who had been at the gates of the Bedouin village when she rode in shaking with emotion, clutching the baby to her chest.

She'd let everyone jump to the obvious conclusion: that Felix Nelson had got himself hopelessly lost after riding off into the desert with no map, compass, or provisions.

The sheikh, she knew, would not risk stirring up trouble by admitting what he had done to defend her. Neither would he lose any sleep over taking the life of a man who had threatened the khatun—the wife of the man whose enterprise he was paid to protect.

As for Nancy, she was in no fit state to hear the news of her husband's death. By the time Max and a gang of Bedouin villagers had managed to haul Queen Mary out of the sand, Nancy was slipping in and out of consciousness. For the past few days she had been lying on a bed of goatskins in a tent, too weak to be moved, with Agatha and Katharine taking turns to sit with her.

The storm had made it impossible to get medical help. On the day before Felix's body was found, Max managed to get Queen Mary across the desert to Najaf to fetch the doctor who had visited Nancy when James was born. He confirmed what they already feared.

"Childbed fever?" Katharine's eyes met Agatha's over the bed.

The doctor gave them a bottle of morphine and told them to keep her as cool as possible. Then he beckoned Katharine to follow him outside the tent. In one short sentence, spoken in Arabic, he said that Nancy was unlikely to make it through the night.

The next few hours passed in a blur of watching and waiting. When they had done all they could for Nancy, Katharine slipped the little ivory amulet out of her pocket, placing it on a wooden stool beside the goatskin bed. She turned it over, so that the carved figure of the hare was on the underside and the image of the snake uppermost.

Agatha spotted it when she came into the tent with a fresh bowl of water. "Do you think it'll help?" She looked doubtful.

"It's all I could think of." Katharine picked up the amulet, rubbing it between her finger and thumb. "It's supposed to protect people."

Agatha nodded. "I've been saying silent prayers ever since the doctor left. But I'm afraid they won't work. I haven't been very good about going to church since my marriage ended. I'm not sure God will be listening."

"I'm not sure I believe in God. Not Len's version of him, anyway: a god who sends floods and famines and plagues of locusts when people don't toe the line."

"Or this." Agatha's fingers traced the outline of Nancy's forehead. She peeled away the warm, damp cloth, dipping it in the bowl of water. "Whatever she's done, she doesn't deserve this."

Sometime during the night, when the only sound in the Bedouin village was the distant bleating of the goats, Nancy suddenly sat up, throwing off the blanket that covered her.

"Where am I?"

Katharine, who had dozed off, woke with a start. Agatha was already on her feet.

"You're quite safe," Agatha said. "We're at the Bedouin village. You weren't well enough to go back to the expedition house."

"Where's James?"

"Fast asleep. One of the Bedouin women is looking after him. He's not far away—just next door." Katharine and Agatha exchanged glances. This was the first time in almost a week that Nancy had been lucid.

"Would you like something to drink?" Katharine reached for a cup of water, but Nancy waved it away.

"Promise me you'll look after him!" The look in Nancy's eyes was heartbreaking.

"Of . . . of course . . ." Katharine cast a desperate look at Agatha. "But you'll be—"

"Promise!" Nancy cut her short, sinking back onto the pillow, as if the effort of those few sentences had been too much for her.

"Try to get some rest." Agatha bent over her, replacing the dried-out cloth that had fallen from her forehead when she sat up.

"You won't let Felix have him, will you?"

"No." Katharine took Nancy's hand in hers. "Felix will never have him. I can promise you that."

"And you mustn't tell anyone about his *real* father . . ." She took a few short, labored breaths. "I can't have him now. No point in . . ." She trailed off, closing her eyes tight, the pain in her body overwhelming her.

"She needs morphine." Agatha unscrewed the bottle, squeezing the rubber end of the pipette to fill the glass tube. "Can you get her sitting up for me?"

Katharine put her hand under Nancy's head. The back of her neck was slick with perspiration. As she raised her up, Nancy's eyes snapped open.

"Don't *ever* let Felix say that James is his. He *isn't*."

"Please, Nancy—don't worry." Katharine held her closer. "He's a beautiful boy and he's yours: that's what matters."

"Just try to drink this." Agatha brought the cup to Nancy's lips.

They watched the pain slowly ebb away as the morphine took effect. When Nancy closed her eyes, Katharine lowered her gently back onto the pillow. She kept hold of her hand, propping herself against the pile of rugs so that even if she dozed off, she wouldn't let go.

Katharine didn't know how long she sat like that, fighting sleep. She didn't think she'd drifted out of consciousness, but she must have done so, because the tent was suddenly flooded with the light of the rising sun. As she felt its warmth on her face, she was immediately aware of something else: something cold and heavy on her fingers.

Nancy was dead.

CHAPTER 31

When the sun rose the following morning, Agatha was alone on the roof of the expedition house. Exhausted to the point of being beyond sleep, she had tossed and turned through the night, racked with guilt over Nancy's death. If only she hadn't brought her to Ur; if only they had stayed in Baghdad, where there was a hospital; if only she had persuaded Nancy to go back to England instead of toughing it out in a foreign country.

She thought of James, asleep in Katharine's room, blissfully unaware of the tragedy that had befallen him, his future blighted before it had even begun. When he had opened his eyes yesterday, his mother's last words were ringing in her ears.

Don't ever let Felix say that James is his. He isn't.

Even on her deathbed Nancy had been absolutely emphatic. Agatha had wondered, fleetingly, if this was a last desperate attempt to thwart Felix's plans to take the little boy. But when James had looked up at her, she had known with sudden certainty that there was no question as to who his father was. Those eyes, cloudy and unfocused in the first few days after his birth, had taken on a startling clarity.

Diamond-bright.

Yes, she had seen those eyes before. In the face of the man on the Orient Express. The man she had mistaken for Archie.

The memory of Nancy's grief that day on the train sent fresh tears streaming down Agatha's face. She tried in vain to rub them away as the colors of the sky melted into a blur of pink and gold.

"Agatha . . ."

She hadn't heard him coming.

Max was suddenly there, kneeling beside her, his arms cradling her shoulders.

"There are no words, are there?" he whispered. He gathered her up, and she cried into his shirt, letting it all out at last. Telling him, in staccato sentences punctuated by sobs, of the guilt that overwhelmed her every time she closed her eyes.

"But you couldn't possibly have known what would happen," he said, stroking her hair. "Did you even know she was expecting a baby?"

Agatha nodded. "B . . . but she said she was only about s . . . six months pregnant."

"You didn't *make* her come with you, though." She felt his chest rise as he took in a breath. "There's more than a chance both she *and* the baby would be dead if you hadn't acted so calmly out there by the river."

Agatha answered with a muffled sob.

"Would it help to get away for a while? Could you manage a bit of mule riding?" He cupped her chin in his hand, his dark eyes searching hers. "I go to the little church at Ur Junction Sunday mornings—gives me a chance to escape this lot for a few hours—and it's a lovely way to travel on a morning like this."

She blinked away the residue of tears, uncertain what to say. She liked the idea of going for a ride across the desert, but she wasn't sure about going to a service.

"You wouldn't have to come to Mass if you didn't feel like it," he went on. "There's a stall on the station platform where you can get coffee and a bite to eat."

"What about James? He'll be awake soon."

"I'm sure Katharine and the others are capable of looking after him for a few hours. Don't worry—I'll leave a note on the table."

~

The air was sharp with the scent of yellow chamomile and wild parsley. The rain that had followed the sandstorm had brought new life to the desert, turning paths into temporary streams where plants sprung up when the water subsided.

They rode in silence at first. She sensed that Max was waiting to see if she wanted to talk. For a while she didn't trust herself to open her mouth. She didn't want to start crying again. She was a few yards behind him, following in his wake, when she saw something drift onto the back of his shirt. At first she thought it was a clump of petals blown on the breeze, but as she drew closer, she saw it move. A butterfly. Unlike any she had ever seen. Its wings were the color of the sea on a summer morning. Turquoise threaded with black.

"Max!"

He turned in the saddle as she caught up with him. Reaching forward, she touched the fabric of his shirt.

"What is it?"

"A butterfly." As she spoke, it crept onto her index finger. Slowly, she withdrew her hand, bringing it round to show him.

"Isn't that beautiful?" He stroked the back of her wrist as she held it out. "You don't see many butterflies out here. I don't think I've ever seen one that color."

As they watched, it lifted a leg to its feelers, as if it was grooming itself. Then it opened its wings and glided away. Agatha felt suddenly uplifted. To put the feeling into words would have sounded mawkish, but she clung to it all the same: the butterfly was like a harbinger of hope.

"I remember watching a butterfly the day Esme died," Max said, as if reading her mind. "It was a beautiful morning—sunny and warm—and it seemed terribly wrong that the world could go on like that when he was no longer in it. I went out into the garden of the villa and sat there for a long time. I felt so guilty just for being alive. Then a butterfly landed on a flower just in front of me." He paused, shifting his weight in the saddle. "It made me think about a story I read as a child, where fairies in a wood came and asked a family of caterpillars if they could have their skins to make fur coats. The caterpillars were outraged. They thought the fairies meant to kill them. But they said no, that wasn't what they meant at all—but they knew a time would come when the caterpillars wouldn't need their coats anymore, because they'd have something much more beautiful to wear."

"What did they say—the caterpillars?"

"They didn't believe it. They sent the fairies packing."

Agatha swallowed hard as tears pricked the back of her eyes. "I used to believe. In heaven, I mean. But now . . ." She sucked in a breath, unable to voice the confusion she felt inside.

Max reached across the space between them, squeezing her arm. "It's not easy to believe in anything when your whole world turns upside down. The main thing is to keep believing in yourself."

~

Katharine was watching James while he slept. One arm was stretched up by his ear, and every so often his fingers opened and closed, like a sea anemone in a rock pool. Sometimes he was so still, she was afraid he had stopped breathing. She'd put her hand mirror over his mouth, unable to breathe herself until she saw the glass mist up.

"Is he all right?" Leonard's face appeared round the door. He had brought her a cup of tea and a plate of buttered toast. "I thought you might want breakfast in here." He set the tray down on the floor, then crouched down beside her. "He's very good, isn't he? I didn't hear a thing during the night."

"Thank goodness he's too young to understand."

At the sound of their voices, James suddenly opened his eyes. He looked from Katharine to Leonard, his mouth puckering in bewilderment as he took in the unfamiliar face with its bushy beard.

Katharine scooped him up before he made a sound, using the trick Agatha had taught her. She stroked his cheek with her thumb, and he nuzzled against it.

"You're very good with him." There was nothing grudging in the way he said it. No hint of jealousy or resentment. It gave her the courage to say what she'd lain awake most of the night fretting over.

"Could we keep him, Len?" The words came out like a genie let out of a bottle. Her mouth went dry as she watched his face. Never in her life had she wanted something so much.

"Keep him?" He was looking at her in the way he looked at objects when they came out of the sand, a mixture of puzzlement and intense concentration as he worked out just what he had unearthed. "But he's not ours."

"He's not anyone's anymore. Agatha and I are the nearest thing to parents that he has."

"But there must be somebody—an aunt or an uncle . . . or grandparents?"

"Nancy was an only child and her parents are dead."

"What about the father?"

"We have no idea who he is, other than that he's a married man who lives in London."

"But surely he could be traced: a notice in the *Times*, perhaps?"

"He already has a child, Len—a little girl. What do you think it would do to his family if it all came out?"

"Doesn't he have a right to know?"

"Nancy didn't want to destroy his family. It was the last thing she said before she died."

Slowly, Leonard lifted his hand. It hovered above the baby's head, as if he was afraid to touch. A look of awe crossed his face as his fingers made contact with the soft black down. "He's a fine little chap. But I . . . ," he faltered as his eyes met hers. "I didn't realize this was something you wanted."

"Neither did I—until now."

"I never told you, but I always hoped to have a child one day. I wanted the chance to be a better parent than my own father had been. When you told me about . . . well, I accepted it then, of course—that it couldn't be."

"But it *could* be, couldn't it?" Katharine whispered. "Think what a wonderful life we could give him, you and me."

His raised his hand a couple of inches, from James's head to her cheek. His fingers felt warm as he touched her. "Yes we could, couldn't we?"

~

Agatha sat on a rickety wooden bench at the end of the platform at Ur Junction, sipping Turkish coffee from a tin mug. The sun felt good on her skin, and she couldn't help smiling at the antics of the stationmaster as he attempted to herd people and animals onto an already packed train—his hat knocked askew as he was prodded by flailing limbs and tumbling luggage. It was like watching an Arab version of *Laurel and Hardy*.

She could hear music coming through the corrugated tin walls of the little church. Max was already inside. She had almost gone in with him, but the thought of doing or saying the wrong thing in a service she was unfamiliar with put her off. She wasn't even sure whether non-Catholics were allowed to attend Mass. Max had assured her that God wasn't bothered about such things, but still she felt uneasy. Deep down she knew that this probably had more to do with her uncertainty about what she believed than anything else.

Max was the only Western person she had seen going into the church. The others were all Indian nuns of various ages and a handful of local people. As the music died away, she saw a group of latecomers hurrying across the rough ground at the edge of the platform. They were young nuns in white habits, followed by a gaggle of small children in Western-style school uniforms. The boys wore gray shorts with white shirts and striped ties, while the girls wore tunics and blouses. Their features were Arabic, like the children she had seen on the streets of Baghdad. As she watched, she saw that one of the nuns was carrying a baby in her arms. It didn't look much older than James. Max had told her that there was an orphanage attached to the mission at Ur Junction. She wondered if these children were from there.

The thought of it stayed with her long after the little group had disappeared through the doors of the church. The sight of a baby in the arms of a woman who couldn't have been its mother had triggered a physical ache that wouldn't go away. What was going to happen to James now? The idea of his being sent to an institution—either here or in England—was unbearable. But what was the alternative?

She thought of the deathbed promise she and Katharine had made to Nancy. They had vowed to look after him. But how? She was a divorcée with a child of her own, and Katharine was a career woman who spent half the year living in the desert. Neither of them was best placed to take on a baby.

She let her mind run on, imagining how it would be if she took him home with her. She tried to imagine how Rosalind would react to the idea of a baby brother. Would she resent him, getting all the attention while she was at boarding school? And what on earth would the papers make of it? She could almost see the headlines: *AGATHA CHRISTIE'S MYSTERY BABY*. It had been hard enough protecting Rosalind from the aftermath of the Harrogate debacle. However would she cope, at school, with more gossip and innuendo?

She thought of James lying asleep in his improvised bed, of the agony of hearing him cry in the night for a mother who wasn't there. Was it cowardly to think of her own situation when his need was so great?

She closed her eyes. In her old life, before the divorce, she would have prayed without hesitation. Now it felt hypocritical. But the words slipped, unbidden, into her head. *Please, God, tell me what to do.*

"Sorry it went on so long!" Max was suddenly there in front of her. "I hope you weren't too bored."

She shook her head, amazed at how quickly the time had passed. She asked him how the service had been, and he made her laugh with a story of a bird that had got in through a hole in the roof and left an unpleasant calling card on the priest's cassock.

She was happy to let him do all the talking on the ride back home. She didn't want to think about the onerous decision that lay ahead, didn't want to feel that ache inside that came whenever James's face flashed into her mind's eye.

When they got back to the expedition house, Michael was underneath Queen Mary, tinkering with the undercarriage. He asked Max to give him a hand to fix the starter motor, leaving Agatha to go in alone.

She found Katharine in the courtyard feeding James. He had got the hang of the muslin teat now—sucking away for all he was worth each time she dipped the screwed-up end of the cloth into the bowl of goat's milk.

"How has he been?" Agatha sat down awkwardly, her legs stiff from the ride.

"As good as gold." Katharine let out a small sigh.

"How are we ever going to explain it to him?"

"I don't know." As Katharine tried to pull the rag from his mouth, James clung on to it, his tiny fist clenched tight. "Perhaps it would be better if he never knew. If he's adopted soon enough, he never needs to."

Agatha frowned. "Do you know someone? People in this country or in England?"

"Yes, I know someone." Katharine looked up as she dipped the rag in the bowl. She wore the same Mona Lisa smile that Agatha had seen on the train. "Me. And Len. We've talked it over, and he's agreed."

"*You?*"

"Don't look so surprised!" Katharine gave a nervous-sounding laugh. "We can't have a child of our own—so it's the perfect solution, isn't it?"

"But I thought—"

"That I wasn't keen on children? Len said that, too. And it's true. I didn't think it mattered, not being able to be a mother. I thought I knew what I wanted: to live like a man, to do a man's work. Until James came along."

"But how will you manage—with the dig and everything?"

"Len's going to talk to Hamoudi about getting one of the Bedouin women from the village to help look after James until we go back to England in the spring. We'll have a couple more seasons out here— three at the most—so by the time he's old enough to go to school, we should be settled back in London."

Agatha nodded, but her stomach was in knots. She knew she should be pleased, but she couldn't help feeling a tug of envy. "What will you do if someone from the British Consulate turns up asking questions? Hugh Carrington might come back: he knows about James."

"I'll cross that bridge when I come to it." Katharine sounded more like her old, determined self now. "We're unlikely to get another visit this season. But if anyone asks, I'll tell them that James is ours."

CHAPTER 32

Two days later, Agatha and Max boarded the train from Ur Junction to Baghdad. Katharine, Leonard, and the baby were there to see them off. As Leonard handed over the gold death mask Max was taking back to London, Agatha bent over to kiss James for the last time. He opened his eyes at the touch of her lips, bringing a lump to her throat.

"You will come and visit when we're back in London, won't you?" Katharine hoisted him onto her shoulder, rocking him gently as she spoke. "We'd love to see you."

Agatha glanced at Leonard, who was talking to Max through the window of the train. "I should have given you something—for the expedition. Perhaps I could wire some money from London."

"That's not necessary." Katharine smiled. "You've given us both something far more precious."

The train gave an ear-splitting whistle, which made James cry out in terror.

"You'd better get on!" Katharine planted a swift kiss on Agatha's cheek.

By the time Agatha was in her seat, the train had already begun to move. Katharine and Leonard were waving. James had stopped crying.

"They look like a proper family, don't they?" Max said.

Agatha nodded. She didn't trust herself to speak. Not yet.

"You mustn't worry." He reached for her hand. "It'll be all right."

~

They traveled overnight on the train, arriving in Baghdad in the early hours of the morning. Their plan was to go on to Damascus later that evening, which gave Agatha just hours to pack up everything in the house by the river.

She couldn't have faced the task of gathering up Nancy's belongings without Max there to help her. In a drawer by the bed she found a photograph wrapped in a moth-eaten silk scarf with a pattern of peacock feathers. It was a holiday snap of a group of men and women. The image blurred as Agatha realized that one of the faces was Nancy's.

"What is it?" Max dropped the bundle of clothes in his arms. Agatha held the photograph out for him to see. He read out the words inked in the border. "Venice Lido—April 1928."

"It's Nancy's honeymoon." Agatha fumbled in her pocket for a handkerchief.

Max studied it for a minute, then pointed to the muscular man to Nancy's right, who was clasping her hand while his other rested on the shoulder of a smiling woman in a kimono. "That must be Felix Nelson. Do you think that's the woman he . . ."

"Probably."

"Who are these others?"

As Agatha looked at the photo properly, her eye was drawn to a man at the far end of the line, on the right. He was wearing a patterned toweling robe and buckled canvas bathing shoes. He wasn't looking at the camera but back at the line of people. Tall enough to see over the heads of the others, he seemed to be staring at Nancy. His high, sculpted cheekbones and diamond-bright eyes made her stomach flip over. It was him: the man on the Orient Express.

"What's the matter?" She felt Max's hand on her shoulder. "You're trembling."

"I . . . It's just . . ." Should she tell him? What would he do if she identified Nancy's lover? Would he feel duty bound to find him? To tell him about James? She had made a promise to Nancy. She mustn't break it now.

"I sh . . . should send this to Katharine." Her voice was on the verge of breaking. "Then she can tell James about his mother when he starts asking questions."

"Do you think she *will* tell him?" Max frowned. "I got the impression she and Leonard were planning to pass him off to the world as their own child."

Agatha folded the photograph up in its shroud of silk. "I suppose that's their business. But if they have this, they have a choice, don't they?"

Max nodded. "Do you have an envelope? I'll go and post it while you finish packing."

~

Four days later, on the twenty-first of December, the Orient Express was gliding through the snow-covered meadows of the Swiss Alps. Dawn came late on the shortest day of the year. Agatha and Max were already eating breakfast when the sky lit up with the promise of sunrise.

"Our final morning," Max said, raising his coffee cup and chinking it against hers. "I know the last few days haven't been easy, but I do hope you've been able to enjoy some of it."

"Oh yes." Agatha gave a smile that didn't quite reach her eyes. "Istanbul was fascinating—and it was a treat to go back to Venice." She bent her head over her plate, buttering a piece of toast to conceal feelings that she couldn't express. There was so much going through her head. Tomorrow she would be back in London, picking up the pieces of her old life. She was desperate to see Rosalind but dreading the moment when Christmas was over and her daughter was back at school. Max would be returning to Mesopotamia. They'd had a wonderful few days together, but there had been no talk about the future. Would she ever see him again? And then there was James. She missed him terribly and wondered how Katharine was coping. Would she get tired of the sleepless nights and the endless round of feeding and changing? What would happen to James if the novelty of having a baby began to wear off?

"You're looking awfully serious." Max put his hand over hers as she laid down the knife.

"I can't help worrying about James." She could admit to that, at least.

"You were very good with him. I can imagine how hard it must have been to say good-bye."

"I did think about offering to take him. That day we rode out to the church, I spent the whole time you were at Mass working out whether it would be possible." She glanced out of the window at the snowy peak of a mountain turned gold by the rising sun. "It wouldn't have been, of course. I don't think a divorcée would be allowed to adopt a child."

"I thought about it, too," Max said.

"You did?"

"I thought perhaps if we were married . . ."

He was still holding her hand. She looked up, astounded, and saw that he was blushing.

"But then I started thinking that if we *were* married, we . . ." He stared at the tablecloth. "I thought we might be able to have one of our own."

"Max—are you proposing to me?"

"Yes." He looked up, a wry smile on his face. "Sorry I'm making a bit of a hash of it. I should go down on one knee, shouldn't I? But I might trip up the waiter." He took a deep breath. "Will you marry me, Agatha?"

EPILOGUE

August 1963

The path from the camellia garden to the house is narrow and winding. My young visitor offers to take my arm. I'm perfectly capable of walking unaided—the stick is just for helping me get up from the bench—but I take his arm when he holds it out, overcome by a sudden, powerful urge to have him close to me again. This was the baby I delivered in the desert, the child I kept alive with goat's milk on a scrap of muslin, the little boy I would have adopted if the circumstances had been different. What a fine young man he has grown into, with his mane of dark hair and those sparkling blue eyes.

I wish that Max was here to see him. But he's in London, delivering a lecture at the British Museum. At this moment he is probably regaling his audience with some anecdote from the time we spent living in Iraq and Syria.

What adventures. Max in charge of his own expeditions, and me at his side as khatun. I learned how to photograph the finds and develop the pictures, and when I wasn't doing that, I was typing away in a mud-brick study Max built for me. They hung a sign above the door, written in Arabic. *"Beit Agatha."* Agatha's house. It was the first proper writing room I'd ever had. I don't think ideas have ever come to me as quickly or easily as they did in that little hut in the desert.

We lost touch with the Woolleys over the years. While Max branched out with new digs in the Middle East, Leonard's work took him to America. The last time we all met, in London in the autumn of 1930, James was nearly two. He didn't remember me, of course, and cried when Katharine tried to sit him on my lap. It would have upset me if I hadn't had a secret reason to be especially happy that day. I was pregnant with Max's baby. For a whole magical month we had been planning a future as parents to a child of our own.

The day after that meeting with Katharine and James, we set off for Syria, stopping for a holiday on the island of Rhodes. I remember going into a little whitewashed church on the island to pray for a son. But I was forty years old. The pregnancy lasted just three months.

It was devastating, knowing that this was probably my last chance. As if to underline our painful loss, Archie's new wife gave birth to a little boy that same year.

Max was stoical, but I knew how much he would have loved to have a baby. It made it even harder to contemplate visiting the Woolleys when we returned to London the following spring—and it was something of a relief when I learned of their move to America.

Thinking back, I can hardly believe how long ago that was. James must be . . . I work it out in my head: thirty-five next birthday. As we walk toward the house, my shoe catches a stone lying on the path and I almost lose my footing. I feel the pressure of his hand under my arm, steadying me.

Yes, I longed for a son.

It became an obsession as I reached my midforties. But as the years ebbed away, I had to accept the bitter truth: that however successful I might be in other areas of my life, this was something I had failed at.

And then something lovely and quite unexpected had happened. Rosalind—at just twenty years old—met and married a soldier in a whirlwind wartime romance. Their son, Mathew, was born in the autumn of 1942. And when I held him in my arms, the ache in my heart simply melted away.

Mathew is a grown man now. I wonder what he would make of this stranger holding his granny's arm. We round a bend in the path. The house appears majestic through the boughs of the magnolias fringing the lawn, its white columns tinged orange by the sinking sun.

"What an amazing place." James stops to take it in. "You can't really see it from the river—I didn't realize it was Georgian."

"We bought it in 1938," I reply. "It was occupied by American troops during the war. They left some artwork behind—you'll see it in a moment."

When we reach the house, I take him through to the library and ring for tea. I show him the mural painted all along the walls, beneath the cornice: a series of illustrations depicting the worldwide exploits of a US landing craft.

"It's the legacy of a homesick lieutenant from New York. I couldn't bring myself to erase it when the house was redecorated—I like to think of it as modern archaeology."

I watch James as he circles the room, studying each stage of the mural. He pauses, pulling at the lobe of his ear—a brief gesture that betrays the fact he is on tenterhooks. He is wondering when I am going to get to the point, whether I really do have the missing pieces he is so desperately seeking.

"I'm sorry I lost touch with your parents," I begin. "We were so busy carving out our lives in different parts of the world. I have a great deal to thank them for: if it wasn't for them, I would never have met Max, my husband."

"Mum often talked about you. She had all of your books."

"It was a shock when I heard about her death. We'd been very close. It must have been terribly hard for you, losing her so young."

"Yes, it was. I was at school here, and they were in America. She'd been ill for a while. The doctors weren't sure what was wrong. It was awful to see her just wasting away, and of course, she hated it. She'd always been so full of life."

He comes over to the chair next to mine, resting his hands on the back of it, as if he needs something to hold on to. "Dad told me that she had a premonition. She sat him down and said, 'Len, I'm going to die this night—and you must promise me that when I do, you'll go on as you always have.' And the next morning she was gone."

I feel a pang of recognition. This sounds so like the Katharine I knew.

"Dad was never very good at expressing his feelings. When Mum passed away, he never seemed to want to talk about their life together. I had no idea they had kept anything from me until he died. When the house was sold, I was going through boxes in the attic and I found those photographs and a letter." His eyes go back to the mural. I can hear him breathing: a soft sigh as he exhales. "It was written by Mum to her sister in March 1929. Apparently, they were planning to stay with her when they finished the season at the dig. The letter said that they'd adopted a baby boy."

The silence in the room is palpable. I can feel my heart beating and a sickening sense of guilt. Will he blame me if I tell him? For what I didn't do all those years ago? For failing to save his mother? And how can I tell him anything without breaking my promise to Nancy?

"There was no clue in the letter about the identity of my parents, other than to say that I was European, not Arab, and had been named after Mum's father. The photographs were tucked inside the envelope." He takes them out of his bag again and lays them on the table between us, his eyes searching my face. "You were there, in Ur, the month I was born. Did she tell you anything?"

I have that ringing in my ears from my blood pressure rising. But there is something else as well. I can hear the voice of Hercule Poirot.

Trust the train, mademoiselle, for it is le bon dieu *who drives it . . .*

Trust the train. My own words, written all those years ago, when I thought my life was over. For the train, like life, must go on until it reaches its destination. You might not always like what you see out of the window, but if you pull down the blind, you will miss the beauty as well as the ugliness.

My finger trembles as it hovers over Nancy's face. "This is your mother."

"Oh . . ." His eyes widen, filming with tears. "She . . . she's beautiful. Who is she?"

"Her name was Nancy. And she wanted you very much. But she . . ." My voice breaks as I try to tell him. We are both crying by the time Jean, my housekeeper, brings in the tray of tea.

We recover ourselves a little as I pour it. Then he listens, sipping mechanically from his cup as I tell the story of how I met his mother.

"She took this photograph." I pick up the shot of Katharine and myself draped in towels. "You were born right there, under that tree, less than an hour later."

He takes the image from me, staring in wonder as I tell him how it happened.

"What about my father?" He picks up the other photograph, the one taken in Venice. "Is this him?" He is pointing to the man standing next to Nancy.

"No—that's Nancy's husband, Felix Nelson. He wasn't your father: she was very clear about that."

"So who *was*?" I hesitate before replying, mindful of my promise. "Your mother never told me his name. All she said was that he was an actor who lived in London, and that he was there in Venice, at the house party."

James runs his finger across the photograph, desperate to know which of the half a dozen men could be the one.

He must use the little gray cells.

Hercule, as always, has the solution: give James the clues to work it out for himself. No need to break my promise.

I leave him pacing the room while I go upstairs. It doesn't take me long to find the photograph. It's in a drawer alongside the bundle of love letters Archie sent me before we were married—something else I could never quite bring myself to destroy.

When I pull out the snapshot of the dashing young pilot, his eyes make crystals of ice bloom in my blood. I had the very same sensation during the last war, sitting in a cinema in London. Max was stationed in Egypt, so I went on my own to watch an adaptation of one of Daphne du Maurier's novels. A few minutes in, I caught my breath at the sight of one of the supporting actors—because he looked exactly like Archie.

When the film ended, I waited for the credits to roll, certain that the mystery of the face I had seen reflected in the window of the Orient Express had finally been solved. I wished I could see the photo I found in Nancy's drawer to prove to myself that I was right—but of course, I had sent it to Katharine.

I take the picture of Archie downstairs and tell James about the man I saw his mother wave at on the train. "I can't be certain, you see," I say as hope flares in his eyes. "It was only a reflection. But he was the double of my first husband. That's why I remember it so clearly."

James nods slowly, holding Archie's image next to the group shot. "This is him: it has to be!" He points to the man in the patterned toweling robe at the end of the line. "He's an actor, isn't he? I recognize him, I think. Do you know his name?"

I go to the bookcase and pull out one of Daphne du Maurier's books, an edition published to coincide with the film. I hand it to James. His father's face is on the cover. He gasps and turns the book over. The blurb on the back tells him what he is so desperate to know.

"Is he still alive?"

I hesitate. When I look at him, I can't help seeing Rosalind. They have the same dark hair, the same bright-blue eyes. James could almost be her younger brother. The thought makes me shrivel inside. Because Rosalind *has* a younger brother: Archie's son from his second marriage. But they were complete strangers until last year, when they met for the first time at Archie's funeral.

That was my fault. I didn't forbid her to see her father's new family, but I made it perfectly clear how hurt I would be if she did. And so she saw Archie on his own in London, never with his wife and son. And by the time she finally got to meet her half brother, he was thirty-two years old. I know how hard she has found it to forgive me for those wasted years.

It was lonely for her, being an only child, when she needn't have been. How much more lonely for James, who has no one now. But he could have a father. And a sister.

"Yes," I whisper, "he's alive."

"Does he know about me?"

I shake my head. "Not yet."

Hercule whispers as I hesitate: *The train must go on. Trust the train . . .*

AFTERWORD

Throughout this story I have mixed fiction with the detail of real lives. My intention was to shine a light on a critical period in Agatha Christie's life by weaving imagined incidents and characters into the recorded history. Readers who long to know what is factual and what is made up would be wise to read Christie's autobiography, followed by Laura Thompson's excellent biography, entitled *Agatha Christie: An English Mystery* (Headline, 2007).

For those who prefer a more immediate explanation, here are the key facts:

Agatha Christie really did board the Orient Express in autumn 1928. Her divorce from Archie was granted in October of that year, and he married his fiancée Nancy Neele two weeks later.

When Archie first confessed to the affair with Nancy in 1926, Agatha suffered a mental breakdown, which resulted in her "disappearance" for ten days to a hotel in the north of England, where she lived under the name "Mrs. Neele" until two members of the staff guessed her true identity and informed the police. She later claimed that the whole episode was the result of amnesia brought on as a consequence of her breakdown, which she attributed to overwork.

Katharine Woolley was a real person and is believed to have been the inspiration for the character Louise Leidner in Christie's *Murder in Mesopotamia*. Her first husband did commit suicide six months after the wedding, although the medical condition I have described is a matter of speculation. In his memoir (Dodd, Mead, 1977), Max Mallowan writes that "she was not intended for the physical side of matrimony."

Agatha Christie met Katharine Woolley when she visited the dig at Ur in 1928, and the two became friends. Max was not at the dig on that particular occasion—Christie met him when she returned the following year. They married in 1930 and spent many years in the Middle East, where Max directed digs in Syria and Iraq. A record of their life at that time is contained in Christie's memoir entitled *Come, Tell Me How You Live* (William Morrow, 1946).

Nancy Nelson is a fictitious character. Her physical appearance is based on that of Archie's lover, Nancy Neele.

ACKNOWLEDGMENTS

In addition to the sources already mentioned in the afterword, I drew on a number of Christie's crime novels in the writing process. *Murder in Mesopotamia, They Came to Baghdad, The Mystery of the Blue Train*, and of course, *Murder on the Orient Express* were wonderful resources for the creation of characters and settings.

Equally important in my research were the books Christie wrote under the pseudonym Mary Westmacott. They give intimate glimpses of her private life, as she began writing them in the aftermath of her breakup with Archie. I drew particularly on *Unfinished Portrait*, a semi-autobiographical novel about a woman contemplating suicide after the failure of her marriage.

I would like to thank my friend and mentor, Janet Thomas, for all the encouragement and inspiration she has given me during the writing process. I'm also grateful to Jodi Warshaw and the team at Lake Union for all their support, and to my editor Christina Henry de Tessan.

Thank you also to my husband, Steve Lawrence, for his love and unfailing enthusiasm throughout the writing of this book. In October

2015 we were lucky enough to have our wedding at Agatha Christie's beautiful home, Greenway, on the banks of the River Dart in Devon. If there could be such a thing as a patron saint of second marriages, I can think of no better candidate than Agatha Christie.

ABOUT THE AUTHOR

Photo © 2014 Isabella Ashford

Lindsay Jayne Ashford grew up in Wolverhampton, United Kingdom. She was the first woman to graduate from Queens' College, Cambridge, in its 550-year history. After earning her degree in criminology, Ashford worked as a reporter for the BBC and a freelance journalist for a number of national magazines and newspapers. She has four children and currently lives in a house overlooking the sea on the west coast of Wales.